Seeking the Dead

Also by Kate Ellis

Wesley Peterson series:
The Merchant's House
The Armada Boy
An Unhallowed Grave
The Funeral Boat
The Bone Garden
A Painted Doom
The Skeleton Room
The Plague Maiden
A Cursed Inheritance
The Marriage Hearse
The Shining Skull
The Blood Pit

For more information regarding Kate Ellis
log on to Kate's website: www.kateellis.co.uk

Seeking the Dead

Kate Ellis

PIATKUS

PIATKUS

First published in Great Britain in 2008 by Piatkus Books

All characters and events in this publication, other than those clearly in the public domain, are fictitious and any resemblance to real persons, living or dead, is purely coincidental

A CIP catalogue record for this book is available from the British Library

ISBN 978-0-7499-0861-4

Typeset in Times by Action Publishing Technology Ltd, Gloucester
Printed and bound by MPG Books, Bodmin, Cornwall

Papers used by Piatkus Books are natural, renewable and recyclable products made from wood grown in sustainable forests and certified in accordance with the rules of the Forest Stewardship Council

Piatkus Books
An imprint of
Little, Brown Book Group
100 Victoria Embankment
London EC4Y 0DY

An Hachette Livre UK Company

www.piatkus.co.uk

To Gillian Green, Sarah Molloy and Euan Thorneycroft
with thanks

Chapter One

Things that frighten the devil away.

The killer grabbed a cheap biro from the box on the table and started to make a list.

Garlic . . . or was that just vampires?

Church bells. Everyone knew they drove evil away. The killer stood on the city walls by the cathedral each Tuesday night while the ringers practised, bathing in the mellow music of the great bells. Safe.

Charms. Coral. And crucifixes. And the sight of an open Bible. And holy water.

With trembling fingers that could hardly form the letters, the killer continued the list. It had to be finished. There would soon be more work to do.

More death to bring to the evil ones.

Carmel Hennessy hurried home, hugging her cardigan around her to ward off the unseasonable chill in the air. As she emerged from the crazy maze of ancient streets on to the cathedral square, she turned her head to stare up at the towers, intricately carved in pale-gold stone, soaring up to heaven like arms outstretched in prayer.

Carmel – who had been raised in Liverpool before moving with her mother and stepfather to a town of concrete and straight lines – loved the centre of Eborby with its network of cramped, medieval thoroughfares where the past hung in the air like a heavy smog. History, from peaceful trade to violent rebellion, slithered through the winding streets and passageways, tending at times to overshadow the present. But then that was why she was there . . . the Heritage Industry. Carmel Hennessy owed her living to the past.

Her flat in Vicars Green stood just a few hundred yards from the great cathedral itself. When she'd moved to Eborby she'd expected to be exiled to the outer suburbs, or to one of the less salubrious streets near Kingsgate, but her new landlady, Peta Thewlis – who was also her boss at the Archaeology Centre – had been looking for a reliable tenant for her vacant flat. Carmel's grandmother, being a great believer in fate, would have said that it was 'meant'.

Carmel was grateful to Peta of course, but she couldn't say in all honesty that she liked the woman. She found Peta cool and uncommunicative. However, she was sure that they could maintain an amicable working and landlady-tenant relationship. No problem.

The Vicars Green flat couldn't be more convenient, but living so close to Eborby's chief attractions did have a few drawbacks. Carmel didn't so much mind the stream of tourists who trudged across the triangle of grass, passing the Roman column standing at its centre without a second glance, as they made for the quaint National Trust tearoom fifty yards along the street. But the ghost tours were a different matter.

They arrived each night at eight o'clock on the dot. A band of tourists marching like a ragged army behind a tall man with a long, pale face who wore a voluminous black Victorian cape and a tall silk hat. He reminded Carmel of an extra from a Jack the Ripper movie. But rather than moving through the swirling mists of Whitechapel, this particular Ripper stalked the summer streets of Eborby recounting tales of spooks and grisly executions. There seemed to be no end, Carmel thought, to the public's appetite for horror. But, as far as she was concerned, the ghouls were welcome to it. After what had happened to her father, she had had her fill of violent death.

One evening she had looked out of her window to see the guide pointing directly up at her flat. And sometimes, if the window was open, she could catch the odd word drifting upwards on the evening air – plague; girl; face. She had no idea what the man she had begun to think of as Jack the Ripper was telling his audience but she was beginning to find his regular visits a little unsettling. If people were staring at her window, she would have liked to know the reason why.

So far she'd discovered that number five Vicars Green had originally been one wing of a larger house, the former home of some prosperous city merchant, built in the late fifteenth century. Her flat, on the first floor of number five, was small – one bedroom, living room, minuscule kitchen and a tiny shower room off the bedroom – but she loved the way the bare floorboards creaked and no two walls stood at exactly the same angle because the house had twisted and settled with the centuries.

If she lay in bed at night and thought about all the people who had lived and died there, her imagination supplied a thousand stories, happy and sad. There were nights when she lay awake listening to each groan of the timbers and each thump of the plumbing. And sometimes there were nights when bad dreams made her wake up in terror – when she saw her father's dead face smiling at her, a trickle of blood dribbling from his lips.

But although the past held terrors, the present too had horrors of its own. The papers were full of Eborby's two recent murders and each day the headlines screeched out more grisly speculation. They had called them the churchyard killings at first. Then some bright spark in a newspaper office had named the killer the Resurrection Man, a catchy label that had caught the public's imagination . . . and stuck.

Carmel did her best to put all this unpleasantness, past

and present, out of her mind as she made herself something to eat. Something warm and comforting. Beans on toast – childhood food. Then at ten past eight she looked out of her small, leaded living-room window on to the green below. Jack the Ripper was there again, talking, gesticulating and pointing up at her bedroom window. Carmel fought a sudden impulse to rush downstairs and find out exactly what it was about her new home that these ghoulish tourists found so very fascinating. Perhaps she'd pluck up the courage to ask Peta Thewlis one day at work. Or maybe she'd join the tour herself one night. She might even learn something about the hidden history of her newly adopted city. The bits they didn't put in the guide books.

After ten minutes the ghost tour moved on, making its way to the Fleshambles, the ancient street of the butchers where the shops' overhanging upper storeys almost blotted out the sky. That thin street, which must once have reeked of blood and rotting flesh, was gloomy even when the sun was shining. No doubt there'd be something nasty there to keep the ghoulish tourists interested, Carmel thought, switching on the TV and settling down on the sofa. As she watched the flickering images she planned the rest of her evening. She would have a shower and an early night curled up with a good book. Then she gave a snort of derision. She was twenty-three – perhaps she should be putting some energy into getting herself some sort of social life. But things are never easy for a stranger in a strange town. And besides, she knew that sometimes she wasn't good company.

At ten o'clock she heard the cathedral clock striking the hour and she turned off the TV before making for the bedroom, wondering why she always felt a thrill of something akin to fear when she crossed the threshold of that small, low-beamed room with its cool blue walls. Ignoring her gut feeling of apprehension, she walked over to the window and lifted her arms to shut the flowery curtains.

Suddenly something caught her eye on the green below.

A movement. A figure stepping out of the shadows. A man in a tall silk hat was standing there quite still, looking up at her. His expressionless face pale as the moon.

Carmel let the curtains slip from her grasp and took a step back, her heart pounding. He looked like death. And he had come for her.

Detective Inspector Joe Plantagenet's eyes were drawn to the photographs pinned on the notice board that covered one wall of the incident room. They held a terrible fascination . . . like the sight of a car crash. After a few seconds he looked away.

Because the victims had been left naked in churchyards, the killer had been dubbed the Resurrection Man by a gleeful press. But the men and women who wrote the reports hadn't seen the pictures on the wall. They hadn't seen the corpses, looking as if they had just emerged from the grave. They hadn't seen the look of horror and despair on those dead faces; the wide, terrified eyes; the gaping mouths set in a silent scream as if they had glimpsed some unspeakable horror before their souls had quit their bodies. Joe had always believed in evil. But he had rarely encountered it before in such a palpable form. So close he could feel it.

The pathologist, a woman of science, had delivered her verdict in a cool, matter-of-fact sort of way. The victims had probably been stunned and tied up before being buried alive. She had shown no emotion as she spoke and perhaps, Joe thought, she had the right idea. Professional detachment was the only way to deal with something like this. You couldn't spend too much time dwelling on the victims' agony. If you did, you'd go mad.

'You OK, Joe?'

The words made Joe jump and he swung round to see Detective Sergeant Sunny Porter standing there. Sunny was a thin, wiry man in his early forties with a prematurely lined face, the consequence of a lifetime's dedicated chain smoking. He had been christened Samson by his optimistic parents but he had only reached five feet eight and the nearest thing he'd ever encountered to a Delilah was a WPC in Traffic who, it was rumoured, had sapped his strength for a few months back in 1995. Samson hardly seeming appropriate, he had been Sunny from childhood, by name if not always by nature.

'I'll feel better when we catch the bastard who killed these two,' Joe said, trying to sound positive.

'Madam wants to see you,' said Sunny with an emphasis on the word 'madam'.

Joe smiled to himself. Sunny was still coming to terms with the fact that the new DCI was female. She was the replacement for DCI Miller, who had been forced to retire suddenly after suffering a heart attack. Whoever had taken over was bound to encounter resentment as Miller had been popular, one of the boys. But Joe was willing to give DCI Emily Thwaite a chance. After all, she had only been in the job a week and it wasn't easy taking over the investigation of two high-profile murders – identical and almost certainly linked – at such short notice.

Joe took a deep breath and made his way to DCI Thwaite's office. After giving a token knock, he walked in and Emily Thwaite looked up and gave him a businesslike smile. 'Joe. Sit down . . . please. I've just seen the Super,' she said. 'He wanted to know if we've made any headway.'

'What did you tell him?'

'The usual. Enquiries are progressing. We're making a fresh TV appeal tonight . . . keeping it in people's minds. We're doing all we can with the manpower available. I've asked for more overtime to be approved.'

'And?'

She smiled bitterly. 'It's being considered.'

Joe looked at her. She was an attractive woman: fair, a little on the plump side and touching forty. Her pale curls framed a pretty, almost doll-like face, and Joe knew that this would count against her with some. But he was determined to keep an open mind.

He looked around the office and saw that she had added some personal touches. Photographs on the desk and an ornately carved letter rack, possibly the souvenir of some exotic holiday. A child's painting had been pinned up on the office wall: five figures of varying sizes, two females – one big, one small – in triangular skirts and three stick-like males stood stiffly in a row. Emily's family, he guessed, although she hadn't made any mention of them so far. The picture, with its enthusiastic innocence, looked somehow incongruous in a place where brutal murders were being investigated. But perhaps they served as a reminder that in the world outside the police station, not everything was dark.

Emily interrupted his thoughts. 'Anything new come in?'

'Nothing important. We've had a team doing house to house near where Uckley's body was dumped but it seems that nobody heard or saw anything unusual.'

Emily rolled her eyes. 'Now why doesn't that surprise me?'

Joe Plantagenet looked at his watch, wondering whether to ask the next question. Perhaps the suggestion wouldn't be welcome. But he decided to make it anyway. 'It's lunchtime. Do you fancy something to eat at the Cross Keys? They serve a good ploughman's lunch . . . and it's about time you were introduced to the watering holes of Eborby.'

She hesitated for a few moments as though she was assessing his motives . . . and the wisdom of accepting the invitation. Then she smiled. 'Why not?'

Joe thought he saw a flicker of something akin to gratitude in her eyes, swiftly concealed. He knew it wasn't easy for her coming in as DCI, newly transferred from Leeds and appointed over the heads of men who thought they deserved the post more than she did. But he'd heard good things about her – that she got results. And he'd also heard rumours on the flourishing station grapevine that she was married to a teacher and had three children of school age.

If this was so, she had a lot on her plate and if anyone was going to give her a hard time, it wouldn't be Joe. But then he had a reputation for being soft. Too soft sometimes.

The police headquarters stood near the railway station, outside the towering grey bulk of the city walls built in the Middle Ages to protect Eborby's citizens - to keep violence out - not that they worked very well these days. As they left the building, Joe saw some young children playing on the steep banks that sloped up to the walls, rolling down the slopes laughing, under their mothers' watchful eyes. Joe had heard that plague victims had been buried beneath these banks in the seventeenth century and he wondered whether the mothers would have let their children play there if they'd known. Probably. The past was the past.

Joe and Emily crossed the bridge over the river and followed the wide road that led into the heart of the city, passing the Museum Gardens and the Victorian red-brick library, dodging the heavy lunchtime traffic: cars, coaches and open-topped tourist buses. The stench of petrol fumes hung in the air until they slipped down a narrow side alley, making for the web of narrow streets at the city's heart - now a pedestrian haven - with their medieval shops and worn stone pavements. Once an unremarkable urban landscape, Eborby's old town was a bustling tourist attraction these days. History sells and city centre pubs took advantage of this fact by retaining their original charm. Theme pubs were banished to the outskirts.

The magpie-timbered Cross Keys had stood at the end of a thin cobbled alleyway for many centuries, quenching the thirst of Eborby's citizens. But the new Thai menu on offer was a recent innovation. Joe, set in his ways, ordered a ploughman's while Emily opted confidently for a Thai chicken curry.

The low ceilings and lighting to match made for an intimate atmosphere. 'Nice place,' Emily said, breaking an awkward silence. She looked at Joe, studying him as she would study a suspect in the interview room. He was younger than she was – around thirty she guessed – with wavy black hair, blue eyes and a pale complexion that suggested Irish blood somewhere in his family tree.

'I suppose we should talk about the case,' Joe said, businesslike, as though he wanted to keep a barrier of formality between them.

Emily pulled a face. 'Not while we're eating, eh. I could do with a bit of a break.'

Joe had to acknowledge that she was probably right. They were getting too bogged down in the details of the case. A rest would do them both good.

There was another silence while Joe searched for something appropriate to say. Small talk to oil the wheels. 'How are the family settling in?'

Emily's expression softened. 'OK. It's the school holidays so my husband's got a few weeks before he starts at his new school. He teaches history.'

'I'd heard he was a teacher. Can't keep much quiet round here.'

'So I gathered,' she said as the food arrived. Joe noticed that she started eating straight away as though she'd suddenly realised she was hungry.

'New house OK?' he asked.

She nodded, her mouth full.

'Whereabouts is it?'

'Near the racecourse,' she answered, playing with her fork. She suddenly looked up. 'Did I hear you used to be a priest or something?' The question was sharp and she looked him in the eye as though he were a criminal under interrogation.

Joe hesitated, wondering how much it was wise to say. 'I was training to be a priest but . . . Well, life has a habit of surprising you, doesn't it?'

'Or kicking you in the teeth,' Emily muttered under her breath. 'So what happened to change your mind?'

'A woman happened,' Joe said after a few moments' silence.

'Is she still on the scene?'

Joe shook his head.

'But there is someone?'

'Not at the moment.' He gave her a wary smile. She hadn't given much away about her own private life but she seemed to want to know all about his.

She tilted her head to one side. 'Do I detect a Liverpool accent?'

He took a deep breath. 'I was brought up there. My dad was from Eborby and my mum was from Liverpool. Her parents were Irish and she was a devout Catholic. That's why I . . .' He let the words trail off. Some things were hard to explain to a woman he hardly knew in a busy lunchtime pub.

'How long have you lived in Eborby?'

Joe didn't answer for a few seconds. A shadow of pain passed across his face. It was barely perceptible. But Emily noticed.

'Almost five years now. I used to be in the Merseyside force but . . . There was an incident. A colleague of mine was killed. I was with him.' He bowed his head, avoiding Emily's eyes. 'He was shot. So was I but they didn't do the job very efficiently in my case . . . only got me in the shoulder. Kevin wasn't so lucky.'

'I'm sorry,' Emily said quietly. She understood. She too had had colleagues – friends – who had been killed in the line of duty. It was never easy to come to terms with. And the anger, the sense of loss and injustice, lasted for years . . . maybe even for a lifetime. You never forget.

'I stuck it out in Liverpool for a few years afterwards but then I decided to transfer to Eborby because I wanted a fresh start. And I've got roots here.'

Emily looked around the pub. 'Yeah, I can understand that.' There was an awkward silence then she gave Joe a shy smile. 'Plantagenet . . . isn't that . . .?'

When Joe returned her smile it was as though a shadow had lifted. 'My dad was from Eborby and Richard III operated in these parts so there are old family stories that we're descended from one of his illegitimate children. But I don't know how true it is. Maybe one day I'll do some research and . . .'

'You should,' said Emily, looking at her watch.

Joe looked down at her empty plate. 'Good curry?'

Emily nodded and arranged her knife and fork neatly before pushing the plate to one side.

'Sorry to talk shop,' he said. 'But I think it might help to go over what we've got so far while we're away from the incident room.'

Emily sighed. They'd had their break and she knew Joe was right. 'OK. I've read all the files but I still need to get my head round the facts. Get them clear in my mind.' She pushed her hair back off her face, preparing to get down to business.

'Right,' said Joe. 'First victim Carla Yates, aged forty-five. Single. Lived alone. Worked at a travel agent's on Westgate and reported missing by her work colleagues. Five days later she was found dead in a village ten miles north of Eborby, lying against the wall of the churchyard. She was naked and there were marks on her mouth, wrists and ankles indicating that she had been bound and gagged with some sort of adhesive tape. There were also contusions on the head which, according to the pathologist, had been sufficient to stun but not to kill. Cause of death probably suffocation. It's likely she was left somewhere, probably in a confined space until the air ran out.'

Joe imagined the unfortunate woman coming round, bound and unable to move, trapped somewhere until death came as a release. It was too horrible to contemplate. He had seen the look of terror on her decaying face. As though she had seen a vision of hell itself.

'Last seen?'

'She'd been to the pub after work on a Friday night with some of her colleagues. She left them to catch the bus home at the nearest bus stop by the Museum Gardens. She lives off the Hasledon Road . . . not far from the university. She was picked up on a couple of CCTV cameras in the city centre and everything seemed normal. We've traced the bus driver and some of the passengers and they didn't notice anything unusual – nobody following her or anything like that. We think she must have been abducted after she got off the bus – the bus stop's about a quarter of a mile from her home. No cameras on the route unfortunately.'

'Private life?'

'Divorced. No significant other. I've got the team making enquiries on that one.'

'Good. Now I've taken over, I'd like to talk to all her friends and colleagues again. There might be something that's been missed. What about the second victim?'

'A man. I suppose that rules out any kind of sexual motive.'

'Not necessarily.'

Joe took a deep breath. 'His name was Harold Uckley. Aged fifty-six. Worked at the head office of the Eborby Permanent Building Society. He was married with two grown-up sons and he appears to have led a blameless life. The word dull springs to mind. But then dull people can sometimes have hidden depths.'

'Mmm. You can say that again. In Leeds the Vice Squad uncovered a network of prostitutes. Most of their clients were solicitors, chartered accountants and tax inspectors. I saw the photographs. I'd never have thought people like that could be so imaginative.'

Joe popped a piece of crusty bread into his mouth and noted that Emily was smirking as if she found the peccadilloes of the upright citizens of Leeds highly entertaining. No doubt they'd provided hours of not-so-innocent amusement for the officers at her last nick.

She leaned forward, her elbows on the table. Joe could smell her perfume, something floral and French. 'Remind me of how Uckley disappeared.'

'He came home from work as usual, had his tea, then he

got a phone call and told his wife he was going out to the local pub for half an hour. We traced the call. It was made by a friend of his, a fellow fisherman. He'd expected to meet Uckley for a quick drink as he often did. Only Uckley never turned up. He left home and never came back. The theory is he met someone near the house and got into a car with them. But who and why we don't know. The friend's certainly in the clear – he was waiting for Uckley in the pub with two other men. Uckley turned up dead five days later in another churchyard. Well, you've seen from the photos up on the office wall how he was found. Exactly the same as Carla Yates – naked with marks indicating that he was bound. Same cause of death. Asphyxiation, as if he'd been closed in somewhere until the air ran out.'

'Nothing from family and colleagues? He'd not been behaving as if there was something worrying him? He'd not indicated that he intended to meet anyone?'

'Nothing. He was a quiet man who kept himself to himself.'

'Aren't they all? Funny that our two victims are so different, don't you think?'

'They must have had something in common. Something they were both involved in, say. We're going through their private lives like my gran used to go through her kitchen cupboards every spring.'

'I had a gran like that.' Emily smiled at the memory. 'Expert on surveillance she was and all. I sometimes wonder whether MI5 have ever considered the effectiveness of the net curtain.'

'So what exactly did you tell the Super about our progress?' Joe asked, dampening the mood.

'What could I tell him? All the usual questions have been asked. The victims' last movements have been traced. But there's nothing that makes much sense. And so far there doesn't seem to be any connection between the two victims apart from how they died.'

'Do you think they were random attacks?'

Emily looked him in the eye. 'Do you?'

'The killings are well organised. He's keeping them somewhere ... watching them die slowly.'

'Or he leaves them and comes back when he thinks they're dead.'

'Oh no, I think he likes to watch them. There's something sick about all this.' Joe pushed his plate away. Suddenly he'd lost his appetite.

'Forensic haven't come up with anything to indicate where he keeps them till they die,' he said. 'However, traces of wood shavings – oak to be precise – were found on both bodies. It's good quality wood but I'm told it's readily available.'

'They're kept in a sawmill? Or somewhere furniture's made? Or coffins. An undertaker's?'

'Could be anything. But I've got people checking it out. Just our luck if the killer turns out to be a DIY enthusiast.'

Emily sighed. 'As far as I can see, every lead's been covered and we're no nearer to finding this lunatic than we were when Carla Yates's body turned up four weeks ago. I've really jumped in at the bloody deep end, haven't I?' She suddenly looked unsure of herself, afraid. But the glimpse of vulnerability only lasted a split second.

Joe gave his new DCI a sympathetic look. 'You look as though you need another drink, boss. Want one?'

Emily shook her head. 'No. We'd better get back.' She gave Joe a sly grin. 'Or people might start talking.'

Joe tried to ignore the remark but he felt his cheeks burning. He suspected that she was rather enjoying his embarrassment. She had a sense of mischief, he thought, which could come in useful in the gruelling days to come ... if only to distract them from their failures.

She stood up, her mouth set in a firm line, and looked at her watch. 'We'd better get a move on,' she said before making a beeline for the door.

Joe followed her out of the crowded pub, weaving through the lunchtime drinkers, wondering fleetingly whether one of them might be the Resurrection Man. Killers, after all, look the same as anyone else.

Carmel Hennessy arrived back at her flat at six.

It had been a satisfactory day, as far as she could tell. She had demonstrated the basic techniques of dating fragments of pottery to a group of visitors and they had looked interested – or perhaps they were just being polite. Anyway, Carmel had carried on regardless because that was what she was being paid for. She knew she was lucky to have the job, especially in a place like Eborby where the relics of previous generations were all around you. Coming back to a lonely flat, miles from friends and family, was a price worth paying – at least for now.

So much talking had left her mouth dry and on her way home she had found herself dreaming of a hot mug of tea like a parched man dreams of water in the desert. As she passed the newsagent's in the little tree-shaded square between the Fleshambles and Marigate, she noticed a board outside bearing the words 'Resurrection Man latest' in scrawled black marker pen but she hurried on without buying a paper. There were some things she preferred not to think about.

She took the quickest route home. She knew the way now. When she'd first arrived in Eborby she'd often got lost in the labyrinth of winding streets. But now they'd become familiar, with their quaint pubs and their quirky little shops. She stopped and gazed in the window of an antique shop at a Moorcroft vase which she knew only too well she couldn't afford – not on her salary. Then she carried on down the street, the golden towers of the cathedral always in view, peeping over the rooftops like a beacon to guide the lost.

When at last she reached Vicars Green, she let herself in with her Yale key and made her way up the steep, carpeted stairs, glancing at the door to the ground-floor flat as she passed. Peta Thewlis had said that Carmel's downstairs neighbour was a quiet old gentleman who'd once had some connection with the cathedral. Carmel wondered whether she should call and introduce herself. It might reassure the old gentleman to know that somebody friendly was living upstairs . . . and make her feel as if she wasn't absolutely alone in that place with only the domestic ghosts for company.

As soon as Carmel reached the top of the stairs she realised that she had forgotten to check if there was any post in the oak letter box fixed to the back of the front door. Not that she was expecting anything important but you never know. Fortune might be smiling in the shape of some invitation or letter from an old friend. Or frowning in the form of a bill.

She hurried back down the stairs and flipped open the lid of the box marked with a large number two, the number of her flat. There were three letters inside. The first was a credit card statement which Carmel stuffed into her pocket, intending to face the awful truth once she'd been fortified by a mug of tea. The second was a letter from her mother enclosing a cutting from her local paper about the glorious deeds of one of her old sixth form college classmates, a young woman who had trekked through the Himalayas for charity in between setting up her own web design company and raising money for some Eastern European orphanage. Carmel had never liked the girl and she seethed with feelings of her own inadequacy as she reread the letter, trying to read between the bland lines.

There was no mention of her stepfather but that was hardly surprising. Carmel had been close to her father – until a bullet had taken him away from her for good – and she had resented Steve, the interloper, from the moment her mother – a widow of less than one year – had brought him home and introduced him to her like a coy teenager. Steve could never be a match for her father, Kevin, the policeman hero who'd died in the line of duty. And Carmel – with the judgemental certainty of the young who have never known loneliness and grief – had almost despised her mother for accepting second best. She put her mother's letter aside and picked up the third envelope.

The address was handwritten, something increasingly rare in the era of junk mail and statements churned out by distant computers. Carmel was about to tear it open when she noticed the name on the front. Miss Janna Pyke. The writing, in bright blue ink, had a certain flourish about it and the thick, cream-coloured envelope looked expensive. She stared at it, turning the envelope over in her hands, wondering who Janna Pyke might be. Perhaps she was the last tenant – Peta Thewlis had never mentioned her name, referring to her only as 'she'. She would ask Peta the next day at work if the opportunity presented itself.

After replacing the letter in the wooden box, Carmel made her way upstairs and opened the door. The flat was just as she'd left it. Clean and tidy. But she always felt slightly apprehensive when she arrived home, remembering what she had seen when Peta had first showed her round the place. Peta had evaded Carmel's inevitable questions about the smashed lock. The last tenant, she said, had left without paying the rent and her things had been put up in the loft, the implication being that the errant tenant had returned and broken in to retrieve her possessions. But Carmel hadn't been altogether convinced. She'd sensed that Peta had been holding something back. Maybe something she'd rather keep hidden.

Carmel made herself a cup of tea and switched on the TV to catch the local news. The sound of voices made the flat seem less empty but the news was hardly cheerful. The police were appealing for more information about the last movements of the Resurrection Man's two victims. Their naked bodies had been dumped in country churchyards and the very thought made Carmel shudder. As both victims had lived in Eborby, it was too close to home for comfort.

She watched the news to the end before switching off the TV and making herself a microwaved baked potato, topped with half a can of tuna – it was hard to put much effort into cooking for one. As soon as she'd finished her solitary meal, she was seized by a sudden need to speak to another human being; anyone who'd make her feel less alone. The faint sound of a TV was drifting up through the floor from the flat below. Perhaps it was time she made the acquaintance of her neighbour.

Careful to lock the flat door behind her, Carmel made her way down the stairs, her heart thumping and her hands tingling with nerves as they always did when she was faced with new people or situations. It was something she put down to the shock of losing her father so suddenly and so violently at the age of fourteen. But over the years she'd found ways to conceal her terror of the unknown and by the time she had reached the hallway she was wearing a friendly, confident expression, hiding the fear inside.

She took a deep breath and knocked on the door of the downstairs flat. Her excuse for calling was going to be the letter addressed to Janna Pyke. She would ask her neighbour if Janna Pyke was indeed the last tenant of Flat 2 and, if she was, whether there was any forwarding address. She stood at the door with her speech prepared and waited.

After a few moments the door opened slowly with a sinister creak: the hinges needed oiling. The elderly man who stood on the threshold was tall with a shock of white hair and the face of a gentle eagle. He wore a checked shirt, grey trousers, tweed tie and new-looking carpet slippers on his feet – and he assessed Carmel warily, as though he was unsure whether to greet her with friendliness or hostility.

'Sorry to bother you. My name's Carmel Hennessy. I've just moved in upstairs.' She knew she was speaking too quickly, her well-rehearsed words coming out in a gush. 'Er, I hope I don't disturb you. I try to keep my music and TV quiet. You must tell me if it ever . . .'

The initial suspicion vanished from the man's face. 'Oh no. I can assure you, I've heard nothing.' He stood aside.

'Please ... please come in. I'm Conrad Peace. Delighted to meet you.' He held out a large hand, mottled with brown liver spots. When Carmel shook it, she was struck by how soft it was. This man was no horny-handed son of toil. In fact by the look of his long, sensitive fingers, Carmel guessed he might have once been an artist or a musician. He looked friendly, benevolent and certainly unthreatening, and Carmel suddenly felt silly for being so afraid.

As she entered the flat, she saw that, although it was old fashioned, it was tidy and spotlessly clean. Carmel asked him how long he'd lived there.

'I moved in when I retired,' he replied. 'About four years ago. I was a verger at the cathedral: there was a house that went with the job but I had to move on when I left. I still have family in Eborby and I wanted to stay near the cathedral. And my wife had passed away by then so I didn't need anywhere big.'

Carmel noticed a photograph standing on the chest of drawers – a smiling girl, aged around six, with blond curls. 'Is that your granddaughter?' she asked, thinking she was bound to be on safe ground. She'd never met a grandparent yet who hadn't wanted to talk about their grandchildren.

But the old man's face clouded and Carmel knew instantly that something was wrong. 'It's my great-niece.' He hesitated. 'She died.'

Carmel cursed herself for her tactlessness. 'I'm sorry,' was all she could think of to say. But it seemed inadequate.

'It was a long time ago,' Conrad Peace said sadly. Then, after a short silence, he gave her a small, sad smile. 'Please don't worry. You weren't to know. Tell me about yourself. You're not local, are you?'

Carmel blushed. 'I'm from Liverpool.'

'I thought so. The accent ... faint but unmistakable. What brought you across the Pennines?'

'When my dad died, my mum married again and we moved down south ... Milton Keynes.'

'But you weren't happy?' The old man was perceptive.

She thought it best to stick to facts. 'When I left university I worked in the Midlands for a year. Then I looked for a job up north and I ended up in Eborby. I've just started at the new Archaeology Centre. I work with our landlady, Mrs Thewlis: that's how I came to know about the flat. She said the last tenant had moved out suddenly.'

'Oh yes. She left without paying the rent.' A glint of mischief appeared in his watery blue eyes. 'I believe they used to call it a moonlight flit. Mind you, I can't understand why Mrs Thewlis let the flat to someone like that in the first place. Then someone tried to break in a few days after she'd left. They smashed the lock.'

'I thought that was the last tenant - I thought she'd come back for something she'd left behind.'

'As far as I know she never returned the key to Mrs Thewlis so I doubt if it was her. It must have been someone else. I was out at the time - a concert at the cathedral. Fortunately, they didn't attempt to break into my flat.'

Carmel suddenly felt uneasy. It was always said that once a thief has broken into your home, they're more likely to return than to seek pastures new. No wonder Peta Thewlis had evaded the question.

'How well did you know the last tenant?'

'I can't say I knew her. I only spoke to her when I had to complain about the noise. She had very odd taste in music. Not very nice, in my opinion,' he added, his lips forming a purse of disapproval.

Carmel was suddenly curious. 'What do you mean?'

'Oh, I've no idea what it was. It just sounded rather ... I don't know. And some of the people who used to call ... Elizabeth, my niece, said they looked like something out of a horror film ... all in black and with their noses pierced and goodness knows what else.'

Carmel flicked her dark hair in front of her ears as discreetly as she could, having a number of piercings herself. She smiled sympathetically, hoping they wouldn't be noticed.

‘Was her name Janna Pyke?’

A flicker of unease passed across Conrad Peace’s pale face for a split second. ‘I think so, yes. You do ask a lot of questions.’

‘My father was a policeman. Must be in the blood,’ she said quickly, the mention of her father producing a suddcn, overwhelming feeling of emptiness.

‘Would you like a cup of tea?’ he asked, suddenly concerned as though he sensed her pain.

‘That would be nice. Thanks.’ She smiled, searching desperately for something to say. ‘Do you know much about the history of this house?’ she asked, thinking the past was a safe topic of conversation.

Peace shuffled over to the window and looked out, concealed from the world beyond the glass by snowy net curtains. ‘What have you heard?’

‘Nothing. I just noticed that the ghost tour stops outside. I wondered whether there was . . .’

‘No,’ the old man said quickly. ‘There’s nothing. It’s all nonsense.’

There was an awkward silence. Perhaps, she thought, he’d felt the strange atmosphere in the house as well. She decided to change the subject and asked him about his days at the cathedral. He sat down again and visibly relaxed.

As she sipped her tea, listening politely as he warmed to his subject, she was aware of the buzz of voices outside on the green. The ghost tour had arrived again.

She excused herself, promising to call again, and went upstairs to watch from her window, wondering about Janna Pyke. And her strange friends.

‘RTA. Eborby bypass. Two miles east of Noyby. Ford Mondeo driven into a bloody great tree. No other vehicle involved. Driver unconscious. Looks in a bad way. Woman passenger hysterical but doesn’t appear to be badly hurt. Ambulance on its way but I reckon we need the fire service with some cutting equipment to get the driver out. And get a bloody move on, will you.'

The constable scratched his head and surveyed the scene. He could make out the noise of an ambulance siren in the distance but it was drowned out by the woman passenger's shouts and screams. He and the young policewoman with him had thought she was screaming in pain when they'd first arrived on the scene but they soon realised things weren't that straightforward.

The woman was blonde, probably in her thirties, slightly overweight and dressed in casual designer clothes. She was out of the car and appeared to be unhurt but she was shouting, screeching, non-stop at the top of her voice, keeping up the constant barrage of high-pitched noise even though her throat must have been killing her. In the constable's opinion his colleague was showing remarkable self control in not slapping her across the face. But then they were all only too aware these days of how easy it was for an accusation of police brutality to stick.

He could hear the policewoman's calm, soothing voice, a drone beneath the soprano screams. 'Just calm down, love. Take a deep breath. Can you tell me your name? Where does it hurt? What happened? Just try and breathe deeply. The ambulance is on its way.'

The radio crackled into life. 'That car number you gave us. It's registered to a Mr John Wendal, fifteen Yarmton Close, Hasledon.'

'Thanks.'

Two ambulances were now in sight, approaching fast, sirens and lights blazing. A fire engine followed in their wake. Mr John Wendal – if it was indeed the registered owner who'd been driving – needed to be cut out of the car if he was to stand a chance.

Suddenly the woman screamed. Her words much clearer this time. 'Keep him away from me. Don't let him near me. He wants my soul.'

The two officers' eyes met. There were a lot of nutcases

around these days. Then, as the ambulance screeched to a halt, the woman picked up a large branch that was lying by the side of the road, knocked off by the collision, and ran to the car.

It took two police officers and two paramedics to stop her from sending the unconscious driver to his final resting place.

The constable had seen some domestics in his time but this one beat the lot.

The killer knew that he had to be patient, to bide his time and wait.

He had watched from the front room window for the paperboy to come up the path and he had sprinted into the hall, snatching the paper before it reached the floor. He fell to his knees and felt the hard chill of the tiles through the fabric of his jeans as he unfolded the paper and scanned the headlines.

It was on the front page again: the Resurrection Man. He didn't understand why they called him that. Didn't they know that he had to leave them in churchyards because they were the proper places for the dead? Proper and fitting.

His hands began to shake and he told himself that he had to stay cool, calm. Nobody must know about the turmoil inside his head – if they did they might guess his secret. He had to put on a show to the world.

She was calling from downstairs. Dinner was ready. But was it true? Perhaps the devil had assumed her voice and was trying to lure him into a trap.

Nothing was ever as it seemed.

Chapter Two

'Police investigating the murders of a man and a woman in the Eborby area by the so-called Resurrection Man have issued a fresh appeal to the public.' The young, dark-haired woman in a pinstriped suit was reading the local evening news with a frown she probably thought gave her gravitas.

'They would like to speak to anyone who knew Carla Yates, aged forty-five, or Harold Uckley, aged fifty-six, and they are urging anybody with information to come forward.' Two photographs were flashed on the screen, a balding man in formal passport pose and a laughing holiday snap of a woman with tousled dark hair, taken in an anonymous bar on some Costa or other. 'Carla Yates was last seen . . .'

Joe Plantagenet picked up the remote control and pressed the red button to silence the TV. Somehow he couldn't face hearing about the deaths of Carla Yates and Harold Uckley just at that moment. He needed a break.

The telephone rang, the sound ripping through the empty peace that had fallen on the room. Joe looked at it for a few moments before answering it, sending up a quick prayer. Please, God, don't let it be another one. He was surprised to feel his hand shaking slightly as he picked up the receiver. But the voice on the other end of the line sounded more apprehensive than he did.

'Joe, is that you? It's Sandra. Sandra Hennessy.'

Joe had recognised the voice at once. Sandra, Kevin's widow. Sandra who'd leaned on him as they followed Kevin's coffin into the church. Sandra who'd cried on his shoulder all those years ago. Kevin and Sandra had been a lot older than Joe, who had only been twenty-three when it happened; a raw young detective constable visiting a Liverpool tower block with his sergeant as part of an armed robbery investigation. Routine. Just to ask a petty villain a few pertinent questions. Routine until the world exploded and Kevin Hennessy hit the damp pavement like a felled tree, blood gushing over the glistening grey concrete like a flowing, scarlet tide.

A few seconds later Joe had felt a sickening pain, looked down at his shoulder and saw the blood where the bullet had hit him. He'd survived but Kevin hadn't. Maybe that was why he'd always kept in touch with Sandra, because he felt responsible for her and her teenage daughter, Carmel . . . even after Sandra had remarried so soon after Kevin's death and moved to Milton Keynes. Responsible and a little guilty. The psychologist he'd seen afterwards had told him these emotions were quite normal. But they didn't feel it.

'Sandra. How are you?' It was a while since he'd spoken to her. The contact had diminished gradually over the years.

'I'm OK.'

'How's Steve?' He asked the question out of politeness. He hardly knew the man who'd replaced Kevin with almost indecent haste.

'He's OK. Look, Joe, I've been meaning to call you. Carmel's got a job in Eborby.'

Joe remembered Carmel. Kevin's daughter had been a shy teenager when he'd last seen her. Gawky and thin with a steel brace on her teeth, she had scuttled away to her bedroom like a frightened crab whenever Joe had visited.

'Good. Where's she working?' Joe dredged his memory. He recalled that Carmel had done well at school and had returned to Liverpool to study archaeology at the university. He knew she'd managed to get a museum job in the Midlands but there'd been no mention of Eborby.

'She's working in some new archaeology centre. Look, Joe, I'm worried.'

He had sensed anxiety in her voice but had hoped it had just been his imagination. 'What about?'

There was a short silence then 'I know I'm being silly . . . It's these Resurrection Man murders. Did the victims know each other or . . .'

Now Joe knew why she had called. Her only daughter might be at risk. This was enough to send any mother reaching for the panic button and Sandra had already lost a husband to murder. She was vulnerable – terrified that lightning could strike twice – so it would reassure her to know that the Resurrection Man's victims had been killed for some logical reason by somebody they knew. If it was random, everyone was at risk. Including Carmel.

Joe thought for a moment. He knew he could lie to make her feel better. But he believed that, in the long run, honesty was preferable. 'As far as we know the victims weren't connected in any way. But I hope we do find a connection.'

'So it's a random killer?'

'Come on, Sandra . . . statistically . . .'

'Sod statistics. Will you get in touch with her? Make sure she's all right. See that her flat's secure and . . .'

He could hear the rising panic in Sandra's voice. It would do no harm to put her mind at rest. And he was the one who'd survived on that rainy night in Liverpool nine years ago. He owed it to her. He told her to give Carmel his mobile number – she was to ring him if she was worried about anything . . . anything at all. And if he hadn't heard from Carmel within the next few days he'd try to find time to call her himself, just to check she was OK.

And warn her to take care.

Carmel Hennessy had slept a little better. Somehow she'd

found her meeting with Conrad Peace reassuring. The knowledge that there was another human being in the same building – a gentle elderly man who'd once been a verger at the cathedral – had brought her back to normality when she'd been in danger of letting her imagination run away with her. Although there was something about her bedroom – something in the atmosphere she couldn't quite put her finger on – that made her restless and unable to relax. She often felt an all-consuming sadness when she was lying there in the early hours which usually seemed to lift when she got up and began the day. She told herself it was probably the move to a new city. But she wondered whether Janna Pyke – the ill-behaved last tenant – had felt it too.

She walked to work – something she had never been able to do in her previous job working at a small museum some fifteen miles from the flat she'd shared with two other girls in a large Midlands conurbation. She loved the walk through Eborby's early morning streets; loved the smell of coffee drifting from the little cafés and the clatter as the shop shutters opened. It had rained during the night and, where the sun managed to shine in over the tangled pantile rooftops, the damp ground sparkled in the shafts of golden light. At this time the streets belonged to the people of Eborby rather than the tourists who roamed, sheeplike, along their worn flagstones later on in the day.

She arrived at the Archaeology Centre at eight forty-five. It was a modern building – tucked between a stone-built medieval merchant's house and a handsome Georgian building that now housed a firm of accountants – so tastefully designed to blend in with the city's architectural heritage that it had won numerous awards. Inside there was a hands-on education centre designed to encourage public involvement in the city's archaeology and much loved by local schools who provided a constant stream of visitors in term time. The other half of the building housed the offices and laboratories of the city's archaeological service but Carmel had little to do with this side of the operation. She was there to deal with the visitors and give demonstrations.

As she put her handbag in her locker, Peta Thewlis entered the cloakroom, her arms folded around her defensively, making a beeline for the toilets. Peta, tall and slim with a helmet of glossy brown hair, had an almost Gallic elegance that Carmel envied and when she spotted Carmel she gave her a cool smile.

'How's the flat? Is everything all right?'

Carmel wondered whether there was something behind her new landlady's question. Then she told herself not to be so foolish. It was an innocent enquiry. Friendly. But Peta was the type of capable, authoritative woman who always made her nervous. And she was her boss as well as her landlady so Carmel always felt obliged to make a good impression: to mind her Ps and Qs.

'It's fine. I met the gentleman in the downstairs flat last night. Mr Peace.'

'Ah yes. Mr Peace.' Peta's expression gave nothing away.

'Er ... a letter arrived addressed to a Janna Pyke and I wondered if you had a forwarding address.'

'No. She left suddenly and she didn't say where she was going ... which is hardly surprising as she owes me a month's rent.'

'So what should I do with the letter?'

The older woman gave a bored shrug. 'That's up to you.'

Peta turned and marched towards the toilet cubicles, leaving Carmel no wiser. Carmel hurried out of the cloakroom towards the interactive education centre where she was to entertain visitors until lunchtime.

She sensed that the subject of the previous tenant wasn't a welcome one. Perhaps there had been some row she didn't know about. Or perhaps there was something Peta wanted to hide, although she couldn't for the life of her think of what it could be.

When Carmel reached the education centre she was relieved to see that Maddy Owen was already there. Maddy had taken her out to lunch on her first day and had showed her the ropes, fussing over her like a mother hen. She liked Maddy. Maddy was OK.

It was Maddy who first told her about the Resurrection Man murders. She seemed worried that there was a killer on the loose in Eborby and every so often she'd bring up the subject, as though it was hovering in her mind like a persistent wasp. Maddy lived on her own and she'd admitted to Carmel that the murders were making her nervous. But that morning Maddy seemed unusually happy. Perhaps the Resurrection Man had been caught.

However, Maddy's good mood owed nothing to police efficiency. An old university friend was coming to stay with her that weekend and Maddy intended to show her the night life of Eborby. But the smile of anticipation on Maddy's face suddenly vanished. 'You are being careful with this killer still on the loose? Keep your wits about you, won't you.'

Carmel nodded, slightly impatient with Maddy's fussing. 'So what's his modus operandi?' she asked after a few moments. 'How does he abduct his victims?' She couldn't resist asking the question, like a child watching a scary film through splayed fingers – horrified yet somehow fascinated.

Maddy shrugged. 'The police are keeping quiet about it which makes me think it must be pretty gruesome. Perhaps it's better not to know, eh?'

Carmel suddenly remembered the white-faced man – the one she called Jack the Ripper – who'd been watching her flat. Perhaps that's how the killer did it. Perhaps he staked out his victims' homes and then followed them. A chill went through her body and she felt herself shudder. Should she confide in Maddy? If she told Maddy and anything happened to her . . .

'I think a man's been watching my flat.' She blurted out the words before she could stop herself.

Maddy looked worried. 'Why don't you tell the police?'

'And say what?' Carmel suddenly felt foolish. She was over-reacting.

'Say someone's watching your flat.

Carmel hesitated. 'My mum called me last night. She's spoken to an old colleague of my dad's. Joe Plantagenet – he's a detective inspector in Eborby. He said I was to call him if I was worried about anything . . .'

'So call him. Ask his advice, off the record.'

Carmel thought for a few moments. 'I haven't seen him in years . . . not since I was about fifteen.' She grinned. 'He must have been in his early twenties then and I think I had a bit of a crush on him.'

'Call him. What have you got to lose?'

'My dignity. I don't want to make a fool of myself. I think it might be the man who leads the ghost tour. They stop outside and he points up to my flat but I don't know what he's saying. In fact I thought I might go along tonight to find out. Perhaps it's not me he's interested in. Perhaps it's something to do with the building.'

Maddy touched her arm. 'I still think you should call this Joe . . . put your mind at rest. And I'll tell you what, if you go on the tour tonight, I'll come with you. Safety in numbers, eh.'

Carmel smiled. 'I'm up for it if you are.' She paused for a moment. 'I spoke to Peta this morning. Not very friendly, is she?'

'You're right there. But I think she has a lot on her plate with her son.'

'How do you mean?'

Maddy leaned forward and lowered her voice. 'He's ill . . . been in and out of hospital. Tragic really. That's why her husband walked out. He couldn't take it, so I've heard.'

Carmel suddenly felt guilty for having judged Peta so harshly. She should have learned long ago never to make assumptions. But she still kept doing it.

A well-dressed couple with a pair of bored-looking children wandered in.

'Curtain up,' Maddy whispered before walking over to greet them with a welcoming smile.

Goths. The desk sergeant recognised the species. But these two seemed older than usual. Well into their twenties. They hovered between the front door of the police station and the front desk, conducting a whispered argument. The sergeant had strained to hear but he couldn't make out what they were saying so he leaned on the desk and assumed a welcoming expression.

'How do. Can I help you at all?'

The pair turned to face him, their faces blank. Both were dressed from head to toe in black; the woman's long curtain of black hair half hid her face while the man's hair stood up in spikes. Their faces were pierced with an assortment of metalware and the woman's eyes were outlined in kohl, reminding the sergeant of an Egyptian mummy case he'd once seen in a museum.

It was the woman who spoke first. 'Er . . . how do we go about reporting someone missing?' She was surprisingly well spoken, not what the sergeant had expected.

He turned and took a missing persons form from the pigeonholes behind the desk. 'So who's missing then?'

'Someone we work with. She's not been into work for a few weeks and nobody's seen her. We went to her flat but she wasn't there. And she was doing a postgraduate course at the university. We asked her tutor but he said he hasn't seen her. I mean people don't just disappear, do they?'

'You'd be surprised what people do, love. I'm sure she'll turn up in her own good time,' the sergeant said. He always told them that. It reassured them and most of the time he was proved absolutely right. 'If you'd like to give me her details . . . Name?'

'Janna Pyke.'

'Address?'

'She had a flat on Vicars Green. Not far from the cathedral. But she moved out a few weeks ago and the old guy downstairs didn't know where she'd gone. He gave us the landlady's address but she fobbed us off. Said she'd disappeared without paying the rent and the place had been let to someone else.'

'What about her things? Did she leave them in the flat?'

'The landlady said she'd left some stuff. She put it up in the loft in case she came back for it.'

The sergeant nodded. If she'd left her possessions, it didn't sound like a moonlight flit. This fact raised the urgency a few notches. 'Where does Ms Pyke work?'

The man and woman in black exchanged glances. 'We all work in the House of Terrors. On Marketgate.'

The sergeant had heard of the House of Terrors. It was Yorkshire's answer to the Chamber of Horrors in London, only more gory. Not the sort of place he'd encourage his two teenage lads to hang around. Who knew what ideas a place like that could plant in impressionable minds?

'Right,' he said with a sigh, his pen poised over the form in front of him. 'What about friends and family? Or boyfriends? Is there a boyfriend?'

'She never mentioned her family except to say she didn't speak to them. And most of her friends seem to be from work.' The pair in black looked at each other.

'Something the matter?'

The young man hesitated, as though making a decision. 'There are a few people she used to hang around with at work who are into . . .'

The sergeant saw the girl give him a vicious nudge. Whatever he was about to say was something she didn't want the police to hear. He wondered what it was. Drugs probably.

'She did have a boyfriend,' volunteered the girl. 'But I think they split up a few weeks ago.'

'Know his name?'

The girl frowned and shook her head. 'We never met him, did we, Steve?'

The young man shook his head. 'Never.'

'She said he was an actor. But I don't know if he worked at the theatre or . . .'

'Well, I'd better take some details. Get her description circulated. You wouldn't have a photograph by any chance, would you?'

With surprising efficiency, the young man produced a photograph of a group of black-clad young people from his rucksack. He pointed to one of the girls. With her long black hair and facial piercings, she looked remarkably similar to her fellows.

'We'll do our best to find her . . . sir,' the sergeant said unconvincingly as he began to record the details.

It seemed that Traffic had washed their collective hands of John Wendal and his car that had crashed so dramatically on the Eborby bypass. But there was something odd about the case. There had been no other vehicle involved, as far as they could tell the car had no faults and, according to the doctors, the driver had suffered no heart attack or fit that might have made him lose control.

Then there was the passenger. The as-yet-unidentified woman who was under sedation after trying her best to send the unfortunate Mr Wendal into the next world with a hefty tree branch. Those who had witnessed her attempted attack on the unconscious man had dismissed the theory that it was a lovers' tiff. Even the most volatile of lovers would hardly react with such fear and loathing. Whatever John Wendal had done to the woman, it must have been bad. Unforgivable. And it seemed it was up to CID to find out exactly what it was.

Detective Constable Jamilla Dal had been about to set off for the hospital alone but DI Plantagenet unexpectedly announced that he was going to take a break from the Resurrection Man investigation and come with her. He wanted to see the mystery woman for himself because, according to the medical staff, she was coming out with some pretty strange statements and this had aroused his curiosity.

Wendal's wife had been informed but she could throw no light on the identity of the mysterious passenger. She was quite sure he wasn't having an affair. Jack wasn't that sort of man. She'd sounded as though she believed every word she was saying. Jamilla hadn't liked to tell her that it wasn't unknown for people to lead secret lives of which their nearest and dearest knew absolutely nothing. Jamilla was a kind young woman and hadn't seen the point in causing unnecessary pain.

The staff at the Eborby Permanent Building Society had been interviewed and the picture they had given of their colleague seemed to back up the wife's statement. John Wendal was a quiet man, devoted to his wife and grown-up daughter. A nice man, interested in DIY, gardening and steam engines – he helped out as a volunteer at the Railway Museum at weekends. A solid citizen, there was no way anybody could see him involved in anything untoward. And as for having a tempestuous affair with a blonde ... The idea was risible. Ridiculous.

'Is she up to speaking to us, do you think?' Joe asked as he and Jamilla walked down the polished hospital corridor towards the side ward.

'The doctor says there doesn't seem to be anything physically wrong with her apart from a few cuts and bruises. She's sedated though. He thinks it might be shock.'

'Most people who are in shock don't try to murder someone.' He smiled. 'But then I'm no expert.'

Jamilla pushed open the door. The sparsely furnished, clinical room was brightly lit. In the bed lay a woman, her dyed blond hair spread out on the pillow like a halo. As she heard them come in, she blinked, as though emerging from a deep sleep and struggled to raise herself. Jamilla hurried over to the bed and arranged her pillows so that she could sit.

'You a doctor?' she said, staring Joe in the eye. 'I keep telling them I'm all right. I need to get home. I've got things to do.'

'Where is home, Mrs ... er ...?'

The woman's lips twisted upwards in a cunning grin. 'You won't catch me out. You're one of them, aren't you? You and her.' She pointed a plump finger at Jamilla.

Joe studied her face and realised that the fear in her eyes was genuine. He took his ID from his pocket and held it up for her to see. 'I'm a police officer. Detective Inspector Joe Plantagenet and this is Detective Constable Jamilla Dal. We're trying to find out how you came to be travelling in a car with Mr John Wendal and what exactly happened to cause the car to crash.'

At the mention of Wendal's name, the woman's body stiffened and her eyes widened with fear. Jamilla and Joe looked at each other. Whatever this apparently respectable husband, father and pillar of the Eborby Permanent Building Society had done, it must have been something truly terrible.

Joe sat down on a chair by the bed and motioned Jamilla to do the same. 'We're sorry to upset you, but we have to ask you some questions. Can you tell us your name?'

The woman clutched at the white sheet that covered her, her tense hands like twisted talons. She gave Joe a sly look and shook her head.

'Can you remember where you live?'

Silence.

'Do you remember anything about last night? About the crash? How did you come to be in the car with Mr Wendal?'

'I'm not saying.'

'Why not?'

The woman looked Joe in the eye. 'Because he sent you.'

'If you mean Mr Wendal, I have to tell you that he's still unconscious. He's in no position to send anyone anywhere. His wife's with him.' He paused, watching the woman's face. 'Did you know he was married?'

She began to laugh, a mirthless chuckle. 'Of course he's not married. How can he be married? Now I know you're lying. Get out.'

'Is that why you attacked him?' Jamilla asked. 'Did he tell you he was married and he wanted to end your relationship?'

She pointed an accusing finger at Jamilla. 'You think you're being so clever, don't you? But I knew who he was. That's why I had to kill him. I knew who he was and what he wanted. It was him or me.'

'What did he want?' Joe asked softly.

The woman looked him in the eye, a smile playing around her lips. 'You know bloody well what he wanted but he's not getting it.'

'What do you mean? What was it he wanted?'

Jamilla sat forward, her notebook to the ready, braced to hear a harrowing tale of sexual violence.

But instead the woman calmly said, 'My soul. He wanted my soul,' before closing her eyes and sinking back on her pillows.

The sound echoed in the silence. The key turning and the padlock falling to the floor. Then the metallic slithering of the chains on the wood, clanking like Marley's ghost as gravity hauled them downwards.

The killer stood and listened. No noise. It was done. Finished.

He didn't like the way they smelled when he opened the lid. But he liked to see their faces. As their souls left their bodies they saw their future. They received a vision of their destination; the final realisation that their actions had dire and eternal consequences. As they died, their bowels emptied and their flesh began to rot. That's why he wore the mask over his face when he went to seek them. And the overalls to protect his clothes and body. Everything had to be done properly. It was necessary. It was his duty.

He put a shaking hand out to touch the lid. The first time he'd seen what was inside he had vomited on to the ground, the acid contents of his stomach burning the back of his throat. But now he found he was almost looking forward to the sight of the face contorted in terror.

His tongue moistened his dry lips as he anticipated the moment. Then, with a sudden burst of effort, he reached forward, grabbed hold of the lid and lifted it up.

And with a groan of satisfaction, he beheld his handiwork.

Chapter Three

According to the posters, the ghost tour began at the side of the cathedral. By the south door. Seven thirty on the dot every night except Sundays and bank holidays. The sun was low now but it still shone on the stones of the cathedral making the building glow like some huge source of warmth and light. Carmel had decided to wear jeans and a T-shirt. And to take a cardigan in case it became chilly as the evening wore on. The posters mentioned that the tour lasted just over an hour and she wondered whether it would be an hour well spent or a complete waste of time. But she was meeting Maddy there so at least she'd have some company.

She hadn't phoned Joe Plantagenet. In the end she'd felt embarrassed about contacting a man she hadn't seen in years and who'd once been the object of her schoolgirl crush, so she'd put it off. And now she had plans for the evening, her fears and misgivings were fading. She'd wait and see.

She told herself that it would be good to learn a little more about her adopted city. She knew about the archaeological evidence and what the history books had told her: she knew how it had been the site of a Roman legionary headquarters before being settled by the Vikings and she was familiar with its role as a staunch supporter of the Yorkist cause during the Wars of the Roses. If you dug a hole anywhere in Eborby you'd find some evidence of the past. But she wasn't well versed on the hidden history. The ghosts that haunted the city's labyrinth of narrow streets and alleys. The soul of Eborby.

When she thought of the break-in at her flat she felt uneasy, even though Peta Thewlis had assured her that the locks had been changed. As she'd left she'd tested the flat door to make sure it was locked behind her and she'd checked that all the windows were shut – even though it was a warm night and she would have liked to have left them open, you couldn't be too careful. She had seen nothing of Conrad Peace that evening, although she had heard the faint sound of voices drifting up from his flat: his TV probably. Maybe she would call in on him again soon, just to make sure he was all right.

She walked slowly towards the cathedral. It had stood for centuries, a thing of beauty and power, and Carmel felt under its protection as she neared the south door. After a few moments she spotted Maddy trotting towards her, waving.

'Is that him?' Maddy pointed to a small crowd of people clustered around a tall man in black who stood beneath an ornate Victorian lamp post at the edge of the cathedral square.

'I think so,' she replied as they slipped in behind a pair of large American tourists, trying to look inconspicuous.

Close up in daylight the man she'd come to think of as Jack the Ripper didn't look at all fearsome. She had only seen him from a distance before and now she took the opportunity to study him, trying not to make her interest too obvious. She wondered whether he'd recognise her. But if he did, he showed no sign of it.

He was a lot younger than she'd imagined, with a shock of fair hair and a long, unnaturally pale face that never broke into a smile. The cloak and the black top hat gave him a funereal look – but that was probably the intention.

He stood quite still while his audience gathered, his cloak held tightly around him, his eyes to the ground, looking like a great, sleeping bat. Once a sizeable party had mustered there on the stone flags, he looked up, turning his head slowly, studying the faces. Carmel felt relieved that he betrayed no sign of recognition as his gaze rested on her. It was as if the sight of her meant nothing to him; she was just another punter.

Suddenly he spread out his arms and the cloak flapped like the wings of some giant crow. 'Welcome,' he boomed. 'This evening I will take you into another dimension. Eborby's secret parallel world.'

He looked around the faces again, his expression blank, his face deadly pale, and Carmel suddenly realised that he was wearing make-up in an attempt to look more cadaverous. But even though he stayed in character, the effect was slightly marred when he announced that he would come amongst them to collect the four-pound fee for the tour. It was difficult for the charging of hard cash to have a sinister edge. The collection was made with discreet good humour and Carmel slowly began to realise this man was partly playing it for laughs. Now she saw him close up, she recognised him for what he was – a young actor playing a part. If she met him without his make-up and costume – in jeans and sweatshirt, for instance – he would look quite mundane. When Maddy gave her an 'I told you so' look, she began to feel a little foolish.

The tour began and their guide fired stories at them with confusing rapidity. A grey lady was seen wailing outside the cathedral, crying because some eighteenth-century clergyman had refused to baptise her baby which had died a month after birth. A man in the dress of a cavalier was seen walking through the front wall of the Dean's house behind the cathedral, just in the place where the old front door used to be until the house was remodelled in Victorian times. They moved on to a nearby alley where two children had been horribly murdered in 1886 – their cries could be heard on a still night. As could the howling of a ghostly dog outside the Georgian residence of the cathedral organist –

but no explanation was offered for the phantom hound's anti-social behaviour.

It was all very much as Carmel had expected. Grey ladies, ghostly cavaliers, howling spectral canines. She was impatient to move on to Vicars Green to hear what their guide had to say about her house. If it was as silly as the rest of the stories, she had little to worry about. But why had he been watching the building? What was his interest? Perhaps she would ask him if she could summon up the courage. Or maybe it was best to stay in the background and leave well alone.

He led the party on without glancing back to see whether his flock was following; rather he stayed in character all the time, marching purposefully ahead. When he reached Vicars Green he climbed on to the bottom plinth of the Roman column that stood in the centre of the grass - a remnant of Eborby's legionary headquarters - and waited for his audience to gather around him.

Carmel stood at the back of the party and held her breath. This was it. She was about to find out why the man she could no longer think of as Jack the Ripper now that she'd seen him in the flesh found her flat so interesting.

He flung out an arm, pointing in the direction of the house. 'Imagine, ladies and gentlemen, being locked in a small room with no way out. Your companions are lying dead beside you, their bodies beginning to decompose.'

Carmel detected a tremor in his previously sonorous voice. This story was different. This one moved him.

'You have seen them die horribly of the plague,' he continued. 'You have heard their cries and been unable to do anything about it. You are helpless. The authorities have decreed that, because you are living there and are likely to spread the infection, you can't be allowed out of the house. They have boarded up the doors and larger windows so you can't escape, leaving only that small window on the first floor for you to look out of.'

Her heart beating fast, Carmel looked up and saw the

small window of her bedroom. It wasn't true, she thought. It was all made up like those grey ladies and phantom dogs. It was just a bit of fun to send a thrill of terror down the spines of the tourists. That's what they paid for. Surely.

'That's what happened to a young girl when the plague struck Eborby in 1603, in the last year of Good Queen Bess's reign. People saw her looking out of that window up there, staring out, her eyes pleading for release. Until one day she wasn't there any more and the boards were taken from the windows and doors. The first people to enter the house were the Seekers of the Dead. These were women whose job it was to discover whether or not people had succumbed to the plague. It was a risky job and it was usually poor women who had to do it.'

He paused for a moment, the air heavy with disapproval. In spite of his role, this man was displaying twenty-first-century sensibilities and Carmel found this rather comforting.

'When they reached the small room upstairs, a horrific sight met their eyes. The family who lived there had perished. Mother, father, their son and their servants, all bearing the unmistakable marks of the bubonic plague which was spreading around Eborby like wildfire that year. But the daughter – the girl by the window – bore no such marks. Instead of catching the plague, she had starved to death, locked in with the corpses of her family.' He paused, this time for effect. 'She was buried with all the other plague victims on the grassy embankments below the city walls – you can see them as you approach the city – and they lie there undisturbed to this day. The girl, however, does not rest. It is said that as you look up at that window, you can sometimes see her staring out, pleading for help.'

He bowed his head and the assembled crowd stared up at the window of Carmel's room. She found herself staring with them. She had just discovered the cause of her inexplicable feelings of sadness when she slept in that room.

As they moved on to the Fleshambles to hear tales of

grisly murders and executions, she noticed that their guide glanced back at her window. Perhaps the story had fascinated and affected him and he was eager to see the ghostly girl for himself. That was probably it. That was why she had seen him standing there alone at night staring up.

'Are you OK?' Maddy asked. She had been so quiet that Carmel had almost forgotten she was there.

'I'm fine,' she answered bravely.

'It's all nonsense, you know.'

'I know,' she said but she found it hard to concentrate on the remainder of the tour. Her mind was on the story of the girl, the story of her flat. She felt reluctant to go home that night. But she had little choice. Besides, even if she had gone on a solitary crawl of the city's three hundred and odd pubs, she'd still have to go back there sooner or later. It was better to get it over with.

As the tour dispersed, leaving their guide at the Fleshambles, Carmel looked at her watch. Quarter to nine. It was still light . . . just. But the doorways and alleys were in deep shadow.

'Do you want to come for a drink?' Maddy asked.

'No thanks. I'd better have an early night.' There was no way she could face going back into that empty flat in the dark but she was loath to say this to Maddy – it sounded so feeble.

'Are you sure you're all right? Do you want me to come up with you?' Maddy asked, concerned.

'No. I'm fine.'

'Do you still think that guide was the man who was watching the flat?'

Carmel nodded. 'He was probably just rehearsing or something. I'm sure there was no harm in it.'

Maddy looked concerned. 'If you're sure.'

'Yeah. I'll be fine.'

They parted in Vicars Green, Carmel telling Maddy to take care going home. Maddy shot off in the direction of the cathedral, walking at a cracking pace. Perhaps, Carmel thought, she was more nervous than she was letting on. Everyone was with the Resurrection Man about.

Carmel opened the front door and crept past Conrad Peace's flat, listening for sounds of human habitation. She could still hear the faint chatter of the TV and the noise seemed somehow comforting. She hesitated before making her way up the stairs. Mustering all her courage she turned the key in the lock and pushed the door open.

She walked into the flat, listening for noises in the still air. She could hear the sounds of the old house breathing and settling. A creak of a board, the scrabbling of a bird in the eaves. She bustled round turning on all the lights to banish the grey dusk that had begun to fall but she left the bedroom till last: there was definitely an atmosphere in there; she had sensed it from the start. A cold sadness. She would sleep with the bedside light on tonight. Or perhaps she'd brave the sofa.

She was about to switch the TV on for company when she noticed the light on the answerphone flashing. She had a message. Eager to hear another human voice, she pressed the switch.

'Janna,' a voice said slowly. 'This is your final warning. You can't escape. Wherever you are, we'll find you. And when we do, you're dead.'

She stood there, frozen to the spot. The voice had been disguised and it was impossible to tell whether it was a man or a woman.

But one thing was certain. The caller had sounded as if they meant every word.

Joe Plantagenet had never found it easy to bring up the subject of souls, even though, for one brief year, they were to have been his chief concern. He wondered how to approach his imminent meeting with John Wendal's wife. How was he to tell her about the woman's claim that her husband was after her soul? Was it just a figure of speech, a way of indicating that they were having a passionate affair? Or was Wendal involved in some sort of Satanic activity? Or perhaps the as-yet-unidentified woman was mentally ill in some way. Something had triggered her strange behaviour and Joe wanted to find out what that something was and clear the matter up so he could concentrate on the Resurrection Man investigation.

Emily Thwaite had expressed a desire to meet Mrs Wendal for herself and when Joe reached her office, he found her standing in front of the small mirror that hung on the wall above the filing cabinet, running a brush through her thick fair curls with a despairing expression on her face. As soon as she was aware of his presence she thrust the brush out of sight.

'I'm ready,' she said briskly.

'Sure you want to come?'

'Try and stop me. I want to get to the bottom of this,' she said with determination, picking up her handbag – a huge, saggy brown leather model, designed to take enough for a week's holiday. 'Nothing new's come in on the Resurrection Man murders. I've got Sunny and Jamilla going through all the witness statements again in case there's something we missed.'

'There must be something. Some link between Carla Yates and Harold Uckley. Unless the killings were random. Anything come in yet from HOLMES?'

'Nothing.' All the data had been put into the national computer system known as HOLMES in the hope that, if their man had struck elsewhere in the country, they would find out about it. Joe and his colleagues found it hard to believe that anyone capable of carrying out these killings wouldn't have some history of violence.

'I was looking at the Forensic reports. There's very little apart from the wood shavings and they could come from any number of places. I don't expect the victims received any unexplained phone calls or . . .?'

'We've been through all their mobile phone records. Nothing. Nothing out of the ordinary on their home phones either. We're still looking at incoming work calls.'

Emily sighed. 'Surely he's made some mistake.' She hesitated. 'If he carries on killing he's bound to get careless. He'll get cocky . . . think he's invincible.'

Joe didn't reply. The thought of a serial killer in Eborby was a bit much for him to contemplate at present.

'You do realise that our car crash man, John Wendal, works at the same place as the second victim, don't you?' she said. 'Harold Uckley worked at the Eborby Permanent Building Society too.'

'Yes. I had noticed. But then so do about two thousand other people. The Eborby operation's the national headquarters. It's a big employer.'

'Still worth looking at though. I don't believe in coincidences.'

Joe said nothing. Somehow he couldn't share his new boss's optimism. Coincidences happened all too frequently in his experience.

As the traffic was unusually light, it didn't take long to reach the suburb of Hasledon, which lay some two miles out from the city centre. The first houses had been built there in the days of Georgian elegance. Then came a brief housing boom in the late nineteenth century but from the 1930s onwards speculative builders had busied themselves, filling former fields with new homes. Creating suburbia.

As Joe drove he was struck by the thought that there was nothing so unglamorous as suburbia. Films are never set there; neither are great novels. Nobody has ever written songs in praise of suburbia . . . or a great symphony. It is a place for living rather than dreaming. A place of reality. And now they were about to come face to face with the reality of John Wendal's life.

His address turned out to be a small semi-detached house in a 1930s cul-de-sac. It was about as far from the Eborby that drew the tourists as it was possible to get. Nobody would go out of their way to see Yarmton Close.

Emily rang the doorbell, having arranged her features

into a suitably concerned and sympathetic expression. Dealing with Wendal's wife would require a delicate touch.

The door opened to reveal a plain, thin woman with lank brown hair streaked with grey. She was probably in her fifties but looked older.

'Mrs Wendal?'

The woman nodded warily.

As soon as Emily had recited their names and held up her warrant card for inspection, the woman's grey eyes widened and flared into panic. 'Jack ... he's not ...'

'No, there's no change in his condition as far as we know. We'd just like a chat, that's all.' She sounded friendly and unthreatening. There were some who'd lean hard on the wife of a suspected attacker, Joe thought to himself, but Emily Thwaite knew instinctively that pressure like that would probably make Mrs Wendal clam up altogether. She had to think that she was amongst friends if they were to get anywhere.

They were led into a generously sized living room. The furnishings looked new ... as though someone had been splashing out. The wall was hung with photographs of a girl: a posed studio baby portrait; the inevitable array of school photos; a formal graduation picture and lastly a wedding picture of the subject with a smiling, handsome husband. An entire life story.

'Your daughter?' Emily asked, sounding genuinely interested.

'Yes, that's our Jennifer.' The woman's strained expression softened as she glowed with tentative pride.

'Does she live near by?'

'Leeds.'

'That's not too far. It must be awful if they go miles away. I've got three – nine, seven and five. Two boys and a girl.' It was Emily's turn to sound proud. Joe, who had never experienced the joys of fatherhood, looked on. Emily had clearly struck up a rapport with the woman so he'd leave the talking to her.

'I presume Jennifer knows about her father's . . . er, accident?'

'Yes. She's coming over to stay with me for a few days. She insisted.'

'Good.'

'Shall I make us a cup of tea?' Joe offered. He might as well make himself useful. Emily gave a discreet nod and he disappeared into the kitchen.

'I'm afraid I have to ask you some questions, Sue,' Emily said as Joe returned with three mugs of tea. She had obviously learned the woman's Christian name while he'd been away. Things were going well. 'We need to get to the bottom of your husband's accident.'

Sue Wendal nodded. 'I don't understand it myself. That woman . . . who is she?'

'You've no idea?'

'Of course not.'

Emily leaned forward and touched her arm. 'Look, I don't like to ask you this but . . .'

'You want to know if Jack could have been having an affair. Well, the answer's no. He's always come straight home from work. Except on the night he goes to the Railway Society. That's where he'd been. They meet at the Railway Museum every Tuesday. He helps out there as a volunteer every other Saturday as well. I think it's good for a man to have an interest.' She glanced at Joe. 'He's never been one for pubs and football.'

'Is it possible he was meeting a woman?' Joe asked gently. The question was tactless but it had to be asked.

'No. I go to the Society socials with him. And one of our neighbours is in the Society too . . . goes to the museum with him every week – although they're on holiday at the moment so he didn't go this week. If he had been . . .' Her eyes began to fill with tears.

Joe and Emily looked at each other. Had both the men been up to something together . . . meeting call girls while their unsuspecting wives assumed they were playing with trains? Such things weren't unknown.

'Do you know someone called Harold Uckley? He worked in the same place as your husband. Did John ... er, Jack, ever mention him?'

Sue Wendal's eyes widened in alarm. 'Isn't that the man who was murdered? Jack said he worked at the Eborby Permanent but he didn't know him. Different department. Look, I've got to get to the hospital. The doctor said if I keep talking to him, it might help.'

'Of course. We'll give you a lift if you like,' Emily offered. Joe knew she was playing the woman's friend – hoping for confidences. And she was playing the part well.

'No. It's all right. I've got my own car.'

'The woman who was in the car with your husband seemed terrified of him,' Emily said gently. 'She tried to attack him. Said she knew who he was and that he wanted her soul. She was behaving very strangely ... even accused my officers of being in league with him. Can you throw any light on any of this?'

A small tear began to crawl down Sue Wendal's left cheek. 'There's only one explanation. She must be mad. Jack wouldn't hurt a fly. Ask anyone who knows him. Ask Jennifer. That woman must have escaped from somewhere. That's the trouble nowadays ... they let them wander the streets.'

Emily gave Joe an almost imperceptible nod. It was time to go. They thanked Sue Wendal and made a quick getaway.

'I'm inclined to agree with her, you know,' Emily said as they climbed into the car. 'She talked about him while you were out making the tea and he doesn't sound the type to go round attacking women. Mind you, the wife's often the last to know.'

'True. And if he's so pure and innocent, what was she doing in his car?'

'I don't know. Maybe he gave her a lift. Perhaps she was hitch-hiking.'

'Doesn't look the type. Besides, I had a bit of a look round while I was waiting for the kettle to boil.' As soon as they stopped at traffic lights Joe put his hand in his pocket and drew out a leaflet. 'This was on top of the drawers in the garage.'

'You searched the garage?'

'It's just off the kitchen and the door was open. I wouldn't call it searching exactly. More being a bit nosey. Killing time.'

'You need a warrant for that sort of thing.' Emily tried to sound annoyed but didn't quite manage it. Then, a few seconds later, she grinned. 'I thought with you having trained to be a priest you'd be whiter than white.'

Joe's eyes met hers and he smiled back. 'I only lasted a year. And the training at the seminary never covered the use of search warrants.'

'So what did you find then?'

He handed her the leaflet and she studied it. 'The House of Terrors. Doesn't seem his sort of thing. Think he had hidden depths?'

'Nothing would surprise me,' Joe whispered as he switched on the ignition.

Chapter Four

Carmel Hennessy had stared at Joe Plantagenet's mobile number, scribbled in pencil on her pad, trying to summon the courage to call him. But she kept making excuses. He'd be busy. He wouldn't want to be bothered with her petty problems when he had high-profile murders to investigate. But in the end she decided that she'd call him later – after work maybe. She had received a threat after all ... or rather Janna Pyke had.

She wondered whether to mention the message on her answering machine to Peta Thewlis. But Peta would only advise her to go to the police. Dealing with tenants' personal problems was hardly in a landlady's job description.

Carmel hadn't slept well the previous night. Apart from the threatening message to Janna, she hadn't been able to get the ghost girl out of her mind. The girl who had starved to death, trapped in with the corpses of her family. Carmel had stared out of her bedroom window, imagining what it would have been like, and she'd found herself shivering with cold even though the night was warm. She was sure she'd heard a muffled sob. Or perhaps it had been her imagination. The dead, she kept telling herself, had gone into the next world. She had always believed that since she had been old enough to work things out for herself. The girl had gone to a better place – just like her dad, Kevin, had done. She wasn't there any more. But if that was the case, why did she feel so afraid whenever she walked into that bedroom? And why had she chosen to spend an uncomfortable night on the sofa?

At least the ghost tour man hadn't appeared on the green again, as far as she knew. But then since she had seen him in the flesh, as it were, she found that he didn't frighten her any more. He was just some actor playing a part. Part of Eborby's tourist industry. Rather like herself.

It was almost lunchtime when her scheduled session – examining the contents of a Viking rubbish heap with a group of children – drew to a close. And when she returned to the office she found Maddy Owen poring over some plans.

Maddy looked up and pushed her unruly auburn curls behind her ears. 'Everything OK?'

'Fine.'

'You look tired. Didn't you get your early night?'

'I kept thinking about that girl.'

Maddy thought for a few seconds then shook her head. 'I shouldn't take much notice if I were you. The first ghost tour I went on they told us about the blue lady of Swinegate and the headless soldier on the city walls ... and the Roman woman who threw her baby in the river. They make them up as they go along.'

Carmel didn't look convinced. 'I couldn't stop thinking about it happening in my bedroom. I slept on the sofa last night.'

Maddy suddenly looked concerned. 'Even if the place is haunted – and I very much doubt whether it is – what harm can a sad little ghost do to you? Try and forget it, eh,' she added with what she considered to be an encouraging smile.

'There's something else,' Carmel said. 'When I got back last night I had a strange phone call. Well, not a phone call. Someone left a message on my answerphone when I was out. It was for the girl who had the flat before me. Janna. It said she couldn't escape from them ... and it was the final warning.'

'Sounds like debt collectors to me. That's probably why she did a moonlight flit.'

'They said they'd find her and when they do, she's dead. They threatened to kill her.'

Maddy's smile suddenly disappeared. This sounded serious. 'Look, Carmel, I think you should tell the police. Call that Joe you mentioned. Please. What have you got to lose?'

Carmel felt her cheeks turning red. 'He'll have enough on his plate with these murders and . . .'

'He won't mind. Wasn't he a colleague of your father's?'

'More than a colleague. He was with Dad when he died. He was shot too but he was luckier than Dad.'

Maddy fell silent for a moment, lost for words. Then she spoke again. 'If someone's threatening this Janna, the police should know about it.' She paused. 'What's Joe like?'

Carmel felt herself blushing. 'It's a long time since I've seen him . . . but I remember he wasn't a typical policeman.'

'How old is he?'

Carmel thought for a moment. 'He must be in his early thirties now. He'd only just started in the police when . . . when it happened.'

'So why isn't he a typical policeman?'

Carmel shrugged. 'Don't know really. He started to train to be a priest when he left university but he didn't stick it. I remember he spent a lot of time with mum when . . . She said he was a good listener.'

'So call him. And don't delete that message. He'll need to hear it.'

'OK,' said Carmel. She had been tempted to delete the message right away, but some instinct had told her not to. 'Should I mention it to Peta?' she asked.

But Maddy shook her head. 'I never mention anything to Peta if I can avoid it,' she whispered with a grin.

*

'Sarge.'

Sunny Porter made his way over to Jamilla Dal's desk. She had just put the telephone down and she looked excited. And it was rare for Jamilla to show much emotion. 'What is it?'

'I think I've found a connection between the Resurrection Man's victims. I've been speaking to Carla Yates's friends again in case there was something we'd missed. Anyway, one of them said that a few years ago she had a job with a building society and I wondered whether it was the same one Harold Uckley worked for. I called the Eborby Permanent and they confirmed that Carla had worked for them from May 1993 to January 1995.'

'That's not long.'

'I know, but it's a connection between her and Uckley. And that man in the car crash, John Wendal – he worked there too, didn't he?'

Before Sunny could say anything, one of the young DCs rushed over to him with a report from Traffic.

A smile spread across Sunny Porter's face. A car had been found abandoned a mile from the scene of John Wendal's crash and, according to Traffic, it had been sitting there since the night of the accident. They'd tried to contact the registered owner but had no luck. It had to belong to the mystery woman, surely. It was a little powder-blue Fiat – definitely a woman's car. And it had apparently run out of petrol. Typical.

He gave Jamilla a brief homily on the dizziness of women drivers but she thought it best to stay silent in case she said something she'd regret. Sunny was an incorrigible male chauvinist. One of the old school. And she despaired of him ever mending his ways, no matter how many equal opportunities initiatives the powers-that-be threw at him.

It was Sunny who reported the find to the new DCI when she returned from interviewing John Wendal's wife. Taking the credit as usual. Jamilla seethed for a few moments at the injustice of it all and returned to her paperwork. But a couple of minutes later she looked up and saw DI Plantagenet making for her desk.

'Sunny's told me about this abandoned car. It's registered to a Mrs Gloria Simpson. Address in Pickby.'

'It might not be the woman in the crash,' said Jamilla, introducing a note of caution. Her male colleagues seemed to be leaping to conclusions she considered to be rather wild. 'Has the car been reported stolen?'

Joe Plantagenet looked a little hurt. 'Do you think that wasn't the first thing I checked?'

'Sorry,' Jamilla muttered. She liked Joe Plantagenet. He didn't patronise her . . . not like some. 'Did Sunny tell you I'd discovered that Carla Yates worked at the Eborby Permanent Building Society for eighteen months in the 1990s? I know it's a long time ago but . . .'

'It's a link between the two victims.'

'Do you want me to go over to Gloria Simpson's address and see what I can find out?'

'No. The DCI's quite keen to go herself. I'll go with her. Wendal works in the same place as Harold Uckley and now we know Carla Yates used to work there too . . .'

'You think there's a connection between the crash and the Resurrection Man?'

Joe smiled. Jamilla was so young and so keen. Or perhaps he was just becoming cynical. Too cautious by half. 'I'm not saying that there's a definite connection,' he said. 'It's a line of enquiry, that's all.' But he was lying. Emily Thwaite was sure there was a connection. But Joe was reserving judgement.

Joe and Emily drove to Gloria Simpson's address in the district of Pickby, a cluster of Victorian streets, just outside the city walls. Many of the larger houses had been converted into B and Bs but Gloria Simpson's red-brick terraced home bore no tell-tale sign outside. It was a well-kept house which, judging from the two doorbells, was divided into two flats. It had a small front garden, gravelled over to save on the spadework, the original sash windows sparkled and the paint was fresh. Somehow it wasn't the kind of house Joe expected the blonde woman in the hospital to inhabit and he had an awful feeling they were barking up completely the wrong tree.

But it was worth checking out. And after satisfying themselves that nobody was at home, their first port of call was the neighbours.

The house on the right was a B and B and the woman who answered the door greeted them by asking how long they wanted to stay because she had two Canadian ladies booked in on Saturday. When they finally got a word in edgeways, their hostess claimed she knew nothing about the woman next door. In the summer she was always too busy with her guests to bother with the comings and goings of the neighbours.

But they had more luck with the house on the other side. This belonged to an elderly couple – the kind of couple who have grown to resemble each other over many years of marriage – and, fortunately, they seemed to act as unofficial caretakers for the landlord, keeping a spare set of keys in case of emergencies. And, as the police had come calling, this constituted an emergency in their eyes.

They were keen to emphasise that they didn't know the tenants personally. A lecturer from the university had the flat upstairs and a woman lived downstairs. Something told Joe that the lecturer met with the couple's collective approval whereas the woman didn't. It was nothing definite, just a look in the eyes and a slight change in the tone of their voices. There was something about Gloria Simpson that they didn't quite approve of. And he wanted to find out what that something was before they proceeded any further.

Emily had let him do all the talking while she watched and he wondered whether she had had the same feeling. When she spoke, he knew that she had.

'Tell me about Gloria Simpson,' she said sweetly. 'What kind of a person is she?'

The elderly couple exchanged a glance.

'Well, she's not really our sort of person. We don't have much to do with her. I mean, people like to live their own lives, don't they?'

That was all the information they were able to extract. Gloria Simpson lived her own life. And the couple hadn't seen her for a couple of days. In fact her cat had come round to their back door demanding food with characteristic feline imperiousness. It was disgraceful that she hadn't fed the creature ... or, if she had gone away, that she hadn't made some arrangements for its care.

Joe's eyes met Emily's. This was their woman all right. The cat's plight confirmed it. Emily asked for the key sweetly, saying there was no need for them to bother themselves. They'd have a quick look around the flat just to make sure everything was all right and return the key later. This seemed to satisfy the neighbours who made it quite clear that they were on the side of law and order.

As they scurried up Gloria Simpson's garden path, Emily tossed the keys in the air playfully.

'I've got a feeling about this one, Joe,' she announced before opening the door.

The hallway was as neat as the house's exterior. There were tasteful watercolours on the pale walls and decorative encaustic tiles on the floor – original features. A flight of stairs ahead of them led up to the top flat while a stripped wooden door to their right formed the entrance to flat number one: Gloria Simpson's flat. Emily tried a couple of Yale keys until she found the one that turned smoothly in the lock.

'Here goes,' she said as she pushed the door open.

As the room was north facing, the interior seemed dim after the bright sunshine outside. The two police officers stepped inside and shut the door behind them. The first thing Joe noticed was a large photograph hanging over the mantelpiece: a studio portrait of a blonde woman, made up to the nines and airbrushed into an unnatural state of youthful glamour. She must have paid a tidy sum for the makeover and the portrait. And she must, Joe thought, have a fair-sized streak of vanity to display her likeness so prominently. It was the woman from the car crash all right. And now Joe wanted to know what made Gloria Simpson tick.

'A couple of years ago my sister-in-law had one of those pictures done for her birthday,' said Emily, staring at the portrait. 'Cost an arm and a leg. Complete waste of money if you ask me.'

'Well, Gloria obviously didn't think so. Wonder what her game is.'

'You think she's playing a game?'

Joe didn't answer. He didn't really know what to think. 'We'd better have a look around.'

'In the hope that we find some love letters from John Wendal?'

'Something like that.' Joe looked at Emily. 'And if the car's registered to a Mrs Simpson, where's Mr Simpson?'

'Miles away, I should think. She looks the divorcée type to me,' was the DCI's snap judgement.

Joe's instinct told him she was probably right. The airbrushed portrait spoke of self-absorption. There might not have been room in her affections for a Mr Simpson.

They began to look around the flat, uncomfortably aware that they had no search warrant. This was to be a perfunctory search, just to confirm the car crash woman's identity and glean any clues they could about her life. The living room was neat, the cream carpet and the feminine nick-nacks testifying to the lack of a male presence. The bedroom was predictably frilly and the kitchen was show-home tidy.

'You can tell she hasn't got kids,' said Emily with a dismissive snort. 'Doesn't really look lived in, does it?'

'Wonder where she works,' Joe mused.

'We'd better have a look through the drawers. I won't tell if you won't, eh. And I suppose she is a missing person . . . sort of,' she added with a knowing grin.

'Sort of,' Joe agreed, looking at the bookcase to his right. 'It looks as if she's interested in the occult and tarot.'

'Each to his own,' said Emily, rolling her eyes to heaven. 'You take the bedroom and I'll take the living room.'

'What's in there?' Joe pointed to a closed door off the corridor.

'Cupboard? Second bedroom?'

Joe strode over to the door, turned the handle and pushed. The door didn't budge. 'It's locked.'

'I wonder why,' said Emily before trying all the keys on the ring in the lock.

When none of them fitted, she fished in her handbag and drew out a bent piece of wire. 'Don't look if you're squeamish.'

Joe watched, fascinated, as Emily Thwaite jiggled the wire in the lock until it turned with a satisfying click.

'Just one of my many talents,' she grinned.

'Do you do safe breaking as well?'

'Naturally.' She pushed open the door. The room was dark and she flicked the light switch. Nothing happened.

Joe went in first, pausing on the threshold as his eyes adjusted to the lack of light. He could make out a chink of light where the thick curtains didn't quite meet so he tiptoed across the room and put his hands up to draw them apart. The curtains were velvet, soft and sensual against his skin like the fur of a living creature and, as he flung them open, the room filled with light.

Emily gave a squeak of surprise before swearing softly under her breath. She turned to Joe. 'Well, you used to be a priest. You're supposed to be the expert on this sort of thing. What does it mean? What's it all about?'

Joe looked around the small room which had probably been used as a dining room or study in less sensational times. The walls were blood red and the curtains dark-blue velvet. A white pentagram stood out on the black-painted floorboards and the walls were adorned with pictures of hideous horned devils, creatures of darkness and nightmares. A goat's skull stood on a makeshift altar and an inverted brass cross hung on the far wall above it. On the front of the altar was a symbol, a triangle in a circle topped by a half circle, like a pair of stylised horns.

'I reckon our Gloria's been in touch with her dark side,' Joe said. He shuddered suddenly, as though someone had laid an icy hand on his heart.

'You can say that again. I think we should have a word with her, don't you?'

Joe had to agree. But somehow he dreaded seeing Gloria Simpson again.

In the end it turned had out to be a good day for Carmel Hennessy. The school kids had seemed fairly interested in the undemanding tasks she had given them to do. And even Peta Thewlis had defrosted a little and made vague noises of approval, which was more than she had come to expect.

Maddy Owen was still quite insistent that she should call Joe Plantagenet to tell him about the answerphone message. In the end she agreed, if only to keep Maddy quiet. There was something of the mother hen about Maddy. But she was good hearted. And besides, Carmel was alone in Eborby and she needed all the friends she could get.

She punched in the number, her heart beating fast. What if Joe resented her mother's presumption? What if he was too busy to be bothered? A hundred what ifs galloped through her head as she waited for him to answer her call.

'DI Plantagenet.' The voice was deep with a residual Liverpool accent, not as strong as her father's had been.

'Joe? Is that Joe?'

'Speaking.' He sounded a little cautious.

'This is Carmel Hennessy.'

'Carmel. How are you?' He sounded almost pleased to hear from her but she couldn't be sure. 'I'm glad you called. I was going to ring you . . . just to see how you were doing.'

'My mum?'

'She called me. She's panicking a bit but I told her you can take care of yourself.'

Carmel smiled to herself. This man wasn't treating her like a child even though he'd only remember her as a silly teenager.

'Look, Joe, I'm a bit worried about something. You're not free tonight by any chance?'

There was a long silence. Then, 'Yeah. Do you want to meet?'

She gabbled the rest, half grateful, half embarrassed. Could he come to the flat? Something had happened and she needed his advice. She was surprised when he said yes. He'd see her at eight thirty and they'd talk then.

On impulse she invited Maddy round for a pizza at seven. She hardly knew anybody in Eborby and she told herself that a little impromptu entertaining would do her good. And besides, as Maddy had said herself, there was safety in numbers.

Maddy accepted the invitation eagerly and Carmel found herself wondering whether there was anyone special in her life – she had never mentioned anyone and Carmel realised that she knew very little about her. But perhaps the coming evening would change that. She began to make plans – she would buy a bottle of wine and a few cans of beer for her guests on her way home and she toyed with the idea of asking Maddy what she liked to drink. But then that might sound too formal. Casual was the watchword here.

On her way home she slipped into a small off licence on the corner of Boargate and bought a bottle of red wine and a bottle of white, not being sure of Maddy's preferences. She also purchased half a dozen cans of Theakstons and two of lager, covering all eventualities. She had a dim memory of her father offering Joe a whisky but that was out, spirits being far too expensive. She bought some crisps and nuts for them to nibble. It would have to do.

Armed with her carrier bag of goodies, she made her

way back to Vicars Green and when she opened the front door, she could hear voices coming from Mr Peace's flat. A man and a woman. Her neighbour had a visitor.

She flicked open the lid of the post box and looked inside. There were two letters lying there. The top one, she knew would be offering a new credit card: she recognised the type as she had received many such offers before. It lay there promising instant gratification like a tart on a brothel bed but Carmel, immune to temptation, tore it up. On what they paid her at the Archaeology Centre, the last thing she wanted was to get herself into debt.

The second letter in the box looked more interesting. The envelope was made of thick cream-coloured paper and the ink used was bright blue. The name Janna Pyke in large, flourishing handwriting, jumped out at her. It was identical to the last one. Whoever had sent it had written again.

After leaving the previous letter in the box for twenty-four hours, she had taken it upstairs and shoved it into an empty kitchen drawer. She was tempted to do the same with this one, forget it in the hope that either it would be claimed or it would somehow disappear mysteriously. Either way she didn't want it to be her problem . . . especially after the phone message.

She was about to make her way upstairs when the door to Mr Peace's flat opened. A female voice was saying goodbye and promising to call in again soon. Carmel hesitated at the bottom of the staircase, curious to see the visitor.

A woman stepped into the hallway, closing the flat door behind her. She was, Carmel guessed, in her forties and she wore a neat sprigged blouse and a pale-blue linen skirt that skimmed her knees. Her straight brown hair was expertly streaked with blond highlights and her make-up was expertly applied, giving her a businesslike look, and Carmel wondered if she was some healthcare professional come to check up on her elderly neighbour. The woman spotted her and smiled.

‘Have you just moved in upstairs?’ The woman had a faint local accent and she sounded friendly.

‘Yes, that’s right.’ Carmel put down her carrier bags as the woman extended her hand.

‘I’m Elizabeth, Conrad’s niece. He said you’d popped in to see him.’

‘Yes.’ Carmel had a feeling this woman was going to do all the talking. But she didn’t mind. After a day’s work she didn’t really feel up to making polite conversation with a stranger.

Elizabeth looked round as though she was afraid of being overheard. ‘I’m glad someone a bit more . . .’ She searched for a suitable word. ‘Sympathetic’s moved in upstairs. The last girl who lived in your flat caused Uncle Conrad an awful lot of trouble, you know. Playing her music at full volume and inviting all sorts round. I had to have a word with her, you know. I told her that he’s an elderly man and she should have a bit of thought for others.’ She pursed her lips in disapproval. ‘But she told me to mind my own business in no uncertain terms. Told me to F off.’ She mouthed the words. ‘Some people, eh . . .’

‘I lead a pretty quiet life,’ Carmel said with a smile and a hint of regret.

‘Good, ’cause Uncle Conrad doesn’t need all that nonsense at his age. I like to pop in most days. I work at the hospital so it’s no trouble really.’ She paused and looked Carmel up and down appraisingly. ‘Uncle Conrad said you work at that new Archaeology Centre. Enjoying it?’

‘Very much, thanks.’

Elizabeth glanced at her watch. ‘I’ve got to get back to the hospital – my boss has a couple of evening appointments.’ She looked at the carrier bags full of bottles but made no comment. ‘Nice to meet you, Carmel. I’ll see you again soon no doubt,’ she said as she opened the front door.

Carmel climbed the stairs wearily, the letter addressed to Janna Pyke stuffed inside one of the carrier bags. When she reached her flat she shoved it into the drawer with the other one, thinking that the place needed noise. Silence brought on the sadness, the heavy atmosphere that oozed from the ancient walls. She switched the TV on, hoping that the sound of the newsreader's voice would drown out the presence of the girl, and for a while it seemed to work.

A rise in interest rates, more explosions in Iraq, some rock superstar standing trial for offences against minors. It was all bad news. Then came the item that interested her. The police had received a good response to their appeal for information about the Resurrection Man's victims and they were pursuing several lines of enquiry. But there had been no arrest as yet. He was still out there, whoever he was. Carmel picked up the remote control and switched to another channel. There was a home makeover programme that sounded relentlessly cheerful – just what she needed.

As Maddy was coming round at seven, she decided to take a pack of garlic bread from her small freezer compartment to go with the takeaway pizzas: there was no reason why they shouldn't indulge themselves a little. She had just taken the pack out when she heard the doorbell. She left it on the worktop and hurried downstairs.

She hesitated for a moment at the front door. She wasn't expecting any visitors just yet. But curiosity overcame her apprehension so she turned the latch and opened the door.

A tall young man stood on the doorstep, the bulk of his body blocking out the evening sunlight. Then he took a step back as the door opened and Carmel could see him properly. He had a shock of fair hair above a long freckled face and his eyes were a piercing blue. He looked familiar, but different in his frayed jeans and black T-shirt proclaiming the virtues of a heavy metal band called the Cynical Dead. She stared at him for a few moments before it came to her. Last time she had seen him he had been wearing much more formal garb.

This was Jack the Ripper. And he was standing on her doorstep.

Chapter Five

Jack the Ripper – she really would have to stop calling him that – looked nervous as he shifted from foot to foot.

'Sorry to bother you,' he began with an anxious-to-please expression on his face. 'But I'm looking for someone . . . a friend.' The voice that had sounded so sonorous, so theatrical, was now lowered to a whisper.

'Don't I know you?'

He looked at her hopefully. 'You probably don't recognise me without my costume and make-up, but I lead the ghost tour. I'm an actor,' he said by way of explanation. 'I have to take what I can get.' He fell silent for a moment, as though he was suddenly unsure of himself. 'I saw you last night.'

'Did you?' Carmel began to feel a little foolish. She'd been misled by the role he'd been playing. Now he seemed unthreatening . . . quite ordinary.

'Look, I don't know if you can help me but I'm looking for someone called Janna Pyke. I don't suppose you know where I can find her?'

Carmel shook her head. 'Sorry. She moved out a few weeks ago. I'm renting her flat but I've no idea where she's gone.'

The young man looked disappointed but resigned. 'I called here last week and the old man downstairs told me she'd moved out but he didn't know any more. I know it's a long shot but has she left any forwarding address or . . .'

Carmel shook her had. 'The landlady said she left without paying the rent and she's no idea where she went. Sorry.' She looked him in the eye. 'I saw you standing outside the other night.'

The visitor took a deep breath. 'I was passing on my way home and I saw a light on in the flat.' The words came quickly as though he'd rehearsed the answer. 'I wondered whether Janna had come back. I was going to call but I chickened out.' He craned his neck to look beyond Carmel at the staircase, as though he suspected she was harbouring the missing girl; that she didn't want to see him and Carmel was colluding in the deception. 'The truth is, she just vanished without a word and I'm wondering whether I should report her missing . . . to the police, I mean.'

'I'm sorry. But, as I said, I really have no idea where she is.' She hesitated. 'Were you and her . . .?'

He blushed 'We split up a while back but that doesn't mean I'm not worried about her.' As he said the words he looked genuinely concerned, somehow vulnerable.

'Look, why don't you come in. I could make us a cup of tea.' Carmel issued the invitation on impulse. But some instinct told her that the man standing in front of her was harmless. A young actor worried about his ex-girlfriend. Nothing more.

'My name's Tavy McNair, by the way.'

'Carmel. Carmel Hennessy.' She held her hand out automatically. Tavy took it and she noticed that his flesh was soft and cool.

With the formalities out of the way she led the way up to the flat and switched the kettle on while he made himself comfortable on the sofa.

'Is it true?' she asked as she put two steaming mugs of tea on the coffee table.

'Is what true?'

'The story about the girl who was left to die here when her family caught the plague. It was my bedroom window you were pointing at.'

Tavy McNair smiled shyly. 'Sorry. Hope it hasn't given you nightmares. Don't know whether it's true or not. It's just something I heard ages ago.'

Carmel could tell he was trying to sound casual, trying to make it seem as if it was something he had made up. But he knew it was true all right.

'In fact that's how I met Janna. She was on one of my tours last summer and she came up to me afterwards . . . told me it was her window I'd pointed out. She asked if it was true as well.'

'And what did you tell her?'

'The same as I told you. I don't know for sure. It might be, but on the other hand it might not be. Who knows? You don't believe in ghosts, do you?'

Carmel didn't answer. She didn't really know what she believed.

After a long silence, Tavy spoke. 'I don't suppose Janna left anything in the flat . . . a diary or . . .' The words were said casually but Carmel sensed an urgency behind them and wondered why. Was there something her former boyfriend wanted? Or wanted to get his hands on so that he could conceal it from the world? She looked him in the eye.

'Someone left a strange message on my answerphone. It was for your friend Janna. Listen.' She played him the message and watched his face.

'Janna. This is your final warning. You can't escape. Wherever you are, we'll find you and when we do, you're dead.' The words echoed, cold and terrifying and, there was no mistaking it, Tavy McNair looked worried.

'Have you any idea what that's about?' Carmel asked, watching his face.

He shook his head. 'I wasn't sure what she was into but I knew it was pretty weird. That's why we broke up.' He hesitated. He looked uneasy, almost afraid. And when he spoke again she could hear the tension in his voice. 'She used to go to a pub called the Black Hen,' he said. 'Some very odd people hang out there . . . you know, they dress all in black and go on about death and . . .'

Carmel grinned. 'I had a friend who was into all that once. She grew out of it.'

Tavy clenched his fists. 'Janna didn't. She took it deadly seriously. Tried to get me involved.'

'Involved in what?'

He looked uneasy. 'There was some strange stuff going on. Satanism and . . .'

'And you said no?'

'I said no.'

There was a long silence. He seemed anxious and she was suddenly afraid of saying the wrong thing. In the end she decided to concentrate on practicalities. 'Have you been to this Black Hen place to ask whether anyone's seen her?'

'I did drop in there a couple of weeks ago. Asked around. But nobody had seen her . . . or at least that's what they said. I got out quick. The place gives me the creeps. That's why I wondered if she'd left a diary. I know she kept one. I thought it might contain a clue about what was going on . . . and where she might be now. She was doing an MA and I went to the university to ask if anyone knew where she was. Nobody did.'

Looking at Tavy McNair now, as his restless fingers twisted a strand of his tousled blond hair, she found it hard to imagine why she had ever been afraid of him: why she'd ever given him the nickname Jack the Ripper. 'What's Tavy short for?' she asked, trying to lighten the mood.

'Octavius. My father was a history professor at the university. His speciality was the Roman occupation.' He looked away and began to bite at a nail. 'He died two years ago. Cancer.'

'I'm sorry,' said Carmel automatically. 'What about your mother?'

He gave her an embarrassed grin. 'Er . . . I still live at home with her. Can't afford a place of my own on what I'm paid for the ghost tours and my weekend job. And I think Mum's glad of the company. Or at least she says she is.'

'Where is it you work at weekends?'

'A kitchen showroom. Nothing exciting.'

There was an awkward silence. After a few moments Carmel looked up. 'What do you think has happened to Janna?'

He frowned. 'I've no idea, but I don't think it's anything good.'

Carmel stood up and walked over to the chest of drawers. She opened the top drawer and took the two letters out. 'These came addressed to Janna. Do you think we should open them?'

Tavy took the letters from her and stared at them. 'Maybe we should,' he said after a few moments of reflection. He slit the first open neatly and took out a sheet of writing paper – expensive deckle-edged paper to match the envelope.

'You have been warned. Jack Wendal demands your silence,' he read before passing it to Carmel. He opened the second. 'The price of betrayal is death. Jack Wendal will collect payment.'

Carmel read the two letters. 'Who the hell's Jack Wendal? Do you know a Jack Wendal?'

Tavy shook his head. 'Look, I don't know anything about this, honestly.' He looked into her eyes as though he was willing her to believe him. But she wasn't sure she did.

'I'm going to show these letters to someone I know who's in the police. If she's really missing . . .' She half expected Tavy to object but instead he nodded.

'Yeah. Maybe you should.'

'This . . . er, policeman's coming round later. Around eight thirty. If you want a word with him, why don't you come back and . . .?'

Tavy made a show of looking at his watch and stood up quickly. 'Sorry. I've got to take another ghost tour soon. But if you find out anything about Janna, will you call me? You can reach me on my mobile.' He wrote the number down neatly on a scrap of paper and passed it to Carmel before standing up.

'Thanks for the tea. Take care of yourself, won't you?'

Something in the way he said the last words worried Carmel. This was no ghostly tale, no spine-chilling story to provide a thrill of terror for the imaginative tourist. This was real.

And for the first time it occurred to her that she might be in danger herself.

DCI Emily Thwaite looked at the tiny jewelled watch on her wrist – a present from Jeff in the early days of their marriage. It was getting late. Six thirty.

'I don't want to be late tonight. Jeff's cooking. It's our anniversary. Fifteen years.' She sighed. 'I've known murderers get less.'

'Congratulations,' Joe mumbled, unsure whether her last comment had been a joke. He thought he had sensed an almost imperceptible trace of bitterness in her voice but maybe that was her way. He didn't know her well enough yet to judge.

They were nearing the hospital now and the traffic was heavy. He concentrated on his driving, keeping his eyes on the road. There were a lot of idiots about. He indicated left and swung the unmarked police car into the hospital entrance.

They had locked Gloria Simpson's strange room up again, glad to leave it behind. And their search of the flat had revealed an address book which Emily now had in her handbag. One of the people listed in it was bound to be their mystery woman's next of kin. Someone had to be told about the state she was in.

'Now we know her name, do you think she'll talk?' Emily asked as he parked in the only available space.

'Who knows?' was Joe's reply. Nothing was predictable in this case.

'Is it worth calling in on John Wendal?'

'Doubt it. He's still unconscious. Someone's going to let us know if he comes round.'

They made their way down the hospital corridors to the ward where they had last seen Gloria Simpson.

'I don't like hospitals,' Emily announced with a shudder as they walked. 'I had all my kids at home.'

'Really.' Joe was uncertain how to react to this snippet of personal information but it hardly surprised him. He was learning that Emily wasn't a woman who would be ordered about by any powers-that-be. And that included their superiors.

When they reached the ward there was no sign of Gloria Simpson. An elderly lady lying in the bed she had occupied eyed them suspiciously as they stared at her for a few seconds before scanning the other beds for Gloria's familiar blond head. It wasn't long before a nurse put them out of their misery. Gloria had been moved to one of the psychiatric wards. There was nothing really wrong with her physically, the nurse told them in a whisper, but she wasn't fit to be allowed home.

Hospitals are always well signposted and Eborby General was no exception. They found the Psychiatry Department housed in a modern, box-like building set apart from the main hospital. Its architecture was calculated to induce depression, even in the most cheerful of souls. Perhaps, Joe thought fleetingly, they were touting for business.

The doors were locked and they had to gain admission by means of an intercom. Once they were inside they were met by a burly male nurse who told them he'd inform Dr Oakley that they'd arrived. They were left waiting in a shabby room that stank of cigarette smoke. The décor, pink and pale green, was scuffed and dirty and there was a hotchpotch of chairs scattered around the edge of the room, worn and broken in places. His eyes met Emily's and he knew she was thinking the same thing. The place made their spirits sink so goodness only knew what effect it would have on vulnerable patients.

The building seemed silent apart from the occasional sound of distant raised voices and it seemed like a long time before they were summoned by a middle-aged woman with an aura of efficiency. She introduced herself as Dr Oakley's secretary and led them through bleak corridors to the doctor's office.

Somehow Dr Oakley didn't seem to fit in with his surroundings. He was a large man with a small beard, a shaved head and a permanent expression of semi-amusement as if he was enjoying some private joke. His blue eyes twinkled as he invited them to sit.

'What can I do for you?' he began, talking to them as though they were seeking medical help.

It was Emily who spoke. 'We believe a patient called Gloria Simpson has been transferred here.'

'That's right. Although she's still refusing to confirm that that's her name. Are you sure about her identity?'

'Quite sure. We've been to her address. It's her all right. What can you tell us about her?'

The doctor smiled. 'I was hoping you'd be able to tell me. All she'll say is that someone called Jack Wendal's after her. She seems genuinely afraid and she's still under sedation. My tentative diagnosis is that she's having some sort of paranoid delusions. I'm told the driver of the car she was in was a John Wendal.'

'That's right. He's John Wendal but he's known to his friends and family as Jack. He's in a coma. We've talked to his wife and she claims he's a model husband and father. Works for a building society. No history of violence. No sexual deviance.'

'A regular guy as they say in the States.' Oakley smiled. 'Think she's telling the truth?'

Joe caught Emily's eye and they both nodded in unison.

'Unless she's an extremely good actress, yes,' Joe answered.

'There is another possibility, Doctor,' said Emily, sounding a little unsure of herself. 'It's only a theory, you understand.'

The psychiatrist crossed his legs and waited patiently,

regarding Emily as though she were a patient, about to spill out her deepest secrets. 'Go on,' he prompted gently.

'Well, it might be nothing but we think we might have found a tentative connection between the driver of the car, this John Wendal, and both the victims of this killer known as the Resurrection Man. I presume you've heard about the murders on the news?'

Dr Oakley sat silent for a second, his expression giving nothing away. 'Of course,' he said. 'It's hard to avoid it. What's the connection?'

'All three, the two victims and the driver, either work or have worked for the Eborby Permanent Building Society.'

Oakley shrugged. 'It's a big employer in Eborby. Lots of people work there.'

'What I'm getting at, Doctor, is perhaps Gloria Simpson had a fright. Perhaps she believes Wendal's the killer and she was next on his list as it were. Perhaps that's the cause of her . . .' He searched for the right word. 'Condition. Is that possible?'

Oakley shook his head. 'In my professional opinion, it's unlikely. I think her paranoia goes a lot deeper than that. I would have thought that most people who escaped the attentions of a murderer would experience shock then relief, possibly followed by flashbacks and maybe panic attacks.'

'We looked around her flat and we found evidence that she was involved in the occult. In black magic of some kind.'

Oakley gave a secretive smile. 'If that's the case it could certainly have some bearing on her condition. I'll investigate that angle next time I see her.'

'You think dabbling in things like that can trigger mental illness?' Emily asked.

It was Joe who answered. 'In some individuals, yes. Definitely. Don't you agree, Doctor?'

'I've known several cases. What starts as a bit of fun with ouija boards and what have you can get out of hand for certain people. Some people are susceptible even if they don't realise it at first. And there are always those who like to exploit their weakness.'

Emily looked at him sharply. 'Have you anyone in particular in mind?'

Another smile, this time wary. 'I'm afraid I'm bound by medical confidentiality. I'm sorry. It would be wrong of me to discuss my patients with you.'

'Can we see Gloria Simpson? We would like to talk to her.'

'I'm sure you would, Chief Inspector, but she's heavily sedated and she's really not up to it at the moment. The last thing I want is for anyone to upset her, you understand. I think it's best if you wait until I've had an in-depth talk with her. As you will no doubt appreciate, these things have to be taken slowly.'

'But you will tell us if you discover anything that's relevant to our enquiries?'

'If it's in her interests. If it helps you to find her next of kin, for instance or to keep her out of danger.'

'And of course if she has some information about the Resurrection Man or about the cause of the car crash, you'll do your best to persuade her to share it with us?'

Oakley hesitated before giving a cautious nod.

'We have her address book so we'll be trying to trace her next of kin as a matter of urgency,' said Emily.

'I wish you luck.' The doctor stood up and stretched out his hand to Emily, avoiding her eyes. That was it. They'd had their ten minutes and were getting no more.

Dr Oakley pressed the button on his intercom. 'Elizabeth, would you show these officers out, please? Thank you.'

The efficient secretary, dressed neatly in a blouse and skirt, led them along the corridor towards the entrance. Joe asked her how long she'd worked there and the answer was ten years. And yes, she liked working for Dr Oakley very much and she didn't find the environment in the least bit depressing. She saw them off the premises with a friendly smile. A breath of sanity in a disturbed world.

'What do you reckon?' Joe asked as they hurried towards the car park.

'You heard what the man said, we have to wait and see.' She looked at her watch and swore under her breath. 'I promised Jeff I'd be back at a reasonable time. I don't want another burned dinner.' She quickened her pace and Joe did likewise.

When they reached the car park Joe's heart sunk when he saw the gleam of shiny yellow metal on his front tyre. He'd been clamped.

'I'd better get a taxi,' Emily said through gritted teeth, staring at the offending article.

Joe reached for his mobile phone and sent up a swift prayer for patience.

The map lay on the ledge next to the Guide to the Churches of Yorkshire. Even though they were evil, they should still be laid to rest in consecrated ground. It was their only chance, their only hope of avoiding the torment to come.

The killer's excitement, his pleasure, had subsided now. It had been intense this time. The best yet. She was young ... and a woman. And her face ... It was almost as if she had shared his ecstasy ... or had it been agony? He preferred to think the former. He'd felt close to her as he'd lifted the lid. He'd touched first her face, then her small breasts, his fingers lingering on their softness. She belonged to him now. And she wouldn't push him away like before. She was his.

He lifted her gently from her sarcophagus and placed her on the plastic sheet. When darkness came it would be time for her last journey.

Chapter Six

Maddy Owen finished her pizza and licked her fingers delicately. They had eaten with their plates balanced on their knees, washing their meal down with a bottle of Chardonnay – the single woman's tipple, Maddy had joked.

When Carmel had seized the moment to ask Maddy if there was a man in her life, Maddy's normally cheerful expression had suddenly turned serious, as if a menacing cloud had momentarily blotted out the sun.

'I did have. He died. Climbing accident.'

'I'm so sorry,' said Carmel.

'That was four years ago and there hasn't really been anyone since. Just the usual assortment of saddos, mummy's boys and married men whose wives don't understand them.'

'Or understand them only too well,' Carmel muttered under her breath. 'What was his name?'

'Angus.' She smiled sadly. 'He was Scottish, as you can imagine. We met at university and we were going to get married but . . .'

'I'm sorry,' Carmel repeated before looking at the plates in panic. 'Look, I'll get this lot cleared up before Joe arrives. And I've got some things in . . . crisps and stuff. Do you think that's OK?'

Maddy looked at her and smiled sadly. 'I'm sure it'll be fine. What time's he coming?'

Carmel looked at her watch. 'Eight thirty. He's five minutes late.' She hurried into the kitchen with the plates and returned with dishes of crisps and nuts while Maddy cleared away the glasses.

'Do you want me to stay or . . .'

'Carmel nodded. 'Please. Unless you want to get back.'

'I'm quite happy to stay if you want me to.' Maddy stood up and walked over to the window overlooking Vicars Green. It was still light and the fine weather had lured the tourists out of their hotels and B and Bs to roam the streets in search of a square meal. They ambled across the green towards the restaurant-lined streets off the cathedral square where diners would be sitting, chatting over their food in the glow of candles. Maddy felt a little envious at the thought of such intimate luxury. It was a long time since she'd been taken out to eat.

She spotted a man walking across the green, making straight for the house. He was probably in his twenties or early thirties at the most, with longish dark hair and the kind of mouth that smiles readily. He wore a light-coloured suit - smart, as though he'd just come from work - and the purposeful look on his face told her that he wasn't one of the tourist throng. Maddy watched him march up to the front door and a second later the doorbell rang, the noise piercing the calm and making Carmel jump.

Carmel ran downstairs and when she flung the door open she looked flushed, her eyes shining with excitement.

Joe studied her as she ushered him into the hallway, noting the bobbed chestnut hair and the anxious eyes that gave her the appearance of a schoolgirl, eager to please a favourite teacher. The sulky teenager was gone and Kevin Hennessy's daughter had become an attractive woman. But she still looked young and vulnerable and he suddenly felt concerned for her, although he wasn't quite sure why.

He followed her upstairs and the first thing he noticed when he stepped into her flat was the array of snacks arranged on the coffee table. He felt almost embarrassed that she'd gone to so much trouble. But she was new in the city and perhaps she was lonely and eager for company – any company. As she asked him what he wanted to drink he was surprised when another woman emerged from the kitchen. She was a little older than Carmel – possibly near his own age – with auburn curls framing a round, freckled face. And she was carrying a half-full bottle of white wine.

'This is Maddy. She works with me,' said Carmel. 'We've just had a pizza and . . .'

'I hope you don't mind me intruding,' Maddy said breathlessly. 'But I was a bit worried about Carmel and . . .'

Joe smiled. 'It's good to meet you,' he said, meaning every word.

He sat down opposite Maddy and caught a waft of her perfume, light and flowery – possibly the same one as Emily Thwaite habitually used. They made small talk as Carmel scurried in and out with drinks and glasses. What was it like working at the Archaeology Centre? How did Joe enjoy police work? Anything but the subjects that occupied both their minds: the Resurrection Man and Carmel's strange message.

But, once the drinks were in front of them and the preliminary rituals had been performed, Carmel came to the point.

'I got home from work last night and I found this message on my answering machine. Listen.'

She pressed the button and the sound of the sinister, androgynous voice filled the room. She played the message twice and awaited Joe's verdict.

Joe glanced at Maddy and took a sip of beer before speaking. 'Well, whoever it is doesn't know that Janna Pyke's moved out so he can't be watching the house or anything like that. And he doesn't know Janna's movements so, if she has come to any harm – and we've no reason to think she has – this joker has nothing to do with it.'

'But it must be why she left the flat. She's hiding from him.'

'Or her. I suppose it could be a woman's voice disguised.' He leaned forward. 'Look, Carmel, I'm sure you've nothing to worry about. If this person does come here, as soon as they find Janna's gone, they'll leave you alone. It's not you they're interested in – it's Janna. Don't you agree, Maddy?'

Maddy nodded vigorously.

Joe looked Carmel in the eye. 'Has that put your mind at rest?'

She nodded. 'I suppose so. But that's not all. I've had two letters.' She had placed the letters in plastic bags, just like she'd seen the police do in television crime dramas, and she felt a small thrill of pride at her own efficiency as she handed them over to Joe.

He took the pair of plastic gloves that he carried round with him for such occasions from his pocket and extracted the letters from their bags.

'Jack Wendal demands your silence,' said the first. Then he turned to the second. 'The price of betrayal is death. Jack Wendal will collect payment.'

As he read the letters, Carmel noticed that his eyes had widened in excitement, as though he'd made some thrilling new discovery. 'Do you mind if I keep these?' he asked after a few moments.

'Please. Take them. I don't want them.'

Carmel looked at Joe and guessed her mum had probably been right when she'd said he was a good listener.

'There's a man called Mr Peace in the downstairs flat,' she said. 'I was talking to his niece and she says that Janna Pyke was bad news . . . caused a lot of trouble.'

'So she could have made enemies?'

'From what Elizabeth said, it certainly sounds that way.'

'Elizabeth?'

'Mr Peace's niece. She's here quite a bit. She keeps an eye on her uncle.' Carmel hesitated then she made a decision. She turned to Maddy. 'Remember the ghost tour? The guide . . . the man in the top hat?'

'What about him?' Maddy leaned forward, listening intently.

'Well, he called round earlier.' She saw the alarm on Maddy's face and thought she'd better put her mind at rest. 'Oh don't worry. He seems quite harmless. He's an actor and his name's Tavy McNair.'

Maddy saw the ghost of a smile on Carmel's lips when she mentioned Tavy McNair's name. She glanced at Joe Plantagenet and he raised an inquisitive eyebrow.

'Why didn't you tell me before?' Maddy asked. She sounded almost hurt.

Carmel shrugged her shoulders. 'The subject didn't really come up, did it? And besides, I thought I'd wait till Joe was here.'

Joe leaned forward. 'So did this Tavy McNair have anything interesting to say?'

'Yes. It turns out he used to go out with Janna Pyke and he called because he's not seen her for a while and he's worried about her. She left this flat a few weeks ago without paying the rent and nobody knows where she is. He thought there was a chance I might have a forwarding address or . . .'

'Could he have sent the letters?' Joe asked.

Carmel shook her head. 'No. I'm certain he didn't.'

Joe eyes met Maddy's and he sensed a scepticism that matched his own. It seemed that the girl had developed a great deal of faith in the young actor on such a brief acquaintance. Maybe she was too trusting, Joe thought. After a few years in the police force, he found it hard to trust anyone.

'Did he say anything else?'

'He said Janna used to hang out with some strange people. She was into the occult. Used to go to a place called . . . oh, what was it? A pub. Can't remember the name. Sorry.'

'There's a place called the Black Hen that has a bit of a reputation for that sort of thing,' said Joe.

'That's it. The Black Hen. She used to go there but Tavy said it wasn't his scene. He says he went there to ask if anyone knew where Janna was. But he drew a blank. Nobody had seen her.'

'Has anyone reported her missing?'

'Don't you know?'

Joe smiled. 'Not my department. Unless her name comes up in one of our investigations we wouldn't necessarily be told. But now we have this Jack Wendal connection, I'll certainly be looking into it. We just have to keep our fingers crossed that we can find her.'

'You think something's happened to her?'

'Most people who go missing turn up safe and well. And from what you've told me, it sounds as if she wanted to go missing. She was receiving threats from person or persons unknown and she left without paying her rent.'

'She left some things. Peta, the landlady, put them up in the loft.'

Joe looked up suddenly. 'Did you tell Tavy this?'

Carmel shook her head. 'I never thought. He did ask me if she'd left a diary – anything that might help to find out what's happened to her – but . . .'

'She might have decided to travel light and left old stuff she didn't want to take with her,' Maddy suggested. 'I don't suppose Tavy or the landlady know anything about her family, do they?'

'Nothing's ever been mentioned.'

'She might have gone back home to her parents. If things didn't work out for her in Eborby she might have decided to cut her losses and run.'

Carmel sighed. What Maddy was saying made a lot of sense. Janna Pyke was probably miles away being pampered by her devoted parents, taking refuge from the fallout of her walk on Eborby's wild side.

But as Joe took another swig of Theakstons, he found it hard to share the women's optimism. The name Jack Wendal had cropped up again. But could there be a connection between the John Wendal lying unconscious in Eborby General and the disappearance of Janna Pyke? Wendal had certainly terrified Gloria Simpson – but had Janna been afraid of him too?

'I'll check Janna out tomorrow,' he said softly. 'See if anyone's reported her missing or if her name's cropped up in any of our enquiries.'

That was the best he could do for now.

All of a sudden a cold shiver passed through his body and he felt a slight pressure on his shoulder. He turned his head and caught a lightning flash of misty grey out of the corner of his eye. He picked up his beer and drank deeply, fighting the sudden feeling of sadness that was beginning to overwhelm him.

Joe had woken up with a headache after drinking too much beer at Carmel's flat the previous night because somehow he had felt the need to dull his senses. Being with Carmel had brought back memories – painful memories of Kevin lying in a pool of blood on the pavement beside him. But he had been reluctant to leave. He hardly liked to admit it to himself but he had enjoyed Maddy's company and felt the old familiar thrill of a nascent sexual attraction. Perhaps he'd call her ... ask to see her again. If the Resurrection Man investigation didn't get in the way.

There had been something unnerving about the flat on Vicars Green. Maddy had told him the story about the plague girl – making light of it but with a hint of discomfort behind the smile – and he wondered whether it explained why he had sensed despair, desolation, inside those four walls. As he had known nothing about the tragedy before, he told himself, it couldn't have been his imagination. Or perhaps he had heard the story once and put it out of his conscious mind. He couldn't be sure.

When he'd arrived at the station, he'd given a pair of young constables the job of tracing everyone in Gloria Simpson's address book before telling Emily about

Carmel's strange letters . . . and the fact that Jack Wendal's name had cropped up again, seemingly making more threats to women. He wanted to find out more about Wendal – it was beginning to look as if the version given by the devoted wife was some way off the mark.

At nine thirty they set off to visit the Eborby Permanent Building Society. The Society's operations were directed from a purpose-built headquarters just south of the river. The impressive building, with its huge landmark clock tower, had been designed by an architect who had possessed the good taste and forethought to use materials that blended well with the local stone and the result was an impressive monument to Yorkshire financial acumen. It was well within walking distance of police headquarters for the health conscious but Emily insisted on taking the car.

On arriving at the grand entrance, Joe pushed at the revolving door and found himself deposited in a towering, marble-lined foyer.

'How may I help you?' The young woman on the reception desk tilted her head to one side in an enquiring manner and tried to look interested.

Joe held out his warrant card. 'We'd like to talk to Harold Uckley's colleagues. I believe he worked in the Home Loans Department.'

The girl eyed him suspiciously. 'Haven't they been interviewed already . . . when he was found?'

'We're pursuing a new line of enquiry,' Emily chipped in with a sweet but determined smile. She wasn't going to be fobbed off. 'I believe a John Wendal works here as well.'

'Which department?'

'Not sure.' Emily spotted the internal phone directory on the desk. 'Perhaps you could look him up for us.'

The young woman obliged. 'There's a J. Wendal in Savings. Would that be the one? He's the only one listed.'

'Where can we find Savings?'

'Third floor.'

'Thanks.' They made for the lift and five minutes later they found themselves face to face with Wendal's boss. The nameplate on his door proclaimed him to be a Mr R. Huggins and he was a little man who reminded Joe of a whippet; thin, sharp and without much hair.

'What can you tell us about John Wendal?' Joe began.

'About Jack? Not much really. Pleasant man. Family man. Interested in trains. Member of the Railway Society, I believe. He wasn't what you'd call ambitious. Quite content to be one of the troops, if you see what I mean.' Mr R. Huggins gave a smile that looked more like a leer to Emily. 'Er . . . how is he? I don't like to keep ringing his wife . . . bothering her.'

'There's been no change in his condition, I'm afraid.'

Huggins leaned forward confidentially. 'Er . . . I heard he was with a blonde.' He had lowered his voice even though he was in his private office and couldn't possible be overheard.

'Word gets round,' said Emily sharply. 'Does that surprise you?'

'What?'

'That he was with a woman.'

'Well, yes, it does. I mean Jack had us all fooled. Sly old devil. He was the last person I would have thought . . . Ask anybody who knows him. They'll all say the same. Jack Wendal was honest as they come. Devoted to his wife and daughter.'

'We don't know the circumstances yet. It might have been quite innocent. He might have just been giving this woman a lift.'

A shadow of disappointment passed across Huggins's face. The thought of his dull underling as a sly old fox with a secret and scandalous love life had obviously brightened his day.

Joe took the leaflet about the House of Terrors that he had found in Wendal's garage out of his pocket and placed it on the desk in front of Huggins. 'Has he ever mentioned this place? Ever said he's been there or . . .?

'No. I wouldn't have thought it would be Jack's thing myself. But he was mad about railways, I can tell you that.'

Emily stood up. 'Thank you, Mr Huggins. We'd like a word with his colleagues if we may.'

'Certainly,' Huggins said obsequiously. 'Anything to help the police.'

Emily was almost at the office door when she turned. 'By the way, did Mr Wendal have anything to do with the man who was found murdered? Harold Uckley. I believe he worked in the Home Loans Department.'

Huggins shook his head. 'Two thousand people work here, Chief Inspector. And Home Loans is on the other side of the building. Might as well be on the other side of the world for all we see of them. As far as I know Jack didn't know this Uckley. Each department tends to keep itself to itself as it were. Of course he might have met him outside work. Was Uckley into railways?'

'Not as far as we know.'

They thanked Huggins for his time and made their escape. They had all Wendal's colleagues to interview and then they intended to venture to the distant wastes of Home Loans and talk to the people who worked with Harold Uckley. They had already been spoken to but there was no harm in the belt and braces approach.

But they came up with nothing. Wendal's colleagues echoed their leader's assessment of the man's character. And they all agreed that any connection to the House of Terrors was very unlikely indeed unless it featured a steam-powered ghost train. And he would certainly have nothing to do with the occult . . . he was a regular at his local church. Jack Wendal was a nice, blameless man, a railway enthusiast and family man. And even the young women agreed that there was nothing even remotely creepy about him . . . unlike some they could mention. Emily and Joe didn't pursue this any further. They didn't want to be sidetracked by office gossip unless it concerned Wendal himself.

The story in Uckley's department was much the same. The murdered man had been an amiable family man looking forward to his retirement. He was interested mainly in fishing, a hobby he pursued with his grown-up sons, and he had never expressed any interest whatsoever in the occult or the House of Terrors. The only thing out of the ordinary about Harold Uckley was that he didn't drive. But then some people don't.

They had drawn a blank. But there was one other line of enquiry they wanted to follow up.

'Why do they call it Human Resources now?' Joe mused as they took the lift down to the first floor. 'It always used to be Personnel.'

Emily snorted. 'It sounds grander. And if human beings are just a resource they feel they can play God with people's lives. Hire and fire when they feel like it.'

'Have you always been this cynical, ma'am?' Joe asked with a grin.

'Not always,' she replied in a way that didn't encourage further questions.

They soon found themselves at the unprepossessing double doors leading to the Eborby Permanent Building Society's answer to Mount Olympus. Human Resources. They didn't bother knocking.

'Yes?' The young woman at the nearest desk barked rudely, looking at them with thinly veiled hostility as though she suspecting they were there to steal the office computers. She was plump and dressed like all the other females in the building in a gaudily patterned pleated skirt and matching top, made out of some silky man-made fibre and designed to fit any figure and flatter none.

Joe showed her his ID. 'We'd like to talk to someone about a former employee. Someone who worked here from May 1993 to November 1995.'

'That's a long time ago,' the young woman said accusingly before pressing a few buttons on the computer keyboard in front of her. 'Name?'

'Carla Yates.'

The woman looked up. 'Isn't that the ... the one who was murdered by the Resurrection Man?'

'Can you look her up, please?' Emily was standing for no nonsense. If the information was in their computer system, she wanted it.

After a few seconds the information appeared on the screen. 'Here she is. You were right. She worked for us from May 1993 to January 1995.'

'We know that. What we'd like to know is which department she worked in.'

'Savings. Clerical Assistant.'

'Can you check which department John Wendal and Harold Uckley were working in at that time, please?'

There was more tapping of keys. 'Harold Uckley – Internal Audit. John Wendal ... he was in Savings.'

Joe kept his face a neutral mask. 'Is it possible to have a list of everyone who worked in the Savings department at the time? Names and addresses if possible.'

The woman scowled. 'I'll see what I can do,' she said as if he had just asked her to run round the circuit of the city walls with her computer strapped to her back.

The drugs were wearing off and Gloria Simpson was once more aware of her surroundings. She'd heard them talking. Wendal was still there. Pretending to be unconscious. But she knew it was just a ruse. He was indestructible. Invincible. He could spring back to life whenever he chose. He was biding his time.

And somehow she had to destroy him.

If she pretended to take the tablets they gave her. If she could somehow fool the nurses into thinking they had her in their power – in his power for he must be controlling them – then she might be able to do it.

It would take all her strength – all her cunning – to destroy Jack Wendal.

*

'Where do we start?' Emily looked at the list of employees who might have come into contact with Carla Yates during her brief sojourn at the Eborby Permanent Building Society, and despaired. There were a couple of people they'd met already. Huggins, for instance. He had been a senior clerk at the time. And one of the women had been a clerical assistant – still was, as far as they knew. But the others would take some tracking down. People move on.

But the building society was a link. It had to be. And it was all they had at the moment. That and John Wendal, the man who had apparently sent Gloria Simpson over the edge of sanity and who had vowed to collect some sort of payment from Janna Pyke.

'We should go back to the Eborby Permanent to have a word with Huggins and get the team to begin tracking the others down. Something must have happened back then. That must be where it all started. And Uckley was in Internal Audit. They'd go round to all the departments, wouldn't they?'

'I suppose so,' Emily said. 'He could have met them both. The three of them could have got together.'

Joe sighed. There was a light in Emily's eyes that told him that she was keen on backing this particular horse. 'Are we sure the victims are linked?'

Emily nodded. 'I think so, yes.'

'And do you think John Wendal's accident's connected with the murders somehow? I keep thinking about those letters that were sent to Janna Pyke.'

'Jack Wendal will collect payment? If it's the same Wendal, it sounds as if he's up to his neck in all sorts. Hidden depths, eh?'

'Wendal's quite a common name around these parts. I've looked in the phone book and it's full of them. There's a Wendal's Butchers in Marigate. And there's a firm called Wendal's Engineering in . . .'

'But there's only one Jack Wendal who terrified a woman so much that she went insane and made him crash the car. He must be a scary individual.'

'He was into trains.'

'He had that leaflet about the House of Terrors.'

'It's a tourist attraction. They give those leaflets out like confetti.'

'He'd hidden it in the garage.'

'It was hardly hidden.'

She looked at him, exasperated. 'What are you saying, Joe? Do you think we're getting this wrong?'

He shook his head. 'I don't know.'

The door to Emily's office opened and Jamilla popped her head round.

She addressed Joe. 'You wanted to know if anyone called Janna Pyke had been reported missing, sir. A missing persons report was filed yesterday. A couple of her work colleagues came into the station.' Jamilla handed him a thin file and he thanked her.

'What's this? Something I should know?'

'Janna Pyke – the woman who received the threatening letters mentioning Jack Wendal. She's been reported missing.'

'That's all we need.' Emily looked at her watch. It was shaping up to be yet another long day.

The lady in charge of the flowers at St Oswald's church in the village of Evanshaw liked to feel indispensable and she guarded her position jealously, keeping her helpers firmly in their place.

This week she had decreed that there was to be a mass of white carnations by the font and a simple arrangement of lilies on the altar. Having examined the available blooms at the florist and made her selection, she had placed the box of flowers on the back seat of her ageing but still immaculate VW Polo and had driven to the church, parking by the lych gate as she did every week, rain or shine, the scent of the fresh blooms in her nostrils.

With the box of flowers resting in her bare arms, she

marched purposefully up the church path to the music of birdsong and a mower from a distant village garden. She stopped at the battered oak door of the small medieval church and put the box carefully on the ground before searching her capacious handbag for the church key. But as she delved into the bag's leathery depths, she spotted something out of the corner of her eye, something out of place in her familiar churchyard.

The birds seemed to fall silent as she turned her head to see what it was. And when the realisation dawned, she put her hand to her mouth.

She had always prided herself on her self-control but the sight of the body lying by the church wall to her left, naked and twisted as though it had just crawled with a great deal of effort from a grave, made her abandon her habitual sang-froid and scream like an hysterical schoolgirl.

Janna Pyke. Aged twenty-three. Five feet five inches tall. Thin. Black hair. Blue eyes. Pale complexion. Studying at Eborby University for an MA in Medieval History and employed part time on the ticket desk of the House of Terrors in Marketgate. Last known address Flat 2, 5 Vicars Green – now the residence of Carmel Hennessy. Reported missing by a couple of her colleagues at the House of Terrors who had been concerned about her absence. She'd had a boyfriend who was an actor but they'd split up several weeks before she went missing.

That was about it. The colleagues who'd reported her missing knew nothing about Janna Pyke's life before she started working at the House of Terrors eight months before. They had implied that she had hung round with some other people who worked there who were into something unsavoury – nothing specific had been mentioned but the writer of the report had assumed drugs.

That was it.

Joe himself, of course, could supply a little more information. Janna Pyke had lived in what was now Carmel

Hennessy's flat and when she had disappeared suddenly, the landlady, Peta Thewlis, who was a colleague of Carmel's, had assumed she'd left to avoid paying the rent. He also thought he knew the identity of the actor boyfriend – he and Carmel's new friend Tavy McNair, jobbing actor and ghost tour guide, must be one and the same person.

He also knew, courtesy of Tavy McNair, via Carmel, that Janna had mixed with some strange friends and had frequented a pub called the Black Hen which had a reputation for being the hangout of misfits and the seriously weird. And McNair had told Carmel that Janna had been into the occult . . . black magic.

Just like Gloria Simpson.

This was getting stranger and stranger. And Joe wasn't sure what it all meant.

Emily Thwaite looked up at Joe and frowned. 'I think we should make it our priority to find this Janna Pyke and fast. And we need to find out all we can about her. Where her family live and who her friends are. I've sent Jamilla over to the university. They're bound to have her home address. I've told her to have a word with Janna's supervisor if possible. He might be able to tell us something.'

'You reckon she's gone home?'

'If she'd got involved with something in Eborby that was scaring her so much that she felt she had to do a runner, she might have cut her losses and gone home to her family to lie low,' Emily said hopefully, although at the back of her mind she knew that the Resurrection Man was still out there somewhere. Maybe waiting for fresh prey.

Joe nodded. He had a bad feeling about Janna Pyke. She was linked with Jack Wendal in some way – receiving actual threats. And Gloria Simpson was afraid of Wendal for some reason. More than afraid. She was terrified.

But could Wendal be the Resurrection Man? Had he been trying to abduct Gloria Simpson? Joe put his head in his hands and took a deep shuddering breath.

'You all right?' Emily asked, watching him carefully. The last thing she needed was her second in command going wobbly on her now.

Joe looked up at her and smiled bravely. 'Just a twinge in my shoulder. It happens now and then. I'm fine. Don't worry.' He straightened his back, trying to ignore the nagging pain around the site of his old gunshot wound. It flared up every so often as if to remind him of the frailty of human flesh.

'You sure you're all right?'

'Course I am,' Joe replied quickly. The last thing he wanted was to be treated as some sort of invalid.

Emily felt relieved. As senior investigating officer, she needed all the support she could get – not that it was wise to show it. 'Have you looked at that list of employees we got from the Eborby Permanent yet? No mention of a Gloria Simpson by any chance, is there? Or it might not have been Simpson back then. According to the neighbours, Simpson's her married name.'

'There's no Gloria Simpson but there was a Gloria Marsh who worked in Accounts for six months in 1996. Gloria's not a common name these days. Could that be our woman?'

'And she had an old score to settle with Wendal? It's a possibility.'

'I'll get it checked out.' Joe was about to add this to his long list of things to do when Sunny Porter burst into the office bearing the pained expression of a messenger who feared he was about to the executed for bringing bad news.

'Sorry, ma'am, but another body's turned up. Churchyard in Evanshaw eight miles east of Eborby. Lady doing the church flowers spotted it and raised the alarm.'

Joe glanced at Emily whose expression gave nothing away.

'Same as the others?' he asked.

'Same as the others.'

'Man or woman?'

'It's a young woman. Fits the description of that lass that's missing. What's her name? Jane . . .?'

'Janna Pyke?'

Sunny nodded. 'Aye. Janna Pyke. That's the one.'

Chapter Seven

It was over for now. Until the next time.

The Resurrection Man – he wished they'd stop using that name. They didn't understand that he only did what had to be done. It was necessary.

He put the scrubbing brush carefully into the bucket and a cloud of filth floated off it into the clear, cold water. Human waste. He wrinkled his nose at the smell then he began to scrub again. Everything had to be kept clean. Fit for its purpose. It was only a matter of time before it would be needed again.

Joe Plantagenet looked down at the dead woman, saying a swift, automatic prayer for her soul in his head while his heart twisted in compassion. She looked so young, this shell that had once been a living being. And the agony on the contorted face told of a hideous and painful death. He asked himself how anyone could do such a thing. It was something he'd always found hard to understand.

Joe knew only too well that evil exists, robust and resilient, deep down in every human being, ready to ripen and emerge given the right conditions. And he knew that when they caught the killer he would look quite ordinary . . . just like everyone else. He wouldn't be some slavering monster with 666 tattooed on his brow. He would be the sort of man you'd walk past in the street without a second glance. The sort of man you'd sit opposite on the train or stand beside at the bar of your local. It was this thought that frightened him most of all.

He watched from a safe distance as the police photographers and the forensic team went about their allotted tasks. And after a few minutes Emily walked over to join him, her face solemn and businesslike.

'I've spoken to the woman who found her,' she said. 'She's not been able to tell us much. But then I didn't really expect she would. She was coming to do the church flowers. Gave her a hell of a shock. Anything to report?'

'Not really. Except that it looks identical to the others. And I think it's her . . . Janna Pyke. Fits the description exactly.'

Emily studied the dead woman's face. 'Doesn't look much like her photograph, does she? But I agree. She fits the description. In the absence of a next of kin, we'll have to ask the friends who reported her missing to identify her.'

Joe nodded. 'They'll probably be at work. I'll send someone round to that House of Terrors place right away.' He took his mobile from his pocket and made the call to the station. Uniform could deal with it.

'Seen enough? Emily asked. Joe sensed that she was anxious to be away from St Oswald's churchyard with its lichen-covered headstones huddled in the shadow of the small, squat-towered church and its glowering yew trees. She knew as well as he did that the body had only been dumped there. The young woman had probably died miles away. And a few days ago judging by the condition of her body.

'Let's go,' said Joe. 'There's nothing more we can do here. We'll need to interview everyone who worked with her at the House of Terrors.' He thought for a few moments. 'Jamilla's already gone to the university to get her home address – once we get that we can contact her next of kin. We need to talk to her supervisor and her fellow students. See if they have anything to tell us about the life and times of Janna Pyke.'

'And there's the boyfriend. The actor.'

Joe said nothing. It was early days. Carmel Hennessy had obviously taken a liking to Tavy McNair. But then the most vicious killers have been known to be charming. He certainly couldn't be ruled out as a suspect. He was an actor after all . . . a trained dissembler. He hoped Carmel would exercise caution and keep him at arm's length until he was cleared of suspicion. Kevin Hennessy's daughter seemed a sensible girl and he could probably trust her judgement. But for Kevin's sake he felt responsible. He would keep in touch with her and check on her regularly. Just to make sure she was OK.

They left the forensic team to their own mysterious devices and, after extracting a promise from the pathologist that she'd perform the post mortem early the following morning, they set off for the university campus at Hasledon, some two miles from the city centre.

As they drove a call came through from Jamilla at the university. In the process of winkling Janna Pyke's home address out of the registry, she had discovered that there was no student registered under that particular name. There was, however, an MA student called Jane Pyke in the Medieval History Department and Jamilla, assuming this was their woman, had noted down the home address she had provided.

Perhaps, Joe suggested to Emily as they drove, she had adopted the more exotic Janna as part of a rebranding exercise. Perhaps she had become Janna, the moody, black-clad enigma, out of some desire to be different. But it hadn't done her any good. If Jane Pyke was indeed Janna Pyke, she had met her death in the most hideous circumstances. Jane Pyke's home address was in a suburb of Leeds but Emily made no sign that she knew the address or the district which Joe found a little surprising as she'd been working in that city until very recently. In fact, she sat there in the passenger seat, unusually silent, preoccupied with her own thoughts.

Emily took the road to the city centre. The university's Medieval History Department was located in an appropriately medieval building not far from the cathedral. It had once been the lodging of the Abbot of St Peter's and, when King Henry VIII had conducted his brutal destruction of England's monasteries, he had left the Abbot's sumptuous quarters intact for his own use when he deigned to visit the north. Eventually the building had passed to the city and then to the university and it was within its mellow stone walls that Janna – or rather Jane – Pyke had studied for her master's degree.

Being a small department, it wasn't hard to track down her supervisor. Dr Keith Webster occupied an office overlooking the stone-flagged courtyard through which all students and visitors were obliged to pass, a good place to observe all the comings and goings. He was a short wiry man in his thirties and he wore a small, dark beard and a wary expression. Joe sensed that he was uneasy in the presence of the police. And this made him watch the man's reactions carefully. As a cat watches a mouse.

Dr Webster hurriedly shifted papers from chairs and invited them to sit down. The small office was cluttered with books and files and all available wall space was filled with colourful posters advertising past theatrical performances and museum exhibitions. It had a cosy feel, as if the man was truly at home there.

Joe glanced at Emily. She had hardly spoken during the journey, which was unusual for Emily Thwaite, who rarely let such a length of time pass without expressing her opinion on a variety of subjects. Joe wondered what was on her mind. Probably the case.

She gave him an almost imperceptible nod which meant she'd leave the questioning to him while she noted all the answers . . . and the things that weren't said – the nervous looks and the body language which would betray Dr Webster as a liar.

Joe began by asking Webster when he had last seen

Janna. The answer, when it came, was vague. She had last met with him at the department for a tutorial about two weeks ago. He had no idea where she had gone after she moved out of the flat on Vicars Green. He hadn't seen her. Webster evaded their questions with unexpected skill, saying only that she hadn't mentioned any accommodation problems to him.

'What kind of person was Janna?' Joe asked, looking at Emily, who was still watching in silence, a preoccupied look on her face.

Webster thought for a few seconds. 'She had a good brain and I was impressed by her work at first but . . .' He glanced at the clock, as though calculating how soon he could make his escape.

'But what?'

'She made a good start but then things started going downhill, as though her mind was no longer on her work. She'd taken a job at that House of Terrors place on Marketgate and it was about that time she announced that she was changing her name from Jane to Janna . . . don't know why. I know students have to work to make ends meet but it seemed to be taking over her life. Then there was her research . . .'

'What was she researching?'

'The plague in Eborby. At first she concentrated on the medieval outbreaks. Thirteen forty-eight to nine.' The man picked a pen up off his desk and began to turn it over in his fingers, faster and faster until it slipped from his grasp. Joe watched his face. Something was making him nervous. 'Then she was er . . . sidetracked,' he continued. 'I tried to get her to focus more but . . .'

'What do you mean by sidetracked?' Something in the way he had said it made Joe suspect this was important.

'She wanted to change the subject of her dissertation. She wanted to concentrate on the plague outbreak in Eborby at the start of the seventeenth century, which wasn't exactly what I'd class as medieval. She began researching a group of women known as the Seekers of the Dead. They used to examine the bodies of plague victims to confirm . . .'

Joe interrupted. 'I've heard of them before. So she took a special interest in these women?'

Webster nodded. 'Yes. There are detailed records of their activities in the city archives. She spent a lot of time there researching.'

'Did she have any special friends amongst the students?'

The answer was a definite shake of the head. 'Janna always kept herself very much to herself. She wasn't one for socialising . . . at least not at the university.'

'Can you let us see her work?'

He shook his head again. 'As far as I'm aware, she has it all with her. I'm sorry but I don't think I can help you.' He fell silent for a few moments, as though he was making a decision. 'To be honest, I'm not really surprised that she's chosen to go missing. She's been losing it since she started working at that House of Terrors place. I tried to talk to her about it but she wouldn't listen. She's over twenty-one and I'm hardly in loco parentis so there's nothing much I can do if someone's on the path to self-destruction.' He leaned forward confidentially 'I had this brilliant student once who started on drugs and . . .'

Joe looked at Emily again, wondering whether to break the news of their find in the churchyard. But she made the decision for him.

'Dr Webster, I'm afraid it might not just be a case of Jane dropping out. Her colleagues at the House of Terrors reported her missing. And a woman's body's just been found in a village called Evanshaw about eight miles east of here. It fits the description we have of Jane Pyke.'

A look of horror passed over Dr Keith Webster's face and he slumped back in his chair as though he'd been punched.

Joe watched him. The pain on his face was more than a teacher's reaction to a student's tragic death. Either he was putting on a show for some reason or she had meant more to him than he'd let on.

'This is a terrible shock,' he whispered after a few moments. 'I don't know what to say.'

'She was found in the churchyard,' said Emily almost brutally.

'I'm afraid there are similarities to two other recent deaths,' said Joe, his eyes still on the man's face, searching for any tell-tale reaction.

Webster looked up, wary. 'The ... the Resurrection Man?'

Joe nodded. 'You don't happen to know whether Jane ever worked at the Eborby Permanent Building Society, do you?'

The man shook his head.

'She moved out of her flat over three weeks ago. Are you sure about when you last saw her?'

Webster pulled himself upright and made a great show of examining his diary. He looked up. 'Yes. It was two weeks ago here in my office. Here.' He pointed at an entry and looked Joe in the eye, pleading, desperate to be believed. Joe knew now that Webster was hiding something. And he wondered what it was.

'And she didn't mention where she was living?'

The answer was a shake of the head.

So Janna had moved out of Vicars Green over three weeks ago and the pathologist had estimated that she'd only been dead for a couple of days. That meant she must have been staying somewhere else in the meantime. Unless the Resurrection Man had kept her prisoner all that time. The thought of such protracted suffering made Joe feel cold inside, almost sick.

Emily stood up. 'Thank you, Dr Webster. We'll send someone to take a statement from you. And we may need to speak to you again.'

'No problem,' was the automatic reply. But Joe sensed a world of worry behind the bland words.

As they left, Joe turned and saw the stunned expression on the man's face. And the tear that had begun to trickle down his cheek.

The children visiting the Archaeology Centre had seemed noisier and more restless than usual that morning and Carmel Hennessy couldn't understand why. But perhaps it was something in the air because Carmel felt rather restless herself. She had done since her meeting with Joe Plantagenet had reawakened memories of her father. She felt she needed some air to clear her head . . . and time to think. So she decided to take a walk around the city walls at lunchtime.

Peta Thewlis was in a meeting with some men in suits. She'd looked harassed from the time she had arrived at work and Maddy Owen had whispered to Carmel over tea that there was something going on; some decision about next year's funding. Maddy looked worried but Carmel preferred to bury her head in the sand and hope that she still had a job. It sometimes wasn't wise to look too far into the future.

At one o'clock Carmel hurried out of the centre to buy herself a sandwich, planning to eat it in the park and take a stroll round the walls before returning to work for the afternoon. Intent as she was on her goal, she didn't notice that someone was waiting for her by the centre's entrance. Until he called her name.

She swung round and she knew at once that something was wrong from the expression on Tavy McNair's face.

'Have you heard the news?' he said, stepping forward.

'What news?'

'They've found a woman's body. It sounds like her. It sounds like Janna.'

Carmel took Tavy firmly by the arm and marched him towards the nearest pub. He looked as though he needed a drink. So much for her lunchtime exercise.

It wasn't until they were settled with beer and sandwiches that Tavy spoke again in a hushed whisper as though he didn't want to be overheard. 'It said on the radio that the body of a dark-haired woman in her early twenties had been found in Evanshaw. In the churchyard.'

'The Resurrection Man?'

'I knew something bad had happened to her. I just knew.'

'It might not be her.'

'She fits the description – height, colouring . . . everything.'

'If you think that you should go to the police.'

He opened his mouth to protest.

'I saw that policeman I mentioned. Joe Plantagenet. He's an old colleague of my dad's. You could talk to him. He's OK. Honestly.'

Tavy looked doubtful. 'I can't tell him anything,' he said quickly. 'I don't know what Janna got up to after we split up.' He hesitated. 'But I know she used to go to that pub a lot – the Black Hen. Will you come there with me?'

'Why? If you think she's dead, what's the point?'

'I need to know what happened to her. Please. Come with me tonight.'

'What's the point? You should leave it to the police. Talk to Joe.'

'If we find something then we can talk to him. But if we don't, he won't thank you for wasting his time. Please.'

Carmel looked at him. It was only a trip to a pub, she told herself. And there was something about his large, pleading eyes that made her say yes against her better judgement.

Sometimes, she told herself, she was too soft for her own good.

'One of her mates from that House of Terrors has identified her. It's definitely Jane Pyke . . . alias Janna.'

DS Sunny Porter looked pleased with himself. Knowing the victim's identity might not be much help if the

Resurrection Man chose his victims at random but you never knew your luck. With the building society connection there might just be some purpose to the campaign of slaughter after all. Someone who'd had their house repossessed by the Eborby Permanent was Sunny's favourite theory until a better one came along. 'The next of kin'll have to be informed,' he said.

Emily Thwaite nodded. She looked as if there was still something on her mind other than the case. But she was new, Sunny thought. Perhaps she was always like this in the middle of an investigation. Maybe she liked time to think.

'Local lads are going over to the address the university gave us to break the bad news as we speak, ma'am.'

Emily looked up. 'Thanks, Sunny. You and Jamilla get down to this House of Terrors with a few uniforms. I want all the staff interviewed . . . yesterday. And send someone over to the university as well . . . the Medieval History Department near the cathedral. I want anyone who ever knew her questioned. Her tutor said he saw her two weeks ago . . . a week or so after she did a moonlight flit from her flat in Vicars Green and left her job at the House of Terrors. I think she was afraid of something and lying low somewhere. But what and where? We've got to find out.'

'If she was lying low, why did she go to the university?'

Emily looked away. 'Don't ask me. Perhaps her research was important to her and she thought she'd risk it. That's what we need to know.' She stood up. 'You'd better get a move on.'

'Yes, ma'am, no, ma'am, three bags full, ma'am,' Sunny muttered under his breath.

'If I'm needed I'll be in my office,' she said before sweeping out of the main incident room. She needed space. And she needed to phone home.

When she reached her office she shut the door behind her and sat down at her desk, taking a deep, calming breath. Then she picked up the phone and hesitated, the hand holding the receiver hovering in midair. Perhaps it wasn't wise to make that particular call from work. There were some conversations that she couldn't risk being overheard. Perhaps she should wait until she got home. Something like this had to be discussed face to face. Besides, through the glass window of her office, she could see Joe Plantagenet marching purposefully up the corridor, heading her way. She put the handset down and pretended to study some papers, her heart thumping against her ribs – she just hoped nobody could hear it.

After the swiftest of knocks, the door opened and Joe entered. He sat down in the chair by Emily's desk, making himself comfortable. Emily took another deep breath and told herself to relax. Act normally.

'The vicar of St Oswald's was at the church yesterday evening,' Joe began. 'There was certainly no body there then. He'll swear to that on a stack of Bibles. At least this means we can rule out John Wendal as he was in a coma at the time.'

'Doesn't necessarily mean Wendal's in the clear. He might have done the dirty deed and got an accomplice to dispose of the body.'

'Who? His wife? She's been at his bedside all the time.'

'His mate from the Railway Society? Perhaps they were into more than engines.'

'He's away on holiday. And it's true. I had it checked out. The Algarve.'

'Nice. Maybe there's someone else. Someone we don't know about. Someone his wife doesn't know about. Remember that leaflet about the House of Terrors. I think it's time we went and had a look at the place.'

'Sunny and Jamilla have just gone over there to question the staff.'

Emily stood up. 'That doesn't stop us poking our noses in. That place has got to have something to do with all this business.' Her eyes flicked towards the telephone.

'Are you all right?'

'Yes. Of course I'm all right. I'm fine.'

Joe sensed that something was bothering her but if she chose not to share it with him, there wasn't much he could do about it.

She slung her bag on to her shoulder. 'Coming?'

He could see she was determined so he didn't try to argue and followed her out of the police station into the traffic-fume-laden air. The House of Terrors was within walking distance and today Emily claimed that she fancied the exercise so they set off down the main road towards Marketgate, crossing the river and turning right into the pedestrianised city centre. It was another sunny day, the eighth in succession, which was probably some sort of record.

Housed in a Victorian red-brick building just outside the medieval heart of the city, the House of Terrors looked rather like a public library and the legend above the door, carved proudly into the decorative brickwork, declared that this had been the building's original function. Now discreet name plates at the side of the entrance indicated that the upper floors were used as offices. It was only the basement that had been given over to horror. Joe followed the arrows that pointed down to the depths and Emily followed close behind, not quite sure what to expect.

A massive, polished mahogany counter blocked the entrance. The ticket desk Janna Pyke had once manned. It looked as if it had once been the bar of some nineteenth-century pub, reclaimed for a more sinister use. Joe flashed a smile and his ID at the young woman behind the counter, dressed, like Janna, in the uniform of the Goth. But her face needed no pale make-up. She looked drained and shaken.

'They're all in the torture chamber,' she said matter-of-factly in a friendly-sounding broad Yorkshire accent, which rather ruined the effect.

'Who are?' The last thing Joe wanted was to intrude on a ghoul's convention.

'Your lot. The police. They've just turned up mob handed. We've had to close to the public. Mr Jevons isn't pleased, you know.'

'Mr Jevons?'

'He runs the place. He's not pleased,' she repeated, as though emphasising the depth of Mr Jevons's displeasure.

'You knew Janna Pyke?' Emily asked.

'Course I did. It was Steve and I who went to the police station and reported her missing. I knew something wasn't right. I can tell these things.' She paused, looking as if she was about to be sick. 'Me and Steve, we've just been to the hospital to identify her. It was awful . . . I don't know how anyone can . . .'

Joe suddenly took pity on her. 'Are you sure you should be here? You look . . .'

'I'm fine,' she said bravely. 'I just hope you catch the bastard and it's not going to help anyone if I sit round moping, is it.' She hesitated. 'Is it the same as the others? Is it that Resurrection Man?'

'I'm afraid it looks that way. Is there anything you can tell me about . . .'

'I've given a statement already. Told 'em everything I know which isn't much.' She leaned forward and spoke in a whisper. 'Like I said to the other one, you want to be looking at the Black Hen. And Mr Jevons. And there's a couple of others too. Hetty Bowles and James Waters. You should be asking them what goes on there.'

Joe glanced at Emily. This was just the sort of witness they needed. 'Thanks for the hint,' he said smoothly. 'Mind if we . . .' He waved a casual hand towards the House of Terrors' entrance.

'Help yourself. Torture chamber second on your left. Can't miss it.'

They followed the young woman's directions and eventually found themselves in a cavernous room, teeming with police officers who were taking statements from black-clad House of Terrors personnel, scattered in pairs. With dim, dramatic lighting and blood-curdling sound effects the torture chamber might have struck fear into the heart of the unsuspecting tourist. But in the cold light of the fluorescent striplights on the ceiling, with the low hum of conversation filling the room, the bloodstained waxwork dummies of the tortured and their sweating, gloating tormentors wielding unspeakable instruments of pain looked exactly what they were – stage props, tawdry and roughly constructed. Joe strode towards the rack where Sunny Porter was taking a statement, his notebook propped up on the wax torso of the naked man stretched out, awaiting the attentions of the executioner.

Sunny was talking to a tall dark man with a small pointed beard. Joe guessed he was in his forties and his once-honed body had begun to run to flab. But there was a power about the man, a presence. Joe thought he saw hostility in his eyes, perhaps even contempt. Certainly not grief.

'This is Mr Terry Jevons, sir,' Sunny said as soon as he had spotted Joe. 'He runs this place. He says he hasn't seen Janna Pyke for over three weeks. Not since she last turned up for work.'

Jevons smiled, a mirthless grimace. 'That's right. I've not seen her since then.'

'Know a place called the Black Hen?' It was Emily Thwaite who spoke, a hint of challenge in her voice.

Jevons glanced at her impatiently. 'It's a pub. What about it?'

'Did Janna go there?'

Jevons shrugged his wide shoulders. 'Sometimes.'

Emily stepped forward, her eyes fixed on the man's face. 'We'd like to ask you some more questions. Is there somewhere more private we can talk?'

'My office. It's this way.' He didn't sound pleased but he led the way out of the crowded room. Joe and Emily followed him, leaving Sunny to look for another victim. They'd compare notes later.

When they reached Jevons's surprisingly well appointed

office at the back of the building he invited them to take a seat. He looked uncomfortable and Joe wondered why. But at least he was going through the motions of cooperation to keep them happy.

'What can you tell us about Janna Pyke?' Joe began. Emily sat behind him, listening intently.

'She was at the university here doing an MA. She was originally from Leeds but she'd done her first degree at Manchester. She worked here part time. We employ a lot of students. They work the hours that suit them in the week and fill in at weekends and holidays when we're busy.'

'All Goths are they?'

'They have to look the part. Wouldn't do to see Mary Poppins in a House of Terrors, would it?' He smirked. 'Some of them are Goths, some just dress up for the occasion.'

'Janna?'

There was a long pause. Then his lips twitched upwards in a secretive smile. 'She was the real thing.'

Joe suddenly noticed something that looked like a business card next to the telephone on the desk. A triangle in a circle, topped by a half circle. Horns. He had seen the same symbol before. In Gloria Simpson's strange room. He glanced at Emily and saw that she had noticed it too. She raised her eyebrows a little and nodded to him to continue.

'Anybody here into the occult? Black magic?'

Joe saw a brief flash of panic in Jevons's eyes, soon suppressed. 'Don't know,' he answered, too casually.

'Do you know a woman called Gloria Simpson?'

'Can't say I do.' The flicker of recognition in his eyes told Joe and Emily that he was lying.

'Does the name Jack Wendal mean anything to you?'

There was no mistaking it. The small eyes widened for a split second. 'No,' was the emphatic reply. 'Who is he?'

'That's what we're trying to find out,' said Emily. 'What about the Black Hen? What goes on there?'

'Drinking. It's a pub.' He smirked unpleasantly, his eyes

on Emily's ample breasts. 'You should come some time.'

Emily pressed her lips together. She was in no mood for playing games. 'Tell us what happened when you last saw Janna Pyke.'

'We cashed up. She said goodnight and left me to lock up.'

'Anyone else around?'

'Can't remember. It was just an ordinary night.'

'Except that she never showed up to work again.'

'Look, I don't know anything. I told that other cop. I've not seen her since that night. Right?'

Emily stood up. 'Thank you, Mr Jevons. We'll be in touch.'

She marched out of the office and Joe followed.

'What's the matter?' he whispered to Emily as soon as they were out of earshot. 'He was lying. I could tell. We should have put more pressure on him. You saw that symbol on the desk . . . the same one we saw in Gloria Simpson's flat . . .?'

'Yes, but I think we should leave him for now . . . make him sweat.' She was hurrying down the corridor, making for the entrance. 'Look, I've got a terrible headache, Joe. Cover for me, will you?'

'OK,' he said as he watched her disappear through the door. But somehow he knew that she was lying . . . just like Jevons had been.

Chapter Eight

Gloria Simpson's address book was hardly filled with the names of devoted friends and family. Most of the entries were acquaintances, tradesmen or work contacts. There were two cousins who'd been eager to emphasise that they hadn't seen her for years and an ex-husband who had moved on to pastures new. He stated that his former partner was decidedly weird and seemed reluctant to elaborate any further.

DC Jamilla Dal, who came from a close and loyal family, found herself feeling a deep pity for Gloria Simpson – a sadness almost akin to pain. She considered that the woman who had attacked John Wendal must have led a lonely and empty existence and perhaps, in the end, it had been that pointless emptiness that had driven Gloria over the edge.

Jamilla had come to the last entry in the book. A Linda Young. She was probably just another business acquaintance, Jamilla told herself, but she dialled the number anyway.

Five minutes later, she replaced the receiver, having struck lucky at last. Linda Young was Gloria's sister and she was driving straight to Eborby from her home just outside Thirsk. She'd sounded shocked by Jamilla's call but, from the tone of her voice, Jamilla guessed that the news that her sister was in hospital after having had some sort of breakdown wasn't exactly unexpected. Jamilla hadn't mentioned the incident with John Wendal. It wasn't something she wanted to discuss over the phone.

She looked around. The DCI wasn't in her office and there was no sign of DI Plantagenet. So, as DS Sunny Porter was still out conducting interviews at Janna Pyke's place of work, it seemed that it fell to Jamilla to use her initiative, something she often longed to do but her superiors rarely gave her the opportunity. She asked Linda Young where and when it would be convenient for them to meet and Linda readily agreed to a rendezvous at the hospital.

There was a café near the hospital's main entrance and it was here she arranged to meet Linda after she had visited her sister in the psychiatric department. Jamilla was familiar with the café's layout and its menu: she and the rest of her close-knit family had spent a lot of time there during her grandmother's last illness, comforting and supporting each other over tea and scones provided by the stalwart ladies of the WRVS.

As Jamilla reached the café, the memories of her grandmother's suffering flooded back into her mind. The pain inflicted on her small, thin body by her cancer; the way sickness had robbed the once all-powerful matriarch of her inherent dignity. Jamilla hesitated on the café's threshold for a moment before marching inside, wearing her bravest face. She was there to do a job; to find out as much as she could about Gloria Simpson.

A middle-aged woman was sitting at a table in the corner. When she spotted Jamilla she stood up and gave a hesitant wave. Her mousy hair was dragged back into a ponytail and the checked shirt, jeans and gilet she wore marked her out as a countrywoman. She looked at Jamilla questioningly, wondering whether she'd got the right person.

Jamilla walked straight up to her. 'Mrs Young?'

'Yes. DC Dal?' Linda Young put out a hand. Jamilla

noticed that the nails were short and unvarnished and the skin was rough.

After the preliminary pleasantries had been completed and the tea, the cure for all ills, obtained, the two women sat down opposite each other.

'You've seen your sister?' Jamilla began.

Linda Young nodded. 'It's bad. The doctor says she'll be in for weeks.'

'What's wrong with her exactly?'

'Some sort of psychosis. I don't think they're sure.'

'Where does Gloria work? Perhaps her colleagues should be told if . . .'

A look of disapproval passed over Linda's face. 'As far as I know she's been working for herself recently. She had all sorts of jobs . . .'

'What was your maiden name?'

'Marsh. Why?'

'Did Gloria ever work for the Eborby Permanent Building Society?'

'Yes, she did as a matter of fact. But she didn't last long there . . . she said it was boring. Soon after she left there she got into all this New Age stuff and started working in a shop that specialised in that sort of thing. That was about the time her marriage broke up. Then she started reading tarot cards for people . . . set herself up in business. And she made pictures for craft fairs . . . that sort of thing.' She leaned forward. 'I'm afraid we rather lost touch. In fact I haven't seen her for over a year until today. Different lives, I suppose.' She sighed. 'I'm married to a farmer and we've got three kids and . . . My husband's never really approved of Gloria. He calls her the weirdo. You wouldn't think two sisters could be that different, would you? Mind you, I was always the sensible one – the eldest.' She gave Jamilla a sad smile, remembering her lost childhood.

'Did you know your sister was involved in the occult . . . black magic?'

Linda's face clouded. 'I'd guessed she was going that

way from things she'd said. Maybe that's why I didn't make more of an effort to keep in touch. Gloria could be – how shall I put it? – a bit obsessive. And she'd always been attracted to danger. She liked pushing the boundaries.' She looked Jamilla in the eye. 'I always found her world uncomfortable. Even though she's my sister I've never wanted to get involved with her life . . . not if she was into that sort of thing. Can you understand that?'

Jamilla nodded. She understood. She'd probably have felt the same even though she came from a culture where family ties were of prime importance. 'Does the name John or Jack Wendal mean anything to you?'

'Was that the man she . . .?'

'Yes.'

Linda shook her head. 'No. I've never heard the name before and she never mentioned him to me. Was he into all that stuff as well?'

'That's what we're trying to find out.'

Linda looked at her watch. 'Look, I'm going to have to get back home.'

'Did you know that one of the rooms in her flat was decorated with black magic symbols? She'd turned it into a sort of . . . temple.'

Linda looked alarmed. 'No.' She put her head in her hands. 'How could she have got mixed up in something like that? How could she have been so stupid?'

Jamilla shook her head. She had asked herself the same question.

'Where's ma'am?' Sunny asked as he poked his head round the door of Joe's office.

'She had to go out.' Joe wasn't sure why he was telling a blatant lie but some instinct told him that any display of weakness on Emily's part would be seized on by some of her underlings and exploited. Even though he was inclined to disapprove of lies on principle – probably a leftover from his seminary days – he knew that little white ones could avoid potential trouble. 'Anything to report on the House of Terrors interviews?'

Sunny sat himself down. 'Half of that lot look as if they could do with a good bath.'

'Apart from that . . .' Joe wanted to avoid one of Sunny's lectures on the shortcomings of today's youth.

'One of them saw Janna Pyke a week ago.'

This was news. 'A week ago?'

'Aye. That's what she said. She was on her way to a pub and she ran into Janna Pyke. She said she looked scared and she tried to slip into a doorway but she caught up with her and asked her why she'd left her job at the House of Terrors. She said she didn't want to talk about it and begged her not to tell anyone she'd seen her.'

'And did she tell anyone?'

'She said not. But I don't know whether I believed her. When I asked her what Janna had been so scared of, she said she didn't know. But she was lying through her teeth, I could tell. She made a statement but I think we should get her in again for questioning.'

'What was her name?'

Sunny consulted his notebook. 'Harriet Bowles.'

'Did you ask her if the name Jack Wendal meant anything to her?'

Sunny shook his head. 'Sorry, boss.'

'Where exactly did she say she saw Janna?'

Sunny consulted his notebook again. 'Boargate. Coming out of a shop.'

Joe knew Boargate well – it was wider than the average Eborby street with an abundance of antique shops – well on the tourist trail.

'Any idea which shop?' Joe asked patiently.

'She said there were paintings in the window.'

'An art shop. And she was sure this was a week ago?'

'Aye, that's what she said.'

Joe thought for a few moments. 'So she left the flat in Vicars Green over three weeks ago, around the twenty-second of June, and her tutor saw her two weeks ago. That means this is the last reported sighting of her and she must have been abducted quite soon after . . . if that's what the killer does to his victims. I'm presuming they don't know him and go with him willingly.'

'Maybe they do. We've no evidence that thcy don't, have we?'

Joe looked up. Sunny could well be right. Perhaps the Resurrection Man knew his victims. Perhaps they'd trusted him. 'Let's doublecheck whether Janna – or Jane – Pyke ever worked at the Eborby Permanent Building Society, shall we?'

Sunny hurried from the office. Maybe his hunch was right after all.

DCI Emily Thwaite parked the car in the drive. She could hear the gravel crunching beneath the tyres as she looked up at the new house. It was a Victorian brick detached villa in one of Eborby's more prosperous outlying suburbs. Not far from the racecourse and the place where criminals were publicly hanged in days gone by. It was about half a mile from Gloria Simpson's flat and even nearer than that to Harold Uckley's house. The thought made her shudder. It was too close for comfort.

She sat in the car for a few minutes and stared at the house. She had lied to Joe Plantagenet about the headache and she felt bad about it. Joe was intelligent and he seemed dependable as well – two things that, in her experience, didn't always go together. But his obvious competence made it more urgent that she should sort her problem out once and for all. Before Joe – or someone else – began to look in places she didn't want him to look.

She glanced at her watch. She had put it off long enough. She climbed out of the car and fixed an expression of benevolent motherhood on her face before marching to the front door and letting herself in with her key.

The children, hearing the door open, rushed into the

hallway, shouting and squabbling, vying for her attention. She scooped the youngest up in her arms and tried to calm the others. There were things she had to sort out.

When her husband appeared, framed in the doorway of the kitchen, she stopped and looked him in the eye. She and Jeff had been married long enough - gone through enough together - for him to understand her meaning. He took charge of the children, shepherding them towards the living room where he switched on the TV. Although neither of them approved of using the box as a babysitter, it had its uses sometimes.

Once the children were settled, Emily and Jeff scurried into the kitchen and sat down at the table. And as she faced him, she suddenly felt afraid.

'It's her,' Emily whispered. 'It's Jane bloody Pyke.'

Jeff looked wary. 'What do you mean?'

'Haven't you been listening to the news? She's the Resurrection Man's latest victim. She was found this morning in Evanshaw churchyard. Some people she worked with reported her missing and her body turned up today. Same as the others.'

Jeff put his head in his hands and said nothing.

'Jane Pyke. They'll find the connection sooner or later.'

'You're in charge of the case. Make sure they don't.'

She hesitated, suddenly uneasy. 'It doesn't work like that, Jeff. We dig into her life: find out all we can about the victim's past. I couldn't stop it all coming out even if I wanted to. There's nothing I can do.'

She stared at him for a few moments. Her husband of fifteen years. He had been remarkably good looking, beautiful even, when they'd married and he was still attractive even though his body was beginning to show the inevitable effects of having lived on this earth for forty-five years.

Emily had sensed a change in him over the past few weeks and had put it down to the move and worry about the new teaching job he was due to begin in September. But now . . .

'Have you seen her since we came to Eborby?'
'Don't you trust me?'
'Of course I do,' she said quickly. 'But if you're questioned . . .'
He looked away, avoiding her steady gaze. 'Of course I haven't bloody seen her. Why would I want to see her after what she . . .?'
'Where were you on Sunday night?'
'You know where I was. I met Paul for a drink.'
'And last night? Where were you?'
'I was here. So were you.' He walked over to the window. On his way he picked up the bread knife lying on the worktop and ran his finger along the blade, as though testing its sharpness.
'You went out.'
'To the supermarket. The weekly shop. Remember?'
'You were a long time.'
'I had to queue up for petrol. This is ridiculous.'
Emily flinched as he threw the bread knife down with a loud clatter before storming out of the room. And as she heard the front door slam she felt tears pricking at her eyes like red hot needles.

It was eight thirty when Joe Plantagenet left the police station. He walked home through the evening streets, dodging the council street-cleaning machines which were out in force, patrolling like robots, and the army of tourists who were still roaming the streets in ragged groups, searching for somewhere reasonable to eat.
As far as days went, it had been a frustrating one. He had been hopeful that Jamilla's meeting with Gloria Simpson's sister would provide them with some clue about why she had attacked John Wendal. But the sister, Linda Young, was a down-to-earth farmer's wife who had lost touch with Gloria long ago and she was as mystified by events as the police were. She did, however, confirm that Gloria worked for the Eborby Permanent Building Society

for a short time which might be significant . . . or not, as the case might be.

The aroma of cooking wafted from the open doors of pubs and restaurants, reminding Joe that he was hungry and had no food in at the flat. Suddenly, on impulse, he took his mobile phone from one pocket and searched in another for the scrap of paper on which Maddy Owen had scribbled her number.

As he stood in the middle of Pottergate, staring at his phone, the tide of ambling tourists parting around him, he experienced a sudden attack of second thoughts. He hardly knew Maddy: he had only met her once and, even though they'd got on well, inviting her out for a meal might be too much too soon. It could be misinterpreted.

On the other hand, they had a concern in common – Carmel Hennessy. And meeting in a pub for a bite to eat would do no harm. Hardly a formal date. No commitment.

In fact it had been a while since Joe had experienced anything approaching commitment. The moment he'd met Kaitlin he'd known that there was no possibility of him staying at the seminary. He'd suddenly had a vision of what a life of celibacy would bring – of the years of loneliness stretching ahead of him with only a housekeeper for human company – and he knew then that it wasn't the life he wanted. He and Kaitlin had married within six months of their first meeting. Then, exactly a hundred and fifty days after the wedding, she'd died – a fall down some cliff steps during a West Country holiday – a stupid accident; a chance in a million. Joe had joined the police by then and he dealt with his grief by immersing himself in his work. Even now he still missed Kaitlin; still found himself thinking of her sometimes in the small hours or when he was alone, wondering what might have been if she'd lived. But usually he tried to forget.

Then came Kevin's death and his own injury when his world had shattered again. There had been women, of course – the periodic brief encounters that could hardly be dignified with the title 'relationship' – but nothing that came remotely close to those heady days of his marriage to Kaitlin. Sometimes, in his darkest hours, he imagined there was some sort of curse on him – the Almighty's revenge on him for abandoning his vocation. But then Joe had never believed that God was vindictive – He left that sort of thing to the opposition.

Joe dialled Maddy's number, telling himself he had nothing to lose but his solitude. And besides, it would be good to have someone there who could keep a discreet eye on Carmel for him – she'd hardly want her late father's old colleague fussing around, cramping her style.

Maddy sounded pleased to hear from him and when she suggested that they meet at the Cross Keys for a meal he accepted. He heard no warning bells ringing and experienced no feelings of entrapment. On the contrary, he found that he was looking forward to seeing her.

When they met at the pub's entrance, she greeted him with a nervous smile and asked him how the case was going. But he sensed she had other things on her mind, things she wanted to share with him. They found a table and picked up the large cardboard menus.

'I heard about the body in Evanshaw churchyard,' Maddy began. 'Is it another . . .?

'Looks like it, I'm afraid.'

Maddy hesitated. 'Carmel told me that the description sounds like that Janna Pyke who used to have her flat . . . the one who received those threatening letters. I told her she should tell you. I said that even if she was wrong, you wouldn't mind.'

Joe sighed. It would do no harm to let Maddy in on the truth as it would be all over the papers the next day anyway. 'Carmel's right. It is Janna Pyke. She's been identified but we don't release the name until the next of kin have been informed.'

'I suppose it puts the phone call and threatening letters in a whole new light then.'

'Apart from the fact she was probably dead when the threats were made. Who'd try and frighten someone they knew was already dead?'

'True.' Maddy looked down and noticed the gold wedding ring on the third finger of Joe's left hand. 'You . . . er . . . must have been close to Carmel's dad.'

Joe nodded. 'He was my sergeant – taught me the ropes. And we were good friends. It hit me hard when he was killed. It's not something you get over in a hurry.'

'I'm a bit worried about Carmel.'

Joe leaned forward. 'Why?'

'She met that Tavy this lunchtime and she's going to the Black Hen with him.'

Joe suddenly felt uneasy . . . and something else: disappointed that Carmel wasn't as sensible as he'd assumed she was. 'When?'

'Tonight, she said. After he's done the ghost tour. She didn't sound too keen on the idea but she said she didn't want to let him down.'

Joe took a drink of beer. 'I'm sure she'll be all right as long as they stick together,' he said, trying to sound optimistic.

'But what if this Tavy's . . .?'

'Let's not think about that, eh,' he said, turning his head away so that Maddy wouldn't see the anxiety in his eyes.

They ordered their meals but neither of them felt very hungry.

Carmel sat down at a table in the corner while Tavy went up to the bar to get the drinks. She sat of the edge of the deeply upholstered bench seat watching him. She didn't want to make herself too comfortable and get sucked into the atmosphere of the place.

At first glance, the Black Hen looked like many other Eborby pubs. Low-beamed ceilings, subdued lighting, a stone-flagged floor and dark-red leather seating around heavy oak tables. There was a fruit machine tucked discreetly in the corner but no juke box or piped music, which some might judge to be an advantage. But in this case the silence only served to emphasise the restless hostility in the air. As though the place held a secret which the patrons were anxious to keep to themselves.

Tavy returned with the drinks. Carmel had seen him chatting animatedly to someone at the bar but she sensed that the conversation hadn't been a comfortable one. She watched his face as he placed the glasses carefully on beer mats. He looked worried.

'What's the matter?' she asked, trying not to sound too impatient and give away the fact that she longed to leave and head for more congenial surroundings.

He sat down and took a sip from his pint of bitter before answering. 'That bloke at the bar . . . his name's Jevons and he was Janna's boss at the House of Terrors. I asked him what she was so scared of.' He paused. 'And I asked him who Jack Wendal is.'

Carmel's sense of unease suddenly increased. 'Was that wise?' She kept her eyes fixed on the tall, bearded man propping up the bar. He was deep in conversation with a couple of Goths, both male; one small, one tall. Occasionally they glanced in Tavy's direction slyly, averting their eyes when they saw she was watching.

'Maybe not. But I thought the straightforward approach might get results.'

'And did it?' As she asked the question, Jevons left his post at the bar and disappeared through an unmarked door at the side of the bar.

'He told me to mind my own bloody business. And he said he'd never heard of anyone called Jack Wendal. But he was lying through his teeth.'

Carmel looked around. 'So where do they hold the black masses then?'

Tavy shook his head. 'Don't ask me. I'm not into that sort of stuff.' He said the words smoothly, confidently. But she wasn't sure that she believed him.

She glanced at the adjoining table. A wiry man with a shaved head was sitting there slumped over an evening paper. His restless hand was drumming on the table and she noticed a rough tattoo on his left forearm: a circle in a square with what looked like horns on top. He looked up and when he caught her eye he began to stare; a strange, assessing stare that sent shivers down her spine. She looked away quickly.

'I don't like this place,' she whispered to Tavy. 'When can we go?'

Tavy picked up his glass and took a long gulp of bitter. 'As soon as I've finished this. Maybe it wasn't a good idea to come. I should have known they'd close ranks.' He put his glass down and looked round. 'Do you know this pub's reputed to have been a meeting place for those dabbling in witchcraft and devil worship? This was in the eighteenth century under a landlord called Jack Devilhorn who also moonlighted as a highwayman. And before that in 1657 the landlady – or I suppose they called her the ale wife in those days – was burned as a witch in front of the cathedral.'

Carmel looked at him, her heart beating fast. 'How do you know all this?'

'When I took on the ghost tour job I did some research into Eborby's grisly past. And believe me, some of it's very grisly indeed.' He drained his glass. 'Come on. Let's go somewhere else.'

Carmel stood up quickly. She wanted to be out of there. 'Did Janna often come here?' she asked as they made for the door, their eyes focused ahead, trying to look casual.

'Oh, yes. She was a regular. I came with her a couple of times but I always felt there was something going on here that I wasn't a part of, if you see what I mean.'

A sudden impulse made Carmel looked round. The shaven-headed man was still watching her, staring unblinkingly at her as though he was trying to see into her very soul. She had been walking slowly towards the door at Tavy's side but now she broke into a trot and forged ahead of him, anxious to reach the outside world.

'Where to now?' she asked once they were on the pavement. It was a warm night, sultry. It had seemed cooler in the pub for some reason, although she hadn't noticed any air conditioning. Perhaps it just had thick walls like many of Eborby's historic buildings.

'We could try this place I know near Wheatley Hall. I sometimes go there after the tour . . . after I've got rid of my costume and make-up.' He smiled. 'We can take a short cut through the snickleways. Come on.'

This sounded more like it. Carmel's heart felt lighter as she followed Tavy to the shadowy entrance of a nearby alley. The short cut. The alley – an ancient passageway between two medieval buildings – was unlit and was almost pitch black, except for a thin shaft of silvery light from the full moon above them. The snickleways of Eborby – the network of inconsequential little alleys and passageways that ran between the huddled old buildings – were picture-postcard quaint in daylight. But they could be dark and sinister at night. She walked close to Tavy so that their hands were almost touching and she felt a sudden desire to take his hand in hers, to seek comfort in the contact of flesh on flesh.

But no sooner had this thought popped into her mind than she heard a sound behind them. Tavy quickened his pace and she did likewise. But the sound was getting closer. Footsteps. Heavy footsteps. Determined. Threatening.

Carmel's heart began to pound. Their pursuers were almost upon them. Nearer and nearer.

'Run,' Tavy whispered. 'Now.'

Her legs felt as if they were weighted down by heavy chains. She had had dreams where she had to flee from some unspecified terror and been unable to move from the spot, but this was real. Tavy had shot ahead but now he had retraced his steps and was yanking her arm. Fear deafened her to his words but she understood the sense of them. They had to get out of there.

A dark shadow suddenly loomed out of the blackness of the unlit alley and Tavy loosened his grasp. Carmel could hear his cries as a boot made contact with his body. His assailant gasped with the effort of attack, panting like a beast in the shadows.

'That's from Jack Wendal,' a voice hissed, vicious as a striking cobra.

Carmel could just make out a figure bending over Tavy's slumped form. She pressed her body into the alley wall, fearing she'd be next. But the assailant, after a second's hesitation, retreated down the alley and left her there listening to Tavy's groans of pain.

And as the sound of the attackers' footsteps faded, Carmel heard herself scream.

Chapter Nine

The killer stared at the card in his hand. At the scribbled, barely legible dates listed, one underneath the other. He had looked at the calendar on the wall, checked it several times, but the answer was always the same. He would have to wait until the next day to know what the future had in store for him.

He longed to know when he could use the equipment again. He had become rather good at it; watching them; following them; getting to know their routines and their habits. Then waiting until they were alone and vulnerable and striking when they least expected it. They were dangerous, fearsome. But he had played his part in ridding the world of their evil. He had done well.

He hoped there would be more tasks for him to perform. If there weren't he might just have to branch out on his own.

Joe Plantagenet had walked Maddy back to her small terraced cottage in the shadow of the city walls, not too far from his own flat. But he hadn't accepted her offer of coffee. He was starting to like Maddy – to enjoy her company – but a small voice inside him told him to take things slowly. When they'd said goodnight, he'd waited outside the house until he knew she was safely inside. While the Resurrection Man was at large, he was worried for her . . . and for all the lone women of Eborby.

He woke up early the next morning and climbed out of bed at six o'clock, feeling wide awake, and, after two slices of buttered toast and a strong coffee, he dressed and let himself out of the flat quietly. He needed time to think.

It was too early for the rush hour so crossing the main road was no problem. As he walked across, his way was barred by the bulk of the city walls. His flat was just outside their protection, a new development, convenient and blessed with all mod cons.

He walked on purposefully, keeping the walls to his left. They looked impregnable, enclosing and defending their own little world. Standing on top of the walls you could pick off your enemies as they clambered up the steep, grassy banks and it was easy to imagine yourself in the defenders' place. That was the trouble with Eborby – and its virtue. Everywhere you looked and trod had thousands of years of history imprinted on it. Roman, Viking, medieval, Civil War. The thought both exhausted and excited him. He was just another link in the chain. Just another official trying to bring wrongdoers to justice. His Roman, Viking and medieval counterparts must have faced the same problems. There would always have been wrongs to right – thieves and murderers to apprehend. It was the way of the world. Always had been since Cain first lost his temper with his brother Abel.

Passing underneath Canons Bar, one of the four intact medieval gates that had been the city's front line of defence in days gone by, he caught a fleeting whiff of urine – last night's revellers had used the shadowy shelter beneath the fierce spikes of the raised wooden portcullis as a convenient place to relieve themselves. He continued down the claustrophobic streets with their little shuttered shops and stone pavements worn smooth by centuries of footsteps, avoiding a small pool of dried vomit outside a half-timbered pub advertising karaoke nights in its small leaded windows.

As he rounded the corner, the narrow street opened on

to the wide expanse of Vicars Green. When he passed Carmel Hennessy's small window he glanced upwards, hoping to see some sign of life in her flat to indicate that she had survived her trip to the Black Hen unscathed. The curtains were drawn across the window which he took as a sign that she had got home safely. Perhaps he was worrying about nothing.

He hurried on past the graceful Georgian symmetry of the cathedral choir school, and at eight o'clock precisely he arrived outside the cathedral's south door, staring upwards at the towers reaching up to the wispy clouds that scuttled across the otherwise blue sky as the great bell tolled the hour. Until a few weeks ago the towers had been hidden by scaffolding, but now they could be seen in their full glory with their elaborately carved pinnacles and their impudent gargoyles that mocked the passers-by below as they had done for centuries.

For a while Joe gaped at the fantastic building, anchored like a gigantic ship floating above the labyrinth of ancient streets, before creeping inside on tiptoe, instinctively silent. There was a service on, sparsely attended because of the early hour, so he took a seat at the back of the huge, airy nave.

A galaxy of twinkling candles lit the cathedral's dark spaces. Maybe he should have lit one for Janna Pyke and the other victims, he thought as he recited the familiar words of the Our Father. He needed all the help he could get.

When the service ended he looked around. There was someone he wanted to see; someone who had been a distant robed figure officiating by the altar during the service. At last he spotted him, a small round man in a black chasuble, bald as a snooker ball, bustling down the aisle. When Joe stood up, the man spotted him and gave a wide grin of greeting.

'Joe,' he said, approaching with an outstretched hand. 'Long time no see. How are you? How is everything?'

'Not bad, George. Have you time for a chat?'

Canon George Merryweather's grin widened. 'Fancy a cup of tea?'

Joe accepted gratefully. He had met George when he'd first arrived in Eborby. He had been investigating a burglary at George's house in the cathedral close and, in his vulnerable state, he had found himself confiding in him about Kaitlin and Kevin – using him rather as a father confessor. George had listened and given the occasional wise word of advice. But he'd mostly listened. There were times when Joe thought that George had saved his life . . . or at least his faith.

He followed George down the aisle and turned left beneath the central tower. Once they had left the main cathedral and passed the chapter house, George produced a large key from an unseen pocket and opened a small oak door at the end of the passage.

'My office,' he said cheerfully. 'Excuse the mess, won't you.'

He switched the light on and stepped inside. Joe followed, suddenly understanding what George meant by the mess. His first thought was that the office had been burgled. But then he remembered that chaos was George's default state. Boxes were piled everywhere and papers lay strewn across the floor. The surface of the desk was invisible under a pile of debris, books and files.

'How do you find anything?' Joe asked, genuinely curious.

'Either divine guidance or luck. Take your pick. I prefer to think it's the former. Sit down, won't you. I'll put the kettle on.'

Somehow a kettle and a couple of clean mugs were produced from underneath a pile of brochures. George had always moved in rather mysterious ways and Joe had learned to accept the fact. He looked at his watch. He had half an hour before he was due at work.

When the tea was in front of him, steaming and still too

hot to drink, Joe came to the point of his visit. 'Hope you don't mind, George, but I want to pick your brains.'

George, who was busy fishing a teabag out of his mug, looked up and smiled. 'Pick away, dear boy.'

'You have a special interest in the opposition, as it were.'

'The devil and all his works. Certainly. In fact they've given me a rather swanky title – Diocesan Consultant on the Occult.'

'And is there a lot of it about?'

'Oh, indeed yes. I'm sorry to say there is. I was called out only the other day. Some poor girl who'd got involved in something because she thought it would be a laugh. Then she found out it wasn't so funny. Her mother consulted her local vicar who came to me.'

'What was she involved in?'

George took a sip of tea before replying.

'It seems she was persuaded to take part in some kind of black magic ritual. I don't know what happened exactly but afterwards she became genuinely disturbed. She started having nightmares: she'd wake up screaming, terrified, and she wouldn't let her mother or a doctor anywhere near her. And then she began to talk in a man's voice, using old-fashioned language she couldn't possibly have known. Her mother said it was as if she was possessed by something evil. That's when she called us in. I don't know whether she believes or not but I don't think she knew what else to do.'

'And did you manage to help her?'

'I hope so. I prayed with her and performed the usual rituals and the girl's had no strange behaviour since. But she's very shaken . . . very fragile. The mother says she'll contact me if there's any change. In the meantime she's seeing a psychiatrist at the hospital. Belt and braces. Science and religion.' He smiled. 'Let's hope she's OK.'

'Have you heard of a place called the Black Hen?'

George's open, round face suddenly looked deadly

serious. 'Of course I've heard of the Black Hen. That place has been notorious since the sixteenth century. Built on the site of a Viking cemetery, so rumour has it. It was OK for years as far as I know . . . just another pub before the present landlord took over and thought he'd revive its old traditions as it were. It's the hangout of all sorts of weirdoes and would-be Satanists. A place best avoided.'

'Is that where this ritual you mentioned took place?'

'I believe so, yes.'

'Ever been there?'

'I reckon I'm persona non grata in that place. But I did pop in once for a swift half incognito – I thought I should size up the opposition. Nasty atmosphere.'

'And they actually perform rituals on the premises?'

'I suspect so but I've no proof. And Amy, the girl who . . . is in no fit state yet to go into details.'

'What do you know about the House of Terrors on Marketgate?'

George shrugged his shoulders. 'It's just a tourist trap as far as I know. Their leaflets are everywhere.'

'Nothing sinister going on there then?'

'I haven't heard anything.' He leaned forward. 'Why? Do you know something I don't?'

'I'm not sure. A young woman who worked there has just been found dead . . . apparently a victim of this Resurrection Man. And we've heard that some of her colleagues frequent the Black Hen.' He delved in his pocket and brought out a small notebook. He extracted a pen from the debris on George's desk and made a rough drawing of the symbol he'd seen at Gloria Simpson's flat and Jevons's office. The triangle within a circle topped by two horns. He pushed the finished sketch towards George. 'Recognise that?'

George stared at it for a few seconds. 'I do as a matter of fact. The girl I was telling you about – Amy – she kept drawing this symbol. I asked her what it meant but she wouldn't say.'

'Did she have any connection with the House of Terrors?'

George's eyes lit up. He had once confided to Joe that he had once considered detection as a career. It seemed the old interest hadn't waned. 'Yes. She worked there in the café. Just on Saturdays. She's in the sixth form.'

Joe suddenly remembered the other thing he'd intended to ask. 'By the way, George, this is a long shot but does the name Jack Wendal mean anything to you?'

George frowned. 'It does seem vaguely familiar. I'm sure I've heard it somewhere but I can't remember where exactly. Tell you what, I'll make some enquiries and if I find anything out I'll let you know.'

Joe smiled patiently. 'If you could, George, it'd be a great help,' he said as he took a welcome sip of tea.

When Emily Thwaite arrived at the police station she hurried straight to her office. She wasn't in the mood to face the team just yet. She needed time to assume the confident persona of leadership her troops expected. After slipping off her jacket she sat at her desk and began to read through some reports that had been deposited there in her absence. But she found that she couldn't get Jane Pyke out of her mind. She thought she'd expunged the girl from her life five years ago. But some things come back to haunt us.

A knock on the door and the appearance of Sunny Porter disturbed her contemplations. She arranged her features into a keen, alert expression and forced herself to smile. There was no way she was going to show any weakness in front of the likes of Sunny Porter.

'Morning, Sunny. Anything interesting come in overnight?'

'It certainly has, ma'am,' he said with relish. Whatever it was he had to report, it was something good.

'Well?'

'A plumber found a carrier bag in a skip and he handed it in at the front desk. It contained clothes and a handbag.

No money or credit cards in it – probably nicked – but there was a cash and carry card with a name on it. Carla Yates. The plumber recognised the name cause he'd heard it on the news. That's why he . . .'

Emily's heart began to beat a little faster. 'Are the clothes the ones she was last seen in?'

'They fit the description, aye. I've sent everything down to Forensic.'

'Good. Where exactly were they found?'

'Skip in Pickby.'

Emily raised her eyebrows. 'Near Harold Uckley's and Gloria Simpson's?'

'Couple of streets away from Simpson's. It's quite a way from where Yates was last seen but it might give us some idea about where the killer lives. Or where he passes on his way to work, for instance.'

Emily cleared her throat. Pickby was too close to her house for comfort. She stood up and walked over to a large map of the city that hung on her office wall. She placed her index finger on the spot where Carla Yates made her last appearance on CCTV then traced the direct route to Pickby. About two miles as the crow flies. She resolved to get herself some coloured pins and see whether there was any sort of pattern to where the victims and the protagonists lived and worked. But then Eborby was hardly a large city. In light traffic a car could travel from one end of the conurbation to the other in under fifteen minutes.

'The carrier bag the clothes were found in was from the gift shop in that new Archaeology Centre on Sheepgate.'

Emily swung round. This was the nearest thing to a solid clue they'd had in ages. 'OK, get someone round there, will you. See if they keep records of sales . . . or CCTV. Anything that'll tell us how our man got hold of the bag.'

'He might have found it somewhere . . . stuffed her things in it because it was handy,' Sunny suggested.

But Emily was determined to ignore this dampener on her enthusiasm. 'Any idea how long the bag had been in the skip?'

'The skip was replaced at nine yesterday morning and the plumber swears the bag wasn't there at lunchtime so, presumably, it was dumped some time yesterday afternoon. He noticed it just before he was due to knock off work and brought it to us first thing this morning. Think he nicked the cash and credit cards . . . that's assuming there were any?'

Emily shook her head. 'He didn't need to bring it in, did he? If he'd nicked them he would have chucked it.' She paused, trying to get things straight in her mind. 'So someone – presumably our killer – keeps hold of his first victim's things for four weeks, pinches her valuables then dumps everything in the first available skip he comes across?'

'That's about it.'

'The only thing is, Sunny, it doesn't quite ring true, does it?'

Sunny said nothing. The theory sounded OK to him.

'I'd assumed the killer kept their clothes as souvenirs. Why get rid of them a few weeks later?'

'Perhaps he waited till the fuss had died down. Thought nobody would notice.'

Emily sighed. Sunny could be right. But somehow the psychology didn't fit. The Resurrection Man was just the sort of sadistic monster who would keep mementoes of his victims' agonies. These things would be precious to him. He would gloat over them, spread them out in front of him and relive his crimes . . . not chuck them in a skip.

'Is DI Plantagenet in yet?'

'Just come in, ma'am. He said he had to see somebody first thing. Want me to muster the troops?'

Emily forced a smile. 'Thank you, Sunny,' she said, still wondering how to conduct a detailed examination of Jane Pyke's life without involving herself.

Chapter Ten

The carrier bag was a breakthrough. Joe could feel it. The killer had made a mistake. And he wondered whether Harold Uckley's and Janna Pyke's clothes would turn up in a similar manner. Patrols had been asked to keep an eye on unattended skips. Just in case.

The connection with the Archaeology Centre worried him a little. It brought it too close to home, too close to Carmel ... and Maddy. He told himself he was being foolish. Thousands of people visited the centre and bought things from the gift shop. He tried to put it out of his mind as he walked down the road towards the Central Library.

The city archives – those that weren't housed in the history department at the university – were housed on the second floor of the library, a red-brick product of Victorian civic pride built on the site of a medieval hospital whose undercroft still stood next door, all that remained above ground of a once vast complex. Twelfth-century confidence cheek by jowl with the nineteenth-century variety. Joe climbed the library's wide marble staircase, passing the fiction section on the ground floor and the reference section on the first, until he reached his goal. Somehow, from what he knew of Janna Pyke, he found it hard to envisage her in these surroundings. But then she had been studying for an MA.

'Can I help you?' A young woman in tight jeans and

T-shirt addressed him quietly. She didn't look like a librarian. But then he supposed he didn't really look like a policeman. He produced his ID and she motioned him to follow her. They ended up in an office packed with files and computers.

'I suppose you've come about Janna,' she began. 'I saw it on the news. Bloody awful. She spent a lot of time here, you know. She told me a while back that she was researching the medieval plague but recently she'd been getting out stuff on the early seventeenth century.'

Joe smiled encouragingly. He knew a good witness when he met one. 'When did you last see her?'

'It'd be a week ago. Aye. It was the Thursday. I remember because that's when some idiot set the fire alarm off. Kids – they say they're here to work but they just mess about half the time.' She rolled her eyes at the folly of youth. 'Janna and Keith were up here in the archives and . . .'

'Keith?'

'Keith Webster. Dr Webster from the history department at the university. He was here with Janna.'

'You're sure about that?'

'Course I am. They seemed to be having a heated discussion about something.'

'Arguing?'

The young woman grinned. 'You can't have a good argument in a library – and believe me, I've tried. More like hushed voices. But I could tell he wasn't pleased about something. When the alarm went off she came back when the all clear was given but he didn't.'

'What did you think of Janna Pyke?'

The young woman pulled a face. 'Bit weird. Intense, I'd say. Not a barrel of laughs.'

'And Dr Webster?'

'Keith's OK.'

'Do you think there was anything between them?'

Another grin. 'Romance, you mean? Or just good old-fashioned rumpy-pumpy?'

'Either.'

She thought for a few moments. 'Wouldn't rule out the latter. But Keith's married. His wife works at the Eborby Permanent. Look, sorry I can't be more help.'

'On the contrary, you've been very helpful.'

A shadow passed over the young woman's face. 'I hope you get this maniac. I'm scared stiff going out at night now.'

Joe didn't really know what to say so he took his leave.

'Are you going to have a word with this Keith Webster? He lied to us. Said he hadn't seen her for two weeks but now we've a witness who saw him with her a week ago.' Emily Thwaite frowned.

'He's out on a field trip at the moment. I'll see him when he gets back.'

Emily had been pacing up and down her office. She suddenly stopped, sat down and put her head in her hands.

Joe sat down on the grey tweed chair next to her desk. He had noticed that she looked tired, as if the strain of the case was getting to her. 'Everything OK?'

She looked up. 'Yes. Why shouldn't it be?'

The tone of her voice told him that it would be wise to change the subject.

He cleared his throat. 'I went to see an old friend of mine first thing this morning. George Merryweather – he's a canon at the cathedral and an expert on the occult. He thinks he may have heard the name Jack Wendal before but he couldn't remember where.'

'Pity,' Emily sighed.

'He was called in to see a disturbed girl who kept drawing the symbol we saw at Gloria Simpson's flat. Remember? She'd undergone some traumatic experience apparently. And there's a possible link with the Black Hen.'

Emily nodded warily. The spiritual and supernatural were uncharted territory for her; things she'd never really given much thought to up till now. And things that made her distinctly uncomfortable.

'Janna Pyke – or should we be calling her Jane? – went to the Black Hen. Her ex-boyfriend says she knew people at the House of Terrors who dabbled in Satanism. If Wendal's somehow involved . . .'

She smirked. 'Are you saying that John Wendal is some sort of grand wizard? Look, Joe, wizards don't work for building societies and play with steam trains in their spare time. Or at least they didn't last time I read a fairy story to the kids. And what about Carla Yates and Harold Uckley? There's no hint that they were ever involved in anything like that.'

'It was just an idea.'

The knock on the door made Emily jump. As she regained her composure and said 'come in', Joe thought again how strained she looked, as though something other than the case was eating away at her. He wondered if he should say anything. But perhaps, he thought, it was better to mind his own business for the time being.

Jamilla pushed the door open and stood on the threshold wearing an eager expression on her face. 'We've drawn a blank at the Eborby Permanent, ma'am. Nobody can remember Jack Wendal having anything to do with Gloria Simpson – then Gloria Marsh – who did six months in accounts. In fact it's more than likely their paths never crossed.'

'Well, something made her attack him,' said Emily.

Jamilla ignored the remark and carried on. 'And Forensic's just called, ma'am. They've got a match on the fingerprints they found on Carla Yates's things.' She paused, as if she wanted to add an element of suspense.

'Well,' said Joe. 'Are you going to let us into the secret?'

'Secret?'

'Whose fingerprints were found on Carla Yates's possessions?'

Jamilla smiled. 'Sorry. It's Michael Friday . . . usually known as Mickey. He's got form for— '

'I know what he's got form for.' He turned to Emily. 'He's one of our regular customers. GBH, robbery with violence. He was done for manslaughter a couple of years back but the jury believed his story and found that he acted in self defence.' He smiled. 'We were just talking about fairy tales, weren't we, ma'am? Well, Mickey can spin them with the best. I wouldn't have put him down for these murders though. Subtlety's not usually in his repertoire. Neither is unnecessary sadism. He's a vicious bastard but this really isn't his style.'

'Get him brought in all the same,' said Emily. 'See to it, will you, Jamilla?' She sounded weary. 'I wish this John Wendal would come round,' she said as Jamilla hurried out. 'I'd love to hear what he has to say for himself.'

'Me too.' Joe hesitated. 'Do you think it might be a good idea if we went over what we've got?'

'It might help.'

'OK. Our man presumably stalks his victims . . . but unfortunately he's never been seen or caught on CCTV doing it.'

'Are we sure about the CCTV? Has it been double-checked? There might be something we've missed.'

'I'll get someone on to it.' Joe wrote in his notebook. Another thing to do.

'Right then, what have we got?'

Joe took a deep breath. 'First victim, Carla Yates. Disappeared after a night out with friends. Found a week after she disappeared in a country churchyard. Naked, signs that she'd been bound. Cause of death, suffocation. Evidence suggests she'd been stunned with a blow to the head then trussed up in a confined space until she died. Clothes have only just turned up. Can we expect the other victims' clothes to appear in due course as well?'

'Let's hope so.' Her eyes wandered to the child's painting pinned on the wall for a second. Then she straightened her back and frowned. 'What about the other victims?'

'Second victim, Harold Uckley. Circumstances similar.

Disappeared on the way to the pub a week after Carla Yates went missing and found a week later. Ditto cause of death and disposal of body. Third victim, Janna Pyke.'

Joe noticed a brief flicker of recognition, of anxiety, in Emily's eyes, swiftly suppressed. 'You sure you're OK, Emily?' he asked, watching her carefully as she rearranged her features into a mask of professional neutrality.

'Yes, of course I am,' she snapped, then immediately regretted her sharpness. 'Go on,' she said. 'What do we know about her?'

'Well, Janna seems slightly more complex than the first two. She did a moonlight flit from her flat almost a month ago and she was spotted in Boargate about a week before she died, around the same time she was seen in the city archives with Dr Webster, her supervisor at the university. We've yet to find out where she was living between her flit from Vicars Green and the time of her death. She had connections with the House of Terrors and the Black Hen but there's no indication that the other victims did. Is this occult connection just a coincidence or is it relevant?'

'Search me,' Emily said, fiddling with a pencil, turning it over and over in her fingers.

'Janna was receiving threats from someone who obviously didn't know she'd moved out of her Vicars Green flat so . . .'

'So they might have nothing to do with her murder.'

'Quite. The threats mentioned Jack Wendal – possible occult connection. In the meantime a John Wendal – commonly known as Jack – is attacked after apparently terrifying the life out of Gloria Simpson. As far as we can see, Wendal is an upstanding pillar of the community. But a leaflet in his garage links him to the House or Terrors . . .' He saw the sceptical expression on Emily's face. 'Or not as the case may be.' He sighed. 'The best thing we've got so far is the fact that the first two victims, plus John Wendal and Gloria Simpson, have all worked at the Eborby Permanent Building Society at one time or another. And

I've discovered that Dr Webster's wife works there too . . . another connection.'

'Carla Yates's things were found in a carrier bag from the Archaeology Centre gift shop.' She turned to Joe. 'I presume someone's checking that angle out.'

'Yes. And there's another thing.' Joe hesitated for a moment. 'That colleague of mine I was telling you about – the one who was shot.'

'What about him?' She could tell the memory was still raw so she asked the question gently.

'His daughter's just moved to Eborby and she's living in Janna Pyke's old flat – her boss at the Archaeology Centre is the landlady and she let Carmel have the flat when Janna did a flit. And there's another thing – Carmel's met up with Janna's ex-boyfriend. He called at the flat.'

The wariness reappeared in Emily's eyes. 'Could this ex-boyfriend be a suspect?'

'There's no evidence to suggest that but I don't suppose we can rule it out.'

Emily sat in silent thought for a few seconds, staring at the pencil in her hand. Then she looked up suddenly. 'We're missing something here, Joe. Some link between the victims. It's not just women he's targeting. Serial killers are supposed to go for the same type, aren't they?'

Joe nodded. 'Young vulnerable women like in the West case. Or kids . . . or homeless young men. There's usually a pattern. But what have we got here? A middle-aged divorcée. A married man nearing retirement. A young woman post-grad student. What makes him choose them?'

Emily sighed. 'If we knew that we'd be halfway to cracking the case. You got any bright ideas?'

Joe shrugged his shoulders. 'Only half-baked ones at the moment but I was wondering whether Janna Pyke ever worked at the Eborby Permanent.' He looked at his watch. 'I'm supposed to be going over to Leeds with Jamilla to see Janna Pyke's parents. Sure you don't want to come?'

'No,' Emily said quickly. 'I'll leave it in your capable hands, eh.'

An hour later Joe parked the car outside a large detached house in a tree-lined suburban street on the outskirts of Leeds. It was a pleasant street, an unremarkable thoroughfare, prosperous but not flashy. Somehow Joe found it hard to associate such mundane surroundings with the troubled Janna Pyke. This was the territory of Jane Pyke . . . her alter ego.

As he and Jamilla walked slowly to the front door, his heart was gripped by a sudden feeling of dread. These people had already been told their daughter was dead – the local police had broken the dreadful news – and he felt as if he was intruding on grief. He hated this part of the job. And he feared that he would have made a bad priest – embarrassed and tongue-tied with the grieving and the needy, absorbing their grief into his soul until he could no longer bear the pain. Maybe it was a good thing he'd decided on the police force.

He let Jamilla do the talking when Janna Pyke's father answered the door. He was a tall man, diminished and greyed by mourning, and he said nothing as he stood aside to let them in. He led the way into the living room with his head bowed.

A woman was sitting on the sofa, flicking through a glossy magazine absentmindedly, keeping her hands occupied while her thoughts were miles away. She was thin with short dark hair. Joe thought she would have been attractive, if sadness and sleeplessness hadn't taken their toll on her face.

The couple motioned him and Jamilla to sit on the sofa opposite them. No tea was offered. With all that had happened, the rituals of hospitality had gone by the board.

'We're very sorry about your daughter,' Joe began after clearing his throat. 'When did you last see her?'

'Not since last September,' the father replied. 'She never came home. Not even for Christmas. Said she was spending it with friends.'

Jamilla looked uneasy as she glanced at Joe. In her family such neglect would be unthinkable. 'Did she telephone you?' she asked, trying her best to hide her disapproval.

'Sometimes. When she wanted money. She last called about . . .' He looked at his wife for help. 'When was it, love?'

'About a fortnight ago,' she said softly. She sounded as though she was on the verge of tears.

'What did she say?'

'I told those other policemen. She just said she'd moved out of her flat . . . said that she'd let us know her new address when she had somewhere permanent. She never did. But that was typical.' Jane Pyke's mother sounded bitter, the sort of bitterness that resulted from long-borne strife. Something in her manner told Joe that in life, Jane had been trouble.

'You didn't get on with your daughter?' he asked tentatively, hoping he'd not misread the situation.

'No. We didn't get on. She made trouble for people. Including us.'

'How do you mean?'

'She always had to stir things up. She was never happy unless . . . She liked to mess with people's lives. I knew she'd go too far one day.'

It was a strange thing for a grieving mother to say. And Joe waited for an explanation. But he didn't get one.

'What exactly do you mean?' he prompted after a few moments.

'She'd push people to the limit. We had neighbours who complained about a couple of parties she had when she was about sixteen. We'd gone out so we didn't know what was going on. Anyway, after they'd complained she used to go and sit on their walls with her radio on full blast. And when she was in the sixth form she caused no end of trouble at school . . . she . . .' She broke off in mid-sentence as though reluctant to speak ill of the dead and looked Jamilla in the eye. 'I suppose you think I'm awful, speaking about her like this.'

'No,' said Joe. 'I don't. She must have caused you a lot of unhappiness. But you still loved her.'

He'd hit a raw nerve. Jane Pyke's mother burst into tears and her father put a comforting arm around her shoulder.

He looked up at Joe. 'We don't know anything about her life in Eborby. We don't know what she got up to or who her friends were. We can't help you, I'm sorry.'

'Had she any friends around here we could talk to? Anyone who knew her?'

'Most of them went away to university. And I don't think she kept in touch with any of them . . . not that we know of any road.'

'There was Gemma,' Mrs Pyke said in a small voice.

'Oh aye, Gemma.' The way he said the name suggested that Gemma – whoever she was – hadn't been regarded as a good influence in the Pyke household.

'Where can we find her?'

Pyke pressed his lips together, stiff with disapproval. 'She works in the chip shop on the Tadcaster Road. The Happy Fryer. But as far as I know our Jane's not seen her for years.'

Joe wrote Gemma's details down in his notebook. It was doubtful whether she'd be able to help them and he didn't think for one moment that the answer to Jane Pyke's murder lay in the suburbs of Leeds, but it might be worth having a chat with her old school friend if all else failed.

'This might seem like a strange question, but did Jane ever work at the Eborby Permanent Building Society?'

'No,' said her father emphatically. 'Her mother worked in the Roundhay branch, didn't you, love? But it's the sort of job Jane would have turned her nose up at. Not her sort of thing.'

'Did you know she called herself Janna?'

Pyke glanced at his wife and shook his head. 'No.'

'Was she interested in the occult at all?'

The man shrugged. 'To be honest, it wouldn't surprise me. She liked all that horror stuff. She was a very clever girl but . . .'

'When can we bury her?' Mrs Pyke said suddenly.

'I'm sorry,' Joe whispered. 'It might not be for a while yet. We'll let you know as soon as . . .' He stood up. 'Did Jane mention anything to you? Anything at all about her friends or where she went in Eborby or anyone she met?'

Pyke stood up. There were tears welling in his eyes. 'We didn't have that sort of relationship with our daughter, Inspector. We didn't sit down for cosy chats over Sunday lunch and she didn't ring her mother to share her news. She led her own life. Her choice . . . not ours.'

'I'm sorry,' said Joe. And he meant it.

Chapter Eleven

It wasn't until midday that Maddy Owen managed to catch Carmel alone. They met in the Ladies at the Archaeology Centre when Carmel emerged from one of the cubicles as Maddy was washing her hands.

'Everything OK?' Maddy asked tentatively as they stood side by side at the mirror. 'You look a bit . . . Did you see Tavy last night?'

'Mmm.' Carmel paused, her face grave. 'If you must know, he got into a fight. We went to the Black Hen and he was beaten up on the way home.'

Maddy's hand went to her mouth. 'Is he all right?'

'I think so, but maybe he was putting a brave face on it. He said he didn't need to see a doctor but I think he should. He went home afterwards so maybe his mother persuaded him. Men, eh?'

'So what happened exactly?'

'We had a drink in the Black Hen. He was asking people who Jack Wendal was.'

Maddy sucked in her breath. 'Probably not the wisest thing to do. He should have left it to the police. What was he thinking of?'

Carmel looked uncomfortable and didn't answer. The more she thought about Tavy's actions, the more foolhardy they seemed to be.

'So did it happen inside the pub or . . .?'

'No. When we left we took a short cut through an alley and someone must have followed us. They roughed him up a bit and said it was from Jack Wendal. I think it could have been a lot worse. It looked as if they were just trying to warn him off.'

'I don't think I'd be taking it so calmly if I were you,' Maddy said.

Carmel managed a weak smile. 'Believe me, Maddy, I'm a quivering jelly inside.' She hesitated. 'Look,' she said after a few seconds, 'do you think these people from the Black Hen, whoever they are, were after Janna Pyke for some reason?'

Maddy shrugged her shoulders. 'It's possible, I suppose. But one comforting thought is that whoever was after her didn't know she was dead – they still phoned and sent those letters – so they couldn't have had anything to do with her murder. And now it's been on the news that she's dead . . .'

'They'll leave her flat alone.'

'Precisely.'

Maddy blushed. 'I . . . er, saw Joe last night.'

Carmel raised her eyebrows enquiringly.

'He's really worried about you.'

'He doesn't need to be,' Carmel said quickly. 'Are you seeing him again?'

'I don't know.'

'Look, Maddy, it was good to see Joe but I don't want my mum persuading him to act as some sort of bodyguard. I can take care of myself.'

'I'm sure you can. But people only worry because they care about you.'

Carmel was silent for a few moments, trying to think of a sharp reply. But she couldn't. 'Has Peta mentioned Janna's death? I thought with her having lived in the flat she might have said something.'

Maddy shook her head. 'I went to her office before to go over some ideas for the Viking Festival but she didn't say anything. Mind you, she might not have heard . . . or she might have other things on her mind.'

Carmel inclined her head enquiringly, eager for gossip about her cool and distant boss.

'I told you she has problems with her son.'

'What kind of problems?'

'She's never really said and I don't like to ask. I heard he's been in and out of hospital, presumably for operations, but she's one to keep her troubles to herself.' She looked Carmel in the eye. 'This Tavy . . . do you trust him?'

'Yes,' Carmel said quickly.

But Maddy sensed a shadow of doubt behind her apparent certainty. 'Look, I think you should tell Joe what happened at the Black Hen.' She saw that the girl looked unsure. 'And if you don't, I will.'

In the face of Maddy's determination, there didn't seem to be any point in Carmel protesting.

Joe and Jamilla stopped off for a bite of lunch in a country pub just the Eborby side of Tadcaster. When they returned to the office in the middle of the afternoon, Joe picked up Carmel's message about Tavy McNair's ill-advised enquiries at the Black Hen and his subsequent beating. Some people, he thought, would never learn.

He tried to put it out of his mind for the time being while he studied the notes on his desk. Some of the investigation team were out trying to trace the whereabouts of Mickey Friday, whose prints had been found on Carla Yates's things.

Joe kept asking himself why the killer had held on to Carla's clothes and bag for so long. Why hadn't he disposed of them in some convenient skip or dustbin soon after her murder? Perhaps he'd wanted to look at them, to gloat, to touch them, to feel their softness and replay her death again and again in his mind. Had she pleaded with him for mercy as she lay naked, trussed up and gasping for air? Had he watched her suffering or had he just left her alone to die?

They knew when and approximately where Carla Yates had disappeared and where and when she was found and, if they could discover where her things had been in the meantime, it might take them one step nearer to the killer. Forensic had examined the bag and its contents thoroughly for any clue, any speck that would give away their secret. But all they had come up with was two prints on the handbag: Mickey Friday's thumb and forefinger.

Joe had had dealings with Mickey Friday on a number of occasions: he was stupid; he was dishonest; and there were times when he'd been violent. But Mickey's violence had always been the straightforward kind – the fist in the alley; the glass in the face. Somehow Joe found it impossible to see him as the Resurrection Man. But then, he had been wrong before. Mickey was out there somewhere and they had to bring him in.

At three forty-five he finally found a spare moment to return Carmel's call and he listened carefully to her account of the attack on Tavy McNair. His first reaction was to feel angry with the young man for playing the hero and putting himself and Carmel in danger. But then he began to wonder whether there was more to it than that. Had Tavy McNair been involved in what went on at the Black Hen in some way and found himself on the wrong side of his former associates? Or had the whole thing been staged for some reason, as yet unknown?

In the absence of Kevin, it seemed that Carmel had suddenly become his responsibility and he couldn't help worrying about her. Perhaps he should advise her to stop seeing McNair. But she was an adult and, of course, there was no guarantee that she would listen.

As he put the phone down Joe felt a strong urge to clear up the Jack Wendal puzzle once and for all. And there was someone he wanted to see at the House of Terrors who might be able to cast a shaft of light into the shadows of his ignorance.

It was a fine day and he felt desperate to get out of the

office again and breathe in some fresh air. After the trip to Leeds he kept seeing the pale faces of Jane Pyke's parents. She had been a nightmare daughter but they had never stopped loving her. Now any hope they may have had that she would grow out of her awkwardness and become a loving child who would settle down and present them with grandchildren was wiped out. He had left them alone to mourn their only daughter, unable to stand their pain. And now he needed a distraction.

He was about to leave his office when Emily poked her head round the door. 'How did you get on?' she asked.

Joe could detect a hint of anxiety in her voice but he put it down to the pressure she was under. 'As you'd expect,' he answered. 'The parents are devastated. But they didn't keep in touch with Jane so there wasn't much they could tell us. They knew nothing about her life in Eborby.'

'What did they say exactly?'

Joe looked up at Emily and saw that she was watching him intently, awaiting his reply.

'Not much. There was an old school friend who worked in a local chippy she might have kept in touch with, but apart from that ...'

There was no mistaking it, Emily Thwaite looked relieved. And Joe wondered why.

'I'm on my way to the House of Terrors,' he said. 'I want to show John Wendal's photograph around ... see if anyone recognises him.'

'Good idea. I've been doing a bit of digging myself. Did you know that the manager, Terry Jevons, has convictions for obtaining money by deception, threatening behaviour and actual bodily harm?'

Joe raised his eyebrows. Somehow the fact that Jevons had a criminal record didn't surprise him. His crimes were hardly in the same league as the Resurrection Man's. But who was to say he hadn't branched out as many criminals had done before him? 'Want to come with me ... have a word with Jevons?' he asked.

Emily shook her head sadly. 'I can't. The Super wants to see me.'

Joe was about to take his leave when he realised there was something he'd forgotten to tell Emily. 'I had a call from Carmel. She went to the Black Hen last night with Janna Pyke's ex-boyfriend, Tavy McNair. Someone jumped him when they left the pub . . . gave him a beating and said it was a warning from Jack Wendal.'

Emily sank back into her seat. 'Is he OK?'

'It looks like he got off lightly.'

'You don't think it was staged for Carmel's benefit, do you?'

Their eyes met. 'The thought had occurred to me . . . but then I've got a suspicious mind. If it is genuine, it looks as if someone's trying to scare McNair off – make sure that he keeps his nose out of whatever's going on there.'

'And what is going on there?'

'I think it's about time we found out, don't you? Fancy a drink in the Black Hen after work?'

Emily hesitated, a smile playing on her lips as though she was uncertain whether the invitation was personal or professional. 'I don't want to be late home.'

'Don't worry. You won't be.'

'OK then. I'll see you later.'

After checking that he had the photograph of John Wendal in his pocket, Joe swept out of the office and headed straight for Marketgate and the House of Terrors.

Joe Plantagenet felt that he had hit a brick wall. When he had shown the photograph of John Wendal to the staff at the House of Terrors, nobody had displayed the slightest flicker of recognition.

He had watched Terry Jevons's sly face closely and he was certain that Wendal was a stranger to him. Perhaps he was barking up the wrong tree altogether. Perhaps he was reading too much into the occult connection. He wished Gloria Simpson was fit to be interviewed, to explain her actions. But each time he rang the psychiatric department the answer was the same. She was still in no state to answer questions.

His next move was to see whether Harold Uckley's family and Carla Yates's friends could throw any light on the Wendal connection . . . if there was one. Joe was beginning to have serious doubts. The fact that George Merryweather thought Wendal's name was familiar was intriguing. But was it relevant?

As he left Jevons's office, Joe thought he'd have one last go. He was halfway out of the door when he turned around. 'That symbol – the triangle in the circle with the half-circle on top . . . looks a bit like horns. What does it mean?'

Jevons looked uncomfortable for a few seconds, then assumed a casual expression. Too casual. 'It's a little society of like-minded people. It's nothing illegal, I assure you.' His lips twitched upwards in an oily, self satisfied smile.

'Black magic? Devil worship?'

'As I said, it's not illegal.' He sounded defensive now.

'Was Janna Pyke a member of this . . . society?'

'We like to keep our membership discreet . . . confidential.'

'This is a murder enquiry,' Joe hissed, suddenly angry with Jevons's evasiveness.

'OK. No, Janna Pyke wasn't one of our number. Is that all?'

Joe knew he was lying. 'What about Gloria Simpson? Or John Wendal?'

'These people expect discretion . . .'

'Are they members?'

Jevons hesitated. 'I really can't say anything without the members' permission. But I was telling you the truth when I said I'd never seen the man in the photograph before.'

'What about Carla Yates and Harold Uckley? Were they part of it?'

Jevons gave Joe another oily smile. 'Now you're pushing

your luck, Inspector. But the answer in both cases is in the negative.'

Joe longed to wipe the smirk off Jevons' face with a well-aimed punch. But instead he took a deep breath and counted to ten in his head – a tactic that usually worked. 'So Gloria Simpson is a member but the others I mentioned aren't?'

'Sorry, Inspector, can't help you. If that's all . . .'

'I need a list of your members.'

For the first time Jevons began to look a little worried. 'That's impossible, I'm afraid. Anyway, most of them either use different names or choose to remain anonymous.'

'Then I'll just have to send a couple of officers to attend your next meeting and take statements.' Joe watched the expression of horror on Jevons's face with a glow of satisfaction. 'I'll be in touch,' he said ominously before sweeping out of the office.

At least he now knew that Jevons was dabbling in the occult, running some kind of organisation from the House of Terrors . . . or possibly from the Black Hen. He claimed that the Resurrection Man's victims weren't members of this shadowy group. But there was certainly something ritualistic about their deaths.

He wondered whether Jevons would have admitted to the group's existence if they had been involved in ritual murder. But then Joe had already let him know that he suspected something was going on and it would only take a small amount of digging to come up with the truth. Perhaps Jevons's candour had been a damage-limitation exercise.

On his way out of the House of Terrors, Joe suddenly remembered what George Merryweather had told him about the girl he had been called in to exorcise. If people of that age were involved, it was no select group of consenting adults as Jevons had claimed.

Someone, he thought, needed to keep an eye on the House of Terrors.

Gloria Simpson tried the door of her sparsely furnished room off G Ward in the psychiatric department. It was unlocked. Someone had been careless. But then they thought she had been taking the tablets that would dull her senses and keep her under their control.

She smiled to herself when she thought of the small pile of tablets pushed inside a gap in the stitching on the bottom of her blue plastic mattress. Somewhere they'd never think to look. She had been so careful to behave as though she had taken her medication. She had slurred her speech and shuffled around, placid and compliant, until they felt confident that she was no threat.

But they had underestimated her.

The Black Hen was hardly Emily Thwaite's idea of the perfect pub. It looked all right from the outside with its old brick and blackened timbers, but the clientele left a lot to be desired. The small leaded windows and dim lighting gave it an aura of gloom rather than cosiness and there were a number of single, overweight men who undressed her with their eyes as she paid a visit to the Ladies. Small gaggles of morose young people with elaborate body piercings and black T-shirts bearing Satanic logos stood around with drinks as though they were waiting for something to happen. There was nobody in there she would have described as normal apart from a couple of American tourists who had wandered in there in search of the typical English pub and wandered out again after one drink, rather disillusioned.

She was glad Joe was there by her side for more reasons than one. Not only did the company of a six-foot male provide moral and physical support, but she needed to question him further about his visit to Jane Pyke's parents. She had to know how much they had revealed about their daughter's life in Leeds. But she had to be careful not to arouse his suspicions.

As they sat there with their drinks in front of them, she

asked her questions with a show of professional interest. But it seemed that Joe had already told her everything he knew. Jane Pyke's parents had chosen not to mention the matter that was preying on her mind. And for this small mercy she was exceedingly grateful.

When they had drained their glasses and absorbed the strange, vaguely restless atmosphere, Joe made for the bar. Emily followed, looking at her watch. She should have been home by now to read her youngest a bedtime story instead of hanging round dodgy public houses with single male colleagues.

She nudged Joe's arm as she caught up with him. 'Don't be long, will you?'

He didn't answer. Instead he took John Wendal's photograph from his pocket and began to show it to the bar staff. But the sight of Wendal's smiling features produced no reaction. Nobody recognised him. He'd never been in there. As far as Joe could tell, they were either telling the truth or they were extremely good liars.

Photographs of Carla Yates and Harold Uckley also produced blank denials. It was only Janna Pyke's image that was recognised. She used to come in occasionally but nobody would admit knowing anything about her disappearance or her death.

The staff suffered a similar attack of mass amnesia when Joe asked them about the attack on Tavy McNair the previous night. One of the barmen admitted that he had noticed Tavy drinking with a girl – he had been in with Janna a few times so he was a familiar face. But apart from that, nobody would admit to knowing anything of what had happened once McNair and his female companion had left the Black Hen. And nobody had seen anyone following them out. Joe knew they were lying but he didn't pursue the matter any further.

'We should have this place searched,' Joe whispered as they left the pub.

'Reason?'

'I think this is where Jevons holds his meetings. And someone attacked Janna's ex-boyfriend because he was asking questions.'

'You think it could have some connection with the Resurrection Man?'

'There is a ritualistic element to the murders.'

'And you think the rituals took place at the Black Hen? You think they were killed there? Locked up in some sort of confined space and left to die?' She stopped and swung round to face Joe. 'Where's your evidence, Joe? We can't organise a search warrant on a whim. I think your talk to that friend of yours at the cathedral has made you over-imaginative. I think we're looking for someone with psychiatric problems.'

'The two approaches aren't mutually exclusive.'

'Trust me to be landed with a bloody ex-priest,' she mumbled.

'I was never ordained . . . couldn't stick out the training,' he replied, a smile playing on his lips. 'I just think you should keep an open mind, that's all.'

Emily didn't answer. Perhaps Joe had a point but she was hardly going to admit it.

'Tomorrow I'll check out the shop on Boargate where Janna was last seen. The shop with paintings in the window. I want to know what she got up to after she left the flat in Vicars Green.'

'Fine. You do that,' she said impatiently. 'I just hope that we find Mickey Friday. Reckon he's into the occult?'

Joe snorted. 'Can't see it myself.'

'Look, I've got to get home,' she said when they reached the police station car park. She fumbled for her car keys, swearing under her breath.

'Is something the matter?' Joe asked.

'Everything's fine,' she snapped before marching off towards her car.

Gloria Simpson had evaded her captors, or at least that's

how she saw it. She had to find him. She had to put an end to this once and for all. For her sake and the sake of the others.

She thought of the others. The women chained up, used by the men in masks who mated with them like animals. Her heart began to pound with the memories. The smell of sweat and blood in that dreadful room.

Sometimes she wondered what had driven her to get in so deep. But then she had believed. She hadn't questioned it until she had seen what was done to the girl whose soul – and body – was given to Jack Wendal. And then there was what they were planning to do next. The ultimate ritual. She had been chosen. And she was terrified.

When she'd accepted the lift, the man had seemed so ordinary, even kindly . . . until the moment he'd revealed his true identity. She knew he was there to carry out the sentence that had been passed on her. He was going to take her soul. And now she knew she had to finish it once and for all. It was survival. It was her or him.

Her escape from the psychiatric ward was easier than she had expected. She had found her outdoor clothes hanging in the wardrobe in her room and had put them on before striding out confidently past patients and staff. She had once heard that if you walked in anywhere with enough confidence, your presence would never be challenged and now she knew it was true. A cleaner leaving the ward had held the door open for her and she had thanked her politely. Then it had been easy to make her way over to the main hospital. Nobody had even questioned her when she had picked up some fresh flowers from a vase in reception and enquired at the desk where she could find Mr Wendal.

As it had been so easy, it was obviously meant to be. She was to be the instrument of retribution. From now on she would be on the side of the angels. She had turned traitor.

When she found Wendal in a side ward she was relieved to see that he was on his own. There was nobody about to disturb her, staff or visitors, so she crept into the room and let the flowers in her hand drop to the floor. The machine by the bed emitted a regular, hypnotic bleep and she could hear him breathing softly. She stood quite still for a while, watching and listening, before she summoned the courage to approach the bed.

She walked towards the patient cautiously, like a child approaching a blazing fire. It had to be done and it had to be done quickly. After steeling herself and taking a deep, gulping breath, she began to pull at tubes and the machine's noise turned into a low whine. A pillow lay on the chair by the bed. She picked it up, placed it over the patient's face and pressed it down, harder and harder until the effort made her breathless.

Then, when the alarm sounded, shrieking in her ear like a demon, she was only vaguely aware of running feet. And rough hands hauling her away.

The Resurrection Man enjoyed his work. He enjoyed the sound of their muffled cries as he fastened the padlocks.

The question of why he hadn't been given more work to do was starting to gnaw at his mind like an insistent rat. He was growing impatient. What had begun as a sacred duty was becoming a pleasure, almost a necessity. It was how he'd heard huntsmen felt as they pursued their quarry. The disposal of vermin had become a thrill to be anticipated and planned with loving care. A beautiful ritual – the chase and the kill.

She would be home at six. She had asked him to do some shopping for her and he'd done it at lunchtime. As he'd wandered around the supermarket he wondered whether anyone could tell that he had a secret. But how could they? He was so careful to hide it, to look and act just like everyone else. There was nothing wrong with his mind, he told himself time and time again. Only when the voices started on at him did he become afraid.

There had been a time when it had been better. Then the tablets had seemed to stop working and the voices, the fear, had returned. But since he had been chosen, he felt he had a new purpose. He was invincible now. He had power over life and death. And as he sat there reading the paper, staring at the photograph of Janna Pyke . . . he longed to feel that power coursing through his body again.

When the call came, he would be ready to rid the world of evil.

Chapter Twelve

The following morning Mickey Friday sat in the interview room and scratched his tattooed arm.

'Where are you working now, Mickey?' Sunny asked, watching the big man's face.

'The Cobweb Club. I'm a doorman.'

'A bouncer.'

'A doorman.'

'Do they know about your record?' Emily Thwaite gave the man a disarming smile. She had a splitting headache through lack of sleep and she knew she looked rough. But, like an actress, she felt obliged to put on a show for her public.

'Dunno.'

It probably wouldn't bother the Cobweb much if they did know Mickey Friday's history, Sunny thought. Occupying the basement of an old warehouse on the banks of the river, at Eborby's Victorian industrial end, it wasn't the most salubrious establishment in town. It was a dive but Sunny had heard the drinks were remarkably cheap.

Emily placed the Archaeology Centre carrier bag and its contents, all neatly encased in plastic bags, on the table in front of her. 'Can you explain how your fingerprints came to be on these items?' she asked with a sweet smile.

'Found 'em, didn't I?' was the rapid reply.

'Where?'

'Outside one of them shops . . . charity shops.'

'You pinched clothes from a charity shop? Can't get much lower than that, can you, Mickey? I mean . . .'

'The shop wasn't open . . . it was just left outside. I saw a handbag . . .'

'And you couldn't resist having a look?'

Mickey nodded.

'And what did you find inside this irresistible handbag?'

Mickey swallowed hard. 'Cash . . . about fifty quid. I chucked the credit cards away 'cause I reckoned they would have been reported missing and I didn't want to be done for nicking 'em.' He sounded disappointed. 'I helped myself to the cash, binned the cards, then I dumped the lot in a skip. That's the God's honest truth. I never touched her . . . never even met her.'

'Did you recognise the name on the credit cards from the TV reports of the murder?'

Mickey's face turned red. 'Yeah. That's why I got rid quick. I never had nothing to do with no murder. I swear on my mother's life.'

Sunny smirked. He knew Mickey's mother from years back. In her heyday she had been one of Eborby's more successful ladies of the night.

'Where was the charity shop?'

'I think it was that one on Little Marygate.' He wrinkled his face in a show of concentration. 'The one for that hospice. What's it called?'

'Mirebridge?' Mirebridge Hospice was a popular local charity. Everyone knew it, even Sunny.

'Yeah. That's the one.'

'You left a couple of prints on her things.'

Mickey shook his head, as though annoyed by his own carelessness. 'I never thought.'

Emily's eyes met Sunny's. There was the shadow of a smile on her lips. Mickey Friday wasn't the sharpest pencil in the box. And she doubted whether he was capable of committing such cruel and calculated murders. It just wasn't his style.

But there were a couple of questions worth asking. 'Ever heard of a pub called the Black Hen, Mickey?'

'I've heard of it,' was the wary answer.

'Ever been there?'

Mickey shrugged. 'Once or twice. I've been to most of the pubs in Eborby in my time,' he added proudly.

'Recognise this symbol?' Emily grabbed a piece of paper and made a rough sketch of the symbol she had seen at Gloria Simpson's flat and at the House of Terrors. She pushed the drawing towards Mickey who studied it for a few seconds.

'What's it supposed to be? A bull's head or what?'

'I hoped you'd tell us. Have you ever seen it before?'

Mickey shook his head and Emily rose from her seat with a sigh. It looked as though they'd hit another dead end.

Emily's thoughts turned to Jamilla Dal, who had been sent to see Janna Pyke's former landlady, Peta Thewlis, about gaining access to the possessions the dead girl had left at her old flat on Vicars Green. Perhaps Jamilla would come up with something. And if she did, Emily thought to herself, it might be wise to get over there.

The last thing Emily Thwaite wanted was an unpleasant surprise.

Tavy McNair had concluded that it wasn't worth getting his injuries checked out by a doctor; after all, he'd only suffered a few cuts and bruises. He'd also said that he was going to tell his mother he'd fallen so that she wouldn't worry.

Carmel Hennessy hadn't seen him since the night they'd gone to the Black Hen and she felt an uncomfortable nag of worry. Perhaps she would ring his mobile later, she thought. Although she was reluctant to seem too keen, too needy. And she couldn't help asking herself how much she really knew about Tavy. He seemed so nice ... so plausible. But then he was an actor; it was his job to pretend.

Sometimes she didn't know what to believe any more.

She had slept on the sofa again because she hadn't been able to face the bedroom and its atmosphere of sadness, and if she didn't hurry, she'd be late for work. Perhaps, she thought, she should get the flat exorcised. She had always thought of such things as nonsense . . . until now. Joe Plantagenet had once started training for the priesthood so maybe he could advise her. But she had bothered him too much already. She had to stand on her own two feet.

She picked up her bag and closed the flat door behind her carefully as the break-in was still preying on her mind, making her uneasy. She hurried down the stairs towards the front door and when she reached the bottom, she noticed that the door to Conrad Peace's flat was open. Conrad's niece, Elizabeth was standing framed in the doorway and she turned when she heard Carmel's footsteps.

'Morning. Another nice day,' she said with a cheerful smile.

'Yes. Let's hope it lasts,' Carmel replied automatically. She stopped in her tracks, wondering whether Conrad knew about Janna Pyke's death. She would have expected something so momentous to have cropped up in conversation but nothing had been said. Perhaps he hadn't heard about it. Perhaps he didn't listen to the local TV news or read the newspapers.

'Er . . . has your uncle heard that the girl who used to live in my flat was found murdered?' she asked Elizabeth in a hushed voice. The last thing she wanted to do was to upset Conrad if it was a sensitive subject.

Elizabeth leaned forward. Carmel could smell her perfume, something exotic and expensive which rather surprised her: Elizabeth looked the light floral type. 'He heard about it on the local radio news. It upset him a bit so I'd be grateful if you didn't say anything.'

'Of course not,' Carmel replied quickly.

'I don't suppose the police are any nearer catching this lunatic. You're not safe anywhere nowadays. I remember when you could walk around Eborby at night and . . .'

The woman was twittering. And she was making Carmel nervous. 'I know. It's awful,' was all Carmel could think of to say.

'My uncle said that you know one of the detectives working on the case.' There was a hint of accusation in Elizabeth's voice . . . as though she suspected Carmel was withholding information deliberately.

'Yes. He used to work with my late father.'

'Has he mentioned anything . . .?'

Carmel shook her head. 'I don't suppose he's allowed to say too much.'

'I'm just glad I don't have to work late at the hospital,' said Elizabeth, wringing her hands. 'Some of the nurses are terrified. Make sure you lock your doors, won't you? And I'd be really grateful if you'd keep an eye on Uncle. Just make sure the front door isn't left unlocked and that sort of thing.'

'Don't worry. I will,' said Carmel, eager to make her escape.

As she made a show of looking at her watch, she thought of Peta Thewlis, sitting in her office near the entrance like a spider in her web, making a mental note of the time each member of staff arrived. 'I'm sorry, if I don't go now, I'll be late for work. I'll keep an eye on Conrad, I promise. Look, next time you're here, why don't you come up for a cup of tea?' She said the words on impulse and she wasn't sure why she'd issued the invitation. Perhaps she was lonelier than she realised and yearning for company – any company. But now she had said it, there was no going back.

'That'd be lovely. Thanks,' Elizabeth said, sounding as though she meant it.

'See you soon then.'

Carmel raised her hand in an awkward farewell and Elizabeth watched her go, a grateful smile on her lips.

*

It couldn't be helped. Peta Thewlis knew she'd be late but some things were more important than work. She put her arms around her son and held him close, just as she had done when he was a small child.

'Why did you do it, Tim?' she asked gently, stroking her son's back. She kissed the top of his head. 'Why did you hurt yourself like that?'

He didn't answer and she felt her heart beating fast. Ever since her husband had left because he couldn't cope with Tim any more, she had borne the responsibility. Responsibility for Tim; responsibility for the financial side of things; responsibility for the house on Vicars Green that she had inherited from her father; responsibility at work where she knew her colleagues at the Archaeology Centre regarded her as a humourless stickler for the rules. But they didn't know that her stiffness was a facade, the only way she could deal with life. If she let the mask slip, people would see the mess inside.

She brushed Tim's cheek with her fingers but he shook off her caressing hand as the doorbell rang, shattering the tension between mother and son. Peta glanced at the clock on the mantelpiece. Tim wasn't the only one who'd be late for work.

'I'd better see who that is.' She hurried out into the hall. She could see a dark shadow behind the stained glass in the door. A smallish shadow. Probably a woman.

She opened the door to find a young Asian woman standing on the step. She wore jeans and a white T-shirt and her jet-black hair was caught up in a ponytail. She held up an ID card and smiled. 'Mrs Thewlis? I'm DC Jamilla Dal. I'm calling in connection with the murder of your former tenant, Janna Pyke. I believe she left some of her belongings at the flat you own in Vicars Green?'

'That's right. Look, I'm late for work and . . .'

Jamilla smiled sympathetically. 'I'm sorry. I won't keep you. I just wondered if we could have access to her belongings.'

'I put them in the loft in case she came back for them. They're packed in two black bin bags.' Peta thought for a moment. 'Look, if I give you the keys, you will let me have them back, won't you?'

'Of course.' Jamilla was pleasantly surprised that Janna Pyke's former landlady was being so cooperative.

Peta disappeared into the house for a few seconds and returned with a set of keys. 'That's the front door key. Let yourself in and go up the stairs. The loft entrance is on the landing. There's a pole you hook through and ...'

Jamilla smiled reassuringly. 'It's OK, Mrs Thewlis. We've got something similar at home. I'll let you have the keys back as soon as possible. Thanks for your cooperation.'

'It's the least I can do,' said Peta half-heartedly as she watched Jamilla retreat down the garden path.

The Resurrection Man's first victim, Carla Yates, had lived alone. She was divorced and her ex-husband had displayed little grief when officers had called to break the news of his former wife's horrendous death. Carla had disappeared from his life years ago, he said, and he had built up a new home with a new, much younger, wife who was now expecting their second child.

Emily Thwaite looked through the file. He had probably traded Carla in for a new model, she thought, her lips taut with disapproval. He had, no doubt, left his first wife for some floozie from the office fifteen years his junior and poor Carla had had to build up a new existence. Start again with a new, much smaller, home and a new job in the travel agency to earn her keep. She had had to make new friends and grab a social life with them where she could. Drinks with the girls, dressing younger than her age, always on the look out for available men. Until a girls' night out turned into a nightmare and she became the prey of a killer.

Emily thought of Jeff and the kids and counted her fragile blessings. They had overcome their troubles ...

even though they'd nearly torn them apart. Even though they were now returning to haunt them.

Tucking the file under her arm, she left her office and went in search of Joe Plantagenet. She wanted him with her on this one. She was new to the case . . . and she'd noted in the file the fact that Joe had met Carla's ex-husband once before when her body was first found. It was always best to have some continuity if possible and Joe seemed to be good at gaining people's confidence.

She found Joe in his office, trawling through some witness statements.

'What's new?' she asked, perching on the edge of his desk.

'Jamilla's just gone to arrange access to the things Janna Pyke left in the loft at Vicars Green.'

Emily experienced a sudden sting of panic. 'I wanted to go with her and have a look at the place for myself.' She took a deep breath. She had to stay calm, in complete control. 'Still, it can't be helped. Tell her to bring the things straight back here, will you? I want to have a look through them.'

'OK, if you wish. But Jamilla's quite capable . . .'

'I want to see them. Is that a problem?' she snapped, suddenly regretting her impatience. The strain was getting to her. She gave Joe a small apologetic smile. 'Sorry. I didn't get much sleep last night. What else is there?'

'I sent someone round to the charity shop where Carla Yates's clothes were dumped in the hope that whoever dumped them was caught on any nearby CCTV cameras but I'm not holding my breath. I've also sent a couple of DCs to the university to interview any students who knew Janna and someone's gone over to the House of Terrors to reinterview some of the staff there. And Jevons of course. I think we should make his life a little uncomfortable for a while, don't you?'

Emily nodded. 'I want to have a word with Carla Yates's ex . . . Show him the clothes. Watch his reaction.'

'You can't think he has anything to do with it?'

'Stranger things have happened. And there's always a chance there's something he's not told us.'

'You mean she might have dabbled in the occult?'

'Have you any better suggestions?'

Joe had to admit he hadn't. He stood up. Carla's ex worked from home these days so they knew exactly where to find him.

Lawrence Yates lived in a small place called Nearland, halfway between Eborby and Thirsk. Nearland was a typical north Yorkshire village with a cluster of stone houses, a village hall and a pub, all huddled around an ancient church. Just the sort of place the Resurrection Man liked to dump the bodies of his victims, Joe thought as he passed the sign welcoming visitors to the village and exhorting then to drive carefully. This part of Yorkshire was stunningly beautiful with its ruined abbeys, rolling, sheep-strewn fields and mellow stone villages but the juxtaposition of beauty and gruesome death chilled Joe's heart.

He glanced across at Emily who was sitting silently in the passenger seat, her eyes fixed on the passing landscape.

'Nice,' he said.

'Mmm. We sometimes come up this way on days out . . . the kids love the countryside. My youngest has a thing about sheep.'

'Is that why you moved to Eborby? To be nearer to all this?'

'Something like that.' She fell silent until Joe brought the car to a halt outside a house that had obviously once been the old village school.

'Is this it?' she asked.

'You sound surprised.'

'It doesn't seem the sort of place I'd associate with Carla Yates, that's all.'

'Perhaps Lawrence Yates's new wife has different tastes.'

'Expensive tastes,' Emily mumbled, sizing up the gleaming arched hardwood windows, and the pair of bushy bay trees in chunky ceramic pots flanking the front door.

The door was answered by Lawrence himself. At just under six foot, he was a well-preserved forty-five with a thick head of hair, slightly greying at the temples. Emily found him attractive and the well-cut jeans and collarless shirt he wore gave him a youthful look. He would have outgrown Carla's tawdry charms quite early on, she guessed. The new wife would be young, svelte, dressed with immaculate simplicity and would drive a large SUV – probably a BMW or a Mercedes.

But sometimes Emily despaired of her abilities as a detective. The second Mrs Yates, when she appeared, turned out to be around ten years younger than her husband, small and plump with brown hair caught up in an untidy ponytail and no make-up on her face. Obviously pregnant, she held a grizzling toddler on her hip. Emily, her assumptions shattered, found herself chatting to the woman, asking how old the child was and when the new addition was due while Joe stood by patiently and waited for the maternal chat to end.

When Mrs Yates – whose Christian name turned out to be Bridget – hurried out to make the tea, Lawrence Yates invited them to sit on the soft leather sofa that stood in the space once occupied by the teacher's desk when the building had been a small, single-class-roomed school.

Emily was carrying the plastic bag containing Carla Yates's clothes in a large briefcase. She pulled it out and presented it to Lawrence. 'These clothes were found in Eborby. They fit the description of the ones Carla was wearing when she was last seen.'

She watched his face for any sort of reaction. But he stared at the bag, impassive, giving nothing away.

After a few seconds he broke his silence. 'How can you be so sure they're hers? They could belong to anyone.'

'There was a cash and carry card in the handbag found with the clothes and it had her name on it. Pretty conclusive, I'm afraid.'

'If you say so. Look, I don't recognise the clothes, but then that's hardly surprising because I haven't seen Carla for a couple of years. It's terrible the way she died but I don't know how I can help you. She was killed by some maniac . . . this Resurrection Man. He's killed other people. I . . .'

'You're quite right, Mr Yates,' Emily said with a sympathetic smile. 'But you do understand that we have to talk to you. You were married to her for . . . how long was it?'

'Three years,' was the weary reply. He sounded as though he regretted every minute of it.

Bridget Yates bustled in with tea at that point and Emily waited till she'd gone before carrying on with her questions. There was no point in upsetting a pregnant woman, she thought. If Lawrence wanted to give her chapter and verse after they'd gone, that was up to him.

'Tell us about her?' Joe asked gently.

'I gave a statement when she was found.'

'Please, Mr Yates. You see, we don't know much about her. We've spoken to her friends but there didn't seem anyone she was really close to.'

Lawrence Yates nodded, resigned to going over it all again. 'What do you want to know?'

'What sort of a person was Carla?'

He inclined his head to one side in a show of thought. 'Fun loving, I suppose you could call it. I was working all the hours God sends and she wanted to be out on the town. Not that Eborby was her ideal town. She used to talk about moving to Leeds. In fact I'm surprised she didn't when we split up.'

'She worked for the Eborby Permanent Building Society, I believe.'

'At one time, yes. Not for long though.'

'Do the names Harold Uckley and John Wendal mean anything to you?'

Lawrence swallowed hard. 'Harold Uckley. He was killed like . . . I haven't heard of the other one.'

'Janna Pyke ... or possibly Jane Pyke?'

'I heard it on the news last night. She's the latest one, isn't she?'

'That's right. When your ex-wife worked at the building society did she mention anything unusual? Anything she was worried about or anyone ...?'

'She said it was boring. She got out as soon as she could because she wanted to get a job in the travel industry.'

'Was she interested in the occult at all?'

Lawrence looked surprised. 'Not that I know of. I think she had her tarot cards read once but apart from that ... Mind you, she'd do anything for a laugh ... for a bit of excitement.' He smiled. 'We weren't really suited, Inspector. That's why the marriage didn't last long. We wanted different things out of life. That and ...' He stopped himself in mid-sentence, as though he was afraid of giving too much away.

Joe leaned forward. 'And what?'

'She had an affair. That's what brought things to a head. She started working in a travel agent's on Sheepgate. Not the one she was working in when she died. This was another one nearby – a small family firm. When she was younger Carla was very ...' He searched for the word. 'Vivacious. Attractive to men. I was working hard as I said, trying to build up my business – I'm a computer consultant. She used to tease me. She used to say I was boring ... getting old before my time. Then the teasing became more vicious.'

Lawrence looked down and seemed to be studying his hands intently. Joe sensed he was remembering a painful period of his life and he needed a bit of gentle encouragement. 'Go on,' he prompted, almost in a whisper.

'There was a married man at work. The boss ... he owned the business. I should have known something was going on because she started getting home later and later. After a while she didn't even bother pretending. She used to go away with him for the weekend. I found out later that he'd told his wife he was going to conferences or to check out hotels. I felt sorry for the wife actually . . . they'd had a child but it had died.'

'So what happened?'

'He finally left his wife and Carla moved in with him.' Lawrence gave a bitter laugh. 'Then came the ultimate irony. He died of a heart attack three months after they moved in together. Of course his wife got the lot - house, business and everything in his bank account - and Carla was left high and dry. Homeless and broke when the wife sacked her from her job.'

'What was the man's name?' Joe asked, thinking it might be worth checking out.

Lawrence thought for a few moments. 'Hill . . . no, Hale . . . Peter Hale.'

'So what did Carla do then?'

'I suppose you have to admire her in a way. She picked herself up and started again. Got herself a new job and a place of her own and I was only too pleased to give her a divorce. I knew it wasn't worth trying again even if she'd wanted to. I put it down to experience.'

'You had every reason to resent your ex-wife. She made a fool of you,' Emily said bluntly, fishing for a reaction.

'Look, I've moved on. I've got Bridget now. A lovely house, a lovely wife, a lovely kid and one on the way. What is it they say? All's well that ends well.'

Joe nodded. He was right of course. He had no reason to kill his ex-wife and even less to kill the others. Their visit had been a waste of time. But he had a couple more questions to ask. Casting his bread upon the waters to see if anything came back.

'Do you know anything about Carla's recent life? Did she have a boyfriend?'

'I don't know and I don't really care. If she'd got herself someone new I would have wished her luck but, as far as I can gather, she lived on her own and she used to go round to pubs and clubs with a gaggle of women much younger than herself trying to pick up men. Who she picked up and whether one of them was a serial killer, I can't tell you, I'm afraid. But it does seem rather likely that that's what happened, don't you think?'

Joe nodded. It seemed as good an explanation as any. Apart from the fact that Carla's friends had claimed that she hadn't talked to anyone when they were out that night. And Harold Uckley hardly fitted into the scenario Lawrence had described.

When they left they said goodbye to Bridget and Emily wished her good luck with the new baby.

'They seem a nice couple,' she commented absentmindedly to Joe as they drove back to Eborby.

'Yes. Do you think we should try and track down the wronged wife? Shouldn't be difficult if she owns a travel agent's.'

'If you think it's worth it,' said Emily, her mind still on other things.

Doris and Ethel, stalwart volunteers of the Mirebridge Hospice Charity Shop on Little Marygate a few streets away from the cathedral, regarded each new bag of donated clothes as potential treasure.

That morning's crop of unattended bags, deposited on the doorstep overnight, had been taken upstairs to the sorting room to await the attention of the ladies. The task of opening the bags – although usually a delight – sometimes held potential hazards. A boiled sweet wrongly placed or a piece of chewing gum could ruin an otherwise desirable garment. Once Doris had discovered something unmentionable in a pocket and it had taken her a week to recover from the shock.

After sorting out the very satisfactory contents of a large Selfridge's bag, Ethel turned her attentions to the smaller bag bearing the name of the Archaeology Centre Shop. She emptied the contents out on to a large table and wrinkled her nose. Trousers – well worn. Shirt with perspiration stains in the armpits. Tie. Shoes – rather scuffed. Socks – obviously unwashed. Underpants – she picked them up with the end of her pen and wrinkled her nose in disgust. She moved the shirt to one side and saw a square of leather peeping out. She picked it up. A wallet.

Ethel hesitated, longing to call down to Doris. She would know what to do. But the shop couldn't be left unattended so Ethel had to take the initiative for once. With trembling fingers she flicked the wallet open and the first thing she saw was a wad of ten pound notes. There was a credit card too. And a bus pass – a seven-day saver ticket with the user's photograph on it. The face seemed familiar. And when she looked at the name she realised why.

She called Doris's name, still staring at the wallet in her hand as though it were a ticking bomb. It was Harold Uckley's wallet. And Harold Uckley had been murdered by the Resurrection Man.

Jamilla hurried up to Emily and Joe as soon as they'd set foot in the incident room. 'There's been a call from the Mirebridge Hospice Shop on Little Marygate,' she said, breathless. 'Harold Uckley's clothes have turned up. Left outside the shop. They found them when they opened up this morning.'

Joe raised his eyebrows. 'Perhaps Mickey Friday was telling the truth about finding Carla Yates's things outside the charity shop.'

'There's another thing,' Jamilla continued. 'Uckley's things were found in an Archaeology Centre shop bag just like Carla Yates's.'

Joe looked at Emily. 'That can't be a coincidence.'

'Is there a CCTV camera covering the shop?' Emily asked.

'The charity shop? Unfortunately no. We checked it out before.'

'What about the shop in the Archaeology Centre? Surely they've got a CCTV camera?'

Joe thought it was highly likely and he said as much to Emily. It occurred to him that he could give Maddy Owen a call and find out for sure. It would be a good excuse to talk to her again. He sat there for a minute or so wondering if he should call her anyway – maybe ask her out for a drink if work permitted. But his thoughts were interrupted by a booming voice.

'The hospital's just been on, boss,' Sunny called across the room. 'Know that John Wendal you're interested in? Well, someone tried to kill him last night. Pulled his tubes out.'

This got Joe's attention. 'Is he OK?'

'Yeah. It was that mad woman . . .'

'Gloria Simpson?' asked Emily.

'Yeah. She's back in the psychiatric ward. Apparently she'd been hiding the pills they gave her. She managed to escape and made straight for Wendal. I don't know what he did to her but it must have been something really bad to . . .'

'Let's hope they keep a better eye on her in future,' said Joe. Gloria had been sly. She'd clearly planned her attack with almost military precision. But he guessed that it was too late to question her now. She'd be sedated: the staff wouldn't fall for the same trick twice.

The phone on Sunny's desk rang and he rushed to answer it. After a brief conversation, he turned to Joe, a wide grin on his face.

'That was the hospital again. Wendal's come round. Must have been the shock.'

Joe smiled to himself. It was about time they had some good news for a change.

The killer wasn't sure what to call it. A box? A sarcophagus? A coffin? It stood there on the ledge. Empty. Awaiting its next occupant. He put out his hand and stroked the wood that he had trimmed and planed with loving care and lined with plastic sheeting. Ideal for its purpose.

The torch was flickering. He would have to remember to buy batteries. In the dim light he could make out the other coffins, the ones that contained the bones of long-dead members of the Gosson family – upright and wealthy citizens of Victorian Eborby who had built the mausoleum in the middle of the municipal cemetery to house their remains and ensure that their memory was held in respect. There they lay sleeping, oblivious to the horrors happening in their last resting place.

When the killer had first found the place he'd gone round the walls reading their names on the small tarnished plaques attached to their coffins: three George Gossons; four Edward Gossons; six Anne Gossons; the names repeated over the generations. The Gossons, so he'd read, had owned a successful shop in the city. They had been 'trade', not old money. Old money built elaborate tombs in churches. The Victorian nouveau riche built their classical mausoleums . . . just like this one.

The last burial in the Gosson Mausoleum – last official one, that is – had taken place in the 1930s, so the hinges and lock on the great iron door behind the classical portico had needed attention. All it had taken was a can of oil and the doors of death had opened to him, welcoming him in.

He felt quite safe there, inside with the sleeping dead. Nobody came to that part of the cemetery any more and he was grateful for its overgrown air of neglect because it meant his work could continue undisturbed.

He stood there in the weakening torchlight, listening. He could hear voices and he froze, not moving a muscle. He waited, alert as a wild animal to the sound of hunters, until the voices had faded into the distance.

He had to be sure that nobody stumbled across this place of death; his special place. He knew that sooner or later the order would come again . . . and that the coffin, so solid and so lovingly fashioned, would have a new occupant.

Chapter Thirteen

John Wendal was in no state to be interviewed just yet, which was exactly what Joe had expected. The man would need time to recover, but time was something they didn't have. The Resurrection Man might, or might not, be associated with Wendal. Or perhaps Wendal himself was the killer and he had an accomplice who'd disposed of Janna Pyke's body and the clothes of the first two victims. The possibilities were endless and Joe was growing desperate. The Resurrection Man was out there. And there was no reason to suppose that he wouldn't strike again. For some killers murder is addictive.

Jamilla's visit to Vicars Green had proved disappointing. She had crawled up into the loft above the victim's old flat and brought two bin bags filled with Janna Pyke's possessions – mainly clothes and shoes with a few CDs – back to the police station as Emily Thwaite had requested.

The DCI had insisted on examining them herself, ordering them to be taken to her office then going through them alone, shunning help, almost possessive. Joe wondered whether she was asserting her authority – demonstrating that she was in personal control of every aspect of the case – or whether there was something else behind her thoroughness; some private knowledge she was keeping from her colleagues so she could claim the glory when the case was cracked, perhaps. But Emily's search proved fruitless and she concluded that Janna's things had been abandoned because the clothes had seen better days. And it was possible that she just didn't like the CDs any more.

Joe felt quite disappointed. He had hoped to find some clue to Janna's life – and possibly her death – amongst her possessions. But if she had left any clues, they lay elsewhere. Probably in the place where she'd spent the last few weeks of her life. Wherever that was.

After checking whether Forensic had found any fingerprints on Harold Uckley's belongings and being told that they were still being examined, Joe decided to check out the art shop in Boargate where Janna had last been seen by her colleague from the House of Terrors. He armed himself with a photograph of Janna provided by her parents – a photograph of a slightly younger Janna with mouse-brown hair – and looked at his watch. It was four o'clock so, with luck, the shops would still be open when he got there.

When he told Emily about his plans she seemed a little distracted. He suspected she was under pressure from above. Or maybe there was something wrong that he didn't know about . . . something at home. People had their problems. Perhaps he'd enquire tactfully, unobtrusively, when they had a free moment. Up till now he hadn't been able to fault the way she was handling the investigation, but if she was being distracted – if her mind wasn't on the job – perhaps he should have a quiet word. He'd see how things developed.

Joe arrived in Boargate to find that the tourists were out in force and the street had an almost carnival atmosphere. Hanging baskets filled with begonias and geraniums dangled from the lampposts, the cheerful colours vying with the bright shirts of a band of chattering Americans. A Roman centurion in authentic costume strolled through the crowd – smiling an unmilitaristic smile as he handed out leaflets advertising a tour of the city's Roman heritage – while a pair of rival living statues struck unnatural poses on their painted platforms in the middle of the street.

As he wove his way through all this milling activity, Joe discovered that there were three shops selling works of art. But he supposed this was only to be expected in a street in the very heart of the tourist area.

He drew a blank at the first shop – a small establishment specialising in watercolours by local artists. Nobody of Janna Pyke's description had visited the premises. The upper floor, jutting out over the narrow street, was used as an office by an advertising agency and nobody there recognised Janna's photograph either.

The second shop was a hybrid – an exclusive gift shop that also sold paintings and sculptures. Hardly Janna's scene. Their upper floor, Joe was told by a snooty young woman, was used for storage. And she had never set eyes on Janna; she was quite sure of that.

The third shop stood at the end of Boargate, almost on the junction with Little Marygate. The window was crammed with colourful oil paintings bearing alarmingly expensive price tags and there was a door to the left of the shop front that looked as though it might lead up to an upstairs flat. Joe stood outside on the cobbled street staring at the paintings in the window for a while. He liked them. The artist had captured the light and landscape of the countryside north of Eborby with great skill. There was a particularly evocative one of Nearland Abbey, showing its great broken arch reaching up to the cloud-spattered sky. But he couldn't stand there appreciating the art all day. He pushed open the door and stepped inside the shop.

A middle-aged, rather camp, man with a ponytail greeted him like a long-lost friend, assuming he was interested in the wares on show. When Joe showed his warrant card, the man became less effusive, but he still remained on the right side of cooperative.

'Yes, there is a flat upstairs,' he said in answer to Joe's first question. 'But I haven't seen anyone there for a week or so.'

'Who lives there?'

'A young woman, I think. She only moved in recently and I haven't seen much of her. I mean, whoever lives up there doesn't have to come through the shop or anything like that so I might not see them from one week to the next.' The man gave a dramatic shrug.

'Do you own the flat?'

The man put a hand to his lips as though he found the suggestion rather amusing. 'Oh dear me, no. I rent the shop but the flat's owned by someone different, I think.' He suddenly seemed to become bored with the subject of the upstairs flat and he turned his attention to the art on display. 'These paintings were done by my partner. He captures the light so well, don't you think?'

'They're extremely good,' said Joe honestly. 'But at the moment I'm more interested in who owns the flat.'

'I don't know his name but I did hear that he has something to do with the university. But don't quote me on that. I could be wrong.'

'The young woman who lives there . . . can you describe her?'

The man made a great display of thought, twisting his features in mock concentration. 'Oh, let me think. She has black hair . . . and dresses in black. What do they call them?'

'Goths?'

'That's right. To be honest with you, she doesn't look as if she could afford a flat like that on her own. But you never know, do you?'

'No, you don't,' Joe replied, searching his pocket for Janna Pyke's photograph. When he found it he held it out. 'Is this her?'

A pair of glasses hung from a chain around the man's neck – he put them on and peered at the picture. 'Possibly. But her hair was darker – maybe she's dyed it black. I only caught a few glimpses of her and they all look the same, don't they?' He took the photograph from Joe and suddenly frowned. 'Hey, isn't this the girl who was on the telly? The one who was murdered?' His hand fluttered to his mouth. 'Oh dear. That's awful . . .'

'Yes, it is.' Joe replaced the picture carefully in his wallet. 'Well, thank you for your help.' He hesitated, his eyes on the painting of Nearland Abbey. 'Er . . . you don't give discounts, do you? Only . . .'

The man gave him an obsequious smile. 'For the boys in blue, anything,' he said with a cheeky wink. 'Fifteen per cent do you?'

'Very nicely, thanks. Put a sold sticker on that one, please.' He pointed to his choice. 'I'll pick it up tomorrow.'

When Joe returned to the police station, rather pleased with his impulsive purchase, he asked one of the DCs to check out who owned the upstairs flat and half an hour later he had an answer.

The flat on the upper floor of number five Boargate was owned by a Dr Keith Webster. Janna Pyke's supervisor at the University.

As soon as Carmel put her key in the door, she was aware of someone in the hallway. For a split second, her imagination supplied a pair of thugs from the Black Hen lurking there, awaiting her return so that they could warn her off as they'd warned Tavy. But, as she opened the door wider, she was relieved to see Conrad's niece, Elizabeth, standing there.

'I hoped I'd see you,' she said quickly, touching Carmel's arm as though she were about to share a confidence. 'Uncle Conrad's having a nap.'

Carmel was tired but she forced herself to smile. 'Do you fancy a cup of tea?' Elizabeth had something on her mind and Carmel was curious to know what it was.

'Thank you. That'd be nice,' Elizabeth said as she began to follow Carmel up the stairs. 'Look, do you know anything about that policewoman who called earlier? She had the key to the front door and she went up to the loft.'

'Sorry, I don't know anything. You're sure she was a policewoman?'

'That's what she told Conrad. She was young, Asian. She showed him her identification and everything and he said she seemed very nice but now he's worrying that she was bogus. You know how these old people worry. I just thought that policeman you know might have mentioned . . .'

'No, sorry.' She hadn't been in contact with Joe Plantagenet for a while and, even if she had, he would hardly have kept her up to date on the minutiae of his investigations.

Carmel unlocked the door of her flat and stepped aside so that her guest could enter first.

'I'll put the kettle on,' she said as Elizabeth looked around, her eyes taking in every detail.

'Thank you. It's very cosy, isn't it? Not as big as Conrad's but . . .'

Carmel wondered whether to mention the girl – her ghostly flatmate – but decided against it. She didn't want Elizabeth to think she was mad. Or going the way of Janna Pyke, obsessed with the dark side. She made the tea and sat down, racking her brains for something to say.

It was Elizabeth who broke the awkward silence. 'How are you settling in? Are you liking Eborby?'

'Oh yes. But it's always hard coming to a strange town where you don't know anyone, isn't it?'

Elizabeth smiled. 'I suppose it is. Not that I've ever done it. I've lived in Eborby all my life. And my family's local.'

'What about your husband? Is he from Eborby?' She'd noticed a plain gold band on the third finger of Elizabeth's left hand and concluded that there was bound to be a husband.

But a spasm of pain passed over Elizabeth's face and Carmel immediately regretted her question. 'He was from Eborby. He died suddenly some years ago. They said it was a heart attack.' She spoke the last words as though there was some doubt.

'I'm sorry,' said Carmel quickly, wondering how she could change the subject. The last thing she wanted to do was to upset the woman. Then she suddenly recalled the photograph of the little girl in Conrad's flat – the dead great-niece – and wondered if she'd been Elizabeth's child. But she wasn't going to ask and risk reopening old wounds. Perhaps that was why she had sensed a hidden sadness behind Elizabeth's cheerful common sense.

For the remainder of Elizabeth's visit, Carmel kept the conversation light, asking about Elizabeth's work at the hospital and learning about the virtues of her boss, Dr Oakley, who was, according to Elizabeth, a wonderful man. She wouldn't be the first secretary to be a little in love with her boss, Carmel thought, but she said nothing. She liked Elizabeth but she couldn't imagine she'd ever be close enough to her to share confidences.

After half an hour Elizabeth glanced at her watch and stood up. 'Thank you for the tea, Carmel. Knowing that Uncle Conrad has a good neighbour has taken a lot of worry off my shoulders if the truth were known. The last girl . . .' She hesitated.

'How well did you know her?' Carmel couldn't resist asking the question.

Elizabeth looked a little alarmed. 'Oh, I wouldn't say I knew her . . . knew of her more like.' She pursed her lips in disapproval. 'She was trouble, that girl.'

'You mean she upset Conrad?'

'That and . . . Well, she caused a lot of trouble for a friend of mine as well.' Her eyes were aglow with righteous indignation. 'She was evil . . . didn't care who she hurt. She—' Suddenly she checked herself and attempted to smile. 'I'm sorry. You shouldn't speak ill of the dead, should you?'

When Elizabeth left, Carmel stood at the window and watched her walk away across the green. She was a sensible woman in sensible clothes. Not one, Carmel would have thought, to overdramatise. Even her personal tragedies had been spoken of with stoical self-control. But she had described Janna Pyke as evil. And Carmel wondered exactly what Janna had done to deserve such a damning description.

Perhaps the evil she sensed in the flat didn't belong to the ghost girl. Perhaps it was Janna's.

Joe had rung Keith Webster's number at the university but there had been no answer. Then, at six thirty, just as he was about to leave the police station, an elderly man had turned up at the front desk, saying that he had seen John Wendal pick up Gloria Simpson in his car. He had only just got back from Norfolk where he'd been staying with his daughter and that's why he hadn't come forward earlier.

He had been walking his dog when he had seen Gloria, a lady in distress, standing by her car looking worried. He had asked her what was wrong and when she said she had run out of petrol, he had flagged down a passing motorist – a man he now knew to be John Wendal through the report in the local newspaper that his wife had pointed out to him that lunchtime.

Wendal had seemed a normal, friendly sort of man and he had offered to drop Gloria off at a petrol station a mile down the road and give her a lift back to her car with a full can of petrol. The dog walker had thought he'd done his good deed for the day by facilitating this arrangement and had gone home, oblivious to the consequences of his actions. He had left for Norfolk a couple of hours later and had only returned yesterday.

As far as the witness could tell, Wendal and Gloria had never seen each other before in their lives. There had been no hint of recognition and any conversation between them had seemed polite and formal. She had expressed her gratitude and, what was more important, she had behaved perfectly calmly.

Joe thought about the man's statement as he walked home. Something cataclysmic must have occurred during the short journey to the petrol station. Perhaps Wendal had tried to attack her. But that didn't really make sense. He had been driving when she went berserk and caused him to crash the car into a tree. If he had wanted to rape or kill her then, presumably he'd have driven to a deserted spot and parked the car before making his move. He pondered this puzzle all the way to his front door but couldn't come up with an answer.

Once he had showered and put on his jeans and white T-shirt, he felt better, as though he was no longer tainted with the scent of blood and murder. He poured himself a Black Sheep Ale and sat down heavily on the leather sofa. From where he sat he could see the city walls through the window, a barrier between him and the city, between his refuge and the Resurrection Man who would surely kill again. The only question was when? And who?

As he drained his glass, his mobile phone began to ring. He looked at the unfamiliar number on the display and answered with a wary hello. When he heard Maddy Owen's voice on the other end of the line he told her he'd been intending to call her, hoping he sounded convincing, and asked her how she was. But they soon got on to the subject of Carmel. She was fine, Maddy said – still a little shaken by the attack on Tavy McNair but, apart from that, fine.

It was a minute or so before Maddy came to the point. If Joe hadn't already eaten would he like to come round for a meal? Nothing elaborate. Joe looked around his empty flat, thought of the ready-meal waiting for him in the freezer, and decided to live dangerously. He told her he'd love to accept her invitation – but he couldn't be late as he had an early start in the morning. He added these last words as an insurance policy. He was wary of involvement. Involvement meant pain.

As he walked to Maddy's house he made a mental note to ask her about the carrier bags. It was always good to have friends in high – or not so high – places. He felt a little apprehensive as he rang her doorbell – like a teenage boy on a date with a girl he'd admired from afar on the school bus. And he had to admit to himself that he admired Maddy. But the past made him cautious. Too cautious perhaps.

Maddy answered the door wearing a long ethnic dress and a shy smile. She looked good and she had a couple of raw steaks sitting on a plate, seasoned and waiting to be cooked. She had already prepared a salad and a crisp French loaf lay on the worktop. On the way Joe had visited the off licence on the corner to buy a decent bottle of wine. It was the least he could do.

They talked of trivialities and Carmel as they ate. Joe never liked bringing up the subject of murder over the dinner table but as the conversation lulled over the strawberry dessert, it seemed as good a time as any. 'The clothes belonging to the Resurrection Man's first two victims have turned up.'

Maddy was about to help herself to more cream but she withdrew her hand. 'Where?'

'Left outside a charity shop on Little Marygate. The Mirebridge Hospice shop. Do you know it?'

She nodded. 'I know it.'

'The clothes were in carrier bags from the Archaeology Centre shop. Both lots. Now if just one lot had been . . .'

Maddy's eyes widened in alarm. Then she frowned. 'So it could be one of our regular customers? It might be someone I've passed or talked to.' Joe noticed she'd turned quite pale.

'It could always be a member of staff.' He watched her reaction carefully.

Maddy put her spoon down and stared at him, horrified. 'You think someone I work with is the Resurrection Man? That's absolute rubbish. There's nobody remotely weird in that place. Some of them are a bit eccentric maybe but not serial-killer weird.'

'How would you know?' Joe was aware that he sounded impatient. But then he suddenly felt strained, tired. Perhaps the case was getting to him like he suspected it was getting to Emily Thwaite. He took a deep breath. 'What about the company that supplies the bags?'

Maddy looked as if she liked this idea much better. 'I'm sure Peta Thewlis'll have their address.'

'Good. I'll send someone round tomorrow and I really must give Carmel a call . . . see how she is.'

Maddy studied Joe's face for a few moments. 'Tavy McNair's not a suspect, is he? I wouldn't like to think of Carmel . . .'

Joe pushed his empty dish away. 'We've not ruled anybody out just yet. But let's just say, he's not at the top of our list. Not that we've got much of a list. This killer's clever. He doesn't leave many clues. We don't even know where he kills them.' He shook his head, longing to change the subject. The thought of his failure so far was too depressing to dwell on over a pleasant dinner.

At ten thirty he left, kissing Maddy first on the cheek then gently on the lips. He promised to call her and he meant to keep his promise. If the Resurrection Man didn't get in his way.

Perhaps Dr Keith Webster would lead them in the right direction when they talked to him the next day. They needed some luck and they needed it fast . . . before someone else died.

Terry Jevons looked round as he locked the heavy oak door of the House of Terrors. He'd felt uneasy ever since the police began sniffing around. Janna Pyke had always been trouble. And now she was still causing him grief from beyond the grave. He wished he'd never taken her on when she turned up at the House of Terrors looking for a job. He wished he'd never clapped eyes on her.

But now Janna was dead and she couldn't bother him any more. The thought gave him a warm glow of satisfaction. A minor irritation had been dealt with once and for all.

He put the keys in his pocket and looked at his watch.

He'd have time to grab something to eat at home before going on to the Black Hen. Ever since the solstice meeting various people had been getting jittery and they needed bringing back into line. Perhaps what had happened with the sixteen-year-old, Amy whatever her name was, had been a mistake. Perhaps in future he'd ensure that he would always be able to employ the consenting adults excuse. Things had gone too far that time, he realised that now. And if Janna Pyke hadn't kept going on about it, he wouldn't have had to deal with her.

He walked quickly down the winding, noisy streets, ignoring the buskers and *Big Issue* sellers, picking his way through the stream of tourists and scantily clad girls. He wondered, not for the first time, whether they'd dress like that, exposing so much bare flesh, if they knew the effect they had on him. Arousing his imagination . . . and his memory of Amy.

As he made for his flat on the river bank, he kept his eyes fixed ahead, resisting temptation, and eventually he emerged from the shadow of the streets and cut across the wide expanse of grass by the museum car park. He lived on the first floor of a Georgian house that stood on the water's edge, a stone's throw from the castle built by William the Conqueror to subdue the unruly north but now reduced by war and time to a solitary tower on a grassy mound. The castle was a shadow of its former self, unlike his flat, which was spacious, with lofty ceilings and sanded wooden floors: the last word in modern living. Terry Jevons considered himself to be a man of taste and the House of Terrors provided him with a lifestyle that he knew his employees envied. He was a good advert for the cause, he thought with a smile. The devil looks after his own.

Once he turned the corner, the river came into view. He could see the ripples, sparkling in the late evening sun as a pair of rowers sped silently along the ribbon of water, like fast-moving insects. To his left, a group of students, chatting in some foreign tongue Jevons didn't recognise, sprawled on the grassy bank beneath the squat grey Norman tower. It was a peaceful scene, a lazy summer evening in a city renowned for its history and its picturesque beauty. Jevons allowed himself a secretive smile. If only the tourists knew what lay beneath.

He was almost home. The Georgian terrace that housed his flat overlooked the river, an enviable position. No wonder it had cost a bomb. There were the occasional floods, of course, but they only affected the cellar – or the garden flat as it was known. On the first floor, he led a charmed life.

He opened the glossy black front door with his key and was about to step into the hallway when he caught a movement out of the corner of his eye. He turned and saw a shadow, there for a split second before it disappeared from sight into the dimness of the little alleyway at the side of the terrace.

Jevons stepped back from the front door and stood scanning the waterfront, shielding his eyes from the low evening sun. This was the third time he'd sensed somebody there. Following him. Watching him silently from the shadows.

Next time he'd be more alert. Next time he'd catch whoever it was. And he'd make them regret that they'd ever been born.

Chapter Fourteen

Joe Plantagenet arrived at the police station early the next morning. Emily Thwaite wasn't in. But then she had kids to see to and a mother's work, so he was reliably informed, was never done . . . especially when that mother happens to be in charge of a major murder enquiry. Joe supposed that her husband, being a teacher, was always on hand to look after the little Thwaites during the long school holidays. There were times he'd sensed that all wasn't well between them. However, he had to acknowledge that he might be wrong.

Emily hadn't mentioned her husband for a while, but then there'd been little time to exchange personal chit-chat. Joe had never met Jeff but, with no evidence whatsoever, he had built up an unflattering mental picture of a hen-pecked husband, a little man who concerned himself with domestic matters while his briefcase-wielding wife pursued her high-powered career as a Detective Chief Inspector. The reality, he knew, would almost certainly be quite different. He was being influenced by long defunct stereotypes which would make the politically correct powers-that-be purple in the face with righteous rage. The thought made him smile, a small secret smile. No doubt he'd meet Jeff one day and all his naughty illusions would be shattered.

It was eight thirty before Emily put in an appearance. She had the harassed look of a woman with too much on her plate and Joe, unlike some, took pity on her. He followed her to her office and she sat down heavily.

'It's been one of those mornings,' she sighed. 'My youngest woke up complaining of a headache. There was an outbreak of meningitis at their last school. I was worried sick.'

Joe nodded sympathetically. Not being a parent himself, he didn't quite understand the implications, but he guessed they were serious.

'I'll ring home later . . . see how he is.'

'I'm sure your husband'll keep an eye on him.'

'Mmm.' She didn't sound altogether convinced. 'Has . . . er, the Super been asking for me . . . or . . .?'

'No, it's been quiet. Is everything OK?'

There was a flash of alarm in Emily's eyes that disappeared after a split second. 'Yes. Why shouldn't it be?' She took a deep breath. 'I suppose I'll have to go in there and rally the troops. Anything come in overnight?'

Joe shook his head. 'Only a report from Forensic saying that there were no fingerprints on the bag containing Harold Uckley's clothes . . . and none on his wallet. Someone's gone to a lot of trouble to wipe them off.'

'Does that mean that the killer has a criminal record?'

Joe thought for a few moments. 'It's possible. But then everyone knows about prints these days. There's far too many detective shows on TV.'

Emily nodded. 'Is there anything you think requires our special attention today?'

'Keith Webster – Janna Pyke's supervisor at the university – owns the flat above the art gallery in Boargate where she was last seen and, according to the gallery owner, the last tenant was a young woman who fits Janna's description. I don't think our Dr Webster has been altogether honest with us. First he claims he hasn't seen her for two weeks and now it looks highly likely that he let her use his flat when she moved out of Vicars Green.' The mention of the flat reminded him that he had to pick up the painting he'd bought before the art shop closed that evening. 'The question is, if the tenant was Janna, why did he lie? What's he trying to hide?'

'We'd better check it out – top priority.'

'I wonder if Webster has any connection with the Black Hen. That place stinks like a barrel-load of rotting fish.'

Emily wrinkled her nose. 'That's one way of putting it. I reckon we should be digging a bit deeper – make life uncomfortable for them.' She paused for a moment. 'We need to find some connection between Janna Pyke and the other two victims. She was receiving threats . . .'

'But there's no evidence that the others were. And we've already established that whoever was threatening her didn't know she'd moved out of her flat.'

'It could be a double bluff to put us off the trail.'

Joe shrugged. It was possible but he wasn't convinced. 'I want to get more background on Janna. I'm going to send Jamilla to talk to that friend of hers who works in the fish and chip shop . . . Gemma.'

Emily leaned forward. 'I think that'd be a waste of time.'

'Maybe,' said Joe, slightly taken aback with the vehemence of Emily's judgement. 'But I'd still like to find out more about . . .'

She didn't wait for him to finish his sentence. 'I'll need Jamilla at Evanshaw to coordinate house-to-house enquiries. I want everyone in the village questioned in case they saw anything on the night Janna Pyke's body was dumped. Someone might have seen a strange vehicle in the vicinity.'

Joe couldn't fault Emily's logic but he still wondered why she'd been so dismissive of his desire to enquire into Janna's past. Perhaps he'd ask her if the moment was ever right.

Emily's briefing took half an hour. Joe's last DCI had liked the sound of his own voice but Emily's manner was brisk and businesslike as developments were noted and plans made for the day. When the team dispersed, she touched his arm. 'You and me should go to the university . . . ask Webster a few pertinent questions.'

Twenty minutes later they'd tracked Keith Webster down in his office. And he didn't look at all pleased to see them.

'I'm teaching in half an hour,' he said tersely after greeting them with a scowl. 'I can't give you long.'

Emily sat herself down on the easy chair beside his desk, a sign that she had no intention of moving. 'I'm afraid you'll have to give us as long as it takes to sort a few things out, Dr Webster. You might have to cancel your lecture.'

Webster opened and closed his mouth like a fish. Then he sank down into his seat, resigned.

Emily caught Joe's eye and gave him an almost imperceptible nod.

'You own a flat above an art shop on Boargate,' he said. A statement of fact.

Webster looked wary. 'I don't see how that concerns you.'

'It wouldn't concern us . . .' He paused for a second. He wasn't absolutely sure of his facts but it was best to sound confident. 'If Janna Pyke hadn't been staying there before she disappeared. Why didn't you tell us she'd been living there, Dr Webster? What were you trying to hide from us?'

Webster put his head in his hands. 'OK, OK. I admit I let Janna use the flat. It was empty and she was desperate to get away from the place she'd been living in. She said she'd been receiving threats and she was scared stiff – really frightened – so I said she could use the flat for a while. I did a student a favour, that's all.'

'She left her other place without paying the rent.'

'That's got nothing to do with me. I didn't know.'

'Did she tell you why she was so afraid?'

'Like I said, someone was threatening her. They kept phoning her.'

'She never said what it was about?'

Webster shook his head. 'Never.' He hesitated. 'This might sound stupid but she thought her old flat was haunted. I told you she'd changed the subject of her dissertation, didn't I? She abandoned her research on the Black

Death in 1348 and started investigating a group of people in the late Tudor period known as the Seekers of the Dead. She became obsessed with a young girl who'd died in her old flat in 1603 and she was coming out with some pretty weird things. She said the girl talked to her and . . . To tell you the truth, I was worried about her state of mind. I thought it would be best all round if she moved into my flat till she sorted herself out. She refused at first . . . then the threats started and she changed her mind.'

'Why didn't you tell us this before? Why did you lie about seeing her?'

'I didn't want to get involved. I thought if you knew, I'd get mixed up in all this mess.'

Joe looked at Emily but neither made any comment.

'Did she leave anything in the Boargate flat?'

Webster looked away. 'I went there when she didn't turn up for our meetings.'

'When was this?'

'It must have been . . .' He thought for a few moments. 'About three days before she was found. She'd not shown up for a while so I thought I'd go and see what was going on. I thought she might have been ill or something.'

'So you went to the flat and let yourself in.'

A nod.

'What did you find?'

'The place was like the *Marie Celeste*. It was as if she'd just stepped out for half an hour . . . as if she'd expected to come back. I looked around but there was no clue as to where she'd gone. Look, when I heard her body had been found I was going to contact you . . .'

'But you never got round to it.' There was a hint of sarcasm in Emily's voice. She'd heard it all before. 'So all her stuff's still there?'

Webster nodded. 'I haven't had the heart to touch it. It's all there. Just as she left it.'

'How long have you owned the flat, Dr Webster?' Joe asked, just out of curiosity.

'I inherited it from an aunt. My wife doesn't know about it so I'd be grateful if . . .'

'So you often let female students use it? Do they pay rent?' Emily asked, looking at him innocently.

Webster's face reddened. 'I sometimes let it out to students,' he answered. 'Not all of them female.'

Joe raised his eyebrows. 'If you'd be good enough to let us have the key, Dr Webster, we'd like to take a look around.'

Webster opened the top drawer of his desk and meekly handed over a Yale key tied to a loop of red ribbon. 'You'll let me have it back when you've finished, won't you? I've a post-grad student who's looking for somewhere to live and I thought . . .'

'As soon as we've finished, I promise,' said Joe with a businesslike smile, not mentioning that if the flat was found to be a crime scene, the wait might be a long one.

It took ten minutes to walk from the university's history department to Boargate through narrow streets and snickleways, and when they arrived at the art shop Joe was glad to see that the picture of Nearland Abbey had been removed from the window.

'I bought a painting here yesterday . . . couldn't resist it,' he said to Emily who was standing beside him, slightly breathless. She had mentioned that she wasn't used to walking briskly. In Leeds she had travelled everywhere by car.

'They're very nice,' she said absentmindedly, turning the key to Keith Webster's flat over and over in her hand. She made for the door at the side of the shop and placed the key in the lock. It turned smoothly.

Joe's heart rate increased a little, as it always did when he stepped into the unknown. He pulled a pair of plastic gloves from his pocket and put them on. It was always possible that the killer had left some trace in the flat, that he had called on Janna and abducted her. Or perhaps he had lured her away somehow.

Their shoes clattered loudly as they climbed a flight of

steep, uncarpeted stairs. The door at the top was shut and Joe turned the handle and pushed it open.

'After you,' Emily whispered.

Joe stepped inside. Keith Webster had been right when he'd described the state of the room. It was furnished with a combination of cheap chipboard furniture and junk-shop cast-offs and the walls were plain magnolia woodchip.

The flat was in a highly desirable location in the heart of the medieval city and, if Webster had taken the trouble to do the place up, he might have earned himself a decent rent from some prosperous young professional. But as it was, only a penurious student or someone very desperate would be willing to endure its spartan conditions. Joe found himself wondering why Webster hadn't made the most of this potentially lucrative asset. But perhaps he had his reasons. A love nest away from his wife's prying eyes might be worth more to him than hard cash.

The debris of a meal lay on the 1970s tiled coffee table in the centre of the room: a takeaway pizza box, empty; a rotting banana skin; and a mug with the dregs of tea or coffee, now turning to penicillin. Magazines and books were scattered about the floor and the threadbare settee was strewn with files and papers. It looked as if Janna Pyke had stepped out for half an hour, intending to return. But she hadn't come back. Instead she had gone to her death and ended up, cold and naked, in a country churchyard.

'I'll have a look in the bedroom,' Emily said.

Joe started to follow her. He wanted to see everything, to glean the slightest clue about the victim's life. But Emily stopped him. 'You do the kitchen and bathroom, will you?'

Joe said nothing. He made for the small kitchen but found nothing of interest to anyone but a microbiologist, who would probably have been fascinated by the contents of the fridge and the condition of the uncleaned oven.

The bathroom also revealed very little about its last user, apart from the fact that she wore heavy, pale make-up – and they'd known that already. The cupboard contained nothing of interest apart from a packet of paracetamol tablets and a bottle of indigestion salts. The sink was grubby and there was a dark tide mark around the bath. Domesticity hadn't been one of Janna Pyke's virtues.

Emily emerged from the bedroom, her face solemn.

'Well?' Joe asked, looking beyond her through the open bedroom door. He could see an unmade double bed, the grey bedding - pristine white in an earlier existence - crumpled and creased as if she had just risen from an afternoon of hot passion. 'Found anything?'

'Her clothes are all there - some in the wardrobe, some on the floor. There's a large packet of condoms in the bedside drawer.' She hesitated for a moment. 'And some used ones in the waste bin.'

'We'll have to get Forensic over. Anything the matter?'

'No, of course not.' She spoke with a vehemence that surprised Joe. 'You're quite right, we'd better call Forensic. And get this place searched from top to bottom.'

'Yes. There might be a diary or an address book. There's no sign of one but she might have kept it hidden somewhere. Or maybe it's in a bag she had with her when she disappeared . . . there's no sign of a handbag, is there?' he said, looking around.

'Tell you what,' said Emily. 'You go and summon reinforcements and I'll have a search round.' She smiled sweetly, as though she expected him to obey instantly. But she avoided looking him in the eye.

Joe took his mobile phone from his pocket, still watching her. He could sense something wasn't right. And he wondered what it was.

'I'll leave it with you then,' Emily said quickly before disappearing back into the bedroom, letting the door swing closed behind her.

As soon as she was certain she wasn't being watched, Emily began to make a methodical search of all the hidden places she could think of. The top of the cheap pine wardrobe, in the lumps of dust underneath the bed, at the backs of the drawers. She found old magazines, an unopened bank statement and various lost items of underwear but there was nothing else; nothing that mentioned Janna Pyke's days in Leeds and nothing that provided any clue to the identity of her killer.

Emily looked down at her hands and saw that they were shaking. She'd have to get a grip on herself before she faced Joe. She took a deep breath and counted to ten.

'It looks like she travelled light,' Joe observed as she emerged from the bedroom. 'There isn't much personal stuff here at all but there's a laptop. We can get someone to have a look at that.'

'Probably just her university work.'

'According to Keith Webster she was researching some people called the Seekers of the Dead. Something to do with the plague.'

'I don't see how that can be relevant.' Emily turned away. Going through Janna's work, she thought, would be a complete waste of time. 'Judging by the used condoms in the bedroom, I think she was doing more with our Dr Webster than a spot of historical research.'

'We don't know it's him. She could have been involved with someone else. Someone we need to find.' He paused. 'Perhaps it would be best if I ask Webster. Man to man.'

For the first time since they'd arrived at the flat, Emily smiled. 'You do that, Joe. I'll wait here for the reinforcements.'

'I'll go and have a word with him then. I still think there's a lot he hasn't been sharing with us.'

As he left the flat he turned and caught a glimpse of Emily's face. She looked haggard . . . and worried. But he was hardly surprised. The case was taking its toll on everyone.

Once he was back on the street, he popped his head round the door of the shop and told the proprietor he'd pick up his painting later. Then he hurried off towards the university. Business before pleasure.

*

Canon George Merryweather left the ordered chaos of his office and strolled into the cathedral. He needed to think, to pray, but the great church was too crammed with meandering, chattering tourists for the pursuit of God's guidance so he wandered back to his office again and sat down at his desk. He put his head in his hands in an attempt to block out the secular world and tried desperately to concentrate.

The girl, Amy, was in urgent need of his prayers. When he'd called on her the previous evening, her condition had much improved. According to her mother, she seemed a lot calmer and she'd stopped having the nightmares. But George could tell that she was still traumatised, afraid of her own shadow.

He was glad to see that Amy's mother, Anne, had a friend there with her to provide support. Elizabeth worked at the hospital and she seemed a pleasant, sensible sort of woman. George had hardly exchanged more than a few words with her but he sensed that she had been through tragedy herself and that she understood what Anne was going through. Perhaps, when he met her again, he'd find out more about her.

According to Anne, the psychiatrist, Dr Oakley, who was also Elizabeth's boss, was pleased with Amy's progress. He was uncovering the story of what had happened to her little by little, drawing it out of her gently, and he thought he was getting near the truth. Anne had blushed when she'd told George, almost in a whisper, that Amy had been raped. But George had already guessed that rape had been part of the poor girl's ordeal.

According to Anne, what had happened to Amy had taken place at the Black Hen but she knew no more. George hadn't yet worked out the significance of the strange symbol Amy had kept drawing in the early days. Now she'd stopped drawing it and George's naturally optimistic nature took this as a sign that whatever power had been possessing Amy no longer had any hold over her. George had told Anne that this was a Good Thing – progress – trying to provide her with some comfort, some hope.

George wasn't sure whether to tell Joe Plantagenet what he'd discovered. All his instincts told him that a rape should be reported and investigated. That justice should be done in this world as well as in the next. But Anne had refused to involve the police, even though her friend, Elizabeth, agreed with George that Amy's attacker should be prevented from doing the same again to some other naïve young girl. Anne was adamant that she wanted to forget it. She wanted Amy to have a new start, she said, without dragging up the horrors of the past. If vulnerable, fragile Amy was made to testify against her attacker in a court of law, who knows what damage it would do to her. Let sleeping dogs lie, she'd said. And she claimed that Dr Oakley agreed with her. Amy's wellbeing was to be their only consideration.

When George had finished his prayers for the unfortunate girl, he began a search of his chaotic desk. He knew the book was somewhere buried in the depths of his paperwork. He had borrowed it from the cathedral library and he knew he had to return it before it went right out of his mind.

He searched through the stratified papers and eventually ran the book to ground in the middle drawer of his desk. It was a Victorian history of Eborby, a dull brown volume easily overlooked. But it had told him a lot about Amy's case. It had told him how, in the eighteenth century, a vicious highwayman known as Jack Devilhorn had been landlord of the Black Hen, then a notorious drinking den reputedly on the site of a Viking burial ground. As well as his lengthy catalogue of serious crimes, this man was reputed to have practised black magic rituals on the premises, plumbing the depths of human depravity and, according to rumour, raising the devil himself - although, in the absence of evidence, George tended to keep an open mind on such matters as the majority of the cases he investigated turned out to have a rational and earthly explanation.

George opened the book and as he flicked through the pages he noticed something, a name that caused him to smile. That was it. He had the answer. He knew where he'd come across the name Jack Wendal before.

He picked up the phone and dialled Joe's Plantagenet's number. He'd want to know about this.

'So what did Webster have to say for himself? Was he screwing his students?' Emily's enquiry sounded more than casual.

'In a word, yes. I had to assure him that his wife wouldn't get to hear about it before he'd talk but he admitted it eventually.'

'I don't know how the university authorities would view it.'

'I don't think they'd be too happy. That's another reason for Webster's reticence. His job and his marriage are on the line.'

'The things some men risk for a quick grope,' Emily said with feeling. Joe looked at her, curious, and saw that her mouth was set in a determined line.

When they arrived back at the police station they made for the incident room, both longing for a cup of tea. The Forensic team was going over the flat Janna Pyke had occupied during the last weeks of her life, although, as far as Joe could see, there was no indication that anything violent had taken place there. He was as sure as he could be that she had been killed elsewhere – stripped and imprisoned in a confined space until the air ran out and she gasped her final breath. But where had she died? And where were her things? Would they too turn up eventually outside the Mirebridge Hospice shop? Only time would tell.

They had their tea in Emily's office, sitting sipping the hot, liquid in amicable silence. Although Joe sensed that something was on the DCI's mind, he was reluctant to pry. It might be something to do with her private life, he thought, and if she wanted to tell him, she'd do so in her own good time. He suppressed his natural curiosity and tried to concentrate on the case.

Emily looked at her watch. 'I need to take Harold Uckley's clothes to his widow . . . get her to identify them. Coming with me?'

Joe nodded. Revived by the tea, he wanted to be out on the trail again. And it would do no harm to find out more about the Resurrection Man's second victim, Harold Uckley. At the moment he seemed to be a respectable enigma.

As they were about to leave the office, Jamilla Dal burst in, brimming with untold news. 'Those house-to-house enquiries I set up in Evanshaw,' she began breathlessly. 'A vet lives opposite the church. On the night Janna Pyke's body was dumped he was called out to an emergency at a farm at three in the morning. As he drove off he noticed a van parked by the lych gate leading to the graveyard.'

Joe suddenly felt excited. This was the best news they'd had in ages. 'Has he given us a description of the van?'

'Something the size of a transit van, he said.'

Joe's heart sank. 'There must be thousands of transit vans in Yorkshire.' He looked at Jamilla, pleading. 'What colour was it?'

'Light coloured, he said. Possibly white. He couldn't be more specific.'

'Not a bloody white van . . . they're everywhere. Please tell me he took the registration number, Jamilla. Please.'

Jamilla smiled apologetically. 'Sorry. He's a busy vet, not an old lady who has nothing to do but spy on the neighbours from behind her net curtains.

Joe sighed. Jamilla was right. But if they had to trace and interview the owner of every light-coloured transit van in the area, the killer would have plenty of time to strike again. And that's what he was afraid of. 'I don't suppose anyone else saw anything?'

'Sorry. No.'

'And the van didn't have any distinguishing features . . .

like a name on the side or damage to the bodywork?'

Jamilla shook her head. 'Sorry. Like I said, his mind was on other things.' She made to leave the office then she turned back. 'I almost forgot, there was a call for you. A George Merryweather. He asked if you could call him back.'

'Thanks, Jamilla. I'll give him a call when I have a moment.' Jamilla gave him a shy parting smile and hurried away.

'Come on, let's go and face Mrs Uckley ... get it over with,' Emily said, sounding a little impatient. Joe sensed that she wasn't looking forward to their visit. But then neither was he particularly.

As they drove to Uckley's semi-detached house, not that far from Emily's own, Joe found himself wondering again about his new boss's home life. Perhaps as they were so near, she'd invite him back for a cup of tea. But somehow he doubted it. He had the vague feeling that all wasn't well. He had picked up undercurrents and he wondered whether the Thwaite marriage was foundering because of Emily's antisocial working hours. However, he hoped he was wrong.

It was Emily who carried the plastic evidence bags containing the clothes and wallet and another containing the Archaeology Centre carrier bag with its large black and white AC logo. Joe knew the visit wasn't going to be easy. He'd met Mrs Uckley before and had found her uncommunicative. Of course her prickly manner might have been due to the circumstances of their meeting. On the other hand, Joe had a nagging suspicion that she was always like that.

Uckley's widow answered the door almost as soon as they'd rung the bell and she stood there staring at them for a few seconds before inviting them in. She was a tall woman, dressed from top to toe in an unflattering grey that gave her flesh a sallow look which suggested some underlying illness. Her hair matched her clothes and was scraped back into a makeshift bun. Perhaps, Joe thought, her monochrome appearance was intended to symbolise that the colour had drained from her life ... or, more likely, that she just didn't care any more.

She led the way through into the living room and invited them to sit. No tea was offered and she stared ahead, waiting for them to say what they'd come to say. She had the air of one resigned to her fate. The worst had happened. Nothing they could say or do could touch her.

'I'm terribly sorry, Mrs Uckley,' Emily began gently. 'But I have to ask you to look at these clothes. Do they belong to your husband? You see, his wallet was found with them and ...'

The woman took the plastic bag and examined it briefly. 'They're Harry's. Where did you ...?'

'They were found outside a charity shop on Little Marygate. The Mirebridge Hospice shop. They were in this carrier bag.' Emily handed her the Archaeology Centre bag but Mrs Uckley looked at it blankly, no recognition in her eyes. 'Your husband's wallet was found too. As far as we can see his money and credit cards haven't been touched so we're ruling out robbery as a motive.' She took a deep breath and looked the woman in the eye. 'I know you've been asked this question before, but can you think of anybody at all who'd want to harm your husband?'

Mrs Uckley shook her head. 'No one. Harry was the most gentle ...' A tear trickled down her cheek and she took a tissue out of her pocket to blow her nose.

'He never mentioned anything unusual going on at work?'

Another shake of the head.

'And did he ever mention a man called John Wendal?'

'No. Who is he?'

'He works at the Eborby Permanent. He was attacked a few days ago.'

'I've not heard the name before.'

'Did Harold ever mention a place called the House of Terrors?'

'No.'

'Or a pub called the Black Hen?'

She shook her head vigorously.

The door burst open. 'What's going on?' A muscular young man with cropped fair hair stood in the doorway, his fists clenched. 'Are you OK, mum?'

Joe stood up. 'Ian? We've met before . . . DI Plantagenet and DCI Thwaite.'

The young man's eyes lit up. 'You've got someone? You've got the bastard who killed Dad?'

Joe avoided his eyes, guilty at having raised false hope. 'Not yet. I'm sorry. But we're following some new leads.'

Ian Uckley sat himself down by his mother and touched her hand, a gesture of support. Joe watched his face as he asked him the same questions he had asked his mother. The answers came in the negative. Apart from the one about the Black Hen which produced a slight flicker of recognition in the young man's eyes, easy to miss unless you were looking for it . . . as Joe was.

Emily turned to Ian. 'Can you think of anything at all that might help us? Did your father go out much, for instance?' She had a sudden flash of inspiration. 'Did he go to the railway museum at all?' she asked. If he had done, it would establish a link between him and Wendal.

'He used to go down to our local, the Drayman's Arms, on a Friday night. That's where he was going on the night he disappeared. But you know that already.'

It was true. They knew all about Harold Uckley's regular visits to the Drayman's Arms to meet his fishing friend, Barry Mere. He and Barry met most Fridays – Barry would have a pint while Harold, the teetotaller, would have a Coke – and on Sundays they went fishing, along with a few others. It was an uneventful life . . . until the Friday night when Harold Uckley didn't turn up at the pub.

'I believe your husband didn't drive.'

Mrs Uckley looked uneasy and glanced at her son. 'Er, no. He had an accident once . . . it put him off. He never drove again after that.'

Joe leaned forward. 'What kind of accident?'

'He ran someone over but it wasn't his fault. He couldn't have stopped in time. But it still put him off driving. He had nightmares about it for years.'

Ian squeezed his mother's hand but she pulled it away.

'Are you sure he's never mentioned the Black Hen?' Joe kept his eyes on Ian's face but this time the young man was prepared.

'No. Dad was a creature of habit. He went to the Drayman's on Friday nights. And the rest of the time he was either at work, at home, or fishing. He wasn't mixed up in anything illegal or—'

'What makes you think the Black Hen's connected with anything illegal?' Emily snapped.

Ian looked uneasy. 'I don't . . . I've just heard it's got a bit of a reputation, that's all.'

'Really?' said Joe, sitting forward, looking Harold Uckley's son in the eye. 'What sort of a reputation would that be then?'

The young man squirmed in his seat. 'Just things I've heard. I've never been in there. I heard someone at work say a load of Goths and weirdoes hung out there. If you think Dad would have gone to a place like that, it's obvious you didn't know him.'

'So he's never been interested in the occult or anything like that?' He saw the shock on the widow's face. 'I'm sorry, but I have to ask.'

'Never,' Mrs Uckley said. 'Harry would never have had anything to do with that sort of thing.'

'No, of course not. I'm sorry.' Joe looked at the wounded expression on the woman's face and felt like a brute.

But Joe felt it was worth having one more go. He took out his a notebook and executed a rough sketch of the symbol they'd found in Jevons's office and Gloria Simpson's flat. 'Do you recognise this at all?' He held out the sketch so that mother and son could both see it.

But there was no reaction apart from a rather puzzled shaking of two heads. Joe looked carefully for some spark of recognition. But he saw nothing.

'Well, that was a waste of time,' he said to Emily as they walked down the neat front garden path. Both Uckleys had seen them off the premises, Ian hovering protectively at his mother's side.

'You win some, you lose some,' said Emily as she climbed into the car. 'I don't think Harold Uckley was a Satanist any more than Carla Yates was.'

Joe started the car. 'So what do you think?'

Emily thought for a moment. 'I think our man selected his victims at random. Carla was walking home on her own after a night out with her work colleagues and Harold was on his way to his local for a quiet drink. And Janna Pyke ... Well, who knows where she'd been? But there's no sign of a break-in or struggle in her flat so it's possible that she'd been out somewhere at night when there weren't many people around and she was abducted off the street too.'

Joe frowned. 'That's all we need ... a random killer taking people off the streets. What about Wendal?'

'We only associated him with the case because he worked in the same place as Uckley. The Eborby Permanent's a big employer. I'm beginning to think it's a coincidence. The two cases might not be linked at all.'

'Jevons had the symbol in his office.'

'So Jevons is associated with whatever's going on at the Black Hen So is Gloria ... and possibly Janna Pyke. But there's no evidence the other two were.'

'Back to square one then.'

'There's always the Archaeology Centre connection. The carrier bags.'

'And don't forget the transit van,' said Joe with a rueful smile. What they needed now was a bit of luck.

The message was still sitting on Joe's desk. Call George

Merryweather. He picked up the receiver but before he could dial the number Sunny Porter rushed in, looking as if he had news to impart.

'Just had the hospital on the phone. John Wendal's feeling better . . . says he wants to speak to someone. Do you want to go or . . .?'

Joe was on the verge of delegating the job to Sunny but his curiosity got the better of him. 'Yeah. I'll go. Fancy coming with me?'

Sunny shook his head. 'Nah. I've got to get down to that archaeology place and get a list of people who might have got their hands on their carrier bags. I'm starting with staff and any customers who've made at least two large purchases with credit cards or cheques. No way of tracing anyone who's paid in cash, unfortunately.'

'Don't forget the company who supply the bags.'

Sunny assumed a martyred expression. 'Give us a chance.'

'OK. Let us know how you get on.'

Joe put the receiver down. The call to George would have to wait until he returned from the hospital. The fact that Wendal wanted to talk to someone looked hopeful. Perhaps when they'd got this one out of the way things would become clearer.

When Joe arrived at the entrance to John Wendal's ward, he didn't know quite what to expect. Was he about to interview a rape suspect? Or maybe the Resurrection Man's accomplice?

But his misgivings were soon put to rest. He found Wendal propped up on a hill of snowy hospital pillows, his eyes closed. His wife, Sue, was sitting by his side, flicking through a magazine. She looked up when Joe greeted her and gave him a shy smile.

'How is he?' Joe whispered.

'He spends a lot of his time asleep but the doctors say he's doing well.' Her voice wavered between relief and a slight distrust of medical opinion. She leaned over and touched her husband's arm, now free of tubes and drips. 'Jack . . . Jack. It's the inspector from the police. You said you wanted to talk to him. Jack.'

The man's eyelids flickered open and he lay there for a few moments as though trying to familiarise himself with his surroundings. He turned his head towards Joe and attempted a smile.

'Good to see you're on the mend, Mr Wendal,' Joe began. 'Are you sure you feel up to talking?'

'Might as well get it over,' the man said in a hoarse whisper.

'I'll leave you to it,' said Sue Wendal, planting a soft kiss on her husband's forehead. She looked as if she was relieved to have someone there to give her a break from her vigil.

Joe sat down in the chair she had vacated. 'Can you tell me what happened?' he asked gently. He took his notebook from his pocket and prepared to write.

He studied the man. In his weakened state he hardly looked capable of participating in the things that had allegedly taken place at the Black Hen. But in health . . .? Well, many harmless-looking people, in Joe's experience, harboured dark secrets.

'There's not much to tell,' Wendal began before indicating that he wanted a drink of water. Joe poured some from the jug on the bedside locker and put the glass to his lips. When he had drunk a little, Wendal continued. 'I was driving along and this woman flagged me down. Her car was nearby and she said she'd run out of petrol and could I give her a lift to the nearest garage. I knew there was one a mile up the road so I said fine. Hop in. There was a man there walking his dog. He spoke to her. He'll be able to tell you what happened.'

'We've already spoken to him. Go on.'

'We were driving along and she seemed a bit edgy . . . a bit nervous. I thought I'd better put her at her ease so I said something like "my name's Jack Wendal, by the way" . . .'

The man lay back on his pillows, staring at the ceiling.

Joe helped him take another drink of water. 'And?' he prompted.

'I can't rightly remember what happened but suddenly all hell broke loose. She started screaming. I couldn't understand what she was saying but she was yelling in my ear, screaming like a banshee. I was bloody scared, I can tell you. Then she grabbed the wheel and I lost control of the car. The last thing I remember was hurtling towards some trees. After that it's all a blank.' He frowned and shook his head painfully. 'What made her do that? Was she mad or what?'

Joe didn't answer. 'She escaped from the psychiatric unit here and tried to kill you. Do you remember anything about it?'

'No, but they told me. I just can't understand it. I'd done nothing to her ... I'd not even seen her before that day. Why did she ...?'

'Ever seen this symbol before?' Joe showed him the sketch in his notebook, the same one he'd shown to the Uckleys.

'No. What is it?' was the puzzled reaction.

'Ever been to a pub called the Black Hen?'

'No. Never.'

'Ever heard the name Janna Pyke ... or Terry Jevons?'

'Can't say I have.

'You had a leaflet advertising the House of Terrors in your garage. Ever been there?'

He shook his head painfully. 'I found one lying about at the museum ... the railway museum where I'm a volunteer. I picked it up but I can't remember why. Maybe I thought it looked interesting. Can't remember what I did with it. I'm surprised I kept it.'

Something told Joe that the man was speaking the truth. 'Did you know Harold Uckley, the man who died a few weeks ago?'

'I knew he worked at the Permanent but I didn't know

him. It's a big place ... can't know everyone. Mind you, it was the talk of the office ... his murder. Dreadful. You're not safe anywhere these days.'

Joe stood up. His instincts told him that he had learned all he was going to learn. And besides, Wendal was looking tired. 'I'll leave you to rest,' he said. 'Thank you for your time, Mr Wendal.'

The man sank back on to his mountainous pillows, exhausted, and Joe suspected that he'd just been in the wrong place at the wrong time. Something had triggered Gloria Simpson's violent behaviour; something that had made sense to her. But that something might not have made sense to anyone else.

When he arrived back at the incident room Jamilla Dal came rushing up to him.

'You know I've been phoning round the names in Gloria Simpson's address book? Well, there was one number with no name by it, just the letter M. I called it but there was no answer. Then I got someone to trace the address.'

'And?'

'You know that man who manages the House of Terrors?'

'Terry Jevons? What about him?'

'Well, it's his number. Gloria Simpson knows him. But why did she list him under M, not T or J?'

Before Joe could reply the phone on his desk began to ring. He picked it up and heard Canon George Merryweather's voice on the other end of the line. He mouthed his thanks to Jamilla who scurried away, back to her post.

'Sorry I couldn't get back to you, George. I've been out most of the day. What did you want to tell me?'

'The name Jack Wendal. I was sure I'd come across it before but I couldn't think where. I found an old history of Eborby and it turns out that he was rather better known by another name – Jack Devilhorn. He was the son of a respectable cleric called the Reverend Charles Wendal ...

rather the black sheep of the family and a great disappointment to his parents, I imagine. Anyway, Jack Devilhorn – né Wendal – was an eighteenth-century highwayman who raped and murdered his way through Yorkshire and was hanged for his crimes at the old gallows that stood near the racecourse. He was involved in Satanic rituals at the Black Hen. There was even talk that he sold his soul to the devil.'

'Is it common knowledge that his real name was Wendal?' Joe asked, curious.

'I shouldn't think so. Jack Devilhorn's quite famous – or should I say notorious – but I think only aficionados of Eborby's darker history would be aware of his true identity.'

'Like the people who frequent the Black Hen?'

'Precisely.'

Joe thanked George for sharing his discovery – it explained a lot. And when he'd put the phone down, Joe sat for a while, considering the implications of George's revelation. Now it looked likely that the letters sent to Janna Pyke mentioning Jack Wendal had been threats from someone at the Black Hen. But threats about what? Perhaps someone wanted to ensure that Janna kept quiet about something she knew ... or something she'd seen. And Gloria Simpson's reaction to the name suggested that whatever had happened there was pretty terrible. Terrible enough to drive a vulnerable woman out of her mind. Maybe what she and Janna had witnessed was murder. Cold, brutal, slow and agonising murder.

The thought sent a shudder down Joe's spine, but human depravity had long ceased to surprise him. He stood up and walked over to Emily's office. She'd want to know about this development. But the office was empty and as Joe was about to close the door, his eyes were drawn to the child's painting pinned on the wall, especially to the tall stick figure with yellow hair labelled 'Daddy'. An innocent sight in a corrupt world. Emily had seemed to be under some strain lately and Joe wondered if it was something to do with her husband, Jeff – some marital difficulty perhaps.

But he hadn't time for idle speculation; he returned to his desk and dialled the number he had for the psychiatric unit . . . for Dr Brian Oakley. The doctor in charge of Gloria Simpson's case should be told of his new discovery about Jack Wendal, the possible trigger for her actions. And perhaps he'd be able to wheedle out of Gloria the truth about what actually happened to Carla Yates, Harold Uckley and Janna Pyke. Janna had been hiding, but now it seemed that whoever had been threatening her had finally caught up with her.

And all roads led to Terry Jevons and the Black Hen. Joe had been so busy that he hadn't had time to organise a search of that particular pub. But he reckoned he should move it up to the top of his list of priorities.

Dr Oakley, he was told, wasn't available. He was with a patient. Joe looked at his watch, disappointed. It would have to wait until tomorrow. And besides, he wanted to pick Maddy Owen's brains about carrier bags.

As he turned the key in the door of the House of Terrors, Terry Jevons looked round. There was a white van directly outside the building, parked illegally, blocking his view of the shops opposite.

Jevons patted his trouser pocket, making sure he had the key to the special place. But he felt nothing. He must have left it inside. Cursing under his breath, he retraced his steps and unlocked the door, not bothering to lock it again behind him because he knew he'd only be a few seconds.

He didn't hear the soft footsteps on the worn stone flags following him as he passed through the darkened torture chamber. He was too preoccupied with what he had to do – and what he anticipated doing that night – to sense that he wasn't alone, that someone was behind him, breathing lightly, creeping on tiptoe.

The blow came unexpectedly. The sudden shock of a heavy object making contact with his skull knocked him forward then, after a few numb seconds, a searing pain engulfed him. He crumpled to the ground in a daze and, as he attempted to rise, he felt strong arms clawing at his clothes. Limbs flailing, he tried desperately to fight them off but his efforts were rewarded with another, harder blow, a blow that rendered him senseless.

When he surfaced into semi-consciousness, he felt the floor, hard and unforgiving against his flesh. To his surprise he found that he was naked. And when he tried to push himself up he couldn't move because he was bound, hand and foot, and there was a gag of some kind cutting into his mouth. His throat was sore and dry as sandpaper as he made a feeble attempt to summon help. But the noise he made was barely audible and he could only lie, trussed and helpless, awaiting his fate.

Then, through terrified, tearful eyes he saw the figure bending over him.

And the last thing he saw on this earth was his captor's rapturous smile.

Chapter Fifteen

The house seemed curiously quiet as Emily Thwaite stepped into the hall. Only the muffled babble of the TV in the living room at the back of the house intruded into the silence. Jeff usually came out to meet her as soon as he heard her key in the door. Then he would switch on the microwave where her evening meal waited for her, congealing, while she tiptoed upstairs to say goodnight to the children.

Perhaps he hadn't heard her, she thought as she pushed the living-room door open. Perhaps he was sitting there in his usual chair, engrossed in some documentary or other.

But as she stepped into the room she saw that Jeff wasn't there. Instead their new next-door neighbour, Mrs Jenkins, rose from the sofa with a cautious smile of greeting.

'You're back then.' Mrs Jenkins, a plump grandmother with the round, rosy-cheeked face of a nursery-rhyme farmer's wife, gathered up the trio of women's magazines she had brought with her to pass the time. 'They're in bed. Good as gold, they were. I said to your husband . . . any time you want me to pop in and look after them, I'm only too happy . . .'

'Thanks, Mrs Jenkins. That's really good of you,' said Emily humbly. Willing babysitters were to be prized and nurtured like precious orchids. 'Er . . . did Jeff say where he was going?'

'He just said he had to go out and asked if I'd sit with the kiddies till you came in. Didn't tell me where he was going and I didn't ask.'

Emily, hoping she hadn't given Mrs Jenkins the impression that all was not well in the marital home, smiled sweetly. 'He'll probably be back soon. Would you like a cup of tea?' The strict laws of Yorkshire hospitality had to be observed.

'No, thank you. I'd better get back to my Norman.' Mrs Jenkins always talked about her husband as though he was completely dependent on her, like a child or an invalid, in spite of the fact that Norman was a hale and hearty sixty-eight-year-old who worked hard in his garden and ran the occasional half marathon.

Emily saw her out and watched as she let herself into her front door. According to Mrs Jenkins, who repeated the mantra each time they met, 'you can't be too careful with this killer about'. Emily was glad she hadn't said it tonight – she felt bad enough as it was.

After creeping upstairs to check on the children, two of whom were fast asleep while the eldest was reading the latest Harry Potter, Emily poured herself a glass of red wine from the open bottle in the kitchen. Then she settled down on the sofa Mrs Jenkins had just vacated and took some reports out of her briefcase. But she found she couldn't concentrate. She kept glancing at the clock, wondering where Jeff had got to.

At eleven she felt her eyes closing but she felt she couldn't go to bed until he was home. She kept looking at the clock. Eleven ten. Eleven fifteen. Eleven twenty. Then eventually, at eleven twenty-five, she heard his key in the door and she leapt off the sofa and rushed out into the hall.

'Where have you been?' was her first question. She tried to sound casual, to keep the anxiety she felt out of her voice. 'And what's that on your shirt? It looks like blood.'

Jeff avoided her eyes. He looked pale and a little shaken. 'There was a bit of trouble at the pub. Someone broke a bottle and thrust it at someone's arm. Don't know what it was all about but . . .'

'Which pub?' she asked.

'Drayman's Arms. I had a call from someone I taught with in Leeds . . . he's in Eborby visiting his brother.'

'What's his name? Do I know him?'

It might have been her imagination but she was sure she had seen a brief flash of panic cross her husband's face. 'I shouldn't think so.'

'What subject did he teach?'

There was a moment's hesitation. 'Er . . . modern languages.' He looked down at his pale-blue denim shirt, spattered with blood. 'I'll put this in to soak, shall I?'

He turned to leave the room but she caught hold of his arm, gripping it tight. 'When was the last time you saw Jane Pyke?'

Jeff's jaw dropped open. He shook off her clinging hand and took a step back. 'Not since . . . I swear, I haven't seen her since she . . .'

'You haven't seen her since we've been in Eborby?'

'Of course not. I swear.'

'Where were you the other night . . . the night before her body was found?'

'You know where I was – I told you before. I went to the supermarket and then I had to queue up for petrol.' Jeff shook his head in disbelief. 'This is bloody ridiculous.'

Her fingers fluttered towards his sleeve. 'I'm sorry. It's just that . . .'

Jeff put his hands on her shoulders, his face close to hers. 'Don't you see, Em? This is exactly what she loved to do . . . to cause trouble. How come she can even get to me from beyond the grave?'

Tears started to prick Emily's eyes. 'I'm investigating her murder. I'm in charge of the case and I don't know how much longer I can keep your name out of it.'

Jeff clenched his fists. 'You know I can't face going over all that again. Try. Please.'

Emily turned away from her husband, wiping a stinging tear away with the back of her hand. And that night she hardly slept at all.

Joe Plantagenet had rung Maddy Owen about the Archaeology Centre carrier bags that afternoon, to see whether she had any suggestions about who might have access to them and to cover any ground Sunny might have missed. Of course it might have been better to ask the person in charge of the shop . . . but he'd wanted another excuse to talk to Maddy, to hear her voice again. Once the questions were out of the way, he'd found himself asking what she was doing that evening and she'd told him she was planning to go round to Carmel Hennessy's flat. She was a little concerned about Carmel, even though the girl kept assuring her that she was fine.

After the call, Joe had felt uncomfortable. The old guilt kept nagging away. The psychologist he'd seen after Kevin's death predicted that he'd feel guilty because he'd survived while Kevin hadn't and he supposed that feeling responsible for Kevin's daughter was all part of the same syndrome.

As soon as he'd arrived home, Maddy called on his mobile to say that Carmel had invited him to join them for a takeaway that evening. Joe was surprised that he felt a thrill of eager anticipation as he examined his image in the mirror and sprayed on the expensive aftershave he'd received from his sister at Christmas. Even though he'd been thinking of Maddy a great deal, he hadn't expected to feel like a callow teenager at the prospect of seeing her again. But life has a habit of surprising you when you least expect it.

It was Maddy who answered the front door of five Vicars Green when he arrived at eight, armed with a bottle of red wine. He'd heard her footsteps thudding down the carpeted stairs and when she opened the door wearing a little denim dress and a wide smile, his pulse rate increased.

She led the way upstairs. 'I ordered Chinese . . . is that all right?' she asked and Joe nodded. Chinese was fine.

When they reached the flat, Carmel stood up and greeted him with a kiss on the cheek and thanked him for coming as Maddy bustled into the kitchen to fetch the plates.

Joe sat down opposite Carmel. 'No more trouble with funny phone calls and letters?'

Carmel gave him a shy smile. 'No. Whoever it was must have heard that Janna Pyke's dead by now.' She shuddered. 'Are you any nearer catching who . . .?'

'We're doing our best.' He hoped he hadn't sounded too defensive.

'I've been feeling pretty nervous when I'm in the flat alone.'

'There's someone downstairs, isn't there?'

'Yes . . . Mr Peace. And his niece, Elizabeth, is there quite a bit. She's very nice.' She gave a shy smile. 'And Tavy's been round a few times.'

'Good,' he said automatically, uncertain whether Tavy's presence was a good thing or not.

'Is Tavy—?' She stopped herself in mid-sentence.

'Is Tavy what?'

'I know it's a strange thing to ask, but is he on your list of suspects?'

Joe leapt on the question. 'You don't trust him?'

'Of course I do. There's no way he could do anything like that.'

She didn't sound altogether convinced and Joe suddenly felt sorry for the girl. She was experiencing misgivings . . . asking herself if she could trust her instincts. But what could he tell her? Tavy McNair wasn't top of their list of suspects, such as it was, at the moment. But he had been going out with Janna Pyke and he'd had some involvement with the Black Hen so he hadn't been ruled out of their investigation. 'You'll have to make your own mind up,' he said to Carmel gently. 'All I can say is that we don't intend to arrest him in the immediate future.'

'But that could change?'

'I really don't know.' He saw the look of disappointment on her face but what else could he have said? He had to be honest. If he'd assured her of Tavy's innocence and then they found evidence against him, she'd have been off her guard. And vigilance was all important.

'My mum's been on the phone, panicking. At least I can tell her you've been round . . . keeping an eye on me.' She grinned and he smiled back as though there was a conspiracy between them to keep Sandra happy.

Joe was relieved when Maddy entered the room with three glasses and a bottle of wine. 'The Happy Dragon said it'd be half an hour.'

Maddy sat by Joe. It was a small sofa and their bodies touched. She made no attempt to move away and neither did he. She turned her head towards him and smiled. 'One of your colleagues came round to the centre just after you phoned, asking more questions about those carrier bags.'

Joe glanced at Carmel. 'What was it all about?' she asked. It seemed the information hadn't filtered down to her.

Joe hesitated. There was no way he could dress this up prettily in tactful words and euphemisms. 'The clothes of the Resurrection Man's first two victims were found in Archaeology Centre carrier bags. We're checking who could have got hold of them . . .'

Carmel's hand went up to her mouth. 'You mean it might be someone who works with us?'

'Not necessarily,' said Joe quickly. 'It could be someone who's bought large items in the shop . . . or someone from the firm that supplies the bags. We've got to cover all possibilities.'

Maddy frowned. 'I can't think of anyone at the centre who could possibly be a killer.'

Joe looked at Maddy. 'Is there anyone at all who might have any connection with the Black Hen?'

Maddy thought for a few moments and shook her head. 'We've got plenty of amiable eccentrics there but nobody seriously weird. Most people tend to drink at the Mitre near the cathedral and I've certainly never heard anyone mentioning the Black Hen.' She looked at Carmel for confirmation and she nodded. She had visited the Mitre with her new colleagues a couple of times and had found them an unthreatening bunch.

'Our boss, Peta Thewlis, was Janna Pyke's landlady,' said Maddy. 'That's a connection. Mind you, I can't see Peta in a place like the Black Hen ... or murdering anyone for that matter.'

'What's Peta like?'

Maddy glanced at Carmel and pulled a face. 'She's known as Frosty Thewlis. Not exactly approachable. But I can't see her being involved in anything dodgy. Anyway, she told me once she doesn't go out much. She has to look after her son.'

'How old is he?'

'I'm not sure exactly, but he's grown up ... not a child. I think he's disabled in some way but she never talks about it. Her husband walked out a few years ago.'

'I feel sorry for her,' said Carmel softly, giving Maddy a critical glance.

'Yes,' said Joe. 'Given her circumstances, it's hardly surprising that the poor woman's not the life and soul of the party.'

Maddy looked uncomfortable but she made noises of agreement. She didn't like Peta Thewlis but it seemed churlish to say so in the face of the woman's misfortunes.

The subject of murder was avoided for the rest of the evening and at ten thirty Joe walked Maddy home.

As they made their way back to her house together, their hands hardly touching, Joe found himself dreading the return to his own small, lonely flat that night. The way he was feeling, he needed some company. He hoped she'd ask him in. He hoped she'd ask him to stay. But he'd always had a fear of taking things too quickly so he said nothing. And when they arrived at Maddy's front door she stood on tiptoe and kissed him on the cheek. She had to work in the morning. Would he ring her soon?

He said he would and, as he watched her disappear into the house, he experienced a feeling of disappointment . . . and deep loneliness.

The hinges on the great iron door of the Gosson Mausoleum had been well oiled and, as it yielded to a firm push, it swung open silently.

The killer had parked the van on the path and opened the back doors, using a torch to see what he was doing as there was no moon that night. The coffin lay there on the shelf just inside the door, open, welcoming, waiting to be fed. It wouldn't take him long to die. They never took very long, although he wouldn't come back for a while . . . just to be sure.

The folded trolley was pitted with rust but still perfectly usable. He manoeuvred it out from beside the coffin and pulled it up until the catch gave a satisfying snap before wheeling it out to the van and opening the rear doors. A parcel, the size and shape of a man, lay on the van floor and the killer stood for a moment, contemplating what was to come. Then, after a few moments of pleasurable anticipation, he dragged the parcel out on to the trolley and wheeled it slowly towards the gaping entrance of the mausoleum, which stood waiting to devour the victim like the jaws of death.

Once the coffin had been closed he stood and listened. He could hear faint sounds of movement . . . flutterings and muffled groans. The victim was coming round. The sound of the chains being wrapped around the box shattered the stale air and the killer looked round nervously as though he was afraid that the noise would wake the rows of decaying Gossons ranged around the walls.

He smiled to himself as he locked the mausoleum door

behind him. Another one done. In a few days it would be time to chose an appropriate resting place . . . a churchyard where the dead could be at peace.

But in the meantime, there were things he had to do.

Chapter Sixteen

Joe rang the hospital as soon as Emily's morning briefing was over. He wanted to speak to Dr Oakley as soon as possible. However, Oakley's secretary told him that the doctor wasn't available until the afternoon. She'd call him as soon as Oakley was free, she said, as though she was doing him a great favour.

Feeling restless at this change to his intended schedule, Joe started flicking through the papers on his desk.

One name leapt out. Janna Pyke. The other victims seemed to have been ordinary, innocent people, possibly chosen by the killer at random. But there was something different about Janna. He remembered years ago, when he was a child, his mother commenting in passing that some local girl who'd gone off the rails was 'the sort of girl who gets herself murdered'. He didn't understand then how his mother had reached this harsh judgement, but in the case of Janna Pyke he suspected that the phrase might just be appropriate. She had been involved with some dubious people, she had received threats, she had been sleeping with her married tutor, she had given her parents hell. Janna Pyke was trouble. Probably had been since the day she was born.

He stared at the file on her murder, deep in thought. He had once read a book in which a killer murdered a series of innocent people unconnected with him just so that he could make the murder he actually wanted to commit look like the work of a serial killer. What if the Resurrection Man had only wanted to dispose of Janna Pyke, and the others – Carla Yates and Harold Uckley – had just been in the wrong place at the wrong time and had been killed to provide some sort of smokescreen? It was a sobering thought and he wondered if he should run it past Emily Thwaite when she returned from her meeting with the Superintendent. However, on second thoughts it seemed too far-fetched; the stuff of fiction rather than fact. But then truth was often stranger than fiction, so they said.

In the meantime he felt that it would do no harm to discover more about Janna's life. He looked through his notes and the name Gemma caught his eye: Janna's old school friend, now employed in the Happy Fryer chip shop on the Tadcaster Road. He smiled to himself. It wouldn't take long to pay Gemma a visit.

He made it to the Happy Fryer in forty minutes but when he arrived he found the place locked with a grubby 'closed' sign hanging in the window. He hammered on the door and his efforts summoned up a thin girl with peroxide hair and a nylon overall who emerged from a door behind the counter and unlocked the door as though she was a zoo keeper about to enter the cage of a particularly fearsome beast.

'We're not open till twelve. You'll have to come back,' she mumbled gracelessly, avoiding his eyes.

He held up his warrant card. 'You Gemma?'

The girl's eyes widened and she nodded. 'Is it about Jane?' she asked. 'I heard about it on the news. It's bloody awful. I just can't believe it.'

'Can I come in?'

She wavered for a second as though she was afraid that inviting a policeman in was inviting trouble. Then she stood aside. A man shouted through from the back of the shop, asking who it was, but Gemma called back that it was OK, it was for her, before sitting down at a spindly Formica table by the window. Joe took a seat opposite her and gave her an encouraging smile to put her at her ease.

'You knew Jane well?' he began.

'Suppose I did at one time. I left school and she stayed on – she were dead brainy. We stayed mates for a while but when she went to Manchester – to university – we lost touch.'

'Was she always interested in the occult?'

'The what?'

'The occult. Black magic, ghosts, that sort of thing.'

'Suppose she was. Aye.'

Joe carried on asking the questions, getting answers that weren't particularly relevant or exciting. Gemma hadn't heard from Jane for years . . . hadn't even known she was in Eborby. Jane Pyke had made no effort to keep in touch with her old school friend. She had moved on and, of late, they'd inhabited different worlds. He'd had a wasted journey.

But just as he was about to cut his losses and leave, he remembered something. 'Jane's mum and dad said she'd caused trouble at school. What did she mean?'

Gemma's eyes lit up at the prospect of gossip. 'She had this teacher in the sixth form. He were quite fit . . . dishy like . . . and she had a bit of a thing about him. She got a bit obsessed if you ask me. Any road, she put it about that she were having it off with him.'

'Why?'

'She did that sort of thing . . . made trouble for people . . . thought it were a laugh. Any road, the head got to hear somehow and the teacher got suspended or whatever you call it. He were off work for a year and Jane stuck to her story . . . played the little victim.' She snorted. 'And the head believed every word, stupid bugger.'

'But you didn't?'

Gemma laughed. 'Did I heck as like? I knew Jane. She were enjoying every minute.'

'But you never thought to tell the head she was lying?'

'She were my mate,' she said by way of explanation as if the schoolgirls' code of honour excused everything. 'Any road, I'd left school by then.'

'So what happened?'

'Well, the teacher, he had some sort of breakdown. I heard later that he was in a bad way . . . in hospital, like. Then one of the other girls decided it had all got out of hand and went to tell the head it were a pack of lies.'

'And Jane?'

'She admitted it . . . eventually.'

'What happened to the teacher?'

'They said he could go back but he never did and I can't say I blame him. I heard he got a job at another school.'

'Do you remember the teacher's name?'

Gemma thought for a while. 'Timmons . . . Mr Timmons.'

'What was he like?'

'He were right dishy, like I said. Tall and blond. He were all right.'

'Not once Jane Pyke had got her claws into him he wasn't,' mattered Joe under his breath.

The shop at the Archaeology Centre sold strange and fascinating things: things unavailable on your average high street, such as reproduction Roman Samian ware bowls and imitation medieval tapestries, reduced to a size that would fit into the modern home. Carmel Hennessy loved this Aladdin's cave of unusual treasures but the only things she had purchased there so far were a small stone gargoyle for her mother's birthday and some wrapping paper decorated with medieval script.

On her way from the office to the education room, she halted at the shop's entrance, full of curiosity. A pair of uniformed constables were talking to the girl at the counter. Normally, Carmel would have assumed there were problems with shoplifters or dodgy credit cards, but she knew they'd come about the murders. The thought that the

Resurrection Man had used the shop's distinctive carrier bags to dispose of his victims' clothing made her shudder. It meant the killer was close at hand. It could be anyone: one of the archaeologists, perhaps; or one of the men who dressed in costume to demonstrate ancient crafts to the visitors; or the friendly security man who always bade everyone a cheery goodnight at the end of each day. It could be any one of them. And the thought brought a chill to her heart.

It was coming up to lunchtime and she was starting to develop a headache. If she nipped back to her flat, took a couple of paracetamol and lay down for half an hour, she knew she'd be OK.

As she hurried toward the entrance, Peta Thewlis came out of her office. Her face was pinched and drawn as though she'd not slept, but then there were police crawling all over the place asking questions and wanting to see sales records and CCTV footage. Peta was in charge so it wasn't surprising that she was feeling the strain.

Carmel walked back to the flat, hoping the fresh air might clear her head. But the narrow streets were packed and the hubbub of noise trapped in by the shops' overhanging upper storeys only made the throbbing in her temples worse. When she reached the quieter expanse of Vicars Green she walked across the grass, making straight for number five, her key to the ready.

But as she opened the front door she sensed that something wasn't right. The door to Conrad Peace's flat stood open and she could hear a sound – a faint moaning like a small animal in pain. Her headache suddenly forgotten, she stepped over the threshold, calling Conrad's name, softly at first, then louder.

The sound seemed to be coming from the living room. Carmel took a deep breath and pushed the door open. There, on the floor in the small neat room, she saw Conrad Peace lying on the patterned carpet, curled up in the foetal position, his eyes closed, his breathing shallow, a set of keys clutched in his hand as though he had collapsed as soon as he had reached the safety of home.

Carmel took a step towards him. 'Conrad. Are you all right?' She knew as soon as the words had left her lips that it was a stupid question.

The man moaned softly and moved his hand a little. Carmel leaned over and touched his wrist, feeling for a pulse. Being no expert in medical matters, she reckoned he was alive but only just, so she mumbled something banal and soothing and searched for a telephone. She needed an ambulance.

The drama of the situation having driven her headache away, she waited with the old man, talking to him gently, unwilling to leave his side in case he took a turn for the worse. She guessed that he had suffered some sort of stroke or heart attack and she glanced at her watch every few seconds, wondering what was keeping the emergency services.

Suddenly it struck her that she should tell Elizabeth. She would want to know as soon as possible and, she thought with a twinge of guilt, it would take the responsibility off her shoulders. Leaving the patient's side, she hurried into the living room and, as luck would have it, she found a battered address book lying by the telephone. As she began to turn the pages, she realised she didn't know Elizabeth's surname, but she gambled on her number being either at the front in a place of importance or under E for Elizabeth. Fortunately she was right on the second count. Elizabeth's name was there beside two numbers, one with the word 'work' in brackets beside it.

She guessed Elizabeth would be at the hospital at this hour of the day, so she dialled the work number and a female voice answered.

'Is that Elizabeth?'

'She's just popped out of the office. Can I take a message?'

Carmel hesitated. Should she blurt out the whole story to

this stranger or should she wait and tell Elizabeth direct? 'When do you think she'll be back?' she asked.

'She's around somewhere. She shouldn't be long.'

This decided Carmel. She would wait to break the news. 'Can you ask her to ring me back as soon as possible on her uncle's number. It's urgent.'

'Hang on. I'm just trying to find some paper.' Carmel heard the scraping of wood on wood as a drawer opened. 'OK. Go ahead.'

'My name's Carmel Hennessy and I live at five Vicars Green.' She recited the phone number. 'Please get her to call me. Tell her it's very urgent.' She could hear the girl – she presumed it was a girl as the voice sounded remarkably youthful – repeating her words as she wrote them down carefully. 'Carmel Hennessy. Five Vicars Green. Urgent.'

Carmel, suddenly doubting the girl's reliability, thought she'd better have another go at emphasising the importance of her call. 'Look, can you try and find her. Like I said, it's really very urgent.'

The girl hesitated. 'OK. I'll do that.'

'Thanks,' said Carmel, hoping the girl would keep her word. As she replaced the receiver, she heard the shriek of the ambulance siren. Then, just as she was letting the paramedics into the flat, the phone began to ring. Her message to Elizabeth had got through.

Emily was out of the office. She was attending a press conference, urging anyone with any information about the Resurrection Man murders to come forward. Appeals like that sometimes worked and sometimes didn't. But it was worth a try. Someone was out talking to everyone employed by the Archaeology Centre and Sunny was following up the supplier of the carrier bags. Things were moving. Joe Plantagenet only hoped they were moving in the right direction.

When he returned to the incident room, he found Jamilla

sitting staring at a TV screen, her chin resting on her hands, a glazed look in her eyes.

'How's it going?' he asked.

She glanced up, then returned her gaze to the screen. 'CCTV footage from a shop that was on Carla Yates's route home. We were lucky to get it. Someone had shoved some of the old tapes at the back of a cupboard so they weren't recorded over.'

'Seen anything interesting?'

'Not yet.'

'Keep up the good work,' he said lightly before making for his desk.

On his way he passed the open door of Emily's office and peeped in, just in case she'd returned from her press conference without letting him know. He wanted to tell someone what he'd discovered from Gemma about Janna Pyke's background ... although he really couldn't see that it was relevant that she'd made some teacher's life a misery all those years ago.

The office was empty but the sight of children's pictures on the wall made him smile. There had been two new additions to DCI Thwaite's little art gallery: a creature that bore a passing resemblance to a rabbit and a figure with yellow hair and an unnaturally large head labelled 'Mummy'.

Then it struck him like a thunderbolt. The young artists' full names were printed underneath this new handiwork. Matthew Timmons and Daniel Timmons. Timmons. Emily's surname was Thwaite. But then women often kept their unmarried names in their professional life. According to Gemma, Jane Pyke had persecuted a teacher called Timmons in Leeds. Emily's husband was a teacher. And she had come to Eborby from Leeds.

His heart beat faster. He had to speak to her. He had to ask her if her husband was the man Jane Pyke persecuted. But he must be. Joe didn't believe in coincidences. And Emily had seemed worried recently ... ever since Janna Pyke's body had turned up.

Jamilla interrupted his thoughts. 'Sir. I think I've found something.' There was a hint of excitement in her voice which made Joe hurry over to her desk.

'What is it?'

Jamilla pressed a button and the picture rolled forward slowly, frame by frame. 'I think that's Carla Yates. Look.'

'You're right. I recognise the clothes.' Carla Yates was hurrying down a street that Joe recognised as Goldgate, a street of cut-price stores and heavy traffic just outside the city's pedestrianised area. She was walking purposefully, clutching her shoulder bag as though she feared it might be snatched at any moment. Joe couldn't make out the expression on her face but the body language told him that she intended to head straight for her destination. No stopping; no deviation. The pub where she spent her last evening was nearby and she was on the exact route Joe would have expected anyone to take who was heading for the Museum Gardens to catch the Hasledon bus. But as Jamilla let the tape roll in slow motion, he spotted something. A white transit van parked at the side of the road. A few seconds after Carla had passed it and had disappeared from the camera's range, the van began to move after her very slowly, almost at a crawl.

'That's it,' Jamilla whispered. 'The van. It's following her.'

Joe reran the tape. It certainly looked that way.

'But if the killer's in the van, we still don't know whether he's targeting her or whether he's just been waiting for any likely-looking victim to come by. If it was that van he must have followed the bus . . . waited till she got off and . . .' Joe stared at the screen. 'Is that something on the side of the van?'

'There is something but I can't tell what it is.'

Jamilla let the tape roll forward a few frames. 'There. It looks like the edge of a letter but the rest of it seems to be covered up by something.' She leaned forward. 'I can just see the outline of the driver.'

'Is it my eyes or has he got a good head of hair?'
Jamilla smiled. 'Certainly looks like it.'
'Could it be a woman?'
Jamilla frowned. 'A woman couldn't do that. Surely.'
Joe said nothing. He knew that in this world anything was possible, any evil, any depravity. And the female of the species wasn't exempt. But somehow this didn't seem like a woman's crime. And whoever manoeuvred the bodies around and dumped them in churchyards had to be physically strong . . . powerful even. Unless he – or she – had help.
He looked at his watch. He had rung first thing to check when Dr Oakley would be available to talk about Gloria Simpson. He was awaiting a call to say the doctor was free but he wanted to speak to Emily first – to put his mind at rest.
'See if there are any cameras on Boargate,' he told Jamilla. 'Some of them might have picked up Janna Pyke's last journey.'
Jamilla nodded, resigned to more tedious viewing.

Joe waited in the office for Emily's return. He needed to talk to her, to find out whether her husband was the same Timmons who'd been involved with Jane Pyke in Leeds. But before he had the opportunity, he received a call from Dr Oakley to say that he was available at last. He hadn't been an easy man to corner, busy as he was with his patients and the hospital's bureaucracy. However, when Joe told him that he had some important information, something he should know, he was happy to spare him ten minutes.
This time Joe made sure he was parked in a legal space – he had no wish to relive the humiliating experience of being clamped. When he arrived at Dr Oakley's office, the seat normally occupied by the doctor's secretary was vacant and Joe had to give a bold rap on the psychiatrist's office door to announce his arrival.
Oakley shook his hand heartily and invited him to sit

down and make himself comfortable.

'Elizabeth, my secretary's been called away, I'm afraid – a family emergency – but I'll see if I can track down a cup of tea,' he said, making for the door before Joe could protest that tea wasn't necessary. But Oakley appeared again after a couple of minutes with a 'mission accomplished' smile on his face but no cups.

'Now then,' he said as he sat down again. 'You said you had important information for me.'

Joe proceeded to relate George Merryweather's discovery. 'I think that's why Gloria Simpson reacted the way she did when John Wendal introduced himself – she associated him with this historic Jack Devilhorn whose real name was Wendal. Do you agree?'

Oakley's eyes flickered with something akin to recognition. Then he rearranged his features into a mask of neutrality and nodded sagely. 'I think it's very possible.' He paused for a few moments, staring at the pen resting in his hand. 'I'm beginning to gain Gloria's trust at last and she told me . . .' He suddenly stopped, as though he'd just remembered the small problem of patient confidentiality. 'Well, of course I can't repeat what she said but . . .'

'Was a place called the Black Hen mentioned?'

Oakley raised his eyebrows. 'It might have been.'

'Am I right in thinking she'd witnessed something there? And that she received threats to ensure her silence?'

'Possibly' was the tantalising answer.

'How is she?'

'Traumatised. But we hope that given time and the right medication . . .'

Joe had a sudden thought. 'Have you any other patients who are involved in the goings-on at the Black Hen?'

Oakley expression gave nothing away. 'I might have.'

After taking out his notebook, Joe found the page on which he'd copied the symbol he'd found in Gloria's flat. He pushed it across the desk towards the psychiatrist. 'Is this symbol familiar?'

Oakley hesitated, then nodded. 'I've come across it on a number of occasions, yes.'

'Through your patients?'

There was a long silence before Oakley spoke. 'I can't give details, of course, but a few of my patients who have been involved in the occult seem to use it,' he said with distaste. 'I believe it's a local symbol used by a certain kind of Satanism. Some appear to use it as a sort of badge and others seem terrified of it.'

'Including Gloria Simpson?'

'You know I can't discuss individual patients, Inspector.'

'Do you think it's linked to the Black Hen?'

There was another long pause. 'Possibly.'

They were interrupted by the arrival of a young woman bearing two cups of tea. As soon as Oakley had thanked her she told him that he had a patient waiting. He'd turned up early for his appointment.

Joe spent a few minutes trying to tease more information out of Oakley without much success. If ever the questions became awkward, Oakley pleaded patient confidentiality. Resigned to the stalemate, Joe stood up to go as soon as he'd finished his tea.

As he left the office, he saw a young man waiting outside, his shaved head bowed, staring at his trainers. Joe sneaked a surreptitious look. The young man was tall and strong and his large hands bore the signs of manual labour. His hands and arms were decorated with a variety of self-inflicted tattoos. A skull, an inverted cross, a pentagram. Then Joe noticed that the skin on his right forearm was a mess of cuts and angry scabs as though he'd tried to obliterate one of his tattoos. Joe's eyes were drawn to the injuries and he couldn't help noticing that the shape of the affected area was similar to the symbol he'd just been discussing with Dr Oakley.

He was almost tempted to sit down beside the young man and ask him about it. But the man looked up and the pale-blue eyes that met his were blank and hostile. And there was something else behind his stare. Fear perhaps ... Joe couldn't tell.

Emily Thwaite stared at the telephone for several minutes trying to summon the courage to call Pickby police station to ask if there had been a fight at the Drayman's Arms the previous night. But she decided against it. There was no reason to suppose that another victim had been attacked on the night Jeff turned up with blood on his shirt ... no reason at all. She was being stupid. She was letting her imagination run away with her. But the discovery that one of the Resurrection Man's victims was Jane Pyke, the one-time scourge of Jeff's life, had thrown her off balance.

Jeff was her husband. She trusted him. However, in the course of her career she'd known enough model husbands who'd been driven to do unspeakable things. Emily had never actually met Jane Pyke in life but, from what she knew of her, she imagined that she could have driven a saint to murder. But even if Jane had made contact somehow and goaded Jeff again until he lost control, there was no way he could have harmed the others. They were innocent people. And then there was the way they were killed.

She shook her head and opened the file that was lying in front of her on the desk. She must be crazy if she thought, even for one second, that Jeff was involved. But even so, it would probably be wise to keep quiet – not to mention his link with Jane Pyke to the rest of the team. The last thing Jeff needed was for the most traumatic time of his life to be resurrected, for old wounds to be picked at by probing questions until they became raw and painful once more. It would only complicate matters. Silence was best.

'Ma'am.'

Sunny Porter's voice made her jump. She took a deep breath and looked up. 'Yes, Sunny. What is it?'

'I've been on to the company that makes the carrier bags for that Archaeology Centre. When they come off the production line they're automatically wrapped in plastic in packs of a hundred or so. They don't just have spare ones floating about. And besides, the firm's in Manchester.'

'There's the M62,' Emily said hopefully.

'Yeah but . . .'

'OK, Sunny, I take your point. It's unlikely. Someone's still going through the list of purchases from the shop?'

Sunny nodded. 'What about employees, ma'am?'

'We're getting everyone who works there to give an account of their movements on the days in question.'

'So it's just a matter of keeping our fingers crossed that this Resurrection Man doesn't take it into his head to kill again in the meantime?'

Emily looked up and attempted a smile. The last thing she needed at that moment was DS Sunny Porter's optimism.

The bonds were tight, cutting off the circulation to Terry Jevons's wrists and ankles. And he felt sick and light-headed. The air was running out.

There was an exhibit in the House of Terrors . . . a reconstruction of a Victorian tomb with a bell above it so that if someone was mistakenly buried alive they could give the signal to the living that all was not well. But here there was no bell . . . and no escape. Just a pitch-black tomb. And death.

He could feel his life ebbing away and he was seized with the bitter thought that it shouldn't have been him who was facing death . . . it should have been the woman. It should have been Gloria. Her life should have drained away with her blood as the greatest taboo of all was broken. Death. He had been so looking forward to it, to wielding that ultimate power. But now the tables had been turned.

He thought of that night when the lights had gone out and the terror had begun. The woman, Gloria, had started screaming while the girl, Amy, had been paralysed, unable to speak . . . as if she had glimpsed hell itself.

In that dark room at the back of the Black Hen he had brought Jack Wendal amongst them – they called him by his real name at the Black Hen: Jack Devilhorn was for tourists – and then Wendal in his flesh, the flesh of the Master, had enjoyed the girl's body. They had touched evil.

And he had planned to go even further, to push the boundaries to their very limit. Everyone had drawn straws for the privilege of taking part in the ultimate ritual and Gloria had drawn the shortest. He had never seen anyone so terrified. But when she had run out he had stood there smiling as if he had some secret knowledge . . . an insight into their souls. He knew she'd be back. She wouldn't be able to resist it.

He had heard rumours that the girl, Amy, had seen a priest . . . the enemy. And a psychiatrist too. The rumours said that Gloria had gone mad and attacked some innocent motorist who'd offered her a lift. The local paper had said that the motorist's name was John Wendal, commonly known as Jack. What an unfortunate coincidence. A turn of fate that would almost be funny if the consequences hadn't been so tragic. The parents of this John Wendal had had no idea what they were doing when they'd given him the same name as the evil one. But they'd had no involvement in the Black Hen's dark world so how could they have known? John Wendal had been in the wrong place at the wrong time and the two worlds – the dark and the everyday – had collided. His name had been his misfortune.

In his domain at the House of Terrors and the Black Hen, amongst his fearful faithful, Terry Jevons had felt all powerful. Even the police hadn't been able to touch him. But now he lay there naked, his flesh soiled with his own excrement, he began to cry, dry, painful tears as he gasped for breath.

It was almost over. And the devil would soon receive his own.

The killer had received the signal loud and clear. Although

he hadn't expected the next one to be named so soon.

Another woman. He liked the women. He liked returning to them after a few hours and lifting the lid. He experienced such ecstasy as he looked into their pleading, helpless eyes, ecstasy that always resulted in an explosion of pleasure in his loins. He sometimes wondered whether he would do it for his own satisfaction if there were no more tasks for him to perform; no more servants of evil to dispose of because they presented a threat to the world and to himself. Maybe he would carry on. He had the equipment all set up. And he'd always choose women.

He looked at the name and smiled. Then he said it softly to himself, relishing the sound. Carmel.

Carmel Hennessy would be next.

Chapter Seventeen

On his way back from the hospital Joe Plantagenet knew he had two choices: he could return to the office to have a word with Emily Thwaite about her husband's past or he could follow up an idea of his own. But, as the question of Emily needed some thought, he decided on the second option.

According to Carla Yates's ex-husband, the Resurrection Man's first victim had once worked at a travel agent's on Sheepgate and had embarked on an ill-fated affair with the owner who had met an untimely, if natural, death, which resulted in his wife inheriting the business, leaving Carla high and dry.

Joe thought it highly unlikely that the wronged wife had opted for the ultimate vengeance - murder. After all, she had had her revenge in the form of her errant husband's will. But there might still be something to discover, either from the widow of Carla's late lover or from one of her former colleagues - if any of them still worked there. These days people moved on.

There was only one travel agent on Sheepgate and that was Corser's. Joe assumed that this was the place where Carla had once worked but it hardly looked like a small family concern. Instead it had a streamlined, corporate appearance, its interior sleek and up to date. The predominant décor was blue and yellow, shades intended to remind the passerby of sea and sun, of balmy days far away from Yorkshire's frequently glowering skies.

He pushed open the glass door and stepped inside. Behind the pale wood counter sat three women; one young and dark wearing lashings of make-up; one young with short brown hair; and the third a plump mother figure with short grey hair and a seen-it-all expression. All three wore an unflattering uniform of navy skirt and blue and yellow patterned blouse and all three looked up eagerly as he stepped over the threshold.

The eldest enquired politely if she could help him as if her seniority entitled her to have first pick of the customers. The other two looked on glumly as their colleague prepared to grant Joe's every holiday wish.

But she was to be disappointed. Joe produced his identification and asked if the owner was about. After explaining that Corser's was now owned by Sunnyside Travel Ltd, a chain that operated all over the north of England, the woman introduced herself as Valerie Johnson, the manageress, and inclined her head, awaiting the next question.

Joe wasn't holding out much hope that anyone at Corser's would be of any use to him. Time had moved on and, no doubt, so had all the staff who'd worked with Carla Yates and her boss and lover, Peter Hale. But he asked the question anyway.

'How long have you worked here, Mrs Johnson?'

Valerie Johnson smiled. 'Longer than I care to remember.' She glanced at her colleagues. 'The girls say that when I first started at Corser's we were offering trips to see the dinosaurs in their natural habitat. It must be thirty years at least.'

Joe returned her smile. 'You'll remember Carla Yates then?'

Valerie rolled her eyes to heaven. 'Oh, I remember Carla all right.' She suddenly assumed a solemn expression. 'I heard about her murder. Terrible. I mean I can't say I liked her very much but you wouldn't wish that on your worst enemy, would you?'

'At the moment we're trying to find out everything we can about the victims; trying to establish a possible link between them. I believe Carla had an affair with the man who owned this place at the time . . . Peter Hale.'

Valerie raised her eyebrows, surprised at the depth of his knowledge. 'I could have warned her it'd all end in tears. It was his wife I felt sorry for. Then he died suddenly of a heart attack and it turned out Mrs Hale inherited the lot. Most people working here at the time thought it was divine justice, I can tell you.'

'So Carla wasn't popular?'

'Not particularly. She was all right but . . .'

'And Mrs Hale? I presume she's not still running the place?'

'She sold the business soon after she inherited. It's changed hands a couple of times since then.'

'What happened to her?'

'I'm not sure. She was a nice woman . . . quiet. Not really a businesswoman so it's probably a good job she didn't keep the place on.'

'So you don't know where I can find her?'

'Sorry, I've no idea. For all I know she might even have moved out of the area. After all she had no ties. She had a child but it died, you know. Tragic.'

'What happened, do you know?'

'Mr Hale never talked about it. But I sometimes wonder if that's what made him start the affair with Carla. I mean, these things can affect people in different ways, can't they?'

'Was Carla ever into the occult or anything like that?'

Valerie shook her head. 'I think she read her horoscope in the paper but that was about it.' Her eyes lit up with curiosity 'Why? You don't think these Resurrection Man murders have anything to do with black magic, do you?' She gave a theatrical shudder and Joe guessed that she was enjoying the tale of horror and murder experienced at a safe distance.

Joe gave the discreet, official reply that they were

following a number of leads and changed the subject. 'What was Mrs Hale's Christian name, can you remember?'

Valerie shook her head. 'No. She was the boss's wife so we always called her Mrs Hale in those days.' She frowned, trying to recall some long-forgotten data from the back of her mind. 'Oh, I remember her coming in after her husband died and someone calling her . . . oh, what was it?' She frowned and shook her head. 'Sorry, I can't remember.'

'It's probably not important,' said Joe. He was speaking the truth. He was clutching at straws, wasting his time. As far as the murders were concerned it surely didn't matter that one of the victims had run off with someone else's husband many years ago. The Resurrection Man murders were the work of a madman. And the victims were probably chosen for a reason other than their past transgressions.

As Valerie Johnson showed him off the premises, his eyes were drawn to the bright posters on the wall, sunbaked scenes of sandy beaches and hilltop villages framed against azure skies.

When they caught the Resurrection Man he might give himself a treat and take a holiday. He just hoped he wouldn't have to wait too long.

When he got back to the police station he found Emily Thwaite in the CID office, checking on progress. He stood in the doorway and watched her for a while, approving of the fact that she was a hands-on boss . . . unlike some.

He steeled himself. He had to tell her what he'd discovered about Janna Pyke's past but he wanted to do it tactfully so he walked up to her and whispered in her ear that he wanted a word in private before drawing her away from the assembled team. She allowed herself to be led to the privacy of her office where she sat down and looked at him, a challenge in her eyes.

'Emily, I need to talk to you about something.'

Her eyes widened for a split second, as though she'd guessed what he was about to say.

'It's about your husband. It's Jeff, isn't it?'

'What about him?' she asked almost in a whisper.

'Did Janna Pyke once accuse him of . . .'

She knew there was no point in denying it; no point in prolonging the agony of waiting while Joe dug further and further until he hit on the truth. 'I suppose that Gemma told you all about it when you went to see her?'

'Yes. She said his name was Timmons. I saw your kids' paintings on the wall and . . .'

Emily leaned towards him. 'Look, it's not something I wanted everyone to know. She caused a hell of a lot of trouble for us and Jeff's never really got over being accused like that of something he never did.'

'So what happened?'

She hesitated.

'Come on, Emily, I know you're the boss but it's confession time.'

Their eyes met and she gave him a bitter smile. 'Once a priest, always a priest, eh.'

'You're either going to tell me everything or I'll have to go to the Super and tell him you're personally involved in the case.'

'After my job?' she said sharply.

Joe shook his head. 'No, I'm just trying to make sure this investigation doesn't get screwed up.' He hoped he hadn't sounded too self-righteous but he had to know the truth. 'Go on. What happened between Jane Pyke and your husband?'

Emily sighed. 'Jane Pyke had a crush on him. Only it was more than a crush, it was more like an obsession. Then when he made it clear to her that he wasn't interested, she made up all these ridiculous accusations. She was a vindictive little bitch with a nasty imagination. When she went off to Manchester, we thought we'd seen the last of her.'

'Until she turned up dead.'

She stood up. 'She was evil, Joe. Nasty. Trouble followed her round like a bad smell. If she saw anything good she had to spoil it. And, by the sound of it, she was involved in the Black Hen business. Still causing grief.'

Joe wasn't sure whether to put his next thought into words. The best place to hide a tree is in a forest – the best place to hide a murder is in a series of murders.

'You can't suspect Jeff, surely?' she said suddenly as though she'd read his mind.

Joe opened his mouth to speak but no sound came out. Of course the idea was ridiculous. The way Janna Pyke had behaved, she would have made plenty of enemies in her relatively short life. Jeff Timmons would only be one of many.

Emily grabbed his arm. 'Look, Joe, you've just got to trust me. I can prove that Jeff has absolutely nothing to do with this.'

He looked into her eyes. She looked tired, as though the weight of the world was on her shoulders.

'He's not involved, Joe. He didn't even know she was in Eborby till her murder was on the news. I can prove it, I know I can.'

Joe knew that at that moment he held the advantage. He could blight her career in Eborby – maybe step into her shoes. All he had to do was speak to the Super – imply she had some involvement in the case that might call her impartiality into question. But he knew all about temptation – how you could be offered all the riches of the world for an act of betrayal. And he knew that riches turn sour and you have to live with yourself afterwards.

Joe considered his options for a few moments. 'I'll leave it with you then,' he said before turning away.

At eight thirty the next morning Little Marygate was quiet. It had rained during the night and the flagstones glistened in the weak sun as Doris hurried to her post at the Mirebridge Hospice shop. As the temporary keeper of the keys while the manageress was away in Tenerife, it was her responsibility to open up the shop and the burden weighed heavy on her thin shoulders. Someone younger should have been given the task. It was really too much at her time of life. And she still hadn't recovered from the shock of discovering Harold Uckley's clothes and her subsequent interrogation by the police . . . although, to give them their due, they had been sympathetic.

She took the keys from her capacious handbag and looked around suspiciously. You heard such awful things nowadays about muggers and the like: for some the temptation of an elderly, defenceless lady's handbag would be too much to resist. But it seemed that her fears were unfounded. The few people around her, hurrying to work and intent on their own concerns, weren't giving her a second glance. She was safe for now.

As she inserted the key into the lock she noticed the black bin liner leaning against the shop wall. Couldn't people read? The notice was up there in the window asking that nothing should be left on the pavement outside when the shop was shut. But people these days thought rules didn't apply to them. Doris pressed her lips together in disapproval as she bent to pick up the offending article. Little pools of last night's rain lay in its folds and crevices and cascaded on to her shoes as she raised it off the ground, causing her to curse its thoughtless donor afresh.

She carried it inside the shop and dumped it on the floor. Ethel would arrive soon to supervise the sorting of donated clothes in the back room. But in the meantime, Doris thought, there was no harm in having a quick peek at what had been left. She opened the bag up and looked inside. And when she recognised the carrier bag lying within, her hands began to tremble. The Archaeology Centre. It was another of them.

Doris took deep breaths. She had to keep calm. She ran to the kitchen and donned the rubber gloves that the ladies wore when washing the teacups. She would feel foolish if her suspicions turned out to be wrong, but she had to check what was inside. It could well be something quite innocent

. . . children's clothes maybe. With gloved hands she opened the bag carefully and her heart lurched. Black clothes. An ethnic bag, glittering with tiny mirrors, with the purse, student ID card and keys still inside.

She dropped the bag as though it was red hot. It was her. The last victim. It was Janna Pyke. 'Not again,' she muttered to herself. 'Not again.'

Doris was shaking as she rang the police. All this excitement was really too much for a woman of her age.

When she arrived at the office, Emily Thwaite had said nothing to Joe about their conversation the night before. She still needed time to think. Jeff had been giving the children their breakfast when she'd left the house at twenty to eight, and she'd given each member of the family in turn a perfunctory kiss before hurrying out to work to a chorus of whinges and bleats of 'Mummy'. She wondered whether Jeff had sensed that something was wrong. The previous evening he'd seemed distant and had said little to her once the children were in bed.

She began the day by asking Jamilla to double-check the alibis of everyone working at the Archaeology Centre on the days the victims disappeared and the time when Harold Uckley's clothes were dumped in Little Marygate. It was a boring, routine job but someone had to do it. She sat down at her ordered desk, knowing that she should make the phone call that would confirm or blow apart Jeff's story about how he came to have blood on his shirt. But when she picked up the receiver her heart sank. She'd leave it till later when she was less busy, she thought, trying to convince herself that she wasn't just making excuses to put off the moment of truth.

Alone in her office, she checked her appearance in the mirror before facing the world . . . and facing Joe Plantagenet, the only one who knew about her sin of omission – the problem she couldn't get out of her mind. Then, like an actor stepping on to the stage, Emily Thwaite left her office and strode into the incident room. The curtain was up.

After a great deal of thought, before going home the previous night she had obtained a warrant to search the Black Hen. She had a feeling Joe was right about the place – there was every reason to suspect that there was some connection between the pub and the Resurrection Man murders. She wanted to introduce an element of surprise and she thought an early morning visit was the best course of action, taking whoever was there unawares. Everybody is vulnerable when they answer the door in their night attire.

So at eight forty precisely, Joe and Emily, with three uniformed officers as back-up, arrived at the front door of the Black Hen. She noticed that Joe was watching her intently as one of the constables banged on the pub door with his fist. And she felt her cheeks flushing as he sidled over to her and whispered in her ear. 'Well?'

'I haven't had a chance to talk to Jeff yet. I'll do it soon. Promise.' She turned to face him and lowered her voice to a whisper. 'Look, Joe, the real reason I'm taking this slowly is that I'm scared for Jeff. He had a bad breakdown once because of Jane Pyke and if he's brought in for questioning . . .'

Joe looked into her eyes and knew she was telling the truth. Her concern wasn't so much for her career as for her husband's mental health and he could sympathise with that. But he still couldn't ignore it. 'OK. But I can't stay quiet much longer. I can't be implicated.'

'You won't be,' she whispered. She saw one of the other officers looking at her and suddenly assumed a confident expression – once more the professional. She pretended to study the name of the licensee above the door. 'Barry George Smyth licensed to sell . . .' The name wasn't familiar. But then she was new to the city. Perhaps in the future it would be . . . if she had a future in CID.

It was a full five minutes before they heard the sound of

heavy bolts being drawn back, a sound that reminded Emily of the times she had had to visit prisons in the course of her work. Ominous and chilling. She glanced at Joe standing beside her. He was staring at the door, his face solemn. She drew herself up to her full height and clutched her shoulder bag.

The door opened a foot or so and a bald head appeared. 'What is it?' The man held on to the door firmly with one tattooed hand.

'Barry George Smyth?' Emily asked sweetly.

'Who wants him?' he grunted with undisguised hostility.

Emily introduced herself and held out the warrant. When he saw it, the man's resolve seemed to crumble and he stood aside to let them in, humble as a Victorian footman in the presence of his 'betters'. Emily was delighted to see that some people still knew when to give in.

All three constables went about their search with gusto but they reported back that they'd found nothing that wouldn't be found in most pubs in the land. Stocks of drinks and crisps; kegs of beer and lager in the ancient cellar; the landlord's surprisingly neat bachelor flat upstairs. The Black Hen, they announced, was clean. Either people had been making up stories or whatever had happened had happened elsewhere.

Emily looked at Joe and shook her head. They were wasting their time. But Joe avoided her eyes and stared ahead, lost in his own thoughts.

'That's it then,' she said. 'Another dead end.'

Joe said nothing. Sometimes his calm manner irritated Emily. She opened her mouth to say something mildly cutting but then she decided against it. She had to keep him on her side. There were so many who'd have already taken advantage of the situation, of having something on their boss, and she wondered if Joe Plantagenet, for all his talk about training for the priesthood, might still turn out to be one of them. Temptation was such a difficult thing to resist.

The landlord was watching them from behind the bar. He had said very little during their visit: he'd just let them get on with it while he stood there, arms folded and a smug expression on his face. He'd known they would find nothing and he looked as if he was enjoying seeing them make fools of themselves.

'Come on then,' Emily said to the three officers. 'We've finished here. She turned to the landlord. 'Thank you for your time,' she said, a note of sarcasm in her voice.

But as she started to make for the door, Joe touched her arm. 'I want to take another look in the cellar if that's OK.'

Emily turned to face him. 'We've searched the place from top to bottom,' she whispered. 'We'd better not push it.'

But Joe had already started to retrace his steps, walking quickly towards the door beside the bar that led down to the cellar. Emily watched him for a few moments, exasperated.

Then something made her follow.

Joe was already charging down the cellar steps and she caught up with him as he came to a halt at the bottom of the stairs. 'See anything unusual?' he asked.

Emily looked round the cellar, taking in each detail. Then she pointed to the cellar's far wall. There was a cupboard pushed against the dirty, whitewashed bricks, a battered piece of dark wood furniture that looked as if it had probably begun life as a wardrobe. 'Those cobbles in front of the wardrobe aren't as dirty as the others. Something's been dragged over them.'

'That's what I thought.'

Emily suddenly felt a stab of irritation that he'd been the one to spot it first. 'Well, are you going to help me shift that cupboard or what?'

Without a word Joe opened the cupboard door and found that it was empty. And when they began to shift the thing together they found that it moved smoothly away from the wall as though it was on some hidden castors.

'Get everyone else down here, Joe,' she said as a dark opening, a doorway, came into view.

As he climbed the cellar steps, Joe allowed himself a rare moment of smug satisfaction. He'd been right.

Emily Thwaite didn't say much on the journey back to the station. She was still annoyed with herself for not spotting the possibility of a hidden room down in the cellar of the Black Hen before Joe had. Maybe she was losing her touch, she thought. Resting on the laurels she had earned during her time in Leeds. But she had to face the uncomfortable truth that her mind had been on other things. She had been distracted by her worries about Jeff; she'd taken her eye off the ball and had missed the obvious. Missed the fact that if terrible things were indeed going on at the Black Hen, then they would hardly have happened where outsiders might see or hear.

The room they'd found behind the cupboard had made her shudder. She hadn't realised she'd be so sensitive to atmosphere, but the stale air in that dark-draped, dim-lit chamber had seemed to hang laden with evil. She had smelled blood. Smyth had claimed it was the blood of chickens but Emily had sent round a forensic team . . . just in case.

Smyth was denying everything. He was saying there was nothing illegal in a group of like-minded people getting together and enacting Satanic rituals. He had even attempted to plead that his religious freedom was being violated. If the RSPCA wished to prosecute him regarding the chickens, he said, they could go ahead. He was saying nothing more . . . and he knew nothing about anything else. As she made her way up to the incident room, Emily felt unclean, tainted by association. Barry George Smyth was a creep and she was only too glad to get out of his company.

Joe had gone off to talk to a witness, a schoolgirl who had allegedly become involved with the goings-on at the Black Hen. Emily had told him to take Jamilla with him. In her opinion these things needed a woman's touch.

On reaching the incident room Emily was greeted by

Sunny Porter, who wore an uncharacteristically eager expression on his face, as though he had some important news to relay.

'Janna Pyke's things have turned up, ma'am. Same place. Left outside the Mirebridge Hospice charity shop some time last night. And they were in one of them carrier bags and all. The Archaeology Centre.'

All Emily could think of was the fact that Jeff had been at home with her all last night and she could prove it – there was no way he could have dumped Jane Pyke's clothes anywhere. But her face gave nothing away. 'Where are they now?'

Sunny jerked his head towards a side office. 'I sent someone to fetch them. The old biddies there are getting jumpy. But one of them had the sense to put gloves on before she handled the bag so there's a chance we might get some prints. I thought you'd want to see the things before they went over to Forensic.'

Her heart was beating a little faster as she walked to the office, resisting the temptation to break into a run. Once there, she found an array of items, neatly bagged in clear plastic and arranged on the long table that occupied the far side of the room. There were dusty black clothes and a pair of down-at-heel ankle boots – also black. Then there was a well-worn shoulder bag – the brightest item in the ensemble with its purple embroidery and its tiny round mirrors set into the material. It was the sort of comfortable bag that held a lot – all the necessities of a woman's life – and its contents were laid out beside it.

A purse containing two ten-pound notes, some loose change and a book of stamps. A student identity card and a library card. Tissues – new and used. Pens. A small diary and a battered address book. Two Yale keys lay beside a smaller key. Emily stared at them, wondering. The Yale keys would surely belong to Keith Webster's flat in Boargate. But the smaller one looked like a locker key. Perhaps she had a locker at the university.

Emily put on a pair of plastic gloves, picked up the diary and flicked through the pages, her hands shaking. But all it contained were scribbled reminders about which shifts she was working and the times of her meetings with Keith Webster at the university. The initials BH featured every so often, presumably the Black Hen.

As she replaced the diary, Emily's eyes were drawn to the address book. She took it out of its bag and began turning the pages. T for Timmons. There was nothing there. Then she turned to J for Jeff, her palms sweating. It was there. His name beside their old Leeds phone number. She closed her eyes for a few seconds. Then when she opened them again she looked underneath the original number. Written there in Janna Pyke's spidery handwriting was her new address and her new Eborby number. The shock almost knocked the breath out of her and she stood there dazed, her heart pounding, nausea rising in her stomach.

Did she dare? She took a few deep, calming breaths and popped her head round the door. 'Er ... has anyone recorded this lot yet?'

It was Sunny who answered. 'I was just going to get someone on to it, ma'am.'

'That's OK,' said Emily, trying to sound casual. 'As long as it gets done in the next half hour or so before it goes down to Forensic.'

She went back into the room, leaned against the wall and closed her eyes for a second. Joe Plantagenet already knew what had happened in Leeds but this was far, far worse. Jane Pyke had their new address which meant that she must have had some contact with Jeff since they arrived in Eborby. Tampering with evidence was serious. But so was your husband being involved with a murdered woman when you were in charge of the case.

She hesitated, turning the implications over in her mind, before slipping the bag containing the address book into her pocket. She needed time to think.

Then, after a few minutes, she called Joe's mobile number. His phone was switched off but she left a message on his voice mail. Could he meet her for lunch? She had something she wanted to discuss with him.

Chapter Eighteen

Joe Plantagenet thought it was about time they stopped pussyfooting around. He knew that if they were to get anywhere with the investigation, the girl who had been traumatised by whatever had happened at the Black Hen would have to be questioned. Gently, of course, with the help of Canon George Merryweather and in her mother's presence.

He had found George at the cathedral and, after a bit of gentle persuasion, he agreed to call the girl's mother and ask if Joe and Jamilla could come round for an informal chat. The mother had agreed ... providing George was there too. Half an hour later they found themselves sitting in the garden of a neat detached house in one of Eborby's more prosperous suburbs.

It was a beautiful day, the sort of blue-sky day when darkness seems to be a distant memory, and the girl's mother, whose name was Anne, insisted on sitting in the shade. She had fair skin, she explained, and burned easily – even in a Yorkshire summer.

She told them that her daughter, Amy, was making good progress and had even mentioned the possibility of going to university again. She wouldn't, of course, be well enough to go the following September as originally planned but, with time and care, she might consider going a year late. She was still very fragile, very vulnerable. And she still had the nightmares, though less frequently now. Anne spoke cautiously as though she feared that the edifice of normality might come crashing down again, just as it had done a few weeks before.

Joe was beginning to wonder whether he'd actually get a chance to see Amy. Her mother seemed to have taken on the role of the guardian at the gate, denying access to all she feared might upset her precious charge. This was quite understandable, of course, but it wasn't much help to his investigation.

Just when he was starting to give up hope, a girl appeared at the French windows, hovering there, as though uncertain what to do. She spotted George and raised a hand in greeting, a shy smile on her face. George waved back and motioned her to come out to join them. The girl opened the glass door and took a tentative step out, like a shy animal emerging, blinking, into the light after a long period of captivity in a dark, narrow cage.

The first thing Joe noticed was how thin she was. Her long fair hair swung forward, half hiding her pale face, as she walked slowly towards them.

George stood up. 'Amy, my dear, come and sit down,' he said gently. 'I'd like you to meet an old friend of mine. This is Joe.' He smiled. 'He's a policeman but he's a very nice one. And this lady is Jamilla. She's with the police as well.'

Joe switched off his mobile phone – this wasn't something he wanted interrupted. Then he gave Amy what he hoped was a reassuring smile and held out his hand. He could feel Amy's mother's eyes on him as the girl took the offered hand and shook it limply. He'd passed the first test.

'George has mentioned you,' she said. Her voice was quiet but more confident, than he'd expected.

'If you don't want to talk about what happened, I quite understand, Amy. Or if you'd prefer to speak to Jamilla alone . . .' He glanced at Jamilla who had assumed a sympathetic expression. 'But if you do feel up to . . .'

Amy looked at her mother. 'I've told Dr Oakley everything and he says . . . he says I should tell the police but I couldn't face . . . giving statements and going to court and . . .' There was a tremor in her voice and tears began to cloud her eyes.

'Honestly, Amy, if you don't want that, nobody's going to make you do it,' said Jamilla. 'If you'd prefer just to have a chat with us now, that's fine . . . really. Or we can leave it till later if you . . .'

Amy's mother leaned forward to push a strand of hair off her daughter's face. Amy had become her baby again. Dependent and helpless.

Suddenly the girl straightened her back, as though she'd come to a decision. 'It's OK, Mum, you can go.'

Her mother looked shocked. 'No, darling. I think it's best if . . .'

'I'll be all right, Mum. Honestly. I'd rather speak to them on my own.' Amy pressed her mouth into a determined line.

'If you're sure . . .'

'We'll call you if . . .' Joe didn't finish the sentence. He didn't like to put the possibility of Amy not being able to cope into words and dent her fragile confidence.

But the woman still stood her ground. Until the telephone began to ring and she shifted, torn between instinct and necessity.

'That might be my friend, Elizabeth. She said she'd ring to see how Amy was. Will you be all right . . .?'

'Of course we will,' said George. 'Amy's quite safe with us.'

Still apprehensive, Anne gave in to the telephone's insistent ringing and made her way inside, glancing back over her shoulder anxiously as she stepped into the house through the French windows.

There was a long silence. Amy sat, studying her fingers. Then suddenly she looked up. 'I don't know what you've heard . . .,' she began, looking Joe in the eye.

'We know that you went to the Black Hen and that something bad happened there. We went there this morning.' He watched her face. 'We found the room in the cellar.'

The girl's face clouded and she gave an almost imperceptible nod.

'Is that where it happened?'

Another nod.

Jamilla leaned forward. 'Did someone rape you?' she asked softly.

Another nod.

'Who was it? You see, I'd like to put this person away where he can't do anything like that to anyone else ever again.'

Amy covered her face with her hands and sat head bowed for a few seconds. Then she looked up. 'It was the Master,' she muttered as though the words were difficult to speak.

'Do you know the Master's real name, Amy?'

There was a long silence and Joe feared they'd pushed her too far. He looked at George and saw that he was sitting on the edge of his seat, waiting patiently for the answer.

Then Amy spoke. 'He works at the House of Terrors. He's in charge. His name's Jevons.'

When the girl's body began to shake, Joe was relieved to see her mother emerging from the house. She rushed over to the girl and took her in her arms, holding her close, whispering words of comfort in her ear.

She looked at Joe. 'Did she tell you who . . .?'

Joe nodded.

The mother looked a little hurt. 'That's more than she's told me.'

George leaned forward. 'Sometimes it's difficult to share these things with someone we love. She's been very helpful. And don't worry, Joe will make sure the man who did this is put away for a very long time.'

'Thank God for that. If she hadn't started going round with that . . .'

Amy winced. 'Oh, Mum. Shut up. You can't blame her for what happened.'

'Blame who?' Joe asked.

It was the mother who spoke. 'One of the girls she worked with at that House of Terrors place persuaded her to go to that place. I blame her for getting Amy involved in all this, I really do.' She pressed her lips together in disapproval. 'But I suppose justice has been done.'

'What do you mean?' Joe asked.

'She's dead, isn't she? She was murdered.'

George Merryweather put a sympathetic hand on the woman's arm as she started to cry.

Lunchtimes were sacred to Carmel Hennessy. A break in the middle of the day when she could pick up a sandwich from the delicatessen and eat it on a bench by the river before wandering around the shops, lost in her own thoughts and daydreams. On one occasion she had met Tavy McNair. They'd gone for a pizza in a cheap café on Hillgate and each day she found herself hoping that he'd ring her to arrange another lunchtime meeting. But the Black Hen incident had left her with a tiny shadow of uncertainty in the back of his mind and, although she hardly liked to admit it to herself, caution kept her from arranging anything which involved being alone with him in the evenings.

Today she had hoped to buy a top she had seen in the sales. She had spotted it yesterday and thought about the economics all last night. It was a particularly nice top in a bold bright print. But her plans of extravagance were thwarted by a summons to Peta Thewlis's office. As she walked down the corridor, she wondered what she had done wrong, racking her brains, going over every little detail of her dealings with the public and the staff. Then she began to wonder if it might be something to do with the flat – some transgression regarding the terms of the lease perhaps – and that hardly made her feel any better.

When she reached the office door she knocked boldly, wondering how soon she could get the interview over with and resume her precious leisure time.

Peta's barked 'Come in' did nothing to inspire confidence. Carmel opened the door and shuffled in like a child summoned to the headmaster. 'You wanted to see me?'

To her relief Peta smiled. But hers was never a warm smile, more like a token grimace. 'I just wanted to tell you that Mr Peace won't be moving back into the bottom flat for a couple of weeks.'

Carmel exhaled, a breath of relief. If that was all, maybe she could go. She took a step towards the door.

'He came out of hospital this morning and he's going to stay with his niece – Elizabeth, I think her name is. You've met her?'

'Oh yes. She's very nice. I do hope Conrad's all right.'

Peta's lips twitched upwards. 'I'm sure he will be.' She hesitated. 'Actually, I thought I'd take advantage of his absence and get some work done on his flat. Heaven knows, it needs doing desperately but I thought it would be a lot of disruption for him. I've arranged to have a new kitchen put in. The one that's in there at the moment must have been in since the 1960s and ... I ... er, hope the workmen won't disturb you too much.'

'I'm sure they won't bother me. I'll be at work anyway.'

'Yes, of course. I know the boss of the firm I'm using so I'm sure they'll be reliable. I just thought I should let you know in case you're worried by all the noise and ...'

'Thanks.' Carmel shifted from foot to foot, anxious to be away.

But Peta spoke again. 'You haven't heard any more about ... about Janna Pyke's murder, have you?'

Carmel noticed the anxiety in Peta's eyes. 'No, I haven't.'

'I just thought ... Oh, it doesn't matter. Thank you, Carmel.'

Carmel made polite noises and hurried off, wondering

why her boss had looked so worried when she'd mentioned Janna Pyke.

But when her mobile phone rang and she discovered that it was Tavy asking her to meet him that evening, she forgot all about it. She had other things to worry about.

Joe received Emily's message when he switched his phone on as he left Amy's house. He called her back immediately and they arranged to meet in the Cross Keys. When he arrived at the pub Emily was there waiting for him, sitting near the entrance on the edge of her seat as though she was preparing to make a quick getaway. She smiled at him nervously as he put their drinks on the table. It was one thirty already – a late lunch – but somehow she wasn't hungry.

Joe came straight to the point. 'You wanted to tell me something?'

Emily took a long drink from her glass of dry white wine. 'Yes.'

'And?'

'I called the local station and they confirmed there was a fight in the Drayman's Arms the other night. Jeff had come home late with blood on his shirt, you see, and he said that was the reason, but I . . . well, I wasn't sure. So I had to check. Apparently it was two blokes with an old grudge going at each other hammer and tongs. One had a broken bottle and there was a lot of blood.' She took a deep breath. 'Jeff gave a statement. That's why he was late home. And the night Uckley's things were dumped, he went out for a drink with an old friend. I found the mobile number in Jeff's address book and called him – I made some excuse that Jeff had lost something and did he remember if he had it with him. His alibi stood up. He was where he said he was all right.'

Joe saw a tear run down her cheek but she wiped it away swiftly with her fist.

'You didn't seriously think he was . . .?'

'No, of course not,' Emily replied quickly. 'The idea was absolutely ridiculous. And he's never driven a white van in his life,' she added with a weak smile.

'I'd still like someone to have a word with him ... see what he's got to say about Jane Pyke.'

Emily sat there for a few moments, quite still. Then she picked up her handbag and delved inside, pulling out a plastic bag containing a small book. She held it out, looking at him through long lashes, her eyes still glassy with unshed tears. 'I found this,' she said quietly, placing it on the table in front of her.

'What is it?'

'Jane Pyke's address book. I won't make any excuses. It was on the table with the other things from her bag. I needed to look at it in private to see whether ... Jeff's name's in it.'

Joe's expression gave nothing away. Emily had gambled on his understanding, his sympathy. But what if she'd miscalculated? What if trusting Joe Plantagenet was the biggest mistake of her career?

After a while Joe broke the awkward silence. 'Well, if she was stalking him, that's hardly surprising.'

Emily looked into his eyes and she thought she saw some sympathy there. It might have been wishful thinking but suddenly she felt reckless. If she didn't confide in someone, she'd go mad. 'It's worse than that, Jane Pyke had our new address ... and our phone number.'

Joe thought he saw a brief flash of pain in her eyes. The pain of the betrayed wife. 'You've asked him about it?'

She shook her head. 'Not yet.'

'There might be an innocent explanation.'

'Like what?'

The question had Joe stumped. He shrugged his shoulders.

She picked up a beer mat with restless fingers and began to shred it, hardly aware of what she was doing. Then, after a long silence she spoke again. 'Will you speak to Jeff?'

Joe considered her proposition. 'Yes. We need to talk to him anyway.' He smiled. 'And it's better if I do the job than some plodding DC who'll enjoy spreading it all round the canteen that he's just grilled the DCI's husband.'

Emily sighed. 'I suppose I'll have to tell the Super about all this. He'll probably take me off the case.'

There was another long silence and Emily wondered whether Joe was secretly enjoying the situation.

'Look, Emily, you've shown me the address book. And if Jeff's alibis for the relevant times are checked and I interview him, then he's hardly being left out of our enquiries, is he?'

'No. I . . .'

He took a deep breath. 'I'll leave it up to you, then.'

'What do you mean?'

'Whether you want the Super involved at this stage. Myself, I think that would cause more problems than it would solve. Of course everything would change if we find that Jeff does have something to hide but . . .'

She looked up warily. 'There are some who'd use this to finish me.'

'Yes, there are. But I'm not one of them.'

'I don't know what to say. I . . .'

Joe leaned forward. 'Before you thank me, we'd better get something straight. If I think that this business with Jeff is affecting the enquiry in any way or if I think for one moment that he's been lying to you, I'll go to the Super myself. You've had a tough decision to make and you've done the right thing. OK?'

'Thanks, Joe.'

'The subject's closed,' he said. 'And unless you do something bloody stupid, we won't mention it again.'

He picked up the address book and put it in his pocket. Then he touched her arm gently and she gave him a wary smile. At that moment she looked much younger than her years, as though she had lost her confidence in her own judgement . . . lost the innocence of certainty.

'I'll need to speak to Jeff,' he said.

Emily nodded. 'He'll be in this afternoon.' She straightened her back, suddenly becoming her old, confident self again before his eyes. 'You haven't told me about your visit to Amy's.'

As Joe brought her up to date, Emily frowned. 'The bastard,' she said. 'We'll throw the bloody book at that Jevons when we get him. She will give evidence, won't she?' She didn't wait for an answer. 'The only consolation is that people who rape young girls have a hell of a time in prison. So Pyke was involved in all this too?'

'It seems she lured the girl there and . . .'

'I told you she was bad news, didn't I? Let's get round to that House of Terrors as soon as we've eaten.'

'Right you are, boss,' Joe said with a smile as their eyes met.

Emily took a deep breath. 'And I think we should dig a bit deeper into the Black Hen. I think these murders have a whiff of Satanic ritual about them.'

Joe nodded. 'Let's have something to eat, shall we?' he said after a few moments, picking up a menu. 'I'm starving.'

They settled for sandwiches: something quick.

As soon as they'd finished eating, Emily spoke again. 'Are you sure that Amy will make a formal complaint against this Jevons? Unless she does he might get away with it.'

Joe knew she was right. Many a rapist got away with it because his victim was too embarrassed or terrified or traumatised to go through the rigorous procedures involved in putting a case together that would satisfy the Crown Prosecution Service.

'But that doesn't stop us putting the fear of God into him.'

He saw the determined look on Emily's face. 'Shall we pay "the Master" a call then?' He said the words with heavy irony as she stood up and swung her bag over her shoulder.

'Why not?' They were both going to enjoy seeing Jevons

squirm. Even the uncomfortable knowledge that Jane Pyke had known Jeff's Eborby address couldn't rob Emily of this pleasure.

They arrived at the House of Terrors just as it was at its afternoon busiest. It may have been bad timing for Jevons but it made no difference to Joe and Emily. In fact it rather pleased them to think of their suspect being hauled off for questioning so publicly.

Joe leaned on the ticket desk and asked if Jevons was in but he was told that he wasn't. He hadn't come in that morning. In fact the girl behind the desk hadn't seen him for a couple of days. She knew nothing.

On further investigation, a man called James admitted going to his flat the day before and finding it empty. No, he hadn't thought to report him missing. He'd probably decided to go off somewhere for a few days. James was his assistant and he didn't mind being in charge of the House of Terrors. In fact he quite enjoyed it.

They all told the same story, almost as if they'd agreed it amongst themselves. Nobody knew anything about Amy being raped, although they remembered her working on Saturdays in the café and they remembered seeing her in the company of Janna Pyke.

'That was what's commonly known as a wall of silence,' Emily observed as they walked back to the car. 'Shall we try his flat?'

'We won't find him there. He's done a runner. Got out before Amy started talking and things got too hot for him.'

Emily said nothing. The scenario Joe described was as likely as any.

And when there was no answer at his flat and they peeped through the letter box only to see a pile of uncollected post on the floor, they knew he had gone. Left Eborby until the fuss died down.

'How about putting it out that he's wanted for questioning in connection with Janna Pyke's murder?' Emily suggested.

Joe looked at her for a few seconds. 'I suppose that's not a bad idea,' he said, noting the look of relief on her face. 'I'll go and have a word with Jeff if that's OK.'

Emily nodded. 'Thanks,' she said almost in a whisper.

Jamilla Dal couldn't get Amy's revelations out of her mind and she lurched between pity for the girl and righteous anger against her attacker. These emotions fought in her head as she settled down to the tedious task of going through all the available security footage from the Boargate area. It was mind numbing but she knew it had to be done – she only wished she hadn't been the only officer available to deal with the task.

She sat there in front of the TV screen, hypnotised by the moving images, uncertain whether she'd recognise something significant if it appeared there in front of her.

The trouble was that they didn't know the exact time that Janna Pyke had been abducted or where precisely she had been abducted from. All Jamilla had was guesswork, a report of a light-coloured van being seen around the time Janna Pyke's body was dumped in Evanshaw churchyard and the white van that had appeared to be following Carla Yates in the security video. And, from watching the videos, it seemed that every other vehicle driving through the streets of Eborby was a white van. The words needle and haystack sprang to mind.

The pictures of Carla Yates's last journey had been enhanced but that hadn't been much help. The figure driving the van was too much in shadow to be seen clearly and it seemed the logo on the side of the van had been covered deliberately by some sort of paper or thin plastic, suggesting that someone had taken precautions.

However, the covering had come away from the first letter of whatever was written on the side of the van. The letter K was clearly visible, unlike the van's registration number, which was too covered with dirt to make out. Jamilla concluded that this could have been deliberate. It was important to the killer that the van shouldn't be identifiable. Precautions again. And intelligence. The police always preferred it when their adversaries didn't think too hard.

Jamilla regarded the pile of videotapes she had already watched with distaste and picked a new one out of the box. After inserting it into the mouth of the machine she pressed the switch, sat back and took a sip of coffee - at least it would help to keep her awake.

She stared at the moving images on the screen. Hussgate ran at right angles to Boargate and was just outside the pedestrianised zone. The digital time in the corner of the picture said seventeen thirty. Rush hour, when the shops were shutting their doors. The date was five days before Janna's body had been found in Evanshaw churchyard. And there was Janna herself, hurrying down Hussgate towards Boargate, head down, intent on her destination, her black skirt billowing behind her and her shoulder bag - the one that had been found with her clothes - slung across her body and clutched to her chest.

Jamilla smiled. Janna was there at last, scurrying along as though she didn't want anyone to see her. She noticed the dead girl was carrying a plastic bag with the name of a well-known convenience store that had a branch on Hussgate. She had been out for provisions; ventured out of the flat above the art shop when supplies ran low. When the bread and milk run out you can't hide away for ever.

Then Jamilla spotted it. Janna was passing a row of parked vehicles, one of which was a white van. A figure was getting out of the van. A hunched figure with longish fair hair and some sort of hooded jacket that seemed too big for him . . . or her. She could only see the figure's disappearing back as it hurried after Janna, following a few yards behind her, barely noticeable amongst the other pedestrians. Then they both vanished from view.

Jamilla sat back and took another sip of coffee before reporting her findings to DCI Thwaite.

*

Jane Pyke had been a manipulative, vindictive, crafty little bitch. But Jeff Timmons was sorry that she was dead, of course. Nobody deserved a fate like that.

Joe Plantagenet had sat in Emily's living room with its stripped wooden floor and original Victorian fireplace, sipping tea and trying to stay patient at the children's frequent interruptions to his strange, almost surreal interview with the DCI's husband.

Jeff Timmons seemed to be an amiable man, glad of Joe's company to relieve the monotony of child-minding and preparing lessons for the following term. But Joe guessed, from the way Jeff talked and from his restless fidgeting, that the subject of Jane Pyke still had the power to disturb him. Jane's lies had almost cost him his job, his marriage and his health and Joe suspected that the man's suffering had given Jane some sort of perverse pleasure. Yes, he told Joe, he still felt bitter but he had moved on. New city. New job. And his relationship with Emily was stronger than ever ... until Jane Pyke had got herself murdered and the events of the past had returned like a dark, evil-smelling flood.

Jeff spoke with straightforward honesty and Joe doubted whether anybody could have put on such a convincing act. As the informal interview progressed, Joe found himself accepting Jeff's version of events, which, as far as he could judge, had the ring of truth.

Jeff swore that he hadn't seen Jane Pyke since his arrival in Eborby and he had no idea how his new details had come to be in her address book. It was a complete mystery and, besides, why on earth should he wish to make contact with the girl who had almost wrecked his life? This was a question Joe had asked himself. It hardly seemed to make sense. In fact he thought it far more likely that Jane Pyke had traced Jeff's whereabouts for some reason known only to herself. Gemma had hinted at an obsession and this certainly fitted with what he already knew of the young woman's strange and disturbed character. It was just Jeff

Timmons's misfortune that she'd chosen him as the object of her twisted affection.

'I hope all this isn't making it difficult for Emily at work,' Jeff said as Joe prepared to take his leave. 'She's worked bloody hard to get where she is and none of this is her fault.'

Joe smiled but said nothing that might be taken down and used in dinner table chat. He had to stay neutral, professional. And there was always the possibility, albeit infinitesimally slight, that his judgement was wrong. Stranger things had happened.

It had all been dealt with. But it had been done much earlier than the killer would have liked. These things were best when there was a long period of anticipation before they were savoured slowly.

The body of Terry Jevons had been taken from its temporary resting place and put in the back of the van, wrapped carefully in plastic sheeting, a transparent shroud that allowed a distorted glimpse of the victim's face ... like a drowned corpse viewed underwater. It was important to get everything right. There must be no fingerprints left or any traces that could lead to his discovery.

The choice of the last resting place was the killer's and his alone. Mabworth church. Fourteenth century. Such a pretty place. Mother had liked it when they had visited a few years ago.

He would move under cover of darkness. That was always best. But he had a dilemma. If Carmel Hennessy made herself available, he would have to strike, to carry her alive in the van along with Jevons's corpse. He didn't like the idea ... it offended against his sense of neatness, of order. But the Seeker knew best. Carmel Hennessy was one of them. And they had to be destroyed before they destroyed him.

The killer climbed out of the van and walked slowly towards Vicars Green. He usually took them off the street, took them by surprise with a blow to the head to stun them. But there was no guarantee that Carmel Hennessy would come out of her flat during the hours of darkness. Maybe it would have to be different this time. Perhaps he would have to come to her.

He reached Vicars Green, walking past the National Trust teashop until he found himself outside number five. He stood and looked up at the house: it stood a little forward from the rest of the row of ancient buildings, its whitewashed top floor protruding slightly over the pavement.

He smiled to himself. His mission would be easy this time. A piece of cake.

Suddenly the killer spotted someone walking across the green, making for the house, and stepped back into the shadows, holding his breath as the visitor rang the top doorbell of number five.

The caller didn't have to wait long before the door was answered by a young, dark-haired woman. She greeted her visitor with a cautious smile and stood aside to let him into the house.

Carmel Hennessy had company. He hadn't taken that possibility into account. Perhaps he would have time to deal with the mortal remains of Terry Jevons before undertaking his next assignment after all.

One thing at a time, he thought as he drove off into the night.

Chapter Nineteen

The call came through at eight twelve a.m. precisely. There was a body in Mabworth churchyard, the caller said, seemingly unaware that this was one of the oldest jokes in the book. But the woman in the communications headquarters knew this wasn't some kids dialling 999 for a laugh. This body in the churchyard was above the ground rather than six feet below. It was male and it was naked. It was another of them.

A couple of phone calls set the full machinery in motion and at eight forty-five Joe found himself driving north to the village of Mabworth with Emily yawning by his side.

'Wonder who it is,' Joe mused as they drove.

Emily didn't answer. She'd had a quick look through their list of local missing persons and concluded that it could be any of them. She was keeping an open mind.

She had left Jeff in bed that morning. He had a headache, he claimed. A slight hangover from the night before when he'd gone to the pub. He'd gone alone because he fancied a drink after a day spent with the kids. Emily had said nothing. Men went to pubs alone to meet people . . . to get chatting over a pint. It was all quite normal, she told herself. But then his name and their new address had been in Janna Pyke's address book and the doubts had come creeping into her brain in the small hours of the morning. Could she really be married to a murderer? But Joe

Plantagenet had interviewed him and he'd seemed satisfied with his story – he had even observed that getting hold of Jeff's new address was just the sort of thing a weirdo like Jane Pyke would do. In the brightness of a North Yorkshire morning her suspicions about Jeff seemed laughable. She knew Jeff wasn't capable of such things. And yet in the course of her career she'd met so many murderers' wives who'd convinced themselves of their loved ones' innocence and this thought made her uncomfortable.

Mabworth was a pretty North Yorkshire village on the edge of the National Park. An area of outstanding natural beauty . . . and the not quite so final resting place of their latest corpse.

Emily and Joe climbed out of the car and assessed the situation. Joe hadn't mentioned Jeff so far that morning and for this she felt rather grateful. She turned her mind to the matter in hand. The local police had sealed off the area in a calm, efficient manner to preserve the crime scene. Not that it was likely that it was the crime scene: if this latest murder followed the pattern, the man – whoever he was – had died elsewhere.

It was a cool morning and a chill breeze blew from the east, whipping round the bulk of the church, which was perched on high ground at the edge of the village. The scenes of crime people and the pathologist had already arrived and Joe and Emily waited, clutching their thin summer jackets around them, until the body had been examined in situ before stepping forward to get a better look.

The corpse lay there naked on the grass in the shadow of a tall memorial, a lichen-covered statue of an angel. His pallid, waxy flesh was stained dark where the blood had sunk and settled and he stared upwards, his lips drawn back in a snarl of agony. His hadn't been an easy death.

'Well, that's a turn-up for the books,' Joe said quietly after a few seconds.

'Terry Jevons,' said Emily.

'The man himself. The Master. The man who raped Amy.'

'He was supposed to be the killer not the victim,' Emily said softly. 'Where do we go from here?'

'Goodness knows,' Joe replied. Things were getting more complicated by the minute. 'How about starting at the House of Terrors?'

Emily nodded in agreement. It was as good a place to begin as any.

James Waters sat at Terry Jevons's desk in the office behind the House of Terrors, twisting the leather swivel chair gently to and fro, relishing the warm glow of being in charge, of telling others what to do. He wasn't particularly worried about Terry. Terry Jevons was a man who could take care of himself. And it was hardly surprising that he'd decided to disappear after what had happened at the Black Hen. It had all gone too far. Especially when Terry had pointed the finger at that woman, Gloria, who, up till then, had been up for anything.

Terry had told her she was going to die and everyone knew he'd really meant it. They had sensed it in the way he pronounced sentence, by the glazed, staring look in his cold grey eyes as he savoured the power he had over life and death. And, in the frenzied atmosphere of that night, it had just seemed like the natural progression ... the next step along the path. A blood sacrifice.

But the next morning, away from the disturbing darkness of that cellar room and back in the sunlight of sanity, it had seemed like a mad dream, an aberration. But James knew that Terry hadn't seen it that way. He had been excited by the power he had exercised over everybody there and over the girl, Amy, in particular. And the thought of that ultimate power over life and death had thrilled and exhilarated him to such an extent that he'd lost touch with reality. James was convinced he would have gone ahead with his plans if Gloria had been compliant and other things hadn't got in the way. There had been a loss of control; an abandonment of all normal inhibitions; a mob following a charismatic and crazy leader. It had happened so easily that it was frightening.

The door to the office swung open, interrupting James's thoughts. When DCI Emily Thwaite strode into the room followed by the man James recognised as Inspector Plantagenet, he stood up, his legs shaking a little with nerves. He looked at the pair expectantly. Maybe it was time to come clean and tell them the lot. After all, it had been Terry's idea. Nothing to do with him.

But Emily spoke first. She came straight out with it. Jevons was dead, seemingly the victim of the Resurrection Man. Did James know of any next of kin? The answer was no. When was he last seen? The answer was three days ago. James had gone to his flat and found it empty. That was all he knew about his boss's disappearance.

The police insisted on closing the House of Terrors while they questioned the staff and James acquiesced without complaint, feeling a little sick. No longer in control.

Joe sat down opposite James and looked him in the eye. 'We know all about the rape that took place at the Black Hen. Were you there?'

James stared at the desk. 'Yes,' he whispered. 'I didn't think he'd go that far, honestly I didn't. Me and my girlfriend gave the girl, Amy, a lift home and dropped her outside her house. She was in a terrible state. Hetty said we couldn't just leave her wandering about.'

'That's very considerate of you,' said Emily. James could hear the heavy sarcasm in her voice. 'You never thought to tell the police that a serious crime had been committed?'

'I'm telling you now,' he answered, the seeds of defiance in his voice.

'Anything else to tell us?'

James nodded and took a deep breath. He might as well get it over with. He proceeded to tell them about Jevons's plans for Gloria; how she'd been chosen for death – to make the ultimate sacrifice. When he had finished, Joe and Emily's eyes met in unspoken understanding. It explained a lot.

They left James uncertain whether charges would be brought against him. But that was Joe and Emily's intention. To make him sweat.

Now that Jevons was dead, the field of suspects was wide open again. There was Joe's tree and forest theory . . . that meant virtually everyone connected with the case might be a suspect. Or there was the alternative, and probably more feasible, theory that the victims were linked in some way as yet undiscovered. Or, of course, there was the most unpalatable theory of all – that the killer was a madman who slaughtered at random for his own twisted reasons. That was the theory that Joe found most depressing – and probably the most likely.

And it seemed that the killer was allowing less time between murders now – he was getting cocky, too confident by half. Which meant he had to be caught quickly – taken off the streets before he claimed more victims.

Just as Joe settled down at his desk, Jamilla appeared, smiling shyly and clutching a thin file.

'Just thought you'd like to know, sir. John Wendal's wife called earlier. He's being allowed home from hospital today. And I rang the psychiatric department. They said that Gloria Simpson's been sectioned and she'll be staying in for treatment.'

'Poor woman,' said Joe, earning himself a curious look from Jamilla. As far as she was concerned Gloria had attacked an innocent man, causing a car crash, and hardly deserved anybody's sympathy.

'And do you remember that travel agent Carla Yates ran off with? The one who died?'

'What about him?'

'You wanted to trace his widow. I've made some enquiries and I've looked through the local electoral register but there's no mention of her. Perhaps she's moved out of the area.'

'Perhaps she has.' Joe felt a momentary pang of guilt for sending Jamilla on a fruitless errand. Suddenly another idea popped unbidden into his head. He looked at Jamilla's eager young face and thought he'd take a chance.

'The killer's been leaving all the victims' clothes outside the Mirebridge Hospice charity shop. Perhaps our man has some connection with the hospice. Perhaps a relative was a patient there. Get on to the matron and see if you can get a list of all their patients, will you, Jamilla? I think the last five years is enough to be going on with.'

Jamilla smiled bravely. It was a long shot but it was worth a try.

Carmel strolled over to her office window and looked out. She was sure that the white van parked outside had been there earlier that morning. But perhaps she was mistaken. One white van looked very much like another. Although this one had some kind of white plastic cover stuck on the side, obscuring a name or logo underneath. But she could still make out the letter that peeped out beyond the edge. The letter K.

She returned to the report she was preparing for Peta Thewlis and thought no more about it. She was anxious to get things right. Peta had been on edge for the past few days and it was rumoured she had berated one of the girls working in the shop for making a mistake which resulted in a till roll being inserted wrongly and several purchases left unrecorded. And the nagging interference of the police, always round asking questions about those carrier bags, hadn't helped her mood.

Carmel sighed and read the report through for a third time. A white van is just a white van.

Dr Keith Webster wasn't one of nature's vandals. He loathed wanton damage to anything. Even to one of the unlovely grey metal lockers that stood in the basement of the history department, placed there to accommodate any possessions the students wished to leave in the department on a temporary basis.

As he approached locker number 379 he looked around to make sure he was alone, all the time listening for approaching footsteps on the stairs. When he reached his destination he produced a screwdriver from the pocket of his linen jacket and thrust it into the space between the frame and the door.

He really wasn't any good at this sort of thing, he thought as he attempted to lever the door open. Up till that moment he'd never regretted his law-abiding youth but now he wished he'd been a little less studious and a little more worldly. But in spite of his inexperience in matters mildly criminal, he felt a glow of satisfaction as the locker door swung open.

It was there ... lying on the shelf in front of him. He had seen it so many times, the file with the pattern of Celtic swirls on the front; the file he knew contained the research for Janna's dissertation. She had taken it out of her bag and placed it on the desk during their many discussions and it had lain there between them as they talked.

His hands shook a little as he took it out of the locker, intending to take it back to his office and study it at his leisure. Then something else caught his eye. A notebook with a padded denim cover. He'd never seen it before and his curiosity got the better of him so he reached in and picked it up.

He looked round to check that he was still alone before opening the small denim book. The lined pages inside were covered with Janna's spidery handwriting. Keith had found that writing hard to decipher when they had first met but experience meant that he now found it easy to understand. And from what he had read so far, he guessed that he had found some sort of diary.

Full of curiosity about Janna's secret thoughts concerning himself, Keith Webster slipped the book inside the file, pushed the locker door firmly shut and headed straight for his office.

That evening Joe Plantagenet took an assortment of files home with him. The atmosphere of the incident room was hardly conductive to creative thought and he needed to go through the files on his own, undisturbed, to pore over them and turn the facts over in his mind until they began to make sense.

After making himself a plate of pasta with a sauce straight from a jar, he switched off his mobile phone and settled down to read the files spread out on the coffee table in front of him.

One by one he read through all the statements carefully, looking for discrepancies. But by seven thirty he'd found nothing and his eyes were beginning to sting with the effort of concentration.

There must be something there. Something he'd missed. In the end he decided that a break would do him good and switched on the TV to find that he was just in time to witness the first scene of a popular soap opera.

He lounged self-indulgently on the sofa, but after ten minutes idleness began to pall and he left the soap opera characters to their own devices for a few moments while he went to the kitchen to fetch a bottle of Theakstons Old Peculier, a glass and a bottle opener. If he was snatching half an hour of leisure he might as well do things properly.

As he poured the golden liquid into the glass he took his eyes off the screen for a few seconds, only to look up again when he heard the squeal of brakes and a dull thud as some actor coming to the end of his or her contract met an untimely end.

Suddenly he put his glass down and scrabbled amongst the files, trying to find the relevant sheets of paper. There was something he wanted to check.

He picked up the telephone and punched out the number that was listed in the file for Harold Uckley's widow. But there was no answer.

If his new idea held water, there might just be a connection between Harold Uckley and Carla Yates, but it still very much a tentative theory. He might be completely wrong and, anyway, it still wouldn't explain why Janna Pyke and Terry Jevons were targeted.

He'd ask Jamilla to check it out tomorrow but he wasn't getting his hopes up. Perhaps some things were destined to remain a mystery.

It was meant to be. He would be like a cat, trapped in a cage with a helpless bird. It would be so easy.

The killer scratched his head. He was hot, even down there in the cellar, but it didn't matter. He ran a finger over the pile of large carrier bags. He didn't really know what they were doing there but they had certainly come in useful.

He put on a pair of disposable latex gloves and picked the top bag off the pile. Terry Jevons's clothes were still in the mausoleum, neatly folded beside one of the rotting coffins which lay on the shelves arranged around the walls. They would be donated to the Mirebridge Hospice shop as usual. Terry Jevons wouldn't be needing them any more, the killer thought, suppressing a giggle. He might have done more harm than good in life but at least his clothes might be of help to someone. He had kept hold of Carla Yates's clothes for a while, wondering what to do with them. Until he had had the idea of putting them to good use. The hospice needed all the funds it could get – he'd learned that the hard way when he had watched someone he loved dying there, his life ebbing away as the cancer triumphed over his weakened body. Every little bit helped.

Once he'd dealt with the clothes, he would be free to concentrate on his next assignment. Free to concentrate on Carmel Hennessy.

He thrust his hand into his trouser pocket and felt the key there. It would be easy this time. There would be no risk whatsoever.

Chapter Twenty

Keith Webster stared at the file containing Janna Pyke's dissertation notes and took a sip of whisky, feeling a glow of temporary comfort as the warming liquid slipped down his throat.

Earlier he'd flicked through the little denim diary he'd found with the notes in Janna's locker but he'd left it in his office – it wasn't something he would risk bringing home. It's contents had made him realise how little he'd actually known about Janna. He'd had no idea what she'd been involved in – she'd always been careful to keep that side of her life from him – but he'd certainly had no reason to suspect that it was anything quite so dramatic. He had always assumed that Janna, with her change of name, was just another self-dramatising post-adolescent. And perhaps she was. Perhaps all the black magic and the rape had been figments of an over-excited imagination.

Did things like that really go on in Eborby? If they did, Keith had never heard of them. Maybe he led a sheltered life, he thought with a twinge of regret as he glanced at his wife who was sitting on the sofa reading an improving biography with an expression of earnest concentration on her plump, pale, once pretty face.

He opened the file and turned the pages until he came to a particular account that Janna had copied out carefully and underlined in red pen.

Mistress Eleanor Buckby did report that the house on the Vicars Green, lately afflicted by the pestilence, was searched most diligently and six bodies examined. One man, one woman, a boy aged twelve years and a girl aged about sixteen were found there with a manservant and a maidservant. The bodies bore no swellings or sores and the corpse of the girl was like unto that of a starved dog. The girl had called from the window many days ago saying that her kin had all died of the pestilence and begging to be allowed from the house. But she was ordered to stay for there was fear she would spread the contagion, and it seems that she died for want of sustenance.

Keith Webster sighed and his wife looked up. Maybe tomorrow he'd treat himself to the vicarious thrill of reading more of Janna Pyke's diary.

Carmel had told Tavy McNair that she couldn't see him that evening. He had asked if he could call round when he'd finished the ghost tour but she had been firm. She had things to do: phone calls to her mother and a couple of friends; catching up with washing and housework and then a long, relaxing bath. Keeping Tavy at a distance for a while would do no harm, she thought. And besides, she suspected he wanted more from their budding relationship than she was willing to give and she wasn't sure how she felt about the situation.

Maybe she should have asked Joe Plantagenet for his advice. But then her feelings for Joe were ambiguous. He was too near her own age to be regarded as a father figure and, although she was reluctant to admit it to herself, she found him rather sexy. Her mother had asked him to keep an eye on her, and Carmel felt some resentment about being made to look like a helpless child in front of a man like Joe. On the other hand, she was glad he was there on the other end of the phone.

Her quiet night in – so attractive in theory – had been fine at first when she had been busy; when she was cleaning the flat, putting the washing in the machine and making her long, chatty phone calls. But when she'd finished her bath and settled down on the sofa in her dressing gown, cleansed and relaxed, to watch TV, the girl had started to make her presence felt.

It wasn't much at first, just a faint scrabbling sound in the bedroom – the room where she was supposed to have been found, starved to death. Carmel hauled herself up from the sofa, walked over to the door and stood listening for a few seconds before pushing it open. But as soon as she stepped over the threshold the noise ceased, leaving a thick silence, as though somebody was watching her from the shadows, breathing very softly.

'What do you want?'

Her whispered question hung in the air for a few seconds before the answering crash came. Something in the room had fallen over. She flicked on the light switch and saw that a box of books had toppled from the wardrobe, strewing its contents on to the floor.

She busied herself, shoving the books back into their box unceremoniously and once the box was back in its place on top of the wardrobe she returned to the living room, leaving the bedroom door open. She turned down the TV and listened. There was another noise, distant yet somewhere in the house. Downstairs. A key in the lock.

But Conrad Peace had moved out and he was staying with Elizabeth while his new kitchen was being fitted. The ground floor was empty.

She held her breath. Someone was opening the front door. She grabbed her keys, rushed to her own door and deadlocked it.

She picked up the phone and dialled the number of Joe's mobile but it was switched off. Then, after a few moments' thought, she tried Tavy's number, listening to the soft footsteps on the stairs getting nearer. She froze, straining to hear, imagining she heard the sound of faint electronic music in the distance. Then, after what seemed like an age, she heard Tavy's voice on the other end of the line.

'Get over here quickly,' she shouted at the top of her voice. 'Someone's trying to get into the flat.'

She heard Tavy saying that he'd be right there. Then she heard the footsteps retreating down the stairs and the front door slamming followed by the thud of running feet and a diesel engine starting up. Her heart pounding, she dashed over to the window just in time to see a white van driving away.

And when Tavy arrived ten minutes later, she still hadn't stopped shaking.

The next morning Joe Plantagenet had just asked Jamilla to check out the idea he'd had the night before about the link between Carla Yates and Harold Uckley, when his telephone rang. After a few minutes he put the receiver down and scratched his head. When Jamilla had hurried off, he stood up and made his way to Emily's office. And as he opened the door she looked up at him expectantly.

'How are things?' he asked. 'How's Jeff?'

'He's OK. Look, Joe, I want to thank you for—'

'Don't thank me. Let's forget it, shall we?'

She shuffled some papers on her desk – something to occupy her restless hands. Then she looked him in the eye, doing her best to put on a mask of confidence. But Joe could see behind it. The Jeff incident had shaken her more than she was ever going to admit to him or to anyone else.

'Anything new come in?' she said after a few seconds, breaking an awkward silence.

'I've just had a call from Carmel Hennessy, the girl who's living in Janna Pyke's old flat. Someone tried to break in last night. Carmel was there alone and she heard footsteps on the stairs. She reckoned whoever it was heard her phoning for help and gave up.'

Emily looked sceptical. 'So they never actually got round

to breaking in. She might have been letting her imagination run away with her. Let's face it, with this killer about, it's hardly surprising. Everyone's jumpy. Could she have just heard the other people in the building?'

'There's only one other flat downstairs and that's empty at the moment. The old boy who lives there was taken ill and he's convalescing with his niece. Carmel says that whoever was there let himself in with a key and was coming upstairs. Carmel locked her door and called this Tavy McNair . . . the one who . . .'

'I remember. The ghost tour man.'

'That's right. He went straight round but by the time he got there the intruder had gone.' He paused, saving he most important bit till last. 'Carmel looked out of the window and saw a white van driving away.'

This caught Emily's attention. 'I don't suppose she saw the registration number.'

'Sadly we don't live in an ideal world,' Joe replied, looking round as Sunny Porter entered the office without his usual perfunctory knock.

Sunny looked excited, which was probably a first for Sunny. 'I've just been out to Mabworth. The door-to-door boys found a witness who saw a white van driving slowly towards Mabworth church on the night Terry Jevons's body was dumped.

'He got the registration number?' The expression on Sunny's face had brought on a sudden attack of optimism.

'No but . . . we've got something almost as good. The witness was a boy of ten. It was the early hours and he couldn't sleep so he decided to look out of his bedroom window. Apparently he makes a habit of it. Likes to look out for owls. There are a lot in the trees round the church, so he told me.'

Emily smiled. 'So what exactly did our budding naturalist see?'

'He saw the van driving past. He said there was something attached to the side that had broken away and was flapping about. Remember on the CCTV footage it looked as if some sort of name or logo had been covered up with plastic. Only this time it wasn't stuck on properly.'

'And?'

'He drew me a picture.'

Sunny had been holding a piece of paper in his hand, half behind his back like a surprise present. He grinned as he held it out to Emily, who took it and studied the clumsily executed black-felt-tip sketch of three intertwining letter Ks.

A triumphant grin lit up Emily's face. 'I recognise it,' she said, handing the paper to Joe. We've been getting quotes from local firms for a new kitchen. This one came round to give us a price last week and this logo's on their brochures. Kathwell's Kreative Kitchens – pardon the spelling. They operate from the industrial estate near the northern park and ride.'

This revelation was followed by a few seconds of appreciative silence. Nobody had expected it to be this easy.

'We'd better pay them a call,' said Joe. 'You didn't ask them to fit your new kitchen, did you?'

'No. One of the other firms was cheaper.' She smiled. 'Perhaps it's a good job, otherwise I might have found myself . . .' She didn't finish her sentence. Somehow flippancy didn't seem appropriate. She turned to Sunny. 'Check whether any of the victims had dealings with this firm, will you? If we find they've all had kitchens installed by Kathwell's we've got our link. In the meantime, Joe and I will visit their extensive showrooms, as it says in the brochure.' She paused, deep in thought.

'Wood shavings,' she announced triumphantly after a few moments.

'Pardon?'

'Traces of wood shavings were found on the bodies. Oak. Kathwell's do a range of solid oak units.'

But before Joe could answer, Jamilla gave a token knock on the office door and stepped inside

'I'm afraid whatever it is will have to wait, Jamilla,' said Emily as she touched Joe's hand lightly. 'DI Plantagenet and I are just off to look at kitchens.'

She picked up her handbag and swept out of the office, as Jamilla watched her open-mouthed.

The northern industrial estate stood on the unlovely edge of Eborby's conurbation, next to a multiscreen cinema complex, a bowling alley, a municipal sports centre and one of the city's four park and rides. There was car parking space in abundance here along with a variety of fast food outlets. Across the newly built and complex traffic roundabout stood a large estate of new houses targeted at the cheaper end of the market. It was only two miles out of town but the contrast with Eborby's historic heart was a stark one. This was the city's backside ... the part the tourists would rather not see.

Compared to the entertainment facilities, the industrial estate didn't look too bad. Emily and Joe drove slowly through its wide, treeless roads and eventually found what they were looking for. The three Ks entwined on the side of a grey building with a glass showroom front. Kathwell's Kreative Kitchens. It was a fairly large unit, but then Kathwell's literature boasted that all its kitchens were made on the premises by master craftsmen. To Emily these words had conjured a mental picture of the likes of Thomas Chippendale or a medieval master woodcarver, lovingly planing each plank of fine wood by flickering candlelight. But she knew the reality would be far more mundane.

The showroom was virtually empty, but then it was a weekday. At the weekend it would be full of eager wives and sulking husbands who'd rather be watching the football on TV and had only allowed themselves to be dragged out to a kitchen showroom to keep the peace.

The man sitting behind the cluttered desk in the office, engrossed in his paperwork, looked rather alarmed when they flashed their warrant cards and asked where all the company's vans had been the night before last. The man, who introduced himself as Baz Teal, senior salesman, seemed anxious to assure them that, as far as he knew, the vans had all been accounted for, parked in the yard outside. However, any of the employees could have got hold of the keys and borrowed one. It wasn't unheard of for such things to happen and the management were pretty easy-going about it. After all, he said, vans were useful for shifting furniture and picking things up from shops to save on delivery charges. Sometimes it did no harm to turn a blind eye as long as the van was returned undamaged in the morning and they paid for their own diesel.

They made themselves comfortable and asked the usual questions before showing Teal the picture taken by the CCTV camera of the man with long blond hair. Teal shook his head: the picture was so poor that the man's own mother probably wouldn't have recognised him and nobody in Kathwell's employ had hair like that.

When Emily asked if anybody was off work that day, Teal rolled his bulging eyes to heaven. 'Only Tim,' he said. 'But then Tim has a lot of time off. He's not been well.'

Joe leaned forward, watching Teal intently, like a cat watching a mouse hole.

'To tell you the truth,' Teal continued, 'His mum's a friend of Mr Bell's, the boss . . . or a cousin, something like that. He did her a favour taking Tim on. He can do the job all right . . . he's not stupid and building kitchens is a doddle to him but . . .'

'But what?'

'He's been in and out of hospital . . . he has problems.'

'What sort of problems?'

Teal shrugged. 'Nerves, something like that. You don't like to pry, do you?'

Joe and Emily exchanged glances. 'Could I have a list of your employees? Especially those with access to the vans.'

Teal produced a neatly typed list of names and addresses from the top drawer of his desk and handed it to Joe, who read through it, holding it so that Emily could see.

It was Emily who spotted it. 'McNair – Octavius McNair.'

'Tavy, yeah. He just does weekends in the showroom. He's an out of work actor.' He grinned. 'He's not a bad salesman actually. Got the gift of the gab.'

'And he has access to the vans?' Emily asked.

'Everyone has, I suppose,' Teal replied. 'I think he's been known to borrow one on occasions . . . to move stuff and that.'

Joe read from the list. 'Thewlis. Tim Thewlis. And the address. Isn't that the same as . . .?'

'Peta Thewlis. Carmel's boss at the Archaeology Centre.'

'And Janna Pyke's landlady. Maddy said Peta had a son who wasn't well.' He looked at Teal. 'Is that the Tim who . . .?'

Teal nodded. 'That's right.'

'Does Tim have access to the vans as well?'

'Like I said, we all do.'

'Did either Thewlis or Tavy McNair borrow one last night?'

'I couldn't tell you. They might have done but they were all present and correct this morning.'

'I don't suppose you've noticed whether any of the logos on the vans have been covered over? If there have been any traces of tape or . . .?'

Teal smiled. 'They've all got hooks on the side that take plastic sheets to cover the KKK logo. The boss has this arrangement: he loans vans to his brother's company but he doesn't like advertising the fact.'

Emily turned to Joe. 'I think we should get a few DCs down here to question the staff and examine the vans while we pay McNair and Tim Thewlis a call, don't you?'

'Most of the vans are out,' Teal chipped in.

Joe nodded. He should have known things wouldn't be that easy. He turned to Emily. 'I'd like to speak to Peta

Thewlis first . . . tell her what we're doing.'

'Suit yourself,' was Emily's reply. 'And while you're at it you can ask her if she ever takes any carrier bags home from work.'

Joe called Carmel at work, just to make sure she was all right. He didn't mention Tavy's new connection with the case. Perhaps he should have done. Perhaps he should have warned her to be careful. But he didn't want her to panic. He just told her to call him if there was anything worrying her . . . anything at all, however slight.

Tavy McNair's address turned out to be a rambling Victorian villa in one of the more salubrious streets near to the university campus. The house was swathed in Virginia creeper and the paint on the window frames and doors was flaking off, revealing the grey wood beneath. The place had an air of neglect, of faded grandeur, Joe thought as he pressed the plastic doorbell.

On returning from Kathwell's, Joe and Emily had paid a flying visit to headquarters. This time Jamilla managed to pass on the information she'd been trying to give them as they'd rushed out. She'd obtained a list of patients from Mirebridge Hospice and there was one familiar name on the list: that of Professor Julian McNair, who had died at the hospice just over two years ago. This discovery added a dash of urgency to their visit. But they hid their impatience from the woman who answered the front door.

The professor's widow was tall, thin and probably in her fifties, and her grey-peppered brown hair was scraped back into a ponytail. She wore a long skirt and bright beads that hinted at Bohemian inclinations.

'Is your son, Octavius, at home by any chance?' Joe asked after the introductions had been made.

'I'm afraid not. Can I help?'

'He works at Kathwell's Kitchens, I believe?'

'Only at weekends. He's an actor, you see.' She said the word 'actor' with obvious pride. 'He has to take part-time work where he can. He has a job leading ghost tours as well.'

'We know. Do you mind if we come in?'

For the first time Mrs McNair looked worried. 'I presume it's about that incident the other night. I'm glad he's reported it at last – I told him he should. It was an unprovoked attack, you know. I'm sure the girl he was with will tell you . . .'

Emily made sympathetic noises but gave nothing away. It would be counter-productive to set the mother on her guard.

Mrs McNair led them through to a once grand, but now rather shabby, drawing room. Joe suspected money was in short supply in the McNair household – but he was sure it hadn't always been that way. As they asked their questions, Mrs McNair sat stiffly on the edge of a threadbare armchair, puzzled at first as to why they weren't concerning themselves with the attack on her son. But she was an intelligent woman and she soon realised that they were there for another reason. As she endured their gentle interrogation, her expression became increasingly strained.

Yes, Tavy was out a lot in the evening but then his job demanded it. Yes, he could drive but he couldn't afford his own vehicle and he sometimes borrowed vans from Kathwell's. No, as far as she knew he wasn't acquainted with any of the Resurrection Man's victims . . . apart from Janna Pyke whom she'd never met. From what Tavy had said, she hadn't seemed a very suitable girlfriend – maybe that's why he'd never brought her home to meet his mother.

When Emily asked as gently as she could if they could see his room, Mrs McNair hesitated, as though she were about to refuse. But then she stood up and said that she was sure he had nothing to hide, before leading them up a flight of sweeping, uncarpeted stairs to a large bedroom at the front of the house.

Sunlight flooded in through two tall sash windows, illuminating a neat room with stripped floorboards, a monumental antique pine wardrobe and a double bed covered by a frayed patchwork quilt.

The walls were adorned with posters advertising various local theatrical productions. 'Tavy had parts in all of them,' Mrs McNair said proudly when she saw that they had caught Joe's attention. 'He's very good. He's just waiting for a lucky break.'

'Aren't we all?' Joe thought, but he didn't put his thoughts into words.

They conducted a perfunctory search under Mrs McNair's watchful eye until Emily lifted the lid of a large oak chest at the end of the bed and summoned Joe over to see what she'd found. Inside the chest there was an assortment of boxes containing make-up and wigs. Joe stared at them for a while, puzzled.

'From his drama school days,' Tavy's mother said, trying to sound casual but unable to keep the anxiety from her voice. 'Look, what exactly is it you're looking for?'

Emily and Joe exchanged glances. 'We need to talk to your son, Mrs McNair. Will you ask him to call us as soon as he gets in?' Joe looked into her worried eyes. 'Your late husband was in Mirebridge Hospice, I believe.'

She nodded.

'Does Tavy have any connection with the hospice charity shop?'

'If we have any donations, that's where we take them but . . .'

'Thank you, Mrs McNair. We'll be in touch.'

When they were in the car Joe turned to Emily. 'What do you think?'

'I think we should check out this Tim Thewlis next. But we need to talk to Tavy McNair and the sooner the better.'

'I'll arrange to have the house watched so he can't do a runner.'

Emily couldn't argue with that. She too wanted to make sure that Tavy McNair didn't disappear into the night.

*

Peta Thewlis had gone home early to catch up on some paperwork away from the distractions of the office. When she opened her front door and saw Joe Plantagenet and his female companion, DCI Thwaite, standing on the doorstep, she tried to hide her irritation. She'd answered all their questions; cooperated when they'd wanted access to the attic in Vicars Green. Why were they bothering her again?

Joe Plantagenet smiled and apologised for disturbing her. She'd heard that he had some connection with the new girl at work, Carmel Hennessy, although she was vague as to the exact nature of the relationship. This link made her feel awkward as she didn't know what Carmel might have said about her. She was uncomfortably aware that some people at the centre thought her cold and hard. She'd heard the names they called her – Frosty Thewlis, the Ice Maiden. But they didn't know that if she bent, even a little, she knew she would break. Hiding her emotions was the only way she could cope.

Emily did her best to sound casual. 'We'd like a word with your son, Timothy, Mrs Thewlis. Is he at home?'

'Timothy isn't here. I think he's at work,' Peta said quickly.

'You think?'

'Yes. He'll be at work.'

Emily, as a mother, could sense worry behind the bald statement.

'Was he here when you left for work this morning?'

'Yes. He had a headache. I thought he'd still be here when I got back but he must have felt better and gone in.' Tim had woken with a headache and she'd rung into work for him, saying that he'd be there later if he was feeling better. When she'd arrived home she'd expected to hear his music playing loud so that it drowned the thoughts and the voices in his head. But he hadn't been there so she'd presumed he'd gone to Kathwell's after all.

'May we have a look at his room?' said Joe. Then he noticed a framed photograph standing on a shelf. Two men

– one young, one old – with their arms around each other, laughing for the camera. The old man had long thick blond hair that looked artificial – a wig perhaps – and the drawn, pale look of the very sick. The young man's hair stood up in dark spikes but last time Joe had seen him he'd been waiting to see Dr Oakley and his head had been shaved.

He pointed at the photograph. 'Is that Timothy?'

'Yes. He's with his grandfather – my father. It was taken shortly before Dad died. His death affected Timothy very badly. They were very close, you see.'

'And your son's been having treatment at the hospital?'

'How did you know that?'

'I saw him there,' he said gently. 'He was waiting to see Dr Oakley.'

Peta looked Emily in the eye as though appealing to her, woman to woman, mother to mother. 'He suffers from schizophrenia but I try to help him lead as normal a life as possible.'

Despite the hint of defiance of her words, it was clear that she was worried.

'He's been having problems with his medication recently but he doesn't want to go back in. Dr Oakley's trying to find the right balance of drugs. He's very concerned but we can handle it.'

Joe spoke gently. 'At the hospital I noticed that he had a tattoo on his arm and the skin around it was swollen as if he'd tried to . . . It was circular with . . .'

Peta looked exasperated. 'He did that to himself, stabbing at his arm with a pair of scissors. I was quite upset about it. I was afraid it would get infected and . . .'

'Had the tattoo any significance?'

Peta hesitated, her cool defiance thawing like snow in sunlight. 'He'd . . . started going to this pub,' she said, her voice quavering slightly. 'He met some people who put ideas into his head.'

Emily caught Joe's eye. 'The Black Hen?'

'I think that's it. Whenever he went there he became very

disturbed and I had to insist that he didn't go again. And before you ask, as far as I know he hasn't. I think that's why he tried to obliterate the tattoo ... to end his connection with that place.'

'So he hasn't been there for a while?'

'No. I think something happened there that frightened him and I was just relieved when he stopped going.' She gave an exasperated sigh. 'Look, I do my best to give him a calm environment. He has a job that suits him ... working with his hands. It seems to calm him and it gives him a reason to get up in the morning. Can you understand that?'

Emily waited for a couple of seconds before she asked the next question. 'Where was he last night, around ten o'clock?'

Peta's eyes widened for a split second. 'Here. He was here in his room.'

'Are you sure?'

No answer.

'Would you mind if we had a look at his room?'

The defiance returned. She pressed her lips together and stood her ground. 'Yes, I do mind.'

'We can get a warrant,' said Emily. Suddenly she saw a flash of pain in the woman's eyes and found it only too easy to imagine herself in that situation, a mother protecting her young.

Peta hesitated for a few moments. Then she nodded. 'All right, but leave everything as you find it, won't you. Tim doesn't like things out of place and it would upset him to think that someone's been searching through his things.'

After assuring Peta that Tim would never know that his privacy had been invaded, Joe allowed her to lead the way upstairs. She pushed open the door to the back bedroom. It was a large room, carpeted in deep blue with walls to match. The walls were plain and looked as though they'd been freshly painted.

'He used to have a picture of the devil on that wall above

the bed,' said Peta as though she'd read their thoughts. 'And a symbol like the one he tattooed on his arm over there. A few weeks ago he painted over them ... thank God,' she added in a whisper.

It was Joe who began the search. He started on one side of the room in the wardrobe while Emily took the chest of drawers near the window.

Peta Thewlis had been standing in the doorway, arms folded, while they conducted their search but now she stepped into the room, chewing her nails. She avoided looking at the walls, at the places where he had painted the terrifying images. Tim had always been such a talented painter. If he hadn't been ill he could have gone to art college. But the world was full of what-might-have-beens.

As Peta watched the search she began to sob. The cool facade crumbled to nothing, revealing the mother beneath. The mother who carried her son's illness on her back like a heavy burden. Emily was just surprised that she'd managed to keep up the act for so long.

Emily found a wheeled box beneath the bed. She pulled it out, lifted the lid and looked inside, pulling on a pair of plastic gloves before examining the contents. But all she found was a collection of CDs – heavy rock. They continued their search under Peta's beseeching eyes but found nothing in Timothy Thewlis's bedroom to link him with the Resurrection Man.

They had drawn a blank. And, for Peta Thewlis's sake, Joe was glad.

Carmel Hennessy looked at her watch. It was seven thirty. Another hour and a half and Tavy would finish the ghost tour. He'd make for Wheatley Hall to give in his takings and change out of his costume before coming to the flat to see her. She turned the page of the local paper, surprised that she was looking forward to their meeting more than she expected.

When she'd arrived back at Vicars Green at six the

workmen downstairs had been packing away and now they'd all gone. They were putting a new kitchen in Conrad's flat and she wondered whether she could persuade Peta to do the same in hers – the present one had certainly seen better days.

The kitchen firm had white vans and she wondered whether last night's visitor had just been one of the workmen who'd come back for something he'd forgotten. It seemed the most likely explanation and she felt a little foolish. Maybe the place – and her ghostly companion – was making her jumpy.

She was about to turn the TV on when she heard a thump. Then another. She froze. The sound had come from the flat below.

She listened but when she heard nothing more, she flicked the TV switch and the flat was filled with the voice of a young woman with a Yorkshire accent, recounting the evening news. When she started to say that the police were no nearer catching the Resurrection Man, she switched to another channel.

It was another half hour before Tavy arrived and suggested that they have a drink at the Mitre by the cathedral. It was quiet, he said. And he didn't feel like facing crowds.

His bruises were still visible. During the ghost tours he could camouflage them with pale make-up but when he was himself, unmasked as it were, he felt rather self-conscious. Carmel watched him as they sat in a corner with their drinks and thought that he seemed a little on edge. The attack had probably affected him more that she'd first thought. Delayed shock perhaps. She joked that the bruises were the honourable scars of battle – a fight bravely fought – trying to lighten the mood, and with the wine her uncertainties and suspicions about him started to fade. Until he mentioned that the police had been round to talk to his mother earlier. They had wanted to speak to him, presumably about Janna. Why was it that Janna Pyke intruded on her life . . . even in death?

At ten, Tavy walked her back to Vicars Green and they said goodnight. Carmel stood with him on the doorstep, wondering whether she should ask him to stay. She would have felt safer if she wasn't alone. But Tavy told her he had an audition for a small part at the Eborby Repertory Theatre first thing the next morning. He had to go because he needed an early night. Carmel was surprised to find that she felt a little relieved. Perhaps the time wasn't right yet . . . not while Janna's murderer was still out there. And as she'd stood there with Tavy in the darkness the old doubts had started to creep back. The tiny, almost imperceptible voice that whispered that he had been involved with Janna Pyke so perhaps he wasn't to be trusted.

She wished him luck with the audition before making her way upstairs, pausing to listen for any sound from the downstairs flat. She heard a faint noise which, she convinced herself, came from next door. And then in the thick, expectant silence that followed, Carmel sensed the presence of the girl. She was waiting for her in the flat. Waiting for company.

The Resurrection Man made his escape through the garden, climbing over the wall at the back and strolling away casually down the back entry, clutching the carrier bag – one of the bags from the Archaeology Centre that he'd found down in the cellar.

He had time to fill before he could act and he wished he could while away the hours in some pub somewhere, chatting with mates like the men from Kathwell's. He would have liked to be ordinary. But the powers that controlled him had other ideas. His was a greater destiny.

He passed a fitful couple of hours on a bench in Robins Stray, dozing off then waking suddenly, startled by unfamiliar noises and shivering with the cold. Robins Stray was a vast area of parkland a mile outside the city walls, more a wild common than a tame municipal park. He liked the place and its desolate history. Victims of the plague had lived there once in wooden huts, well away from the city's population. There was even a stone known as the plague stone, a flat stone with a shallow depression. He had once been told that the depression had been filled with vinegar to disinfect the money left by the unhappy plague victims in exchange for their food. He had also heard that there were bodies buried there and he wondered whether their spirits still walked, restless and resentful at their untimely end.

He took the key from his pocket and turned it over in his hands, staring at the thing, preparing himself.

The coffin had been cleaned out ready for its next occupant. The Seeker, in his wisdom, had named her as one of the evil ones who had to be destroyed. He had her name safe in his pocket and when it was over he would put it with the rest, with the Seeker's instructions and his register of the dead . . . of souls reclaimed. And after death he would do her the kindness of laying her on consecrated ground, a kindness the poor victims of Robins Stray had never been given. He always made certain that their souls were saved, which demonstrated that he was on the side of good against the creeping slick of evil. An enemy of Satan.

At ten minutes past midnight he began to walk the two miles to the industrial estate. He had to pick up the van and the equipment he kept in the disused cupboard at work. The battered old trolley he'd found during one of his visits to the hospital, missing a wheel and destined for the skip. He knew that it had been put there for him to find and, after making a few repairs, he used it to transport them to and from the van. It had been meant.

He had left the tape in the cupboard along with the wig; the one he'd bought for the dying man as a joke when he'd been in Mirebridge Hospice. When he donned the wig, he felt strength flowing into him. A power beyond his understanding. The wig was to him as ritual robes were to a priest or a witchdoctor. It made him special. Lifted him above the everyday.

He was relieved to see that nobody was watching the workshop car park. He'd been afraid that the devil's followers, who had assumed the form of policemen, might have been lying in wait for him there. This stroke of luck increased his feelings of omnipotence. Soon he would feel all powerful. Invincible.

It was almost time for him to fulfil his next task. Almost time to deal with Carmel Hennessy.

Chapter Twenty-One

The killer's mother recognised it at once. It was the special box. Oak inlaid with brass; quite old. When she was a child all the important papers had been kept in there.

She wondered why it had been shoved underneath the bed in the spare room. Last time she'd seen it, it had been in a drawer in the dining room. She sat staring at it in the heavy silence. It was after midnight now and he still wasn't back. She was worried sick.

She opened the box and found a small, hardbacked black book inside that she'd never seen before. A notebook with ruled pages. Filled with curiosity, she took it out of the box and opened it carefully.

The pages were filled with writing, carefully and neatly printed in blue ballpoint pen. She began to read and at first the contents just seemed to be paranoid ramblings. But as she read on, the words seemed to make a horrible kind of sense. Eborby was being infiltrated by the agents of the devil and they had to be destroyed. Someone would be chosen for the task by the Seeker . . . the Seeker of Souls. Her hands began to shake at this first glimpse into the mad world of her son's mind.

She stared at the notebook, puzzled. There was something wrong. Somehow it didn't look like her son's writing – he had never formed his letters so neatly and precisely. Unless his illness had caused it to change in some way . . .

she didn't know much about these things.

As she turned the page, a few loose sheets of paper fluttered to the floor. On each sheet was a name and address, all printed in the same neat handwriting. She flicked through the papers. Carla Yates. Harold Uckley. Janna Pyke. Terry Jevons.

She sat there shaking, trying to think. Her first instinct – her mother's instinct – was to keep silent, to protect her child. But as the minutes wore on, it dawned on her that for his own good, he had to be stopped. She had no choice.

With tears rolling down her cheeks, she telephoned the police and fifteen minutes later, she was sitting face to face with Detective Inspector Joe Plantagenet, bleary-eyed, hair unbrushed as if he'd just been roused from sleep.

He leaned towards her, his eyes fixed on hers. 'Where is he, Mrs Thewlis?' he asked gently. 'Where's Tim now?'

Peta Thewlis shook her head, pain and fear in her tear-filled eyes. 'I don't know. That's the truth. I just don't know,' she muttered, bewildered as a lost child.

She looked into Joe Plantagenet's anxious eyes and cried out. A howl of grief. The primitive cry of a mother who had lost a child. He hadn't come home. He was out there somewhere doing goodness knows what. She didn't deserve this.

Tim was out there somewhere. And she was terrified for him.

Carmel's throat had begun to hurt. There were a lot of people at work complaining of vague, flu-like symptoms and she'd feared that she might be going down with some sort of virus. She decided to go straight to bed, hoping that an early night and a couple of paracetamol would keep whatever it was at bay.

So, after making sure the lights were switched off and the door was locked securely as Joe Plantagenet had instructed, she had undressed, read for fifteen minutes and snuggled down. She was now using her bedroom again after telling herself firmly that the girl couldn't harm her in any way. The poor, lonely spirit would probably just be glad of her presence. At one time she would have been terrified of a ghost. But now she had lived with her for a while, she had become used to her. Like a flatmate who was unusually quiet and didn't leave wet towels in the bathroom.

Once the light was off, the moonlight seeped through the thin curtains covering the small window where, according to the story, the girl had gazed out sadly on to the green below. But Carmel closed her eyes. She was going to get a good night's sleep and nothing would stop her.

She didn't know how long she'd slept before she felt someone shaking her awake. Disorientated, she opened her eyes and saw a pallid face close to hers.

She was dreaming. She must be. The girl was there, leaning over her, her bloodless, pinched lips mouthing something Carmel couldn't understand. Then Carmel woke with a start and the red glowing letters of the alarm clock told her it was five past four.

She lay there and listened, her ears suddenly sensitive to the slightest sound. A key was being turned in the door slowly, stealthily. Hardly daring to breathe, she lay frozen, her heart pounding as she heard soft footsteps crossing the living room floor. She put out a trembling hand and reached for the phone by her bed. She had Joe's number written down somewhere but there was no time to find it. She managed somehow to punch out the numbers 999 and she just had time to whisper her name and address before the bedroom door opened slowly to reveal a tall, long-haired, figure framed in the doorway, outlined against the moonlight.

Carmel never thought that in a situation like that she'd be unable to scream. But all the clichés were true. She let the receiver drop from her hands and opened her mouth but no sound came out as the figure paced slowly, purposefully towards the bed. She heard herself whimpering, a pathetic sound, but she was paralysed with terror and she could only watch as he raised his hand.

As the blow was struck she felt no pain. But she glimpsed the girl for a split second out of the corner of her eye. And saw the fear and pity on her dead face.

'At least she managed to dial nine nine nine,' Emily said as she steered her way through streets that were silent as the grave. 'We might still be in time.'

'Put your foot down, will you?'

Emily glanced at Joe and thought that he looked remarkably alert for one who'd hardly slept.

'Is Peta Thewlis meeting us there?' Emily asked, her eyes on the road.

'Yes. I'd say the truth's just dawning on her.'

'That her son's the Resurrection Man?'

'Well, Tavy McNair's out of the frame. The patrol watching his house said he arrived home last night at ten thirty like a good boy and didn't go out again.'

'It's Thewlis all right. That notebook his mother found – I didn't believe her for one second when she said it wasn't Tim's writing. She was trying to cover up for him ... like mothers do.'

'Not just mothers,' Joe muttered under his breath, regretting the jibe as soon as the words had left his mouth.

Emily felt her cheeks redden but she said nothing. As they pulled up at the edge of Vicars Green he saw that a patrol car had arrived there just ahead of them and a pair of constables were standing by the door of number five with Peta Thewlis. Her hair was unbrushed, she wore no make-up and her clothes looked as though they'd been thrown on in the dark.

'She's not answering,' she said weakly to Joe as he reached the front door. 'I've brought the key.'

Joe took the key from her. Her hands were shaking so much that he reckoned she'd probably miss the lock and she looked as though she'd aged twenty years since they'd last seen her. He was glad to see that Emily had placed a comforting hand on her shoulder and was leading her away.

The last thing she wanted was for Peta to be present if they made a gruesome discovery.

Joe made his way up the stairs, calling Carmel's name. He had started to pray; urgent, anxious prayers shot upward like arrows. Please let her be all right. Please let it be a false alarm.

A brief search of Carmel's flat didn't tell them much apart from the fact that her bed had been slept in and she'd neglected to make it after getting up. But a closer examination of the bedroom revealed a few spots of blood, dried but recent and the long T-shirt she wore as a nightdress lay discarded on the floor in the living room. Joe called out the Forensic team. This wasn't right.

As he stepped outside into the morning sunshine, he caught Emily's eye and gave a slight shake of the head. Emily's arm tightened around Peta's shoulders as she whispered something in her ear.

Peta shook her head furiously. 'I've no idea,' she almost screamed. 'He could be anywhere. I don't know.'

Emily left Peta in the care of a nearby policewoman and joined Joe at the front door.

'There's no sign of Carmel. There's a bit of blood but . . .'

Emily instinctively touched his arm. 'We'll find her, Joe. We're one step ahead of the bastard. You OK?'

Joe nodded but he felt anything but OK. Sandra had trusted him to keep an eye on Carmel and he'd let her down.

'Let's not stand here,' she said decisively. 'You find out whether any of Kathwell's vans are missing. And I'll get on to Dr Oakley. Tell him what's happening.'

Five minutes later Joe discovered that one of Kathwell's vans had gone AWOL. But they had the registration number. It was just a question of finding it.

After driving round and round for what seemed like an age, Tim had reached the cemetery, only to find that the gates were shut and fastened with a chain and padlock. This was the first time this had happened in months. He'd read in the local papers that there'd been problems with vandals, not that he'd ever seen anything amiss. And now it looked as though the council had decided to take action. Which meant he had problems.

He parked in a lay-by for a while but when he heard muffled cries from the back of the van, he decided to try the cemetery again. The sooner he acted, the better.

This time his luck was in. The gates had been flung open and he drove through them at a stately pace, hoping the sight of a plain white van wouldn't attract attention. He'd tied the plastic sheeting on to the hooks at the side of the van to cover the logo just like he always did: one white van, he told himself, looks much like another.

There was nobody about as he drove along the wide, wooded pathways to the oldest part of the cemetery. To the overgrown place where worn gravestones, their lettering illegible through wear and lichen, stood or lay covered by nettles and bindweed. The place where the Gosson Mausoleum stood. He backed the van almost to the doors slowly and warily, careful not to hit any of the tall grey headstones lining the path, and sat there for a few moments contemplating his next move. She had gone quiet, which was good. He liked it when they didn't make a fuss. When they accepted their fate.

He pulled off the wig and scratched his head. On a warm day it was uncomfortably hot to wear. But he needed it to give him power. It was a disguise to throw his enemies off the scent. And it made him feel somehow closer to his grandfather. Closer to the dead.

He looked at his watch. Seven thirty. If he waited any longer there would be people about and his work might be interrupted. He climbed out of the van and walked slowly to the great rusty iron doors of the mausoleum, looking around to make sure he was unobserved. He could hear no human sound, only the high-pitched mocking of the birds in the trees and bushes round about. But he couldn't see them. They were hiding from him, watching from concealed branches, hidden in the foliage like observant enemies. Guerrilla fighters on the devil's side.

For a split second he thought that it was just another bird, chirruping insistently in the background of his mind. But then he realised the sound owed nothing to nature. It was the ring tone of the mobile phone that lay on the dashboard of the van. He stared at it for a while, hoping the noise would stop. The girl in the back had started making muffled sounds again, strangled screams. The sound of the mobile, the thought that he was in touch with the outside world, must have given her fresh courage.

He had to shut it up and shut her up. He pressed the button that would silence it and held it to his ear. He had half expected it to be someone from Kathwell's Kreative Kitchens but instead he heard a familiar voice.

'Please, Tim. Come home. If you've got Carmel don't harm her. She hasn't done anything. Please.'

He felt his body shaking. His mother didn't understand. She didn't know how evil they were. She didn't realise that they had to die. And she couldn't take this away from him. Not now. Not when he had her there and the mausoleum was prepared. The Seeker had given him her name - made a gift of her. He had a job to do and nothing would stop him.

He was vaguely aware of screaming the word 'no' into the telephone, a primitive cry of defiance, before switching it off and throwing it into the passenger foot well. He had come too far to stop now.

He climbed out of the van and took the large iron key from the pocket of his overalls. When he inserted it into the newly oiled lock it gave a faint click and the doors to the mausoleum swung open smoothly and silently. The box was standing open to receive its latest visitor and he gazed at it for a while with a contented smile before returning to the van and opening the rear doors.

She lay there naked on the plastic sheet, wriggling like a maggot hooked on the end of a fishing line, her limbs bound with parcel tape and her mouth taped to ensure silence while he worked. He put his face close to hers and she could smell the faint aroma of garlic on his breath. His gloved hands touched cheeks that were damp with helpless tears.

'Don't worry, you'll be put somewhere nice ... somewhere proper,' he whispered in her ear as her eyes bulged with terror.

He said no more as he rolled her up in the plastic sheet and pulled the collapsible trolley out of the van before manoeuvring her on to it. Her body stiffened and her resistance excited him. But he tried to put it out of his mind. There was work to do.

He wheeled the trolley into the mausoleum and tipped her into the box he'd made so lovingly: the box he'd created in the workshop at Kathwell's after everyone had gone home. He'd had a copy made of the keys and he'd returned there in the evenings. He'd used the best wood – solid oak off-cuts from kitchen doors – and made it virtually airtight by lining it with plastic sheeting. They didn't last long once he'd put them in there and shut the lid, securing it with chains and a strong padlock so escape was impossible.

She lay in the bottom of the box, wriggling helplessly as he pulled out the plastic sheet she had lain on in the van. It would be needed for the next one.

Then Carmel's world went dark as she listened to the chains being fastened and the dull clang of the mausoleum door shutting. Suddenly all was silence.

The last silence before death.

'The van was picked up by traffic cameras travelling south on Eborby Road at five to seven this morning.' Joe tried to sound calm although his stomach was churning. But giving in to panic wasn't going to help Carmel. He'd toyed with the idea of calling her mother, Sandra, to tell her what was happening but, if he was going to channel all his energies into finding Carmel, he didn't have time to deal with Sandra's desperate worry. And at that moment, he didn't feel he could face breaking the news.

Emily pored over the large map of the local area that lay on her newly cleared desk. Some things were more urgent than paperwork. 'Any other sightings?'

'No, it disappeared before reaching the ring road. Must have turned off somewhere.' He ran his finger along the straight line that was Eborby Road, the old Roman road approaching the city from the south. The van had been recorded by one of Traffic Division's cameras but it hadn't reached the next camera half a mile further on.

Joe studied the map. Where had he taken her? Then it jumped out at him. 'There's a cemetery . . . there down Gosson road. Left off the main road and about half a mile further on. Could that be where he's taken her?'

'Hardly a country churchyard.'

'He keeps them somewhere before dumping them. Maybe somewhere in or near this cemetery. There's nothing else around there, only residential housing.'

'He might be using a house. An empty or derelict one maybe.'

Joe shook his head. 'There won't be too many derelict places round there. The house prices are too high. As for empty ones, I'll get someone to ring round the local estate agents . . . and I'll send a patrol round there to see if they can spot his van. But my bet's still on the cemetery.'

'If that's the case, why doesn't he just dump them there instead of using country churchyards?'

'Don't ask me, but he must have a reason . . . maybe a twisted one that only makes sense to him, but there'll be one.'

'Let's get out there, then.'

Emily made a couple of calls before bustling out of the incident room, Joe by her side. They had debated whether to take Peta Thewlis with them – after all, her murderous son was vulnerable in his own way – but they had decided that it was best that she stayed at home for the time being with the policewoman who had been assigned to look after her.

Patrol cars had been sent ahead of them with instructions to look out for the van, and officers were making for the cemetery to begin a search.

Carmel Hennessy was out there somewhere. Joe just prayed that she was still alive.

The two constables said nothing as they climbed out of the patrol car, slamming the doors shut behind them. The van had been exceeding the speed limit by at least twenty miles an hour. If it hadn't been, it wouldn't have lost control on the bend and ended up slewed across the dual carriageway, holding up the traffic. Lucky it wasn't rush hour or they'd have had real problems.

The driver was slumped forward, his shaved head in his hands. The taller constable walked slowly over to the vehicle and wrenched the driver's door open. They'd been on the lookout for this particular van and they'd felt a flush of triumph when they'd spotted the registration number and switched on the lights and siren, entering into the chase like hounds after a fox, adrenalin pumping. But the pursuit hadn't lasted long before the driver, their incompetent quarry, had miscalculated a sharp bend and taken it too fast. Now they had him. And he seemed more frightened of them than they were of him.

'Timothy Thewlis?' the taller officer said roughly as his colleague produced a pair of handcuffs. 'Come on. Out you get.' He put an assisting hand on to the man's thin arm and noticed the mess where he'd tried to obliterate the home made tattoo. He pulled at the arm but the man stiffened as the sound of approaching police sirens drifted towards them on the warm summer breeze. Reinforcements.

The constable looked at his companion and grinned.

Resisting arrest. They'd enjoy this one. They told the hunched creature in the van that he was under arrest and recited the words of the caution before dragging him out and bundling his limp body into the patrol car, leaving the long blond wig on the passenger seat like some decaying animal.

'They've got him.' There was no satisfaction in Emily Thwaite's voice, only worry. 'They're bringing him in.'

'And Carmel?'

Emily shook her head. 'He's refusing to say where she is. We've got to talk to him.'

Joe knew she was right. With considerable effort he'd fought the impulse to stay at the scene to help with the search and headed back to the station. Every available officer was searching the area so they'd be more use trying to get the truth out of the Resurrection Man.

Once the duty solicitor had been called, they made their way to the interview suite. The incident room was buzzing with an almost party atmosphere. But there was a tension behind it. The girl was still missing. Emily found herself making the pessimistic assumption that Carmel Hennessy was already dead. Joe Plantagenet, on the other hand, hadn't given up hope but he knew that the sooner they persuaded Thewlis to talk, the more chance she had.

Tim Thewlis looked rather pathetic as he sat slumped on the hard plastic seat. He had blank, closed-down eyes which stared ahead, ignoring the tall, grey-suited solicitor by his side.

Joe sat down and switched on the tape. Emily sat beside him, making eye contact with the prisoner. But he averted his gaze. He wasn't playing that game.

'Where's Carmel Hennessy?'

Thewlis looked up. 'I know who you are,' he said.

Joe leaned forward. 'Who are we?'

'Enemies.'

'Whose enemies?'

Thewlis raised a finger to his lips, smiled, and shook his head.

'We've seen the instructions the Seeker gave you. Did he tell you where to take Carmel?'

The smile disappeared from the prisoner's lips.

'Your mother said the instructions weren't in your handwriting. Is that true?'

No answer.

'We can easily find out.'

Again silence.

'If you didn't write them, who did? Who gave you the names of the victims?'

Thewlis pressed his lips together tightly. He knew the Seeker was a man of influence and considerable intelligence. A man in touch with higher things. He had chosen him specially to do his work. To purge the world of the infection of evil. He had hinted as much last time they met. The Seeker trusted him and he wouldn't betray that trust.

'That tattoo on your arm . . . Did you used to go to the Black Hen?' Joe leaned forward. 'You killed Terry Jevons, didn't you? He called himself the Master.'

Thewlis nodded vigorously. 'I had to kill him.'

'Why?'

'He was evil.'

Joe tilted his head to one side. 'I'll ask you again, Tim. Where's the girl you abducted? Where have you taken her?'

Emily nudged his arm. They were getting nowhere. She decided on another approach. 'Who gives you the names, Tim? Or are you the Seeker? Do you decide who's going to die?'

Tim looked at her and frowned. 'No. He gives me the names.' The matter-of-fact way he said the words made Emily shudder.

'Who gives you the names, Tim?'

A sly grin.

'Does he know where you take them?'

'Of course he does. He gave me the key.'

Joe and Emily looked at each other and a few seconds later Joe left the room, breaking into a run as he made for the custody suite. If there was a key it might be among the prisoner's possessions. If.

As it turned out there were several keys amongst Tim Thewlis's belongings. House keys, keys to the white van. And another. A large, iron key, slightly rusty. Probably Victorian. A key to somewhere old. Joe stared at it for a while, imagining what sort of place would still use such a key. A church perhaps – although nowadays most churches – in fact most ancient buildings still in daily use – would have added something more modern to secure their premises.

He returned to the interview room and placed the key on the table in front of Thewlis. 'Is this the key?' he asked casually.

There was a flash of recognition followed by a long silence and Joe knew he'd got it right.

'Tell us where Carmel is.'

'If I tell you, he'll take my soul.'

'Who will?'

Silence.

'Does the key belong to the Seeker?' Emily asked.

The answer was a nod.

'So he tells you where to take them? Somewhere that belongs to him? Where is it, Tim?

Tim Thewlis pressed his lips together like a stubborn child. 'I'll never tell. You can't make me.'

Emily realised that they were getting nowhere. She needed to change tack again.

'Where does he give you your instructions? At work? At Kathwell's?'

Tim shook his head.

'Does he send them to your house?'

Another no.

'Is there a pub you go to?'

Tim shook his head vigorously.

'Where else do you go regularly?' Joe thought for a few moments. 'The hospital?'

Tim looked wary and shook his head again but there had been a flash of recognition, almost of alarm, in his eyes that told Joe he'd hit the target.

Joe leaned forward. 'Does he work at the hospital or is he one of the patients?' he asked.

Thewlis hesitated then shook his head. 'I don't know.'

Emily produced the sheets of paper with the victims' names and addresses on from a folder in front of her and lay them out on the table. 'These were found in your house. Are these the names he gave you?'

Thewlis looked at them and nodded.

'You say he gives them to you?'

'He leaves them for me.'

'Who is it, Tim? Who leaves them for you?'

Thewlis shut his mouth tightly. They weren't going to catch him out so easily.

'Is it Dr Oakley?'

Joe looked at her. She had put into words what they were both thinking. Thewlis's eyes widened in alarm and they knew they had hit the target.

'Where did you take Carmel Hennessy, Tim?'

He looked at his solicitor and grinned. 'No comment,' he said before bursting into laughter. They had no evidence. He was winning . . . him and the Seeker.

Emily stood up and Joe followed her out of the room, his fists clenched with frustration. They were running out of time.

'We've got to bring Oakley in,' he said once they were out of earshot. 'I reckon he's been using Tim Thewlis to do his dirty work. Putting it into his poor addled head that these people have to die for some reason.'

Emily looked sceptical. 'Tim's a paranoid schizophrenic. Surely he doesn't need anyone controlling him to give him ideas like that.'

'No, this is organised. The names and addresses.'

'Maybe Tim wrote them himself. Maybe it's all in his head.'

'His mother swears it's not his writing ... and we're just waiting for Forensic to confirm it. Someone else is in on this, Emily. Shouldn't he be taking medication to control his schizophrenia? He sees Oakley regularly. His mother makes sure he keeps his appointments. But if Oakley's giving him placebos so he's still ...'

Emily nodded. She had to acknowledge that Joe had a point. But they still had to find Carmel Hennessy. 'He's not going to talk, is he?' she said quietly.

Joe shook his head. 'I reckon our best hope is getting to Oakley. If we're right, he knows where Tim's taken Carmel. We've got to find her, Emily. I don't care what it takes but ...'

'OK,' she said. 'We'll bring Oakley in for questioning. But I can't think what he could possibly have against Carmel Hennessy. Have you told her mother yet?'

Joe shook his head.

'Tell you what, I'll do it.'

Joe shook his head again. 'No, it should be me. I'm the one who's supposed to be keeping an eye on her.'

Emily put her face close to his. 'She's a grown woman, Joe. You couldn't watch her twenty-four hours a day ...'

He knew she was right but somehow it didn't make him feel any better.

Suddenly the door burst open. DC Jamilla Dal was in a hurry, her eyes aglow with untold news. She'd run all the way down the stairs from the incident room and she stopped to catch her breath for a few seconds. This was important.

She addressed Joe. 'You know that thing you asked me to check on, sir. Well, it's taken a while but I've just found something that could be important. A link between the victims.'

'Go on,' Emily said impatiently. She really didn't have time for this now.

'That person Harold Uckley ran over ... remember? It

was a little girl called Imogen Hale. I did some digging and I found out that her father owned a travel agent's in Sheepgate – the one Carla Yates used to work at.'

She had Joe's full attention. 'Peter Hale. He left his wife for Carla Yates.'

'Well, as you know, I looked for Peter Hale's widow – Imogen Hale's mother – in the electoral register,' Jamilla continued. 'But I couldn't find her. Then I thought of seeing if she'd married again but there was no record so I presumed she'd left the area. Then I had the idea of checking on her maiden name.'

'Which is?'

When Jamilla said the name, Joe knew it sounded familiar. But it wasn't until he'd spent a few moments dredging his memory that he realised why. He experienced a strong temptation to hug Jamilla for bringing the news that had made everything fall into place. But he thought better of it. Rumours started so easily in police stations.

Emily frowned. 'Is this going to help us find Carmel Hennessy?'

'If Tim won't tell us where she is, our best bet is to find the person who's controlling him, who thought all this up. I've just got to make a phone call . . . check something out.' He picked up the phone and made a short, hurried call. When he put the receiver down, he looked up. 'We're off to the hospital.'

'Yes. It is about time we had a word with Dr Oakley,' Emily said, puzzled by the bitter smile on Joe's lips. 'What is it? What's the matter?'

'I'll tell you on the way,' said Joe, making for the door.

Carmel felt hot as she made the effort to breath, to stay alive. She could feel the sweat on her body and her arms, secured behind her back, hurt. She knew she shouldn't cry or shout out – the slightest effort would only use up precious oxygen.

She had to conserve energy. She had to live.

Chapter Twenty-Two

Emily strode into the office first, a look of fierce determination on her face. Joe walked slightly behind her.

'Is he expecting you?' Dr Oakley's secretary looked up at the newcomers and inclined her head politely. 'He's in with a patient at the moment, and I don't like to disturb him.'

Emily stepped forward. There was no time for niceties. There was a young woman somewhere, dying or possibly dead already. 'Elizabeth Anne Hale?'

'No, my surname's Peace.'

'That's the name you use now but Hale was your married name, wasn't it?'

'I decided to use my maiden name again when my husband left me. Why do you ask?' She sounded wary. As though she had something to hide.

'You had a daughter called Imogen. She was killed in a car accident.'

She lowered her eyes. 'Yes,' she said in a whisper.

'A man called Harold Uckley was driving the car. And your husband left you for a woman called Carla Yates.'

'How do you . . .?'

'I expect you're familiar with the conditions of Dr Oakley's patients.'

She looked uneasy. 'Not really. I . . .'

'You needed someone who'd be suggestible, someone

you could manipulate to do exactly what you wanted. When you found a paranoid schizophrenic who'd become involved in what was going on at the Black Hen and wanted out because he was terrified, I bet you couldn't believe your luck. You knew from the taped interviews he'd had with Dr Oakley that he imagined himself to be in danger from a man who called himself the Master and from then on it was a piece of cake. You left messages from a supposed agent of good who opposed "the Master". You called your creation "the Seeker". Rather corny but it worked. You gave him messages suggesting the Master's agents were after him and it was his duty to destroy them or they would destroy him. Did you make sure he didn't take the drugs he was prescribed? Did you take the prescriptions off him and give him placebos instead?'

Emily waited for an answer but when none came, Joe took over.

'As far as you were concerned, Uckley got away with killing your daughter, didn't he? He never paid for what he did. Then someone told you they'd seen Carla Yates out on the town having a good time. She'd destroyed your marriage . . . took your husband. If it hadn't been for her and all the stress she caused, he'd be alive today.'

He saw that tears were welling up in Elizabeth's eyes.

'You made them pay, didn't you? It took a while but you had your revenge in the end.'

Elizabeth Peace pressed her thin lips together. She wasn't giving anything away.

'What about Janna Pyke and Terry Jevons?' Emily asked, a note of aggression in her voice. She was aware that the clock was ticking for Carmel. She needed answers fast.

It was Joe who spoke. 'You and Amy's mother are good friends, aren't you? I remember you phoned her while I was there.' He was trying to sound confident but he knew what he was saying was largely guesswork. He watched Elizabeth's face carefully, looking for some sign that he'd got it right, but he saw nothing. 'Janna Pyke pretended to be Amy's friend, didn't she? But she was only grooming her for ... She took her to the Black Hen – and Terry Jevons raped her. You knew all about the Black Hen, didn't you? You knew it was that place that had tipped Tim over the edge. And you made sure you kept him there. You used him. You took your revenge on these people through him.'

Elizabeth shook her head. 'You can't prove any of this. You know you can't.'

'What about Carmel Hennessy?'

Elizabeth looked up, puzzled. 'What about her?'

'Why did you set Tim on her? What did she do to you?'

'Absolutely nothing. Why do you ask?' She suddenly sounded unsure of herself. 'Carmel lives upstairs from my uncle and I certainly didn't set Tim on her, as you put it. Why on earth should I? She's a nice girl. It just proves you're talking nonsense.'

'So why has he abducted her?'

Joe and Emily could tell that the shock on Elizabeth's face was genuine. 'That's ridiculous. He can't have. You're lying.'

'It's true,' said Emily leaning forward until her face was close to Elizabeth's. 'Tim's abducted her ... taken her somewhere. Now where is she? If she's still alive, she won't have long.'

Elizabeth shook her head. 'I told you, I don't know what you're talking about.' Her hand suddenly went to her mouth and her eyes bulged with terrible realisation as if she'd just glimpsed a vision of hell.

'What is it?'

She shook her head.

'You'd better tell us. If Carmel dies ...'

Elizabeth was silent for a few seconds, trying desperately to regain control of herself. Then she took a deep shuddering breath as though she'd reached a decision. 'Carmel rang the other day. My uncle was taken ill and one of the other secretaries wrote her name and the address on a piece of

. . . Tim was there that day for an appointment. If he . . .'

Joe interrupted. 'You wrote Tim's instructions down and left them for him when he came out of Dr Oakley's office. Is that how you communicated with him?'

One look at Elizabeth's face told him he was getting near the truth. 'Then someone handed you a sheet with Carmel's name and address on it and your mind was on your uncle. If you left it in the office and Tim picked it up . . .'

'I don't know. I . . .' Elizabeth's face was frozen between horror and self-pity. Joe knew he was right.

'We've questioned Tim and he's refusing to say where she is. Where is she, Elizabeth? Where does he take them?'

Emily stepped forward. 'Where the hell is she?' she shouted, making the woman flinch. This was no time for good manners.

Elizabeth began to wring her hands. 'It's not my fault. I never meant . . .'

'There's a girl out there dying. Tell us where she is.'

Elizabeth looked up at Emily, who was descending on her like a fury. 'OK. I'll tell you. My mother was a Gosson. They were an important family in this town once and they had a mausoleum in Briargate Cemetery. When . . . when it started, I left the instructions in the pocket of Tim's jacket – he always took his jacket off and left it in here, you see. I explained about the evil people who had to be destroyed. Later on I left him an envelope containing the key to the mausoleum and instructions about what to do – I told him to destroy the instructions in case anyone found them. The key had been passed down to me, you see.' She sniffed and raised her head. 'My mother was very proud of her family.'

'Never mind that,' Joe snapped, making the woman jump. 'How do we get there?' They were wasting time.

Suddenly the reality of the situation seemed to dawn on Elizabeth and she told them, meekly, repeating almost after every sentence how sorry she was. But Joe had no time for her contrition. Ignoring the hospital's ban on mobile phones, he made the calls that would send patrol cars and an ambulance round to the Gosson Mausoleum, remembering to tell Sunny to take the old iron key with him. He'd need it.

'You OK, Emily?' Joe asked as they led Elizabeth out to the waiting car.

'I will be when they find the girl alive,' she replied with a worried smile. 'Thanks for asking,' she added as the prisoner slid into the back seat.

Cemeteries are quiet places, the territory of the sleeping dead. But today the blanket of deep peace was slashed by insistent sirens and running feet. The Gosson Mausoleum, in the oldest part of the burial ground, now disused and overgrown, was the focus of all the activity. The ambulance stood there, lurking like a nervous onlooker, behind the patrol cars. Waiting for its cargo . . . dead or alive.

Sunny Porter placed the key in the lock in the centre of the great iron door and hesitated. It was the sort of place that spooked him. There would be rotting coffins inside containing the dead. He didn't want to go in there. But he knew he had no choice. This was the place where he kept them. The killing chamber.

His hand was trembling as he turned the key, expecting his efforts to meet the resistance of years of rust and disuse. But the key turned smoothly. The mechanism had been oiled, as had the hinges of the heavy door which swung open in response to his tentative pull.

Sunny turned to the pair of uniformed constables who were hovering just behind him. 'OK. In you go.' There was no way he was setting foot over that particular threshold if he could help it.

But a few seconds later, in response to shouts of 'In here, Sarge,' Sunny ventured reluctantly into the darkness, trying not to look at the rows of stacked coffins containing long-dead Gossons, intent only on the focus of attention. The long, roughly hewn oak box with the chains wrapped around it.

'Don't just stand there. Get it open,' he barked at the constables, who forced the padlock with sheer brute strength and let the chains slide noisily on to the flagstoned floor before lifting the lid.

'Get the paramedics . . . quick,' someone said to Sunny, who was standing there frozen, staring in disbelief. He rushed outside and from that moment things seemed to happen at double speed. Before Sunny knew it, the girl's nakedness was covered deftly with a blanket and she was bundled on to a trolley and into the ambulance, which sped off, all sirens blazing.

The silence that followed seemed almost unreal as the Forensic team moved in to seal off the crime scene.

Carmel opened her eyes and saw only white light. Her first thought was that perhaps she was dead. Perhaps this was it. The end. But then, as her eyes adjusted, she could make out a bright rectangle, possibly a window, and a fair-haired woman in pale blue with a stethoscope slung around her neck bending over her. An angel, perhaps.

'Hello, Carmel,' said the angel. 'My name's Dr Hughes. You're in Eborby General. You're quite safe now.'

Carmel tried to smile but wasn't quite sure whether she'd managed it. She moved her legs. Soft sheets. That was good. Somehow she'd always imagined that heaven would have soft sheets.

'How are you feeling?' the angel asked.

'OK.' Her own voice sounded faint and distant, as if somebody else had spoken and she had mouthed the word like a ventriloquist's dummy.

The angel leaned over her, her pretty face full of concern. 'The police would like to talk to you but if you're not feeling up to it . . .'

'That's all right. I'll talk to them,' she heard herself saying.

'And there's someone else who wants to see you. Are you up to receiving visitors?'

Carmel mouthed the word yes. She wanted someone to tell her what had happened, to return her to the land of the living.

'OK. I'll tell Sister.' The angel smiled. 'You're doing well. You'll be out of here in no time but in the meantime, take it easy, eh.'

Ten minutes later Tavy McNair rushed into the room and took Carmel in his arms, his eyes full of tears.

Chapter Twenty-Two

Dr Keith Webster sat alone in his office, thinking of Janna Pyke. She had been trouble, he had known that instinctively from the moment he first met her. But something about her had entranced, almost hypnotised him. He had engineered meetings, extra sessions to go over her work. And then the final triumph of getting her into the flat, a favour that had left her in his debt. But now, when he thought about it, he felt such a fool.

He began to read the first page of her diary again, trying to make sense of it. *'She has a little, thin face,'* Janna wrote. *'Very pale. The eyes are sunken and dark like the coal eyes of a melting snowman and she has long hair, unbrushed and so matted with dirt that it looks almost grey. Her lips are as white as the rest of her flesh. There's no blood in them. In fact she looks dead. But then that's probably because she is.'* He'd read through the diary several times and the references to this ghostly girl puzzled him.

Then there were the entries about the Black Hen. And her flight from the Vicars Green flat and her fear that a woman called Elizabeth who'd seen her in Boargate would tell her ex-landlady, Mrs Thewlis, where she was. But that was Janna. Running, afraid. Always trying to escape from something or other – usually a disaster of her own making.

Then there were the bits about Tavy McNair, but Keith had known all about him. And she wrote about a man called

Jeff Timmons. She'd followed him home one day and had rung directory enquiries to get his number - Keith wondered what their exact relationship was but he supposed he'd never get to find out.

There were times when he'd contemplated giving the diary to the police. But someone had already been arrested for Janna's murder - a psychiatric patient and an unidentified woman, the papers said. And besides, there were the sections about himself. About his lacklustre performance in bed and Janna's threats to tell his wife what a dirty old man he was. She had written some humiliating things. Hurtful. And the prospect of his personal embarrassment being pawed over in a police station - maybe even used in evidence in some court - was more than Keith could cope with.

After discarding Janna's diary in the bin, covering it with waste paper so that he wouldn't have to look at it and be reminded, he turned his attention to the file containing her work ... her research. As her supervisor, he had been aware of the subject matter - the Seekers of the Dead. But he knew now that she had kept things from him.

He re-read her work avidly, with an interest that was both professional and personal. This research had been important to Janna. It had almost been part of her.

Her notes were written in a conversational tone - almost like a second diary - but she wrote as though the subject matter was real to her, almost as though she knew the protagonist personally.

The truth came as a complete surprise, she began. *I presume the Seekers of the Dead were accustomed to death in all its forms but what they found in the house on Vicars Green must have shocked them. You can tell that by the language used in their report. They were women, ordinary women of the time doing an extraordinary job.*

The account of one Eleanor Buckby, who was the

first to enter the house doesn't make for easy reading. She describes the bodies, their position and their state of decomposition. The father and mother were found in the downstairs room, their faces hideously contorted but their bodies bearing no sign of the buboes that were the normal symptoms of the bubonic plague. A twelve-year-old boy, in a similar state to his parents, was also found downstairs and two servants in the attic room. When Eleanor Buckby ventured upstairs she found the girl who had raised the alarm that her family had succumbed to the plague. The authorities had decided not to allow her out of the house and her pleas to be released were in vain as she was considered a risk to others. It seemed that for weeks she would call from the window, saying that as she had no symptoms she should be freed, her cries becoming more and more desperate as the bodies of her family rotted around her. But still they would not let her out and when she was found by Eleanor, it seemed that she had starved to death as nobody would venture close enough to that house of pestilence to provide her with food.

It seemed that the girl could write and she recorded her thoughts and her suffering. It was this brief account that I discovered in the archives with Eleanor Buckby's report . . . and it altered everything, all my assumptions. How wrong I was. If I had known the truth, I would never have contemplated setting foot in that flat.

Keith sighed and put the papers to one side carefully, fighting a strong temptation to take her research and claim it for his own. After all, nobody else was aware of her findings and if he put the material together in a coherent form, it would do his academic reputation no harm whatsoever. Perhaps when a decent amount of time had passed and he had added some original research of his own to Janna's . . . She was dead so she could hardly accuse him of plagiarism.

Keith's thoughts were interrupted by a knock on his office door. He called out a curt 'Come in', shoving Janna's notes to one side. Somehow he hadn't expected a visit from the police. With Janna's murderers arrested, he'd thought that his tentative involvement was over. So when the door opened to reveal Joe Plantagenet standing on the threshold, he was surprised . . . and a little alarmed. He found himself instinctively covering up Janna's notes with a file – hiding his guilty secret – as the detective sat down and made himself comfortable.

'I don't know if you've heard that we've arrested Janna's killer,' Joe said. 'I thought that as you were close to her . . .'

Keith felt himself blush at the implications of the words. Had he been close to Janna? Had anybody ever been close to Janna, who lived on that edge between darkness and light?

'I read about the arrests in the paper,' Keith said. 'So what was the motive, do you know?'

Joe hesitated. What he was about to tell Keith Webster wasn't pleasant and it would probably shatter any illusions he still harboured about his former lover. He took a deep breath and recited the bare facts.

Keith already knew most of it from Janna's diary, which now lay beneath a screwed-up draft report at the bottom of the waste bin. But he wasn't going to let Joe know this so he feigned surprise. 'I'd no idea she was mixed up in anything like that,' he said, trying to sound convincing. But he wasn't sure he'd fooled Joe Plantagenet.

The two men sat quite still for a few moments before Keith broke the awkward silence. 'Janna was a bright girl, you know. Her thesis was very promising. She was researching the history of her old flat in Vicars Green – a girl who supposedly starved to death there after her family died of the plague.' He looked up at Joe and saw that he was listening intently. 'Only they hadn't died of the plague. They were murdered.'

Joe leaned forward. 'That's interesting.'

Keith hesitated. This policeman wasn't involved in the world of academic research and learned papers so it would do no harm to share the story Janna had uncovered. Besides, he was so excited about the discovery that he longed to tell someone.

'A woman called Eleanor Buckby – one of the so called Seekers of the Dead – reported on the deaths to the authorities. She concluded that the victims had all been poisoned, apart from the girl who had starved to death, and she found poison underneath the girl's bed. The girl had reported that her family had died of the plague – not that they were ill, but that they were already dead. What she can't have known about was the practice of locking any family members who hadn't succumbed to the plague in with the dead to prevent infection spreading. By lying she had signed her own death warrant.'

'But why would she kill her family?'

'Her father was a wealthy merchant and, with her parents and brother dead, she should have inherited the lot. And according to neighbours there had been family conflict about an unsuitable boy – one of her father's apprentices. Janna was working on the theory that he put her up to it.'

'Looking at it from a policeman's point of view, that sounds likely,' said Joe. 'Did Janna discover the girl's name?'

Webster nodded. 'Elizabeth. Elizabeth Melchet.' He hesitated. 'Plantagenet. Any relation to . . .?'

Joe shrugged his shoulders before standing up to leave.

On the day Carmel Hennessy returned to her flat it rained. Number five Vicars Green looked innocent enough as she stood at the front door with Tavy McNair by her side, his hand hovering by her elbow as if he was afraid she would collapse.

Carmel's mother, Sandra, and her stepfather, Steve, had rushed up to Eborby from Milton Keynes as soon as Joe told them what had happened and they'd stayed in Joe's flat until they were sure she'd made a full recovery. But Carmel was relieved when they returned home. She couldn't stand people fussing over her: it made her feel like breaking down in tears.

When Joe met Sandra he embraced her, saying over and over again how sorry he was that he hadn't kept Carmel safe from danger. But that, thought Carmel, was Joe all over – all that guilt. Perhaps Maddy Owen would be good for him . . . if she could ever get them together properly. The relationship was still tentative – like the start of some elaborate courtship ritual on a wildlife programme – and Carmel wished they'd just get on with it.

Tavy interrupted her thoughts. 'You ready?' he whispered in her ear.

She tried her best to give him a brave smile. 'As I'll ever be,' she said, her voice emerging stronger than she'd expected.

As she put the key in the lock the cathedral clock began to chime the hour, the sound distracting her for a moment, giving her courage. It was twelve o'clock, midday, and by the tenth chime Carmel was at the top of the stairs, staring at the door to her flat.

When Tavy took the key off her and opened the door she gave him a shy smile. Since he'd started rehearsals for the new play, he'd seemed more confident, more positive. He'd told her that he'd never really enjoyed the ghost tours. And Oscar Wilde was a useful antidote to death.

Maddy Owen had been in to tidy up and she'd made a good job of it. The flat was neat and clean and there were fresh flowers on the coffee table. But Carmel still couldn't help shuddering when she looked at the bedroom door.

'It's OK,' said Tavy as though he'd read her thoughts. 'Maddy's cleared up in there. Changed the bed . . . everything.'

Carmel managed a weak smile. 'You will stay tonight, won't you?'

Tavy put his arms around her and held her close. 'If you

want. But I'll have to let mum know that I won't be home. She worries.'

Carmel gave him a swift kiss on the nose and began to wander around the flat, looking in cupboards, examining the bathroom, trying to come to terms with the fact that it all seemed so very normal. She could hear the sound of voices drifting in through the open window from the pavement below. Another guided tour of the city was passing by, taking in the notable sights. Carmel wondered whether they would mention the Resurrection Man killings and point out number five as the place where the only victim to survive was attacked. But she doubted it. Such things would hardly be good for Eborby's tourist image.

When the doorbell rang Carmel jumped. Her nerves were still bad. Her heart still raced at the sight of a white van or the thought of confined spaces. She could no longer travel in a lift and she hated the very thought of an aeroplane. Life would never be quite the same again. Some scars never quite heal.

Tavy left her alone to answer the door and she wandered into the bedroom, testing her courage. She'd always sensed the girl in there, even in the middle of the day. There had always been a feeling of not being alone, of having an unseen companion. And somehow she needed one now.

But standing in the middle of the room, she felt nothing. There was nobody there, nobody watching her, half seen in the darkest corner. All she was aware of was sunlight streaming in through the small window and the sound of bustling, living humanity below on the green. The girl had gone.

When she heard voices she returned to the living room. Maddy Owen was standing there with Joe Plantagenet, holding out her arms, and Carmel hurried over to her to submit to her comforting hug.

Joe leaned towards Maddy and whispered in her ear. 'Shall we tell her?'

Maddy nodded and Carmel sensed a rapport between them that hadn't existed before her attack.

'I've found out who your ghost girl is,' Joe began. 'I know the whole story.'

Carmel turned and saw that Tavy was watching her anxiously. 'Well?' she said. She could feel her hands shaking and at that moment she wondered if she really wanted to know the truth. Sometimes it's better to remain in ignorance.

Joe told her to sit down and Maddy rushed to put the kettle on. Whatever it was, this was serious.

She listened as Joe recounted the story of the girl, of her terrible secret and her horrible death. No wonder, Carmel thought, her spirit couldn't rest. It explained everything.

Carmel looked Joe in the eye. 'When I went into the bedroom before, I sensed she wasn't there any more. Maybe I'm wrong but . . .'

'While you were in hospital I asked someone to come over – someone who knows about supernatural phenomena. He . . .' Joe didn't know quite how to say that Canon George Merryweather had prayed in the flat and ordered the girl to leave, to be at peace. In the everyday atmosphere of modern Eborby it seemed a little strange. But it had happened. Joe had seen it with his own eyes. He'd felt the oppressive presence vanish.

'He exorcised the place?'

'She's gone now. She won't bother you again.'

Carmel said nothing. She wasn't sure how she felt. After all, the girl had tried to warn her of the danger she was in. Maybe she had been trying to do a good deed to make up in some way for the sins she had committed in life. Who knows? Carmel certainly didn't and she felt a small twinge of resentment that Joe had interfered.

'Will you be OK staying here?' Maddy asked anxiously. 'You don't think you'd be better moving or . . .'

Carmel shook her head. 'Someone should keep an eye on Conrad downstairs. After all, he won't have Elizabeth now, will he?'

The matter-of-fact way she said it surprised Joe. She

looked at him as though she could read his mind. 'I can't stop thinking about Elizabeth. What made her . . .?'

Joe glanced at Maddy. 'We won't know for sure until we get the full psychiatric report.' He fell silent for a few moments, imagining the bitterness that must have gnawed away at Elizabeth for years like a hungry rat before she hit on the idea of avenging herself by proxy.

'Well, I think she was an evil bitch,' said Carmel with the certainty of youth, her voice trembling a little.

Joe said nothing. He turned to Maddy. 'How's Peta Thewlis?'

'I've not seen her,' Maddy replied. 'She's not been into work since . . . And someone said she was moving away.'

'Tim will probably go to a secure hospital,' said Joe. 'Perhaps she'll want to be near him.'

He half turned his head and thought he caught a fleeting glimpse of a pale shadow in the corner. Maybe the girl hadn't gone away after all.

Perhaps she never would.